SHADOW RISE

AUDREY GREY

STARFALL PRESS

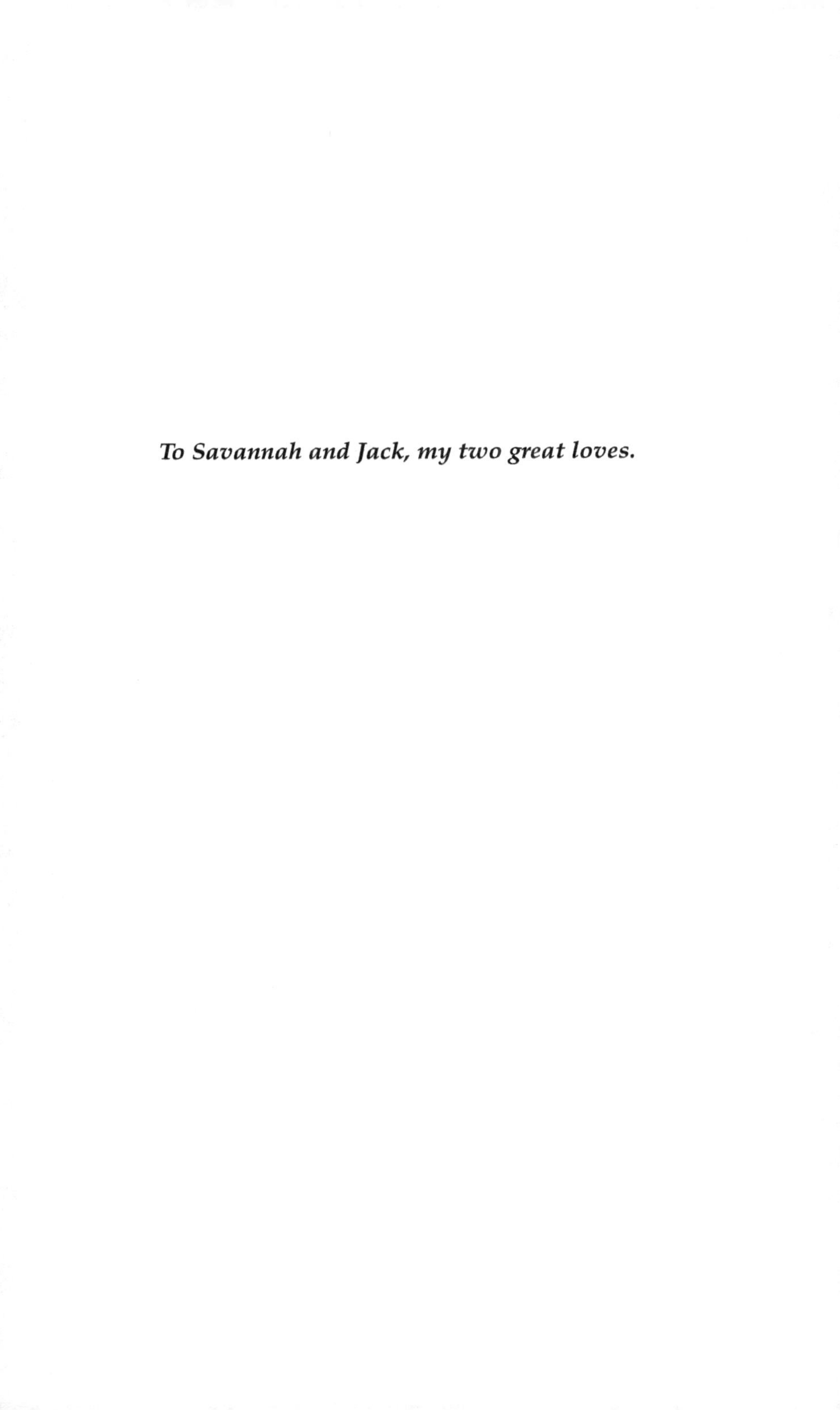

To Savannah and Jack, my two great loves.

PROLOGUE

I've been prepared to die for half my life. There were hundreds of options to choose from in the pit—starvation, dehydration, disease, murder—and once I escaped the disgusting hole, the Royalists came up with even more creative setups to kill me.

But of all the ways I imagined I could die, all the scenarios I forced myself to envision, none were ever as brutal or horrifying as this.

Pain like nothing I've ever felt consumes me. My screams ravage the air, slick with mold and the coppery tang of blood. *My blood.* I buck and writhe against the altar I'm chained to; gritty stone scrapes the flesh off my shoulder blades, the top of my spine.

Every part of me shivers and burns with agony.

"Where are the Rebels, you vile worm?" the Archduchess demands.

I blink, my gaze roving around the shadowy room. I've been here before, but how many times? When?

"What's your name?"

"Screw . . . you."

She reaches back, and her fist connects with my temple, knocking the vision from my eyes as pain ricochets inside my skull. "How many Rebels are there?"

I groan. "None."

"Are there more on the Island?"

"No."

"Where are they hiding? Who's their leader?"

Resist. The word is burned into my soul.

Resist. *Resist.*

But it would be so easy . . . so damn easy to give in. The pain could stop. It could all go away.

Just the thought of stopping the torture leaves a crack in my will, an ever-widening chasm that threatens to shatter my resolve.

"Please . . ." Fire burns a path down my throat. "Water. I need . . ." I convulse into a fit of coughing, and I'm shivering down to my bones, my teeth slamming together, even though my flesh feels as if it could cook an egg. "Please stop."

"Please," she mocks in a whining whisper that scrapes down my spine. "*Please* stop."

I flinch against the sound of her voice, every cell, every fabric of my being shuddering at her presence. My pleas for mercy only seem to make her angrier, yet I can't stop.

The Archduchess's heels make sharp clacks against the filthy stone floor as she circles to my right. My mind knows I can't escape my chains, but my body tries anyway, yanking and pulling on the heavy manacles shackling me to the stone. Steel bites into my bruised wrists.

She leans over me, so close I can feel her hot breath on my cheeks and smell the powder of her wig. Her long nose is shiny in the torchlight.

"Who is Riser Thornbrook?"

My heart punches into my throat. I feel like she's asked

this question before, like it's important. I pull in a breath to steady my heartbeat and look away, a tear gliding down my left cheek because I remember what happens now.

I know the pain that's coming. I know I'm not strong enough to take it.

I've tried—gods, have I tried not to scream when she hurts me, yet each time I fail. Each time she tries a different way to hurt me, and afterward she has my bones mended and skin healed back together so she can do it all over again.

An endless loop of agony and doubt, the only certainty that the pain will be intolerable.

Riser's face flashes in my mind, his green eye bright and calming, his blue eye mirroring the storm inside me.

"Fight," he whispers. "Fight until your very last breath, Digger Girl."

Something taps against the stone. A hammer. The Archduchess hits the blunt steel instrument by my feet, each blow striking a hole in my courage. Then she brings it down on my flesh and a wave of blackness washes over me.

I come to a few seconds later. An unearthly scream rips from my chest. The sound goes on for countless minutes, in between moments of nothing.

Dark, beautiful, silent nothing.

I scrape my eyelids open. My throat is swollen nearly shut, exhaustion swallowing my scream. I shiver and groan as she runs her fingers over my forehead, gently, pushing my sweat-drenched hair out of my eyes.

"There, there," she says, leaning down over me. "Let's start again, shall we? What is your name?"

Nausea burns in my belly, my skin drowned in sweat.

Fight, Digger Girl.

All my anger and pain and fear collide, creating a whirlwind of fury that dulls the throbbing pain.

Pushing up on my elbows, I growl through the roaring

agony and meet her gaze. "I'm the Digger Girl who survived the pit, who survived the Trials and eluded you for years. You can have my screams, but that's all you'll get."

The Archduchess grins and lifts the hammer. "We'll see."

ONE

They come for me at dawn. The rats squeak and scrabble their claws over the stone floor as they flee, and I eye them with jealousy.

What I wouldn't give to be a rat right now.

I would escape. Not just my cell inside the Tower with its dark corners and damp air and bone-aching chill—or the iron shackles that etch bloody bracelets into my flesh. Not just the insane Archduchess and the barbaric tools she uses on my flesh, or the asteroid named after the gods that's weeks away from raining death onto my world.

I want to escape me. What I've *done.*

The labyrinth consumes my nightmares. Not the real one, but a warped, hybrid version, half-pit, half-maze, half-Tower.

Every time I close my eyes, I'm there. Trapped in darkness, drowning in it, the fires crackling all around me. My dead friends scream for help. Princess Ophelia. My best friend, Merida. Riser.

But I can't see them. Can't find them. It's too dark; there are too many twists and turns, too many prison bars and crooked stairwells and flames, so many flames.

Every night I relive this new form of the labyrinth constructed to mutilate and kill us. Every time I close my eyes, it's like I'm inside the Trials again.

I try to fight sleep, but my weakness and the drugs the emperor gives me make that impossible.

Then there are the voices. They crawl through my brain when I'm in my cell, hundreds and hundreds of voices, begging me to wake them up. As if it's them and not me stuck in a nightmare.

Most times I pretend they're real, if only to not feel alone. Desperate, I know. But my circumstances call for a little desperation.

There's no escaping the voices or the nightmares. Not when I'm asleep. Not when I'm awake. Not ever.

It's this fun little loop of, *let's see how crazy we can drive Maia before we kill her.*

And they will, eventually. Every night, when they drag me to the Archduchess, I think it's finally time. They're going to make good on their promise and execute me.

But they only make me wish I was dead, the Archduchess finding more and more elaborate ways to inflict pain.

When she's done toying with me, they mend my ruined flesh with handheld Reconstructors, the pain almost as bad as the torture itself, leaving me drugged and weak.

At least when they drug me, I don't see Pit Boy. Silver linings, right?

Sometimes they parade me in front of angry crowds and cameras. Sometimes they ask me questions. Sometimes they kick me or hit me, but it all just feels so far away.

The days are lost to me, drowned in a feverish storm of agony and fear and memories.

How many days have I been here?

Hard to tell. From the hollow, relentless ache of my belly, it's been at least two days since I ate anything other than the few morsels Bramble sneaks past the guard into my cell, the brave idiot.

Still, his gifts usually come back up.

A faint laugh escapes my raw throat. It's like I'm in the pit all over again, Bramble scavenging for food to keep me alive. I swore I'd never end up in this position again, yet here I am.

The sound of a door opening down the hall makes me focus on reality. My head spins as I stand, my body aching from being continuously broken and put back together. I inhale a choppy breath and bite my cheek to focus, waiting until the halo around my vision is only a faint onyx shimmer before letting go.

I need to be alert, ready, so I go over the plan.

Stun the first guard with a shot to the throat. Use that moment to take out the second one. I may not be able to escape my nightmares, but maybe I can escape *this* particular nightmare.

Luckily, Bramble is off scavenging, so I don't have to worry about him.

Something jangles outside my door, and then the click of the key turning the lock wets my palms with sweat.

My cell gate creaks open, and two Centurions pause just inside, their fingers curled above the pistols at their hips.

The larger man whips his head toward the door, his eyes shining with undisguised loathing. "Move it, Fienian scum."

I blink at the word I used to despise. Fienian. Then there's terrorist. Rebel. Murderer. And my new favorite—prisoner.

"Okay," I whisper in a weak voice.

I make a blade with my bent knuckles and pop the first guard's Adam's apple, dropping him to the floor. The other guard's eyes widen, and he goes for his gun, but I bring my foot down just above his ankle. There's a sharp, sickening crack, and the man screams and falls, grabbing his broken leg. A well-aimed kick to his jaw does the rest.

Once he's prone on the ground, I take his pistol, reveling in the weight of it inside my hand.

The first guard writhes around, lips yawned open like a fish out of water trying to breathe.

I take his pistol and run, bare feet slapping over the stones worn smooth by the heels of thousands of nameless prisoners just like me. An ache tears through my bones, my head spinning as I vault down the spiraling staircase.

I need to slow down, to breathe, but I can't afford to.

Darkness laps at my periphery, my heart shuddering as it struggles to provide enough blood to my muscles. A sharp burn fills my lungs.

Every step closer to freedom drains the weight from my shoulders, the fear from my heart. I must be close.

Free. Almost free.

The door! I remember this door. I yank it open with a grunt, blinking against the sunlight—

Only to see the wide-eyed face of a guard.

TWO

The guard blocking my way has thin lips and cruel eyes. *Crap.* I bring my pistols up, but my muscles are too tired, too slow, and I cry out as something sharp cracks against my skull.

Half conscious, I feel the guard grab my hair, and he drags me back up the winding stairs I fought so hard to descend.

Each step that hits my failing body is a blow of defeat.

Still, I fight. My fingernails scrape at his leather doublet. I kick and buck, gouging and clawing at anything I can, but I'm too weak to do much damage.

The guard laughs as he flings me back into my cage. I curl into a ball, my muscles trembling with exhaustion, and spew a string of curses at the guard.

For a time, there's nothing but blackness. Then my cell door clinks open, the sound scraping down my spine, and I scramble to my feet. The ground spins, and my head throbs as more guards haul me away.

I try to look unafraid, but my mouth is sticky with fear. Where are they taking me?

I count everything to stay sane—or as sane as I can be with voices talking to me.

Two guards. Eight cells. One measly barred window. Three hundred and twenty-two crumbling steps and one iron door. Five hundred more dizzying footfalls across the well-kempt lawn sheened with dew and through the array of fragrant gardens.

Seven holly bushes. My head grows heady with the smells of hyacinth and jasmine as I scan the crowd beyond the stone wall cloaked with white roses.

For a moment, I think I spot my mother's sharp features in the wall of faces, and my heart flutters sideways in my chest.

Mom. Help me.

But it's not her. Of course it's not. While she has no problem designing a death maze to kill finalists in the most gruesome of ways, she would never stoop to watching a prisoner be dragged through the estate and ridiculed. Not really her style.

I blink up at the sky. Pandora watches the spectacle behind a veil of wispy clouds, larger than I imagined she would be.

Could it already be too late to stop her?

A little girl throws something red at my face—a spoiled tomato, by the putrid taste. Its slimy innards drip down my jaw and neck. Pity and self-hatred form a pit in my core as I lick what I can.

More spectators join in, chucking whatever they have handy until I'm covered with goo. I ball my hands into fists. How many people in Cypher could this feed?

I smell the cherry trees before I see them, their stunning blush-white blossoms stirring on their branches as if trying to escape the horror they're about to witness. A wooden scaffold waits for me in the shade, cherry petals clumped in little piles along the pale wooden floor, swirling in the sporadic breeze.

When the group of onlookers ringing it catches sight of me, they erupt in jeers.

Even though it's early morning and the sun is weak, the Archduchess waits for me in the shade of one of the slender, gray trees, as if her papery skin will catch fire in the soft light. She's pale, her irises blanched, lips the color of old bone—as if every drop of blood has drained from her body. A casket-black mourning gown drapes her sharp figure.

If someone told me she was a wicked spirit raised from death to haunt me, I would believe them without question. As if she knows I'm thinking about her, she flicks her cruel gaze to me.

Her eyes light up; her plaything is finally here.

I cringe as her long strides gobble the space between us. "Hello, worm. Lovely morning for a hanging, isn't it?"

My breath catches in my chest; they're going to *hang* me.

Despite the cloying oleander perfume she wears, the faintest tendril of death reaches my nose, and my stomach clenches.

"Don't pout. You knew this would happen. How could you not? Or were you really stupid enough to believe you could get away with attacking the emperor on his own Island? But you don't get to die just yet, worm."

That's when I notice the group by the scaffolding. A chasm of dread splits open inside my chest.

"Don't . . ." My voice is a broken rasp. "Kill me. *Me*. Not them."

"Oh, I will. Slowly, with absolute pleasure. But first you have to choose. From now on, every time you disobey me, someone dies. Every time you do not answer a question correctly, someone dies. Every time you try to escape, or even resist, someone dies. Now *choose*."

Centurions in sleek black military jackets with golden buttons that shine in the sun parade the prisoners in front of us. Just like me, most wear fancy dresses and waistcoats from the celebration, the luxurious silks and velvets ragged from days of wear, spots of blood and charred smudges hinting at the horror from that night.

They plead, their focus flitting between the Archduchess and me.

"Choose the first to die for your mistake," the Archduchess orders.

Despite the chill, sweat dribbles down my shoulder blades. I can't see the cameras, but of course they're here somewhere, filming everything.

The entire world is watching me choose who lives and who dies.

My heart roars inside my chest as I force my gaze onto the prisoners. There's the finalist I recognize whose name I can't recall, her dark fishtail braid hanging nearly to her waist. The wrinkled, sun-hardened woman with gray hair and gnarled fingers, obviously from across the fence. A young dark-skinned man in a tattered, navy-blue jacket with matching eyes that rake my face.

I take a step and fall to my knees. Laughter and taunts from the Royalist crowd fill the air, mixing with the daybreak noises of chirping birds into a horrible, cruel song. Even though the sun burns against my cheeks, my flesh is clammy and ridged with goose bumps.

The Archduchess's shadow creeps over me. "Choose."

"No."

"Then I will choose for you—only, maybe I'll choose five instead of one."

Hollowness fills me, a deep, unbearable ache. My fingers sink into the grass as I pray to the gods to let the earth swallow me up.

"Please."

"You're boring me, worm. Perhaps I'll take ten. Yes, ten is a good number—"

"No."

"Or, perhaps I'll hang them all one-by-one and have you pull the lever. Wouldn't that be fun?"

I count the prisoners. Twenty-four. Thank the gods none of my friends are here. I hate the tiny whisper of happiness this realization brings.

Some I recognize from somewhere—the Trials, maybe? Some look new. It's hard to remember. Every time I glance too long at one person, they shake their head and cry, their eyes piercing me with accusation.

A few refuse to look at me altogether.

I glare at the Royalists flocked around us in their mourning finery, searching for the camera. Gods only know how they're presenting this to the world.

I should refuse, but I can't. I will not be responsible for any more deaths than I have to be. Even if the prisoners will hate me for it.

Even if *I'll* hate myself for it.

An older man stands off from the rest, his eyes glassy with pain. He clutches his chest, a dark cherry-red stain spreading out from his fingers. His gray flesh shines with sweat. He's feverish. Weak.

He may die anyway.

At least this is what I tell myself as, staring down at the grass, I point a shaking finger at him.

"Is that any way to condemn a man to die for your sins?" the Archduchess asks. "Go to him. Look him in the eye."

I take a step toward the man. Another. My feet are impossibly heavy, weighted down with guilt.

When I come within a foot of him, I see the worn picture he clutches, the hand-sewn seams of his ill-fitting tunic that shows someone used to care about this man.

"Him." My voice sounds hollow, raw.

Despite his pain, despite his fear, he nods to me as a Centurion forces him up the steps to the scaffolding. All the same, I know I'll see him again soon, in my nightmares along with the others.

A murmur of excitement ripples through the onlookers. The Archduchess grabs a fistful of my dress and forces me to join them.

Tiny, threadlike red capillaries lace her chest, her excited breaths coming out in short bursts. "Watch, maggot."

And I do. Forcing down the shame and guilt, I make myself watch the man I condemned to die. After it's over and the crowd thins, I close my eyes and say a prayer for the man and any others to come.

Because I won't stop trying to escape until either I make it out and find the Mercurian, or they *kill* me.

THREE

I'm barely back inside my cell when two Centurions I've never seen before come to collect me. The rusty door grates open. I must not move fast enough because the larger man reaches his huge fist over and grips my hair, yanking me out.

I stumble forward, grinding my teeth against the dull pulse of fire in my leg, phantom pain from my Reconstruction. Near the top of the stairs, the idiot shoves me. My fingers scrape against the stone wall to keep from falling, adding dark scum to the dried blood and filth beneath my fingernails.

An underground tunnel waits. Flickering torches sputtering in the wet darkness. Rats squeak in the corners. The bigger Centurion taunts me the entire way. Sometimes with his fists. Sometimes with his harsh words and rotten breath. Hatred rolls off him like fog.

I take the abuse, welcoming the sharp spikes of pain that set my bones on fire and the blinding momentary nothingness.

Each blow fuels the flames inside me and reminds me I'm not dead.

As long as I'm not dead, I can escape.

Something metallic flashes in my periphery. Bramble. He's following us, clinging to the shadows with the vermin and whatever ghosts haunt this place.

As our feet clop across the wet ground, I say a silent prayer to the gods to keep him safe.

We slink farther through the famed red tunnel, where the emperor has prisoners from the Tower secretly brought to the castle for interrogation. After several nights being taken to see the Archduchess, I know the way.

Except when it comes time to take a right down the cramped stairwell, we keep going. As we enter another stairway leading up, the air thinning and warming with each step, I consider every possible reason for veering off course.

The Fienians could have captured someone important, someone dear to the emperor or the General—hopefully the Countess Delphine, Caspian's betrothed—and perhaps they're trading me for her.

But as soon as the thought comes, it goes. The emperor would never negotiate with the Fienians, even for his favorite Chosen and soon to be daughter-in-law.

I'm wheezing from the climb. How high are we ascending? Perhaps we're going to one of the many terraces that adorn the palace. To show the people how the emperor caught the evil Fienian responsible for the bombing and the deaths. Parade me around like a trophy again.

He did that once, in the beginning . . . I think. With the pain and the drugs, I can't remember exactly.

Despite my fatigue, I straighten my spine and pull in deep, steadying breaths. Wherever the guards are taking me, I need to be ready to fight. I grind my wrists against the cuffs, growling at the pain.

"Stop moving," the guard growls, knocking me into the wall.

My head cracks sideways into the stone. I bring my manacled hands up to fight, but he's already opening the door to a long corridor.

From the corner of my eye, I catch Bramble scurrying over the steps to protect me, the delicate antennae jutting from his head sticking straight up in anger.

I jerk my chin in a subtle command, stopping him on the last step.

Go, idiot, I mouth.

I swear I hear a tiny, rebellious chirp in reply.

Golden rectangles of light pour from the windows lining the hall. My gaze cuts to the burnished-yellow sky as I instinctively search for Her. Pandora.

My promise to stop Her seems silly now, a childish taunt.

Except it's not silly because if I can just escape here, I'll dedicate the rest of my life—however short—to obliterating Her.

But first, I have to take care of these two idiots. Swiping the hair from my eyes with my forearm, I glare at the cruelest guard.

You'll be the first to die.

I keep my gaze sharp, on the lookout for anything I can use as a weapon as we wind through torch-lit hallways and antechambers. The castle is quiet, a sense of mourning haunting the air. A few servants in homespun tunics look away as we pass, their shoulders hunched and eyes timid.

How many Bronze servants did the emperor punish because of the Rebel attack?

A sharp left turn brings us to a larger hallway. Attendants stand outside thick oak doors with iron locks, and fresh-cut red roses line hammered-silver vases in the alcoves, the flowers' alluring scent mixing with the strong perfume of frankincense and vanilla.

A hunched servant with gray hair snips more roses for a vase and pauses as we pass. My gaze flicks over the wood-handled gardening knife he sets on the table, the serrated blade the size of my pinky.

Hardly breathing, I stand as close as I can to the table without drawing suspicion. The Centurion knocks softly on the third door on the left, cutting his eyes at me every few seconds as if I'm going to bolt or do something stupid.

Which, hopefully, I am.

Muffled steps from inside. My heart is a wild drum against my ribs, and my mouth turns to cotton. I'll only have half a second when everyone's attention is on the opening door to grab the knife.

The gold handle turns. As the door parts, I lean back, slip my arm under the huge canopy of flowers, and take the knife.

Carefully, I wedge the blade into my bust and release a breath.

Both guards bow, but the angle I'm standing makes it hard to see who's inside.

"My Liege," they say in unison.

Liege? Oh gods, no. The emperor. Probably the emperor *and* the Archduchess.

Tingly fear pulses through my limbs. I fight as the guard wraps his arms around me and hauls me forward, bucking and kicking through the threshold and into the large room.

His ear passes in front of my face, and I clench the fleshy cartilage between my teeth and bite down. Hard.

"Bitch!" he screeches.

The guard shoves me down. I thrust out my cuffed hands, but my feet entangle with the torn hem of my dress and my face collides with the white marble floor.

I spit out blood, both mine and the guard's, making a bright stain on the otherwise pristine flooring.

Silence. Kicking my feet out of my ruined dress, I lift my manacled hands, ready to die fighting the emperor and Archduchess. "If you think you can—"

Breath flees my lungs. I never thought there could be anyone I'd hate to face more than the emperor and Archduchess, but as my gaze trails the fine leather boots and over the gleaming doublet and land on his face, I'm frozen in place with shame.

Prince Caspian stares down at me, his curved lips pressed into a tight line. "Hello, Maia, or whoever the Fienian hell you are."

FOUR

A wave of emotions crashes over me as I stare up at the Crown Prince. Sorrow for tricking him, making him feel responsible. Shame for playing a part in Ophelia's murder . . . but the emperor killed her, not that Caspian would believe me.

Mainly, though, I feel longing for things to be different.

I study the prince I was once supposed to marry. His hands are clenched into fists at his side, his breathing shallow and choppy as he inspects me much the same. I can't stand his stare, the condemnation in those beautiful champagne eyes rimmed in golden lashes. Lines seem to have creased his eyes since the bombing, and his cheeks are hollow and sharp.

An invisible wall has grown between us, making him unreachable.

A muscle in his neck flickers. "Who are you?"

"Maia—"

"No." His voice is quiet, clipped, none of the warmth or amusement from before the bombings. "You're not her, whatever you say"—he rakes a hand through his golden hair—"it's all lies, anyway."

I try to stand as he paces, but the Centurion I bit launches forward with his fist raised, only too happy to hit me again. His other hand is pressed into his bleeding, mangled ear.

The second Centurion is nowhere in sight—probably outside guarding the door. Goading the guard into attacking me might be beneficial. If Caspian has any decency left, he might send the soldier away, giving me full access to the prince.

But one look at Caspian's face, the ruthless cut of his mouth, and I know my plan won't work. Not that I blame him.

Scowling, I ease back onto my rear as shame tightens my chest. My dirty fingers—still stained with grit and blood from the bombing—worry at the silken shreds of my dress, twirling them like ribbons of blood.

I'm sorry, I want to say—*would* say, if he would believe me.

Only the emperor was supposed to die. Not hundreds of innocents. Not Ophelia, the sweet Rebel princess who perished within arm's reach of me. But the words sit heavy and sour on my tongue, and I force them back down.

Don't focus on that. Find a way to connect with him again.

I release a breath and allow my eyes to feast on the opulent room, a jarring contrast to my time inside the Tower. High marble ceilings, rich ivory panels, and gold converge to create a thing of beauty.

And the space . . . you could fit twenty Tower cells inside this chamber.

In place of the bars I'm used to, windows spill warm light over Caspian and paint a burnt-orange shadow across the too-white floor, bright compared to my dingy cell. A pale marble sphinx over the wall glares down at an enormous, gold-veined marble bed, as if sneering at the clumps of over-sized fur pillows the color of snow.

Silence snaps my attention back to Caspian.

His dark, accusing gaze pins me to the tile. "Why?"

"I . . . I . . ." I lick my dry lips. "It wasn't supposed to happen like . . . I mean, I knew, but I thought . . ."

My excuse sounds pathetic, even to me. I drop my face into my hands as the screams and smell of burnt flesh pierce my mind.

Footsteps echo across the marble. A hand pulls me to my feet.

"No," Caspian says as he drags me up and across the floor to the window, my feet making *thump-thump* sounds against the tile, "you don't get to close your eyes and pretend what you did doesn't have consequences."

Even though I know what to expect—I was there—the sight still makes me gasp. What once was an entire wall on the east side of the palace is now jagged chunks of marble speckling the green lawn. Blackened craters mar the grass like the pox. Dead horses still lie where they fell, shadowed by clouds of flies. Servants pick through the rubble, clearing body parts and gathering corpses into wheelbarrows.

Somewhere in the distance, dark smoke churns the sky.

The Royalists must be burning the bodies.

How many are my friends? The thought makes it hard to breathe.

I turn to face him. "Caspian, if I could go back in time and stop it somehow, if I could trade my life for any one of the innocent courtiers who died, I would, gladly."

His jaw is clenched. "Like O? If only you could."

Shouts draw my gaze down near the cherry trees where we dined not four days ago, where O smiled and glowed like a benevolent goddess from the pages of a book and Caspian didn't hate me.

And Riser . . . Riser.

But now instead of the cherry blossoms falling on long oak tables full of food, they flurry over the tall scaffolding from earlier. Ten people stand on the scaffolding, nooses around their throats. I squint as I make out boys and girls around my age, some crying, others stoic.

They watch wide-eyed as the Archduchess grabs the lever.

No. I pound the glass with my fists. She said if I chose, I would save the rest. But it must have been all for show. A cruel trick.

I pound my fists again and again, rattling the window, and although the thick marble walls hide the sound of the planks beneath the prisoners' feet giving way, I can still *hear* them, the sound from earlier engraved inside my head.

Nausea churns my belly. Why would Caspian show me this? "She said only one would die if I chose."

"She lied."

"She's a monster," I snarl, unable to contain the fury in my voice. "And so is anyone who doesn't stop her."

"Monsters come in all different forms."

I glance out the window. "Is that what will happen to me after the Archduchess grows bored of my screams?"

His cheek twitches, but his eyes remain hard. "Yes, if you're still alive."

We both know if I'm lucky, I won't be.

And any chance of saving the empire will die too. My heart sinks. My father spent a large chunk of his life building the device that could possibly save us.

How many hours did it take for him to hide the Mercurian here? How many times was he almost caught, an offense that would have earned him a spot on the Archduchess's torture table?

Caspian watches me with his golden eyes. But there's a flicker of . . . something. Sadness?

Even after everything that's happened, the pull between the prince and me remains strong. I have to try to break through to him.

I reach out a filthy hand. "Please, Caspian—please help me."

He inhales sharply, his gaze flitting over my hand before lingering on the dried blood that darkens the creases between my knuckles.

He draws himself up tall, shoulders rigid, looking every part the prince in his black doublet threaded with gold. "If you address me as anything other than Prince again, I'll have you whipped."

A spark of anger burns through my chest. "Yes, our actions led to O's death, but it was the emperor who ultimately killed her. Yes—I deserve to pay for my actions, but *so* does the emperor. And what about the hundreds of Bronzes the emperor has enslaved, imprisoned, tortured, and killed. What about them? Are they not as deserving as O?"

Caspian glowers at me, and I realize his mind is already made up.

"Why did you bring me here, *Prince*?" I lift up my shackles. "To see me bound and helpless before the Archduchess tortures me?"

He flinches at the chains, taking a quick step back. "Take them off."

Before I can grasp what's happening, the guard has unshackled my chains. Mirroring my surprise, he glares at me as he pockets the cuffs.

"Leave us," Caspian orders.

The guard hesitates. "Beg your pardon, my—"

"*Leave us.*"

My pulse drumbeats inside my skull, and I wring my hands. *Am I being freed? Is he going to kill me?*

I ready my hand over my hidden knife. But could I kill Caspian if it came to that?

Yes, I realize, hand shaking as I slip it over the handle. *Yes I could.*

FIVE

The Centurion slips out the door but not before one final warning look back at me. If I murder the prince on the Centurion's watch, surely he'd be hanged.

My fingers twitch above the dagger.

Caspian walks to the window.

Sighing, I try to cover my relief with small talk. "Not afraid to turn your back on me?"

Tilting his head to peer at the ground below, he chuckles darkly. "Do you have a knife hidden somewhere I don't know about?"

"No," I sputter, *too* quickly. The knife suddenly feels hot, as if it wants me to pick it up. I shift on my feet, hoping he doesn't notice how fast I denied it. "Why free me?"

When he turns, my chest tightens at his stiff mouth, the sheer sadness in his eyes. "I'm not. But I can give you a moment of peace before she takes you."

She. He can't even say the Archduchess's name.

"You think removing my handcuffs will give me *peace*?"

He frowns, his gaze flickering over the entertainment buffet by the door. Fluffy pastries and colorful cakes mound the gilded china, and a porcelain teacup gushes steam, making my belly tighten. How did I miss those?

Without looking at me, he waves his hand, the golden phoenix cufflinks adorning his sleeves winking. "Whatever you like."

"A last meal?" I snort. "Do you really think a cup of tea can absolve you for loosing that—that monster on me?"

Anger flashes in his eyes. "That's more than the three-hundred-twenty-two souls you murdered received. I had them set your leg and mend the hole in your side—"

"The hole the Archduchess made when she stabbed me."

"Yes, well I did everything in my power to keep her away from you, even though that delay gave the Rebels time to escape!"

Escape? Does that mean they're not *all* dead? A flicker of hope tickles my chest.

"Why?" I say. "If you despise me so much, why not get it over with?"

The waning light glints off the almost-tears in his eyes. "Whenever I . . . Whenever I look at you, I see the Rebel who murdered my sister. But then"—he takes a step toward me, arm out—"in the same instant, I see the girl I was meant to be with and I . . . I . . ." His shoulders slump. He lets his arm fall, his fingers curling into a fist. "You're a weakness, a blight in my character. And you almost cost me my kingdom, my life, my *everything*."

All at once, I want to drop to my knees and beg him to help me find the Mercurian. We could save everyone, fix it all. And maybe—maybe I could redeem myself to him. The Mercurian is on these grounds. The guards wouldn't question him if he took me away . . . We could search . . . but no, I don't even know where it is.

Use his weakness, the reconstructed part of me whispers. *It's the only way.*

I stroll to the buffet and poke one of the pastries. His intense focus burns into my shoulder blades. "Prince," I say, twirling a flaky tart stuffed with raspberry jam, "you can still take me to the Sim." I take a bite and turn. "Once they . . . Once *I'm* dead, the thing my father created will be useless. Help me save our people."

He blinks, swallows, a shadow passing over his face. "Like before, right? When you tricked me?" His mop of golden hair glints as he shakes his head. "Drink the tea before it gets cold."

The pastry tastes like ash in my mouth. I wash it down with warm, bitter tea as Caspian watches me, and I let myself hope.

Maybe I won't have to use my weapon. Maybe if I tell him about Ophelia, how his father murdered her . . .

Sighing, I plop the cup back on the tray and turn. Then I cross the floor to the prince.

Caspian stiffens, his mouth parting slightly.

When I'm close enough to feel the warmth of his breath, I stop. "Caspian, no more lies. No more pretending. Only the truth."

His eyebrows gather above a smirk. "Are you even capable of that?"

I grit my teeth against the snappy retort on my lips. "Princess Ophelia Laevus was a Fienian Rebel. She was helping the—helping us, although I didn't know it at the time."

He opens his mouth and then closes it, exhaling through his nose. His eyes search my face.

"Somehow, your father found out. After the bombing, she was hurt but alive. Your father . . . the emperor killed her."

I pore over his face, trying to read his thoughts. Everything rests on him believing me. His fingers have curled into tight fists, but that could mean anything.

"What I told you that night before the bombing was true," I continue, my voice gaining confidence. "My father built something that can stop the asteroid. Your father knows, and he wants to destroy it. I didn't tell the Rebels about it because I'm afraid they'll use it as a weapon."

His jaw grinds back and forth. *What is he thinking?*

I reach a pale hand out, ignoring the dirt and blood darkening the creases, and touch his shoulder. "You are the only person who can help me. Please, Caspian. We can stop this madness together."

The *tick-tock* of the clock on the wall marks his silence in time with my heart.

His lips twitch, and then he grabs my wrist and plucks my hand off his shoulder like I'm something disgusting. "I thought I told you what would happen if you didn't address me properly. Guards!"

I find the knife in my bodice, my fingers hesitant around the handle, and pause. But he's left me no choice, so I slip behind him and wrap my arm around his neck.

He moves to fight, but then freezes, as if he's felt the blade at his throat and knows he's lost.

I press my lips to his ear just as the two guards burst in. "And I thought I told you I didn't have a knife? I guess we both lied, *Prince*."

The guards reach for their pistols, and I press the tip of the blade into the side of Caspian's neck. "Stop, or the prince dies."

Their eyes widen, and slowly they lift their hands.

"Think about what you're doing, Fienian," the larger guard spits.

"Oh, I am." Using the knifepoint to guide Caspian, I circle around the guards and to the door. "Take out your pistols and slide them across the floor."

The smaller guard looks to the large man, who sighs, his

massive shoulders heaving, and sends his gun skidding toward us. The second revolver follows.

Forcing Caspian down, I grab the first weapon and tuck it into my bodice. There's no room for the second, so I open the cylinder and tilt it, spilling the bullets, which I keep.

We stand. "Now the keys."

After I have them, I force Caspian out the door and make him lock it. At first he tries to fool me by barely twisting the rusted iron key, but I push the knifepoint a little deeper and force him to comply.

For a few pounding heartbeats, I'm lost, torn between finding the Mercurian and escaping. But the door locking the guards in won't hold for long, and I still have absolutely no idea where the Mercurian is.

Perhaps Caspian might have a clue—but by the taut muscles of his jaw and neck, I can guess he's feeling a bit uncooperative at the moment.

"Move," I growl, forcing him down the hall as my gaze darts over the doors and corners, my stomach lurching at every sound. "You know, it didn't have to be this way."

"No?" Caspian says. "Am I really to believe you with a blade at my neck? And, while we're discussing the way things are, perhaps you can ease up on the knife a bit? I rather like this shirt."

Blood dots his collar, and I realize the knife has broken his skin. "Well maybe if you weren't about to order me *whipped*, I would take it easier on you."

A bitter laugh slips from his throat. "Gods, how did I ever believe a word you said? You sent me a poem, one stupid poem, and I just blindly fell at your feet. You and your traitorous father must have laughed at me. The poor, dumb prince."

I clench the knife at the word traitorous. Before I can

correct him, voices trickle from the end of the hallway, and I yank him into an alcove, flattening against the wall.

"I won't hesitate to kill you," I whisper.

I have no idea if that's true. I thought I could hurt him earlier, but who knows what I'm capable of right now—especially with Caspian warm against my chest, smelling of sandalwood and horses, a vast improvement on my locked-in-a-tower aroma.

Luckily the voices disappear around a corner, and I don't have to find out. I wait a few seconds, and then we continue moving, retracing my steps to the red tunnel.

If I can just make it there, I can have a moment to think without fear of being caught. The knife goes into his side now, so it will look less conspicuous.

Rats squeak and flee as we enter the red tunnel, the heavy iron door grating shut behind us. I loosen my grip on Caspian a hair and let out a ragged breath.

He shifts, growling as the knife presses into his side. "You won't get away with this."

"Watch me."

I try to move again, and again he resists, just slightly, glancing down the long tunnel at a darkened stairwell.

"What's down there?" I demand.

His silence tells me perhaps something important. I force him closer, the moldy stone floor slippery beneath my feet. A torch sputters in the moist air, and I pluck the flame from the wall. The steps are steep and crumbling, shadows pooling to veil whatever lies beyond.

Halfway down the stairs, the torchlight illuminates a steel door, rust bubbling over its surface.

"Where does this door lead?" I ask.

Caspian sighs. "I don't even know if it works."

"But if it does work, *where* would it lead?"

He stares at the door for a too-long second. Then his

shoulders sag. "To the other side of the mountains—but the tunnel has probably collapsed by now."

All I hear is mountains, which means off the Island. Freedom.

I fish the keys from my pocket and hand them to Caspian. "Open it."

Gritting his jaw, he turns the lock. There's a mechanical click, and then the door pops open with an inrush of cool, dank air.

I give Caspian a little push. "After you, Prince."

As soon as the door shuts behind us and the small space comes into view, my body trembles and sweat drenches my armpits. I can barely pull in enough air to satisfy my lungs.

I shift, my elbows scraping the tight tunnel walls. Just like the pit. Like the labyrinth of horrors during the Trials. Despite my resolve, my lungs are beginning to freak out, sucking in air like I'm drowning.

"Well, this is cozy," Caspian quips.

I gulp another ragged breath.

"What, no snappy comeback?"

But I'm only halfway listening as I force more air into my chest and try to slow my pounding heart. Sweat drenches my forehead.

I cannot have a panic attack when I'm this close to freedom.

Inhale. Exhale. Survive.

All at once, his back stiffens. He slows, just enough that I notice. Before I can react, his arm darts to the knife.

I press the blade into his side. "Don't."

"Ah!" His angry scream bounces off the walls. "If you're going to kill me, just do it already!"

I pull the blade back slightly but keep it at his side. Eventually the walls widen, and the pit and the labyrinth fade into the dark recesses of my mind. The torch crackles and sputters in the wet air, orange light dancing inside the pale strands of the prince's hair.

Water trickles from far off, and a cold stream runs over my bare feet.

My mouth aches. When was the last time I had a drink?

Caspian halts, and I nearly collide with his broad shoulders. "Do you hear that?"

"What?" My grip tightens on the knife. At this point, my trust in the prince has withered a bit, and I let him feel the sharp end of the weapon.

The blade quickens his step again, but his head cants to the left, as if he can see something at the base of a knee-high mound of stones. "Something's following us."

My chapped lips ache as they spit into a grin. "That's probably Bramble. He's a friend."

"Bramble?" When I don't elaborate, Caspian snorts. "If he's a friend, why is he hiding?"

"Because he doesn't trust you." I take way more pleasure in this then I should.

Caspian's shoulders stiffen, and I brace for an argument. But then he clears his throat. "So . . . what happened back there?"

I shrug, even though he can't see me. "This place reminds me of something."

"The labyrinth."

It isn't a question. "You watched what happened, what we all had to endure. You saw me kill my best friend. So, I don't know—what do *you* think?"

He threads a hand through his hair. "I think that anyone who went through that would come out traumatized."

"Understatement of the century," I mutter under my breath, thinking about the voices. Traumatized may not be the right word for me. "Did you know my mom created that maze of horrors? Never mind. Of course you did."

"I'm sure that's hard for you."

"Yeah." My hand tightens around the knife handle as I remember that Caspian's mom and baby sister died tragically from a bomb, just like Ophelia. Perhaps he understands more than I give him credit for. "Can I ask you a question?"

"Ask away."

"After your mom's death, and your sister's, did you ever . . . I don't know. Hear voices?"

He pauses for a moment. "Voices? No. I'm grieving, not insane."

Right. We duck low beneath fallen beams, and I rub the knuckles of my free hand over my temple, as if somehow that can explain the voices I hear.

By now, I've allowed space between us. This far in, if Caspian runs, I can still probably get away. In fact, I know I'm only keeping him with me now because I can't bear the thought of being alone in the darkness.

His profile comes into view as he glances back. "What happened to you after your father died? Where did you go?"

"To hell."

He halts, his gaze slanting back at me. "I'm sorry."

"No," I counter, sounding angrier than I mean to. "You're not. Because you have no idea what that means. You can't even fathom what my life was like then, so saying you're sorry is just empty words, a way to make yourself feel better."

After that, we walk in silence, until a faint trickle of light up ahead catches my eye. My pulse quickens as the sound of birds chirping fills the air. Hurrying Caspian forward, I practically run to the hole four feet up along the tunnel wall, just big enough for a body to fit through. Blue sky and green leaves call to me. A burst of fresh air blows over my face.

After a quick prod, Caspian jumps through, and I follow.

The crevice hides behind a large gray boulder, on an outcropping below sheer-faced mountains. A rock-strewn hill leads down to trees; the sound of a rushing stream trickles in the distance.

Slipping and sliding down the hill, I manage to land behind Caspian with the knife just as my gaze flicks to the sky. Drones could be nearby. The Royalists could already be looking for me.

I can't let the prince go free, not yet.

Caspian sighs as I press the knife gently into his back, prodding him forward. I keep a step behind. As we make our way out of the valley, the forest changing to sloping meadows that wave in the breeze, my bruised, beaten, starved body lets go of the tension and fear I've been hoarding for days. Especially once I catch sight of Bramble darting through the tall grass a few feet away.

Every few steps, he pokes a blade of grass with his antennae, his chirps filling the air.

I smile, the tension around my heart lifting.

I want to revel in this newfound freedom. But without the adrenaline that's kept me going, I feel everything. The bones that were shattered and mended back together countless times ache with each step, every inch of my flesh twitches with pain, and a headache presses behind my eyes.

"What now?" Caspian asks.

His question highlights my lack of a plan. Honestly, I didn't think I would get this far. Without an idea where the Rebels are hiding, or even where *we* are, I'm lost. Not that I will admit that.

I'm about to answer when a soft buzzing noise from over the hill makes us both freeze. Bramble chirps twice in alarm and then scuttles around my feet before climbing up my leg and onto my shoulder. I pull Caspian close, sweat slicking my hand around the handle of the dagger.

"Swifters," Caspian breathes as sleek metallic vehicles zip over the hill toward us. All five of them glitter in the sun, and their riders are just as bright in their red jackets and vests. They must be incredibly fast because I barely blink and they're on top of us.

Rebels. They have to be. No one would flaunt the color red otherwise. They form a circle around us. One of the riders looks familiar—

"Rhydian!" I cry. My voice is hoarse, hardly a whisper. "Is it really you?"

Merida's brother tilts his head and squints at me, his sharp gaze sliding to Bramble on my shoulder. "Everly?"

I nod, relief giving me a burst of energy. "Yes. I escaped. Oh, gods, I can't believe you found me."

I go to take a step, but the female rider points a crossbow at me. "What's that thing on her shoulder?"

I clench my teeth, glaring at the girl. "Rhydian, tell her who I am."

"That's the prince," one of the Rebels hisses.

Rhydian scratches his neck, a line creasing his forehead as he studies me.

"Rhydian, it's me. Tell them to put their weapons down."

With a heavy sigh, he turns to the others. "Take them both."

The girl lunges at me. On instinct, I smash my palm into her face. There's a crack, and blood spurts from her nose as she screams.

At the same time, Caspian knocks the closest Rebel from his seat and slides onto the back of the silver machine. He grasps the handlebars and shoots through the circle, knocking Rhydian into the Swifter beside him.

One of the Rebels lifts something shiny—a pistol—and aims it at Caspian's retreating back.

Without thinking, I bat the weapon away just as a shot splits the air. Bramble flinches into my neck. Grass and dirt explode on the hillside where the bullet hit. Gunpowder fills my nose.

By the time the Rebel aims again, Caspian slips over the hill.

"Should I go after him?" one of the Rebels asks Rhydian.

Rhydian's gaze is on me as he shakes his head, slowly. "No, there could be other Royalists around. We need to get back."

"And her?" the girl with the broken nose asks.

"The traitor comes with us."

Traitor? I open my mouth to reply when there's a sharp crack, and a white-hot bolt of pain splits my skull. A gasp escapes my throat as I fall to my knees, and I manage to call out Rhydian's name again before my world goes dark.

SEVEN

erida is alive. Her eyes are wide and pleading as they peek from beneath the mountain of burned, bloodied corpses. Her lips form the same words over and over. Help me. Other voices join hers, begging me to save them.

"Help us," they whisper. "We're trapped. Please, help us!"

Screaming, I jerk up in bed. A sweat-soaked sheet tangles around my legs, my stomach clenched and trying to heave up my last meal. My flesh shivers even though the air is stuffy and hot, and my head feels as if it's been crushed with a mallet.

Where am I? What's happened?

Caspian. The tunnel. Bramble.

Escape.

Free. I'm free. I'm . . .

But am I? Pulling back the faded cardinal-red duvet lined in gold—*Who would dare flaunt the banned color?*—I slide from the bed and take in the cramped, red-paneled room.

Wherever I am, it's not under Royalist control. Everything red was burned after Ezra's final betrayal, the Fienian leader's House Color strictly forbidden. Eventually, the color became synonymous with rebellion.

Flurries of dust stir as I follow shafts of light to the massive window behind my bed. A deep grate of wood, carved and glossed into a lattice of sorts, blankets most of the glass. Trapped slivers of the window peek beneath its cage.

I blink as something begins to take shape in the wood. Some sort of beast, with a short, curved tail and a . . . a barb.

Scorpion. I pick out hundreds of the poisonous creatures. Some small and strange and spindly, others large and cruel, their thick, curved pincers large enough to amputate a person's limbs. The detail put into the beasts must have taken years to complete.

Knots twist my gut. The room feels too much like a cell, and I still have no idea where I am or what happened to Bramble.

Muffled shouts and sharp laughter draw my gaze to the thick redwood door. More carvings mar its surface. I rub a palm against my forehead, massaging the knot left where I was struck after Caspian escaped. I wince as my fingers trace over a small, raised incision on my left temple.

Microplant. They must have taken one out . . . and probably put another one in, knowing Nicolai. Especially if he thinks I'm a traitor.

Traitor. The word clangs around my skull, not helping my headache.

Perhaps Rhydian didn't recognize me, dirty and bloodied from days of torture. It's the only thing that makes sense . . . and then, when I helped Caspian escape, it confirmed I was someone else.

First on my agenda is finding Rhydian and letting him know it's me. Then . . . then I have to face my fears and ask about Riser. My stomach churns just thinking about the possibility that he didn't make it, and I twist the tangled strands of my hair inside my fingers.

Riser has to be alive. He has to be.

I need to get out of this room. My dress is trashed, so I rifle through a wardrobe brimming with old, out-of-fashion dresses that I imagine my mother wore when she was my age. I roll my eyes at the full corsets and long sweeping skirts. Like the room, the gowns are dark, my gaze catching on the embroidered red flowers and patterns that pop against the charcoal-and-black silk.

I choose the least cumbersome, a gray dress of cotton with black silk panels and red piping. Shiny black boots sit neatly at the foot of the bed. They're tight but not unbearable.

After searching for a few minutes, I discover a pearl-handled letter opener and slip it in a small slit sewn into the inside of my bodice. *That should make the Fienian happy.*

Even with the metal heavy against my breast, I feel empty, exposed without a dagger or pistol.

Finding an effective weapon goes to the top on my list, right after finding Bramble and Riser and discovering *where* I am.

The heavy door groans open beneath my fingers. A long swath of burgundy carpet stretches down the hallway. Circular iron chandeliers hang from the arched ceiling, the candles imparting a buttery glow over the rich wood walls. The smells of polish and something else—perhaps ancient leather—fill my nose, wakening the ghost of a headache.

Just like my room, the windowless hallway has an old, heavy feel, as if hundreds of souls have walked along these corridors.

The hallway curves to the left. Every time I think it's going to branch off, it turns again, a never-ending circle of burgundy and gleaming panels. Doors much like the one from my room appear, each one with similar, cruel carvings that send shivers down my spine.

Voices echo down the hall, and I stop to stare as two older boys walk toward me. My gaze slides to their entwined fingers. Both wear leathers similar to mine, with high-collared silk tunics of scarlet, their pitch-black hair jetting at odd, fierce angles. The taller boy lifts his brows at me, the six silver studs rimming his brows flashing. The other boy chuckles and leans in, nuzzling the taller boy's cheek, and I quickly focus on my boots.

I can hear their whispers even after they disappear around the curve. Blood warms my cheeks, but I force myself to continue, desperate for something, anything I can anchor myself to.

This is another form of torture. Not as bad as the Tower, but at least there I knew where I was and what to expect.

Here, it's like I've stepped into another world.

Other groups pass, all dressed in tight leather pants and brightly colored tunics. *Does Color not matter here?*

A break in the curve reveals a large room on my right. Tall bookshelves march across the floor in rows.

I blink. They're brimming with books. *Real* books.

Mouth hanging slightly open, I approach the nearest shelf, a ten-foot tall wall of faded leather-bound manuscripts.

How could so many books have escaped the Great Purge?

My heart flutters as I skim my fingers over their spines, and I let out a tiny gasp of joy.

For some reason I remember Riser. I scoffed at him when he tried to touch the hologram bookshelf in my mother's office.

They're not real, I teased.

But these, these are very much real. Their scent swells inside my nose, a hint of stale paper and citrus, filling me with an indescribable emotion. I reach out to touch another worn book when my periphery picks up something red to the right.

A painting takes up nearly the entire wall. I draw closer, lured by the rich, dark colors. My attention whips to the stunning woman inside. Midnight-black ringlets cascade from the rim of a gray hat and spiral down to her slim waist. She wears a low-cut gown the color of charcoal, the blood-red roses that line her corset the only bright color on the canvas, besides her sea-blue eyes.

I frown at her cruel, jagged beauty. The sharp planes of her face, her piercing stare.

Something familiar about her tugs at me.

My stomach hollows at the scorpion choker nestled in the indent of her pale neck. At the familiar sting of her gaze, as if even through the old oil paint, she's slowly peeling away at me, searching—

Dragging footsteps against the stone have me snapping around. My hand is already on the letter opener inside my corset, my fingers cold against my flesh.

An older boy with warm, dark eyes and a wild crown of rich, curly copper hair rakes his gaze over me. "Are you March?"

My mouth parts; it takes a second for my synapses to fire, reminding me that March is my new last name. "Call me Maia."

"O-kay . . . *dandy lover.*"

The insult cuts deep, but I try to blow it off. He must think because of my brand I'm a Royalist. "Can you tell me if Riser Thornbrook is . . . Well, is he alive?"

"The Blood King?"

"Blood King? I don't know what that is."

The boy cuts his eyes at me, two lines creasing his forehead as his gaze slides to the emperor's brand at my neck. "He's alive."

I let out a deep sigh. "Thank the gods. What about my friends? Brogue, and Rhydian."

"Friends?"

"Yes. You know. People you care about. *Friends*."

He toys with the top button of his tunic. "Couldn't say."

"What about the . . . the machine that was with me. Bramble?"

"Machine?" The amusement in his voice is at odds with his tight mouth. "Enough chit-chat, love. Nicolai wants to see you."

He turns on his heel before I can raise my eyebrows, not looking back to see if I follow. One of his legs drags the floor, just slightly. The worn stone is slick beneath my boots as I scramble to catch up.

As much as I want to take in my new surroundings, I can't focus on anything long enough to get much of my bearings.

Alive, Riser is alive. The words speed up my footsteps. Although I won't let myself believe, won't allow myself to really hope until I've seen Riser. I picture him, his irreverent grin.

Digger Girl, he'll say. *What took you so long?*

Despite what I assume is a pleasant, even handsome face, the boy's lips are pinched together in a scowl, his shoulders taut, discouraging conversation. Obviously he won't lower himself to talk to me.

Not that it matters. I'm practically floating now. Outpacing him. If Riser is alive . . . No, of course he's alive. Pit Boy has more lives than a cat.

Despite my weak condition, I leap down the wide, curving steps that lead to the lower level, pausing only to take in the huge open chamber, a balustrade making a giant circle overlooking an arena of sorts.

The boy follows, gritting his teeth and favoring his leg.

The sharp bite of steel clanging together draws me to the

railing. Even from here I can smell the sweat from the bodies and hear the grunts.

Peering over, I catch sight of a group of fighters surrounded by onlookers on three sides. Five steps lead to a dais that disappears from view. Most of the crowd is dressed in red tunics and leathers. But the fighters wear protective armor across their torso. They brandish weapons—short swords, whips, and long double-edged blades—the sounds of their lethal instruments reminding me of the battle on the Island.

A bead of sweat trickles down my back; my hands are clenched around the banister.

Lifting an impatient eyebrow, the boy sighs.

I release a breath. *They're not fighting. This isn't a battle.* But the noises twist into a knot inside my stomach, every groan of metal or gasp of pain tightening the knot, conjuring images from the bombing.

A girl swings a flail over her head, once, twice, and then releases it on her opponent. The silver ball on the end of the stick whips into her partner's armored chest plate with a *clang*, and she drops to the ground. A few of the onlookers cheer, but I feel like puking.

Training. Just training.

Before I can ponder why, a figure enters the arena. Everyone freezes, a hush falling over the floor. All I can see is the back of him, but I can't tear my gaze from his wild, ink-black hair, the way he seems to float down the dais steps, his body claiming the space around him with smooth, measured movements.

The crowd responds to him, giving him space, as if one flick of a pinky finger could bind them all to his will. He wears a simple onyx tunic lined with red, no armor or shield —but just like the others, I'm both drawn to him and over-whelmed with a sense of *fear*.

And then something—his ivory skin, the way his head turns at an angle as he scans the crowd—strikes deep within me, and I lean over the railing and scream, "Riser!"

His head whips up, his one green eye pale against the stormy-blue one as they search my face. I try to say something, but a warm ache tightens my chest and makes it impossible to breathe.

Behind him, a girl parts from the clump of fighters, her flesh pale against a gold breastplate, her dark hair streaked the color of ash.

A cold feeling wriggles beneath my skin, one name screaming inside my skull like a warning: *Lucy Redgrave, the ex-Chosen girl from the Trials who tried to burn down an apartment building with innocent people inside. A die-hard Royalist and Lady Delphine lackey.*

The long sword she holds glints as she lifts it into the air.

The blade is pointed at Riser.

EIGHT

I turn and spring down the stairs, landing with grace I never knew I had, my boots squeaking over the marble floor. I've never moved so fast in my life.

The wall of onlookers gapes at me. I can't breathe. Can't scream. Can't stop it.

In my mind, Lucy has already killed Riser. His being alive was too good to be true. I deserve this for letting my father down. Letting Merida die for nothing. Killing the prisoners.

I *deserve* to lose Riser.

I push and shove my way through the bodies, the boy from upstairs right on my heels.

He grabs my arm. "Whoa! What are you doing, crazy?"

I rip from his grasp. A lanky boy with tattoos spiraling down his cheeks and neck puts his arm out to stop me, and I drop him with a fist to the gut. The rest back away to form a tight tunnel, but their eyes are full of suspicion as they follow me, lingering on my dress before finding the brand at my neck.

"Dandy whore," someone spits.

More taunts are hurled at my back. *Whig-lover. Royalist bitch.*

Traitor.

The letter opener is cool inside my palm. I break free of the crowd, sprinting toward the dais just in time to see Lucy's sword scrape against the pale stone floor, sparks flying, nearly missing Riser's head. He finds his feet with feline grace, a calm, lethal smile tugging his jaw.

"Stop." The air seems to whoosh from the room until the only sound I hear is my ragged breath rattling inside my chest. "Stop her!"

Lucy ignores me, stalking Riser, but no one lifts a finger to help.

Don't they know who she is? That somehow, somehow, the Archduchess snuck assassins in here?

Lucy takes another crude swing at Riser. He lithely retreats a hair, just enough that the tip of her blade brushes his tunic. He still wears a saccharine smile that seems to infuriate Lucy as she recovers and chops again at him.

I frown. Doesn't he remember her?

And then a boy yells, "She's got a weapon."

What the Fienian hell took so long? I swallow with relief and take a step toward Lucy in case the fools need help—

A flash in my periphery.

I pivot, but it's too late. Hands lock onto my arms, two on each side, and the floor greets me. Fingers yank my hair and twist my head around. I grunt as a hand forces my cheek into the rough stone floor.

Someone pries the letter opener from my hand. Two boys lift me to my feet and drag me all the way to the dais.

I angle my head back to Riser. His eyes flick over mine, but there's nothing there. No recognition. No emotion. He squints, as if trying to remember who I am.

Riser, I mouth.

But he looks away without so much as a blink.

And then Lucy *smirks* at me.

All at once I'm released, guards blocking me in on either side. Three thrones crown the dais, carved from the same deep-redwood the walls are made from. Tall white pillared-candles line the stage, spilling an orange-reddish light over them. A figure draped in a crimson robe sits on the throne to my right; Flame sits on the one to my left.

Footsteps echo behind me, and then Riser ascends the steps and slides into the largest throne in the middle. He's hardly broken a sweat. Both hands rest over the carved scorpions sitting atop each thick arm of his throne, his fingers drumming the wood, as if sitting in one place, even for a moment, makes him restless.

When he finally rests his gaze on me, my heart drops to my stomach.

An inky-black lock of hair falls over his forehead as he cocks his head to study me. His thumbs rub in tiny, bored circles over the scorpion carvings.

I search his face, begging, pleading with my own. But there's no recognition in those eyes. Eyes that once begged me to trust him. No half-smile on those lips I once kissed. Nothing of the past, the bond we shared.

Done with his assessment, he glances at Flame. "Is this the traitor they brought back?"

He doesn't remember me. The realization hits me like a knife to the heart.

What did they do to you, Pit Boy?

Whatever happened after he was injured, however they fixed him, they did more than treat his wounds. They erased me from his memory.

His *heart*.

Two Rebels grab me, and I buck and kick as they drag me down the hall.

He erased me.

No, I don't want to believe it. I can't. One of the Rebels leans forward and orders me to be still, so I crack my forehead into his face. He falls to the floor, screaming.

The sharp end of my elbow connects with the second Rebel's eye. His grip loosens just for a heartbeat, but I take it, pulling from his grasp and running.

Somehow I end up turning into what has to be the kitchen, big steel pots boiling over fires. I knock into a girl wearing a stained gray apron, sending a stack of plates to the floor in a *crash*. More halls, more rooms. All I hear is the sound of my heavy breathing.

Out, I need out of this place.

Slamming open another door, I fall into a storage room and immediately turn—and come face-to-face with Flame and her favorite crossbow pointed at my eye. "Where you going, Princess?"

"I want . . . out of here," I pant. "I want—"

"Always wanting something, aren't you?" Flame purrs as she approaches, her velvet white cape scraping the floor and leaving a thick trail in the dust. Like Riser, her hair is short on the sides and longer on top, fluffed into a wild mane. A rose-gold scorpion cuff slinks up her left ear. "Because you think you're better than us."

"Better?" I clench and unclench my fists at my side. "You . . . killed all those people, Flame. Innocent citizens. You played right into the emperor's hands."

"With the help of you and your Gold prince."

"No."

"You think we're savages," she sneers.

"No."

"Even Riser finally saw the truth."

"*No.*" Beneath my fury, a whisper of hurt tightens my chest. "How could you mess with his mind like that?"

She circles me, that damned cape swishing the floor. A red scorpion crests the back, bright as blood on snow.

The soft scarlet leather of her pants and vest rustle softly. "Did you think the emperor would welcome you with open arms once you told him about the bombs, about *us*?"

"I didn't tell him anything, Fienian," I snap, but it's the wrong answer, and she stops her circling to face me full on, her wrath evident in her quiet stillness, the artery throbbing over her forehead.

Her eyes are bright and accusing. "Just like you executed the False Prince?"

"The—"

"Prince Caspian," she clarifies, his name coming out like poison on her tongue. "The *second*-born son of the emperor. You know, the boy you keep protecting."

Riser is the first. I blink, trying to get a glimpse at what's going on inside Flame's head, but her expression is unreadable.

That's why Riser was on that throne. Why they took him first and left me behind.

"We all saw you point out Rebels for the Archduchess."

"What? I would never—"

"I saw them hang! We all did. You pointed your traitorous little finger, and they died."

The Archduchess. She must have released the videos to make it look like I was part of the hanging.

"Flame, please." I hold up my hands in a soothing motion. "You're right. I couldn't kill Caspian. But I didn't tell the emperor about the bombs . . . He already knew. And I certainly didn't point out Fienians to hang."

"So it wasn't you we saw choosing who hung?"

I shake my head. "I did, but I had—"

"The others voted for your execution."

A chill scrapes down my spine. *Even Riser?* "So, what? You

wanted to look me in the eyes before you strung me up?" I hold my arms out, palms up, exposing my bruised, scabbed wrists. "Here I am. What are you waiting for?"

Flame goes still, except her fingers twisting the cinched leather sleevelets creeping from her wrists to her elbows. "You'll get the same offer the other Royalists who joined us got: take the brand, and publicly declare your allegiance. The ceremony is in four days."

"Where's Brogue?"

A tight, sad smile. "*Indisposed.*"

What does that mean? "I want regular clothes like the rest of the Rebels."

"But you're not a Rebel yet. You proved that when you let Caspian live *twice*. So, until you prove otherwise, you get to wear Royalist garb."

My jaw tightens. The dress is a mark against me. I'll be paraded around, spat on, forced to prove myself at every turn . . . I realize my teeth are clenched so tight they ache, so I relax my jaw and smooth my face, hiding my frustration.

She moves to leave.

I quickly call out, "What did you do to him?"

A pause. "Nothing he didn't ask for."

"Liar."

She snaps around. Despite her small demeanor, the look she gives has me searching the room for a makeshift weapon.

"You think this is a game, Princess? That you can do what you want without consequences?" She toys with her crossbow. "Riser saw you on the balcony with the False Prince and the emperor. He knew you'd turned on us, but he still tried to save you."

My mouth opens, but the protests swirling inside my head die on my lips.

"When he had a chance to kill the False Prince, you stopped him." Her lips pucker into a scowl. "We barely escaped the Island. Riser was half-dead when we got him into the Reconstructor. But he managed to beg us to excise you from him, to scrape every trace of you from his mind, even if the added strain from the procedure killed him."

"No!" Desperate, I grab her arm. "I would never—"

The crossbow is inches from my face, the arrow gleaming a hair's breadth from the tip of my nose. "Don't ever presume you can touch me, dandy lover." Her voice trembles with rage. "You were never good enough for him. Never."

NINE

The two now very angry Rebels from earlier drag me to a room and push me inside, shutting the door in my face and locking the handle with a *click*. I pound on the door. When that doesn't work, I switch to screaming every violent thing I'm going to do to Lucy and Flame and the whole damn lot of them.

Fists throbbing and throat raw, I release a long sigh and slide down the door. Visions of Riser wounded and in pain flash through my mind.

He thinks I tricked him. Tried to kill him. Did he truly believe I had betrayed them? That I could do that? He must have not noticed the ties on my hands when he spied me on the balcony.

Fienian hell, did he think that and still try to save me?

Wiping at my eyes, I glance around. At least my new cell is fancier than the Tower, with a large sitting room sporting more dust than chairs. Rage at being locked up *again* propels me around my new cell. I check for hidden doorways. I yank and twist the wooden grate covering the windows. I look for anything that could become a weapon.

But there's no way out, and nothing worthy of a weapon.

If I wasn't locked up, I'd rip their hearts out.

I pace the dingy floor, my hands balled into fists. I need to get to Riser. I'm sure if I can talk to him, alone, I can make him remember.

"You can't just erase a person," I yell in a voice nearly hoarse from screaming.

Even the real Everly March, that bright, ferocious girl whose life and identity I stole lingers inside me, a wraith of shadows and barbed taunts.

But if she's here, then surely I'm still inside Riser, somewhere.

I jam my fingernails into my palms to keep from punching the wall. But no matter what I do, the fury grows.

After everything I did for them, everything I sacrificed, what I *became*, how can they do this to me? And Riser, sitting on his throne, his bored eyes glancing over me as if I'm some . . . some . . .

I scream again, my raw throat burning. Nothing makes sense. The Riser I knew would have never believed I could be a traitor, and he would have never willingly forgotten me. I was part of his past, and, according to him, part of his future.

But he did, meaning he isn't the person I thought he was. He erased me from his mind, not knowing if I was dead or alive, being tortured.

I thought of him every minute of every hour we were apart. I cried for him, prayed for him. I made bargains to long dead gods to keep him alive. I would have gladly given up my life to save his.

And he *erased* me and went on with his.

Growling, I circle the room, looking for something to bust down the door. I've nearly gotten the leg of one of the wooden chairs broken off—one more kick will do it—when the door creaks open and Lady Teagan, the finalist who helped with the bombing, saunters in.

Her crown of dark hair is slicked down to a point over her forehead, and a man's emerald-green tunic swishes over her matchstick frame, a thick, knotted braid of black pearls circling her thin, elegant neck.

The only hint of red she wears is the ruby-red lipstick matted across her full lips, but that only seems brighter and more of a statement than any of the others could ever make.

It's hard to remember she's considered a Subversive, the lowest member of our society. A girl who loves other girls, who chooses to live outside Royalist rules.

She gifts me with a radiant smile. "Hello, darling."

Feeling like a savage creature next to a beautiful swan, I tilt my head and stare dully at her.

She eyes the splinters of wood scattered across the floor.

Then she smiles again with those beautiful, ferocious lips, and holds out a slender hand dripping with gold. "Care to accompany me?"

I don't ask where because it doesn't matter. "Are you . . . freeing me?"

Something flickers inside her caramel eyes, and she chuckles. "Guess I am, March. You're not going to run again . . . are you?"

I shake my head, marveling at the absent Lady before my name. This isn't the Island, after all. A fact I'm grateful for as I follow her out into the small antechamber abutting this one.

"Don't call me that anymore," I say, cutting my eyes at the boy from earlier who still waits for me. "My name's Maia Graystone."

Teagan runs a hand over her pearls, her lips curled at the sides. "Okay. Hear that, Lash?" She glances at the boy. "Call her Graystone."

The boy shoves his hands into his pockets. "Flame didn't—"

"Tell Flame," Teagan purrs, "I'm taking her prisoner to *eat*. And she's promised not to run."

"But—"

"She's been locked up and starved by the Royalist pigs enough to last a lifetime." Teagan's lips press into a furious line that dares him to challenge her. "If you must tell our little commander something, tell her that."

Little commander? I bite down on my smile as the boy flicks his gaze between us.

Running a hand through his thick hair, he sighs. "You're going to be a pain in my ass, aren't you, Graystone?"

I afford him a smug grin as Teagan takes my arm in hers and leads me into the hallway. The boy struggles to catch up, his boots squeaking against the stone floor.

Teagan slides her gaze over our shadow and chuckles. "Lash here takes his job very seriously." She pats my arm. "You do have a desperate glint in your eye"—her voice grows soft—"but I know hunger when I see it. Anyone becomes feral after a few days without food."

Feral? I run my fingers over my ratty hair caked with food from the gallows and dried blood; I touch the sharp planes of my jaw and collarbone. My stomach rumbles again, an ache lodging below my ribs.

I don't remember *obsessing* about food in the Tower, even when the food was being hurled at me. But now that being filleted alive is less of a possibility, it's as if my body has reanimated, and every cell inside me begs for nourishment.

We round a corner, the hallway opening up into a large convex chamber with the windows also covered by wooden carvings, but these twine and grow along the walls, the creatures depicted in the carvings so lifelike they could almost be real. A crude monstrosity of iron and glass hangs from the arched ceiling, throwing meager bits of amber light around.

A huge blood-red banner with a black scorpion hangs limply from the rafters.

Near the back, the sound of weapons and bodies clashing drifts from the thick wooden doors. My shoulders loosen as we veer to the left, away from the fighters—and Riser—the noises dampening with each step up the carpeted stairs.

"I didn't tell the emperor," I say, my voice sounding more hurt than I'd planned.

"I know." Teagan halts, the boy, Lash, nearly colliding into our backs. She throws him a sharp glance. "But a lot happened that night. It's hard to know who to trust."

A cold chill ripples down my spine as I remember the horrible, horrible screams. And Ophelia . . . the miniature roses that once adorned her golden hair . . . I exhale just as we top the stairs, shuddering.

Lunch is served in the Great Hall on two long oak tables. It's not much—black cauldrons full of thick, steaming vegetable stew, and a hard biscuit—but it's hot and filling.

Teagan and Lash watch me eat. Normally I would take more care to seem like I possess manners. But my hollow stomach demands it all right *now, now, now*, and after I've inhaled two helpings, I notice another helping has made it onto my dress.

The stew settles uneasily in my gut. I lay my hands flat on the table and slide my gaze to Teagan. "Where's Brogue?"

Teagan's dark eyebrows gather, but she stays quiet.

"Okay. Anyone know what happened to the machine that was with me?"

More grating silence.

My lips twist to the side. "Fine. At least tell me where we are?"

"Bloodwyn Hall."

My stomach clenches, threatening to return the stew.

"But that's . . . This is"—I pause to examine the dark windowless room paneled in wood the color of clotted-blood, more iron lighting that seems moments from sputtering us into full-blown darkness—"the dead Fienian leader's cursed estate."

"Ezra Croft," Lash says, his voice coated in reverence. "They say he and the executed men of House Croft haunt this place, ready to murder Royalists and their sympathizers."

I ignore how his gaze shifts to me on the last word.

Teagan snorts. "Thanks to superstitious ninnies like Lash here, Bloodwyn Hall makes the perfect place to stash our forces." *Forces?* "The Centurions won't search it. Hell, they won't even come *near* it for fear of the curse."

I scratch at some of the stew splattered on my dress. "But people have to come and go. How do the drones not spot them? Or see the smoke from the chimneys?"

Teagan shrugs her wide, square shoulders. "There are hundreds of holographic lasers that cover the entire estate. Anyone looking will see an old, abandoned ruin more likely to be cursed than the center of the rebellion."

I remember how well hiding in plain sight worked for me the last time, but I don't mention it, because now that my belly is full to bursting, a thousand questions invade my mind. "How many of you are there?"

She raises an eyebrow, as if to say *don't you mean us*? "Nearly seven hundred Fienian Rebels live in the castle. A few hundred more inhabit the grounds. Hundreds more are hidden around the southern cities to supply us with goods and information."

My mouth goes dry. "That's almost enough for an . . . army."

"Exactly, darling." Teagan drums her manicured fingers over the table. "We march on the empire in four days."

TEN

March on the empire? Even with a thousand Rebels willing to fight, I doubt they would get past the gates.

I glance over at a few Fienians. "Where do they come from?"

Lash leans his broad frame over the table, scratching at the rust-colored stubble covering his jaw. "I came from Longview, a Royalist city a few miles north of here."

"So you're a Silver?"

"Was." He shrugs. "Now I'm a Rebel."

"They come from all over," Teagan adds. "The villagers who fought on the Island and survived the bombing are here too." She eyes Lash. "Some are more experienced than others, though, hence the training you witnessed today."

Training. A sour taste coats my tongue as I recall how they threw me to the floor as if I was going to hurt Riser. And Lucy Redgrave *smirked* at me.

"Why is Lucy Redgrave here?"

"After the bombing, we were trapped between the mountains and the water with no way out. But the Redgrave twins know the mountains, and they led us through a small, hidden pass to safety. Lucy even dressed Riser's wound so he wouldn't bleed out." I roll my eyes, and she elaborates. "I don't trust either of them, Graystone, but they saved us . . . and it's because of them we got Riser to a Reconstructor in time to heal him."

The tip of Caspian's sword, thick with Riser's blood, come's unbidden to my mind. I scrunch my eyes closed to try and erase the memory.

Everything has changed since the night I wore the red dress and set off to assassinate the emperor. Everything except the monstrous rock still plodding its way toward our little planet—and the Archduchess who is probably right this second scouring the hills for me.

"Why don't you go take a bath and recover a bit," Teagan says. She's watching me as if I might break apart at any moment. "Afterward I'll find you. There's something else we should discuss."

I want to argue, but she's right. I'm bone-weary, every muscle in my body aching, and the thought of a hot bath nearly buoys me out of my seat. I'm halfway up when the door slams open with a crack and the fighters from today enter, led by Flame.

There's something near comical about watching Flame lead the Fienian fighters, a foot shorter than her fellow soldiers and trailed by her too-big cloak—but then I remember earlier when she leveled the crossbow at my nose, the steely look in her eyes, and decide she's not out of place after all.

I scan the sweaty would-be-soldiers for the Fienian army. Though they don't wear uniforms, most don similar red tunics with leather vests and pants, and all sport baldrics glittering with blades. A few look strong and weathered— perhaps young Mercs or loggers from the northern Blue Horn

Mountains—but the majority of the fighters hardly look capable of defeating the Royalist Army.

The table next to us fills, and the tang of hot, sweaty bodies cuts through the scent of stew and fresh bread.

My focus is drawn to a boy near the end. He's young, although not the youngest, no more than fifteen, his curly blond hair darkened at the temples with sweat. He casually runs a hand through his mop and laughs at something the girl across the table says.

Watching him, a deep ache fills my chest.

The boy steals a biscuit from the girl's plate, dodging her playful swat, his eyes sparkling.

I can't breathe. Can't fill my lungs with enough air.

I slide from my chair. "Max?"

Teagan stands, her chair scraping the floor. "I was going to tell you . . . I just thought . . ."

My feet move. Taking me to him. I call his name again, but my throat closes around the word like it's barbed, and I only manage a rasp.

From the corner of my eye, I see Flame frowning at me, but I don't care.

"Max?"

Except as soon as I say his name again, he flicks his gaze to mine, his eyes catching on my Royalist brand, and I want to unsay it.

Guilt slams into me. I left him on his own. I abandoned him. Made him wait for me gods know how long to come back.

What horrors did he suffer because I let us get separated? Did he think I just left because it was easier without a crying seven-year-old?

Max huffs a nervous laugh, his gaze darting around the table. Everyone is staring at me now, their expressions accusing.

You left him, you left him, you left him—

I hold out my hand, embarrassed by the tears burning my eyes. "Max, it's—"

"Only my friends call me Max." His tone is clipped, dismissive, and despite how his words cut me, a part of me beams with pride. Not even fifteen and he's already so sure of himself.

I wipe at my eyes. "What about your sister? What do *I* call you?"

Silence. A few of the soldiers cough.

"Traitor," someone whispers, and the word circulates in cruel little whispers just loud enough for me to hear. The girl Max stole the bread from snickers under her breath.

Then they all watch him to see how he'll react.

Clenching his jaw, Max tears his gaze from my face and studies his plate. Then he swipes another biscuit from the girl and dips it in his stew.

As if I'm not standing here. As if I'm not *real*.

Just like Riser.

The rest do the same. Noises of spoons scraping bowls and slurping and laughter make a cruel song around me. Not a single person glances up as I stand here, fists clenched, fighting warm tears with every breath.

Look at me, Max. Forgive me.

The world around me fades to black. Only my brother is in focus. The one person left on this earth I can call family, that I can call home.

I bang my shin on the table as I flee, the pain in my leg nothing compared to the agony inside my heart.

ELEVEN

The sting from Max's rejection stays with me after I've fled the mess hall. I charge blindly up wide stairs and through narrow halls. Past more Rebels, a blur of red leathers and cruel taunts.

Where's my room? But every door looks the same. As I stumble through the halls, rage and sadness wash over me.

I want to sink down into some dark place, crack open my chest, and spill out the pain.

Candlelight flickers through my tears . . . the library. The tables are empty, a soft breeze blowing from a faraway window. I snake between the maze of bookshelves, glad for the lurking shadows and cool, dank air.

When I'm deep within the stacks, so deep that no one can hear me, I drop to my knees.

For a heartbeat, nothing comes out, as if my heart has literally lodged in my throat. I can't breathe. Can't make a single noise.

A quiet sob grows in my chest, trickles from my throat. And I let myself cry, silently, so hard that my vision blacks out and I nearly faint. I want to cry it all out until my throat aches and my eyes burn and there's literally nothing left to give.

I want to purge every drop of my pain.

In the pit, the only thing that got me through was Max.

I had to be strong for Max.

I had to get out for Max.

When I jumped from the cliff into the freezing ocean, it was for Max. When I let them change me, make me into a stranger, a killer, it was for Max.

The trials, killing Merida, everything was for my brother.

Now I don't have that anymore. I don't have *him*, the little boy who needed me. He's gone.

They took him from me.

I release a shuddering sigh. Maybe Max is smart to pretend I don't exist. Look at all the things I've already messed up. I disobeyed the order to kill Caspian. I failed to save Merida. I nearly got Riser killed. And I failed, utterly *failed* to find the one thing that my father died for.

The thing that can save us all.

There's a faint, diffuse buzzing in my head. From the crying, probably . . . except it gets heavier. Fuller. Then the voices start, first dull and far away, as if I'm underwater and someone is screaming at me. The voices get louder. Begging for help. For me to save them.

The intense cries flood into my brain, too much—

Just like that, it's gone. I press my thumbs into my eyeballs. The voices are getting stronger.

Or, maybe, I'm getting crazier.

I wipe my nose on my sleeve and scramble to my feet. I need to go back to my room and take a bath, maybe sleep, so I can refocus on my plan, but I barely have the energy to retrace my steps through the bookshelves, much less find my room and search for a suitable tub to bathe in.

Amber candlelight flickers near the entrance of the library, illuminating the painting from earlier. As I approach, I notice a man in a black tunic lined in red, his ink-black hair darker than the deepest shadow.

I stop dead in my tracks behind Riser. He has one arm stretched behind his back. The other holds a candle up to the painting of what has to be his mother, Amandine.

I see the resemblance now. Ivory skin. Midnight hair. Ruthless, dark beauty and sharp eyes.

Riser shifts on his feet slightly. There hasn't been one indication that he's heard me. But, of course, he has.

He doesn't turn around. He just keeps staring up at that stupid painting. Pretending I don't exist. That I didn't just wail my heart out.

"You know," he says without turning around, "usually when someone watches me from behind, they plan to do me harm."

If only. My jaw grinds. *Screw you, Pit Boy, and the Reconstructor that erased me and your smug, arrogant voice and your—*

I grab the nearest object—a heavy, leather-bound book—and hurl it at him.

As I stalk away, I hear him grunt in surprise. A smile twitches my lips.

"Try to *erase* that, Prince," I mutter under my breath.

I feel somewhat better now.

My mood only improves when Lash finds me and leads me to a bathing room—after scolding me for a good minute about what a pain in the ass I am. Together, we carry buckets of fire-warmed water until the bath is half-full.

Lash seems a bit hesitant when I force him out of the room to undress, but I assure him there's nothing harmful I could do in the bath, other than drown myself—and I'd much rather burn this whole crumbling castle down than give them that satisfaction.

After I'm clean, clothed in a similar poppy-red gown, my

wet hair twisted into a tangled bun, I try to make some sense of my situation so I can make a plan. Even though my body yearns to find a bed and sleep away my aches, there's a sense of urgency stirring my blood, electrifying my bones, making it impossible to rest.

I'm on a dead Fienian leader's cursed estate, surrounded by Rebels who don't trust me and are training for a battle against the emperor they're going to lose.

I release a long breath.

I should be back at Emerald Island, searching for the Mercurian. And Max—my heart flutters at his name—Max holds the map. If I can somehow get him to see me as his sister again and not the enemy, maybe I can figure out how to access it.

I open the door to my room. "I want to see Flame and Nicolai."

Lash jumps to his feet. "Yeah, no. Out of the—"

"Now." I cross my arms. "I'm prepared to make a scene."

Fixing me with an annoyed stare, he releases a now-familiar sigh. "Go ahead, love. I promise you I've seen it all before."

"Not likely." I push past him. "Where are they?"

"Wait!"

"Anyone seen Flame around?"

He grabs my wrist. "Stop, this won't end well for you."

On instinct, I twist my arm from his grasp and grab the back of his bicep, hook my leg behind his knee, and take him to the ground.

With one knee perched on his chest, I grin down at him. "Then take me to them, or this won't end well for *you*."

"Take me to them, she says." His eyebrows shove together above a frown, his gaze rolled to the ceiling. "And by them, she means the Rebel Commander and General."

"Who are you talking to?"

"She asks who I'm talking to." He rips his stare from the ceiling. "The gods say I'm being punished."

"Right." I dig my knee into his flesh, ignoring the way he grimaces. "Did they also tell you what will happen if you don't take me to Flame?"

Sighing, Lash pushes my knee away and jumps to his feet, turning without a word to lead me through maze-like corridors thick with lamp oil and dust. Long shadows spill from corners.

I crave windows. Light. Fresh air that smells like grass and earth. This place, with its dark, ancient wood and seemingly endless passageways, feels like a sarcophagus. I pull at the hem of my bodice, fighting the urge to claw my way to the outside.

Voices trickle from a heavy door. Lash pauses, shakes his head, and raps on it.

As soon as it creaks open, some of my bravado ebbs. Ten Fienians stand around a large table. I recognize some—Flame stands near the head of the table, right next to the cloaked form of Nicolai, his red mask glinting in the dingy light.

Riser stands at the other head, facing the door—a leftover habit from the pit—and his gaze flicks to me, his hand already on the dagger at his waist.

A spark of anger grows in my chest as I spot Lucy Redgrave beside him, her pale, ashen face smirking at me once again.

Gods! Is her face stuck that way?

I search for a friendly face. Brogue. Teagan. But the table brims with anything but friendly. They're all frowning at the intrusion.

Before I have time to change my mind, I push past one of the younger fighters acting as guard. My gaze slides to the hologram castle shimmering over the table. I recognize the pale turrets, the mountains looming behind it.

Laevus Castle. Why would they be meeting about that, unless . . .

Nicolai waves, and the monstrosity disappears. Inside the mask, his gray eyes are stark against the red, and they pin me to where I stand.

"Lady March," he purrs in that warbling, electronic voice. "I don't recall summoning *you* to this meeting."

I stride to the table and slam my fist down, never taking my eyes off Nicolai. "I'm not a traitor, Nicolai, and my name is Maia Graystone, not March."

His face is unreadable beneath the mask. "But isn't that what a . . . traitor would say, *Maia Graystone*?"

Smug bastard. "What about my Microplant? Surely you could see what happened?"

"Oh, no, dear. Your Microplant was conveniently cut off before the bombing."

Beneath Nicolai's smugness lingers something else. Something dangerous. When our only interaction was through Microplants, it was easy to miss the darkness Nicolai's feigned manners veil.

But now . . . now I watch the way the others look to him first, the way his voice says one thing, but his cold, calculating eyes say another.

"Am I free to leave?"

A few of the Rebels chuckle.

"This room? Yes, immediately, please."

"No. The castle. Am I free to leave the castle?"

"Now why would I let you go, when you may very well tell the emperor about this place?" Nicolai gestures around the room. "We all watched how easily you turn under pressure. Besides, you do hold the key to a very powerful weapon, one—"

"Then why aren't you having a meeting about that?" I scan the faces around the table.

Except for Flame, every face holds confusion. So they don't even know there might be a way to stop Pandora. But Nicolai called it a weapon, so maybe he doesn't want to stop Her at all.

"Yes." Nicolai's voice is breathy with impatience. "The weapon that no one can find, that no one's seen, supposedly put together by a dead man." His chuckle grates down my spine. "I should plan an entire war around *that*."

The others laugh, perhaps too loudly. Sycophants.

At least Riser isn't laughing. No, he's studying me with his usual candor. Probably still wondering why I chucked a book at him.

I lob a feral smile at Pit Boy and enjoy the confused tilt of his head.

"Take the oath and the brand, Princess," Flame says, perhaps a bit too quickly. "Prove yourself like the others did, then it won't matter what you've done."

What I've *done*.

My jaw grinds, and I fight the urge to lunge at Flame, swallowing it down like glass. "I'll take the brand, the oath. I'll wear this dress, work for you, fight for you. I'll do anything you want. Just send Max away so he's not here when . . . when . . ."

Can't they see how foolish this is? The Royalist army will crush them.

"That's Max's decision," Nicolai says in a dismissive tone, focusing on the stack of maps by his elbow.

"Then help me get back inside the castle."

"No. Now run along."

I refuse to move. "Where's Brogue? What have you done with him?"

"The Twitcher? Chasing the black, I imagine."

A reference to getting high. Crap. I wasn't expecting that.

"And Bramble? The little sensor I was with when you kidnapped me?"

Chuckles fill the room. They think I've lost my mind.

Flame lifts an eyebrow, her amusement evident in the curve of her lips. "Anything else, Princess?"

"Yeah," I cut my eyes at Riser, "you might want to assign guards for the prince, or next time it might not be a book I throw at him."

A smile broadens my face as I stalk away, even though I technically just threatened the *prince* in front of witnesses and confirmed their suspicions about me.

They want me to be the bad guy? Fine, I'll be the bad guy, the traitor they can't trust. The loose end. And I'll do whatever it takes to stop this stupid, hopeless war and get back to the Island.

Even if it means destroying the Fienian Rebels from within.

TWELVE

After unsuccessfully storming my way to my room and getting lost, Lash decides part of his job includes giving me the royal tour, which takes ages and does nothing more than confuse me. The house is a maze of snaking dead-end corridors, stuffy chambers, and empty antechambers. Other than the depressing oil paintings that dress some of the larger formal rooms and the heavy red rugs that settle over the worn floors like bloody carcasses, there's nothing to see but wood and stone and shadows.

Lash pauses beneath a tall wall of landscape paintings, all dark and dreary and morose—just like he is now. "You know, next time you're going to piss off Nicolai and threaten the prince, don't make me a part of it."

"What?" I murmur.

But I'm still only half listening. I need to get inside the council room and see how they're planning to storm the Island. Now that I know Max will be involved, I have to know the risks. If Nicolai and the Fienians want to die in an impossible battle, fine.

The world might be a better place. But I'll be damned if I let them drag my brother down that martyr's path.

I refocus on Lash—the green flecks in his dark brown irises that I missed earlier, the head thick with hair the same rich, deep color as the wood on the walls.

"You're not listening to me at all, are you?" His brows gather together. "The gods warned me you'd be trouble. Before I was assigned to babysit *you*, I was in the armory. Basically, you know, my dream job."

"You can't really believe you talk to the gods?"

"Don't change the subject, love." He limps away faster than he walked during the entire tour.

I hurry to catch up and reach out for him. "I'm sorry, okay?"

His shoulder stiffens beneath my fingers.

"It's not you. I'm just . . . tired."

"You meant what you said? You're not a traitor?"

"I'm not a traitor." My voice comes out a whisper, even though I want to scream it. "And they can all just go to Fienian hell."

Lash chuckles. "Did you really throw a book at the prince's head?"

I release a half-sob, half-laugh. "Yep."

"Why?"

"Because he hurt me."

He stops at the foot of the wide stairs that lead up to my room. "So you know him, then?"

The awe in his voice grates on my nerves. I knew Riser when he was simply Pit Boy. Not Prince. Not the Savior-of-the-World. Not Would-be-Emperor.

"I thought I did."

"Huh," Lash says, flicking up his eyebrows. "Who would have guessed?"

We walk the rest of the way in silence.

I SPEND all of five minutes in my dim, cramped chamber before I leave again in search of Teagan and Brogue, who no one seems to know anything about. I have no idea what time it is, or when Shadow Fall hits. Being inside this windowless mausoleum seems to have frozen time, as if days don't exist.

Lash's awkward gait makes a soft dragging noise across the floor as he follows, yawning and looking like he'd rather be anywhere but here.

When I find Teagan, I'm going to ask her for a job. Something that will give me access to the rooms and maybe get Lash off my back.

Next, I have to find a way outside. If I don't see the sun, I'll go mad. Or, madder than I already am—although I can't imagine there's much crazier than hearing voices.

The armory is a long, windowless, rectangular room behind the arena that spans the entire wall. Two guards monitor the door, but they nod to Lash and let us pass. The scent of oil and gunpowder permeates the room, and metal sparkles over the walls.

Lash's eyes light up as they appraise the racks of weapons. He moves along an invisible current drawing him deep into the racks and out of sight.

Teagan bends over a girl no more than fourteen, adjusting the too-long baldric drooping awkwardly over her shoulder and chest. Two daggers and a short-sword hang from the leather band.

Teagan glances over her shoulder. "Hello, darling. I see you survived the tour."

"I need a weapon," I say by way of greeting, my gaze flitting over the gleaming wall of knives in every size and style imaginable.

There are chiseled edges, hollowed edges, flat edges.

Jeweled metal finishes catch my eye, while others shine with decorative patterns of file work, and a rare few are Damascus steel, two metals forged to make a striking pattern.

Teagan, brow furrowed at the buckle on the baldric, snorts. "Anything else?"

I twirl, glaring at the flare of my dress. "Something other than this dress. And a job, too."

Teagan stands, waving the girl away. "That all?"

"Well, I'd like to feel the sun on my skin."

She retrieves a sword from a rack, steel clanging. "I can do two of those things." With smooth, careful movements, she begins to slide the edge of the blade over a whetstone. "What do you have in mind for work?"

Think. Something that requires you to have a key . . . "Making beds and cleaning rooms?"

Her fingers pause over the razor-sharp edge, and her eyebrows lift. "That's the job you want?"

"Sure."

"O-kay." Although her focus is back on the weapon, her lips twitch upward. "You can start today." The blade glints in the low light. Once it's back on the wall, Teagan nods to me. "Follow me."

"What about the other thing?"

"This *is* the other thing."

I scramble to catch up with her long strides, my heart pounding as we near two tall, arched doors of gold-veined marble. Sunlight trickles from a thin crack between them, and my breath catches in my throat. A guard unlocks the doors with a thick iron key, and slowly, slowly, they grind and creak open, flooding the room with warm, golden light.

As soon as the sun warms my cheeks I feel a release, as if I'm finally able to take a full breath. The air tastes like salt. I blink and wait for my eyes to adjust. A stone railing . . . blue sky . . . I release a disappointed breath. We're on what appears to be a huge stone balcony overlooking the sea. Below, the ocean roars and beats against the cliffs.

There's no way out.

The stone has been carved into a ring of steps that lead down to the arena below. Three thrones similar to the ones from the indoor arena sit on a black fur rug near the front in the shade.

As we pass, I make eye contact with Flame, the spikes curving over the shaved area of her head sparkling beneath the sun's glare. Her gaze slides from me to Teagan, and something unreadable sparks inside Flame's blue-gray eyes.

Teagan smiles that slow, inviting, red smile at Flame . . . and Flame glances away *too* quickly.

What's that about?

Once we're seated with the rest of the crowd around the arena, I find the courage to look up. Pandora hovers near the sun, a dark cancer creeping toward the light.

Shadow Fall is coming.

I bite my cheek. I'm nowhere near stopping Her. The promise I made to my father rings in my ears, and I loose a breath against the frustration filling my chest.

I need to find a way back to the Island and the Mercurian, but how can I do that when I don't even have a weapon?

"What about my weapon?" I ask Teagan.

"By the gods, you are persistent, darling." A wry smile brightens her face. "Sorry, but no weapons and no leathers until Flame puts the word out otherwise."

Muttering under my breath, I sink into my ribcage, a headache starting to form behind my eyes. I rub my temples and crack my neck. Probably the sunlight.

Lash slides in next to me, eliciting more than a few curses as he wiggles to make room. He fixes me with a stern, handsome glance.

I smile. "What? It's not my fault you weren't watching me close enough."

"You know, you may be pretty, love, but that doesn't mean I won't put you on a leash if I have to."

"Aw." I punch his arm. "You think I'm pretty?"

His lips part, revealing a row of straight white teeth only a Silver and above would have. "Yeah, a pretty pain in my ass."

I feel bad for him, *almost*, but before I can respond, the wide set of iron doors below open and fighters spill out. I scan the heads, looking for Max's blond curls. Instead I spot Rhydian, all sharp angles and fierce stares, a totally different person from the sad, beaten boy from before.

I wave, trying to catch his eye, but his gaze is fixed on the fighters stalking the sand.

Max enters the arena, followed by Riser. Lucy and Hugo Redgrave are a step behind.

I go rigid at the sight of Max around all those warriors. The Max I remember was too preoccupied with toys and sweets to take anything seriously, much less train to fight. But he's different now. Taller than most fourteen-year-olds, with wide shoulders and sinewy muscles that can easily heft a blade.

I squint as my gaze begins to blur. Pain pulses through my skull, and I clench my teeth, trying to drive the pain out. I blink until my eyes refocus, but a pale red light halos my vision.

"You okay, darling?" Teagan asks.

"Yeah." I drag my arm across my eyes. "What is this?"

"The Blood Court. Anyone can enter. They fight until the last man"—she cracks a sly smile—"or woman is left standing. The winner takes the Scorpion Throne, and Riser's place."

"And what is Riser's place, exactly?"

Teagan glances at the three thrones. "Flame, Riser, and

Nicolai rule as a triumvirate. Flame is the commander. Riser, the Blood King."

"And Nicolai?"

"Nicolai is whatever the hell he wants to be."

"Why would Nicolai allow someone to challenge Riser's rule?"

"The Fienian's call the cost of ruling the blood price. Blood proves your worth. Besides, it's only for a day. A century ago, House Croft held a Blood Court on the last Sunday of every month. This is an extreme version of that. It keeps the Rebels happy."

I peer down at Riser standing casually in the middle, his shoulders loose, stance wide. He wears an expectant grin, but the smile doesn't reach his eyes, and something darker hides behind his arrogant mask.

The smell of yeasty dough hits me. The crowd passes around braided ropes of bread. They glisten with salt and butter.

"Blood bread," Teagan says, in answer to my curious stare.

I pluck half a rope of blood bread from Lash's fingers, stuffing the dry twist in my mouth. "Has anyone taken the Scorpion Throne yet?"

Teagan steals the other half from Lash. "Not even close."

I scan the fighters again. Not a single blade. "Where are their weapons?"

Lash has managed to find another blood bread, and he leans forward to get a better view of the arena. "As soon as we sat down," he says, "we entered a Sim field. When Shadow Fall hits, each fighter will get a simulated weapon to destroy the other with."

Right, we couldn't have them killing each other every day before the real battle starts, so they use simulated weapons.

I stand up. This is a fragmented Sim—but it's still a *Sim*. My father's message might reach me here.

I stare into the arena. Truth be told, the last thing I want to do is fight. After the bombing, after witnessing what *real* fighting looks like, the blood and the cries and the terror, the thought of entering a battle—even a simulated one—terrifies me.

But what choice do I have? I push the fear down into some dark recess of my mind. Down, down, *down* until it is only a whisper of panic.

Wiping my greasy hands on my dress, I take a step toward the arena.

Lash is up in a flash. "Don't do it, love."

"Why?" I challenge. "What are the gods saying?"

"Oh, they promise your cheek will kiss the sand before the shadow rises."

"Tell the gods I don't answer to them."

Teagan calls out my name, but the air has already started to darken, and I pick my way through the curious crowd. Before Pandora completely blots out the sun, I glare up at Her. A reminder of the promise I made in the Tower.

Whatever it takes, whatever I have to do, I will destroy you.

This is just one step closer to that goal, I promise myself, leaping the final steps down to the arena.

As my boots sink into the sand and everyone turns to gape, I can't help wondering if I've just made a huge mistake.

THIRTEEN

The others stare at me as if they can hear my heart knocking against my rib cage. Lifting the hem of my stupid dress, which insists on snaking under my boots, I take a place next to Rhydian.

"Traitors don't belong on the Blood Court," he whispers from the corner of his mouth without taking his eyes off the others.

"I missed you too—" I gasp as a shock radiates behind my eyes, and tendrils of electricity zip through my skull.

I grab my temples. There's something wrong with me . . . with my head. I grit my teeth and force my hands back down to my side.

Don't let them see that you're hurting . . . and weak.

Rhydian glances back. "What? The truth hurts?"

"I'm not a traitor, Rhydian. And I want my sensor back."

He raises an eyebrow. "Now?"

He's right. Now's not the time. "No, later. But if you've hurt him . . ."

Rhydian studies me carefully, as if I'm a bomb that could

explode at any time, but I retreat a few steps to align with Max's shoulder before he can respond.

My brother's chin juts out and he gets that stubborn look, like when he was little and I ordered him to do something. I fight the urge to run a finger over his pale curls as he looks straight ahead, ignoring me.

Fine. These are his friends. I can't just pop back into his world and demand he give all that up for me, a supposed traitor.

I flick a glance at my brother. *I'll earn that love back if I have to fight every one of these Fienian idiots.*

One moment it's shadowy and pale, like whispers of dusk. The next, we're cloaked in darkness. The walls erupt with flaming torches in a soft *whoosh.*

Through the grainy air, I make out Max. The simulated long sword clenched inside his grip looks so real that orange torchlight dances inside the shiny steel. The others have weapons as well.

But my hands remain glaringly empty.

"Where's my weapon?" I hiss up at Flame, where she and Nicolai peer down at us from their shadowy thrones.

"I said you had to earn a weapon." She shrugs and tosses me a lazy smile. "Rules are rules, Princess."

Crap.

I turn just in time to see Max's *too-real* sword arcing toward my neck.

FOURTEEN

I drop flat and roll to avoid Max's sword. Displaced air from the blade caresses my cheek as the fine edge whispers over my head. The darkness around me buzzes and moans with the sound of steel on steel and the twang of arrows loosing from crossbows.

As soon as I jump to my feet, Max swings again, his sword barely missing my side.

Now that I've had a moment, my heart has found a steady course, and my body responds to his attack with ease.

He's relentless, but he's also emotional and sloppy. Some instinctual big-sister part of me even begins critiquing him. Aim too high. Grip too low. Sword needs to be shorter to align to his height. Less weight on the heels. Fights with too much feeling.

His cheeks redden, and he stumbles forward, huffing.

On instinct, I grab his sword hand, take the pommel of his sword with the other, and fold it over. Guilt pricks me as he cries out and releases his grip, his pale-blue eyes sliding over the weapon now in my possession.

Gods above, why don't you embarrass him in front of his friends and see if he loves you for it.

I frown at a girl approaching Max from behind. I should give his sword back to him, but I tighten my fingers over the sweat-damp leather pommel. It feels good to hold it.

So damned good.

I toss the sword handle first at him, but he just watches the blade pierce the ground at his feet.

"Pick it up, Max!" I shout, trying and failing not to make it sound like an order.

A steely look glitters in his eyes, the same look I've seen a million times before when I bossed him around, and he glares at me with an expression half betrayal, half rage.

The girl smiles at Max's head. It's the same girl he stole bread from earlier, her coppery hair pulled into a tight braid.

"Sorry, Graystone," she murmurs as she plunges her short sword into his back.

His eyes go wide with pain. A grunt escapes his lips, and he staggers for a moment before stalking out of the arena.

I blink. Max's abandoned sword screams to be taken. But all I can see is Riser as the memory of Caspian's sword coated with blood invades my mind. The sounds of that night echo inside my skull—the screams from the bombing, the sound of horses charging—and my headache returns.

Maybe it's been here the whole time and adrenaline masked it. I can almost taste the blood in the air as a wave of nausea rolls over me.

Then the girl leers at me.

One second I'm helpless, my feet stuck to the earth.

The next, the sword is in my hand, and I'm swinging it at her neck. Her eyes widen in shock. She tries to duck, but it's too late.

The simulated blade meets her lithe neck.

If it were a real blade, her head would be rolling across the sand.

The thought sends a euphoric feeling crashing over me.

Before the girl has time to recover, I'm stalking the grounds. Gritting my teeth against the pounding inside my skull, I find an empty bit of wall to protect my back and begin circling to my left. My boots churn the loose dirt, my head swiveling left to right.

A loud *boom* shudders the stone behind me. I turn to see Hugo bathed in orange firelight, his pistol raised, pale smoke leaking from the muzzle.

Bastard.

I dart into the melee, slipping through two fighters locked together in a sweaty, primal embrace. Another shot. One of them yells out, and I turn to see him grabbing his leg.

Hugo points his revolver at me again, his dark eyes flat above curled lips—

I drop and roll. The sand explodes inches from my face, hurtling tiny grains of shrapnel into my cheek and eye. I snap to my knees, and fire slices over my forearm as another shot reverberates against the walls.

How many is that? Four?

He has to be out soon. My gaze tumbles over the fighters, the only cover in the arena. I lunge into more bodies, surrounded by an orchestra of clanging steel and shifting sand and hard, tired grunts.

Vaguely I register the throbbing behind my eyes, the pressure inside my skull.

Where is Hugo?

A flash of silver. I barely get my sword up before a short, dark-haired girl's blade bites into mine. The shock works its way into my shoulder.

Simulated pain. But it *feels* real, and I wince as I grasp her boot and lift, standing.

Now she's hopping on one foot, trying to yank her boot free, and I chop her other leg out from under her and then run my sword through her heart.

It's a simulation. But as her mouth parts and her body convulses, I squeeze the pommel, the pain in my head roaring; I'm sure I've killed her until she stumbles from the arena.

Where is Hugo? Where is Hugo? Where is Hu—?

Cla-ack. The sound sends a finger of terror scraping down my spine.

FIFTEEN

My heart rams into my throat as I turn to face Hugo. His breath washes over me, his pale, ashen skin flushed. He presses the cold muzzle against my forehead. Flames twinkle in his all black eyes. Beneath his red leather vest, his chest heaves, a bizarre, excited laugh parting his mouth.

Just a Sim. Just a Sim—

A zinging noise splits the air, forcing my eyes shut.

When I open them, Hugo has fallen to his knees, his face twisted in a snarl of rage. Rhydian throws me a quick glance, the crossbow he holds still pointed at Hugo's back.

"Fienian hell, that felt good," Rhydian says, smiling bigger than I ever remember seeing him on the Island. He nods to the pistol still pointed at me. "Take it. His weapon is yours by right."

"I thought I was a traitor?"

Rhydian shrugs. "The only thing I hate worse than traitors are the Redgraves."

Ignoring Rhydian, Hugo glares at me with his reptilian

gaze. Pointing the pistol at his feet, he discharges the last remaining bullet into the sand.

Then he offers it to me, that awful, rasping laugh spilling from his lips.

A few of the crowd applaud his decision, their cheers of praise turning into ugly insults hurled at me. I try forcing down the anger and shame their voices conjure, but the taunts only seem to get louder, the crushing pain inside my skull worsening with each curse.

And then I spot Riser near the back, clanging swords with a tall gangly boy. Every part of me goes still as I watch Riser, captivated. The bigger boy runs at him with murderous intent, and a tiny gasp escapes my lips, but Riser sidesteps, a bored grin on his face, and runs the boy through.

Two others replace Riser's opponent. They share clumsy turns slashing at him, nearly injuring the other in the process.

Riser evades with ease. He's like smoke, a slippery shadow, moving with an unnatural grace so fast I can hardly track him. It takes him to the count of ten to administer killing blows to his attackers.

What did they do to you, Pit Boy? Anger courses through me, sharp and relentless. *You promised me you would never hurt me . . . but you did.*

As if breaking free from a trance, I stride toward him. My feet move fast, faster. My breath steady, the pain in my head drowned out by my fury.

You erased me.

There's ten feet between us. It's as if an invisible string of betrayal and rage draws me to him.

You erased me like I was nothing.

I lift my sword, my intent clear. Riser swivels his head to appraise me, a slight quirk in his lips, his face lighting up with amusement.

Yes, Pit boy. I'm the girl who threw a book at you, and now I'm going to—

The blow knocks me senseless.

For a heartbeat, I'm gone. Just gone.

Then voices claw into my head. *"Help me!"* they beg. *"Wake me up!"*

I'm groaning. Cheek pressed into the sand. I spit blood —*real*, tangy blood. I struggle to my knees. The pain in my head vices until I can hardly see. Cruel laughter from behind wheedles into my skull.

Lucy Redgrave stands with a flail poised to brain me. I drag my forearm across my mouth, leaving a smear of red, sticky sand. She must have punched me, because the flail would have knocked me out of the game—and hurt like hell —but it wouldn't have broken my skin.

Gathering my strength, I glare up at her.

Against the shadow murk, Lucy's bloodless face is pale and wraith-like.

Large black eyes blink at me, her lips curled in derision. "Aw, is that your mean face?"

"Finish her!" Hugo yells from somewhere above.

Someone repeats his bloodthirsty plea. It begins to echo across the arena.

Finish her! Finish her! Finish her!

Frustration and anger pour through me. I search the crowd for Max, for Teagan, for a friend, but there are none. Only hateful, derisive faces, red from chanting for my simulated death.

Lucy raises the flail, the sadistic, spiky ball attached to the end glimmering maliciously in the amber light of the fires. Excited screams thrum the air. A bead of sweat trickles down my spine.

I glance at Riser. He's frowning, looking just past me at something. Refusing my gaze.

And then, for a fraction of a second, his focus shifts to my face, and I remember his words from what seems like years ago: *Fight until your very last breath, Digger Girl.*

But I'm tired of fighting.

I'm tired of *failing.*

It's too much. I can't do it anymore.

Something flickers across his expression, an unreadable emotion. I anchor myself to his green eye, bright even in the darkness.

I have to be in there somewhere. As my image races along his optic nerve into the dark recesses of his brain, some part of him has to recognize that I've been there before. That he's tasted my lips and smelled my skin. That his fingers have traced along my flesh.

Try to remember me, Pit Boy.

"Riser," I whisper.

Try.

"*Riser.*"

He squares his shoulders and looks away.

The flail makes no sound as Lucy swings it at my head, but I hear their jeers—*traitor, dandy whore, Royalist bitch*—and the voice of someone else, someone deep inside my head, screaming for hel—

The pain splits my skull.

SIXTEEN

I'm vaguely aware of being helped off the arena floor. Lash limps to my left, his arm hooked beneath my armpit, and Teagan steadies me on my right. We exit through an iron door that leads into a dim hallway with one sputtering torch. Chambers line both walls, and I sigh with relief as they help me into one of the rooms and onto a hard bed.

"Why in Fienian hell would you want to fight in the Blood Court?" Teagan growls.

"It was a bad idea," I admit, rubbing my head.

She plucks the sole torch from the wall and waves it over my face. The flame stings my bruised, scraped cheeks. "A horrible idea, darling. Even so, Redgrave took it too far."

Lash kneels in front of me. "Head shots are supposed to be against the rules. Sometimes the brain doesn't reset itself like the rest of the body after a simulated blow."

That's why they're hovering over me.

I push the torch away. "I'm already broken. There's something wrong with my . . . my head. I heard voices for the few seconds I was unconscious. Is that normal for simulated blows?"

Teagan's eyes are tight as she studies my face. "No. Could it be something else? Maybe something the Archduchess did to you when you were at Laevus Castle?"

"Not that I remember . . . but I heard the voices then, too —when she was torturing me. Maybe that made me, I don't know, lose my mind?"

Lash and Teagan both avert their gazes.

"I didn't give her anything about the Rebels, if that's what you're wondering." Teagan opens her mouth to say something, but I stop her with a shake of my head. "Anyway, that's in the past. But these voices, they're so real. Could it be Sleepers still uploaded to me from the Island?"

"I'm no expert, darling," Teagan drawls, "but nothing about that whole wretched business would surprise me anymore."

"They keep asking me to help them, to wake them up." I scratch my nose. "My dad left a letter for me and said the same thing, sort of."

Teagan purses her lips. "When do you hear them?"

Lash dabs a cloth over my cheek, and I wince. "When I'm in pain. When I'm scared. You know, basically all the time."

"Well, it would seem to me if you're the most connected during traumatic moments, then that's when you would most likely be able to wake them."

"And that's what they want?"

"Darling, I have no idea about that."

I chew my lip as Teagan and Lash exchange concerned glances.

Then he holds up four fingers. "How many fingers, love?"

Sighing, I flash my middle finger. "I'm not imagining things . . . Well, other than voices."

"Cute." He presses my hand down. "Any pain?"

"What are you, a healer?"

His mouth twists into a frown. "Gods, no. My father was .

. . I was in training before . . . well, before. To make him happy."

I don't press him. I know when someone doesn't want to talk. "I'm fine," I say, pushing past him to my feet. Sand rains from the folds of my dress and patters to the floor. "You know, despite having millions of voices inside my head."

Teagan holds out her hand. "Ready to go back out there?"

I glance at the door, my fingernails digging half-moons into my palms. "I have to face them."

Teagan's silk blouse rustles as she holds out her elbow, her red smile like a beacon in the dark. "We'll face them together."

After a reluctant pause, Lash takes my other arm. "Might as well escort a beautiful woman."

As the door parts and we climb the stone steps up to the dais, I wonder why they're declaring their solidarity with me. *Me.* A supposed traitor and dandy sympathizer.

But why? How could it possibly benefit them?

I cut a glance at Teagan, her head held high on that long neck of hers, mouth set in a firm smile as she meets the eye of every Fienian who dares look our way, somehow managing to appear both murderous and regal.

Merida's voice sparks in my head. *People will surprise you.*

We get behind a line of Rebels waiting to greet the winner on their throne. Teagan still holds my arm. A few Rebels pass by and open their mouths to hurl what would undoubtedly be creative insults, but Teagan silences them with a haughty stare.

The Fienians wither beneath her amber gaze. Most have only been Rebels for a few weeks; she's had an entire lifetime to learn how to be strong, forged by discrimination and intolerance. As a suspected Subversive, even her parents would have considered her an abomination.

Perhaps that's why she's befriending me. Because she knows how it feels to be the outsider, hated and alone.

She pats my arm. "Botchers. Half will piss their knickers at the first hint of real battle."

"Not me," Lash says, puffing out his chest.

Teagan raises an eyebrow. "Lash, they still haven't cleared you for battle—"

"But they should. I can fight, and I won't run." Lash draws up in front of Teagan, careful to hide his limp. "Just let me *try*."

Teagan's eyes are warm, but her lips are firm. "For the hundredth time, Lash, no. Your skills are needed elsewhere—"

"I'm lame, you mean. Broken. Useless."

Her gaze follows his skulking form as he stalks to the railing and glares down at the sea. "If only we had a hundred with his spirit."

"Why can't you fix his leg?"

"Not everyone's body can handle the massive influx of nanites used during Reconstruction. Lash has a rare blood type that prevents it."

"So he works in the armory?"

She chuckles, the sound both masculine and refined. "On occasion, when the infirmary is slow, he's allowed to assist me in the armory."

"And now he's my babysitter."

A wry smile finds her lips. "Following you is his punishment."

"For?"

"Entering the Blood Court, *again*, after being ordered not to, *again*."

I'm about to respond when the line moves and suddenly I'm facing three thrones. Nicolai sits to the right, cloaked and veiled in onyx-and-flame silk from head to toe, the sun's rays swimming along the smooth curves of his mask. Only his eyes peek out: lidless, near-pigmentless orbs that crawl over my skin with scrutiny. A silver fan whirs to his left, spitting misty air over him.

Flame is curled up inside her throne, her cloak pooled around her like cream. Beneath the sun, her red leathers shine like polished wood.

But it's Riser who captures my attention—Prince Dorian Riser Laevus. Not a single part of Pit Boy is left in this distant, dark figure perched on the Scorpion Throne, legs shifting, long fingers once again furiously tapping the wooden arms beneath his palms, as if he churns with too much energy, a bomb seconds from igniting. Sweat drips from his raven-black hair—half still constrained by a leather tie, the other free and wild—onto his red leathers.

He watches me with a sharp, unreadable gaze that makes me want to strangle him with the shreds of my dress.

"Blood for freedom," Teagan says in a clear, strong voice.

I follow, stumbling over the Fienian motto.

Riser is supposed to answer back so we can be done with this foolish charade, but Nicolai leans forward before Pit Boy can respond. "Now that's the spirit, Maia. Your enthusiasm overwhelms us."

Ignoring Nicolai's taunt, I shift my gaze to Flame and raise my eyebrows. "Think I can get that weapon now?"

Flame unfurls, stretching out her arms and legs. As she does, she steals a furtive glance at Teagan, before looking back to me. "Normally you would take any demands you have to the Head of Recruits, who would in turn relay your request. But since you know nothing of our ways, I'll give you your answer now."

"If you would just—"

"No."

I blink. "But—"

"No." Flame sits on the edge of her throne, daring me to challenge her. Tension crackles the air.

You—You . . . I dig my fingernails into my palms and force a shuddering breath into my shaking body, holding it until the words I want to say sink back down into my brain.

A snicker comes from behind me, nearly loosing my rage. But I push it down, swallowing the emotion like glass.

Before I say something I'll regret, Teagan steps forward. I do the same, staring at my feet the way Teagan does, and Riser quickly bids our departure with the response, "Death for Honor."

I make it two steps before Riser says, "Wait."

Sighing mid-step, I resume my place in front of him.

"Why did you enter the Blood Court?" His mismatched eyes peel away at me, sharp and searching, whittling with his uncanny skills.

One glance at Teagan's lifted eyebrows says she's interested in my answer as well. I kick at an invisible rock at my feet.

If I look at him, I'm afraid the rage brewing inside me will be too much to restrain.

"I was bored, your Liege—or is it My Prince?" I shoot a murderous glance at Flame. "I'm new to these kinds of things."

The line behind me goes quiet, but I swear a corner of Riser's mouth twitches in what *could* be amusement. "Riser is fine. Now, back to my question. What did you stand to gain by entering?" He goes still for once, every part of his body settling into the space it occupies. "Did you plan to win and take this throne for yourself?"

My lips part. Of course they wouldn't know the real reason: my failed attempt to connect with my father, like I did on the Island during Caspian's Sim. Yes, *failed.*

I grind the toe of my boot into the balcony floor. As if I

would want some stupid, uncomfortable Fienian throne, to bark orders and . . . and . . .

Command. I would command. And if I were in command, I would have influence. Influence enough to gather a small crew and go back to the Island to find the Mercurian.

"Yes." As soon as the word spills from my lips, my body lightens a little and the semblance of a plan takes hold.

"Be careful, girl," Nicolai purrs behind his mask, the awkward timbre of his Electro-Larynx dulled by sounds of the sea below. "A statement like that could come off rather . . . *traitor-ish.*"

But my attention is on Riser. He has reclined into the back of his throne, and although it's impossible to read his eyes, he's no longer smiling.

"Good luck . . . What was your name again?"

"Maia Graystone." Each syllable is a declaration, a threat. "I look forward to taking your throne, *Prince.*"

Slowly he leans forward, resting his elbows on his knees. A nearly dry strip of hair blows across his forehead. "And I look forward to you *trying.*"

SEVENTEEN

There's some ridiculous ceremony after Riser's win, but I don't stay to watch Pit Boy crowned. Three words rattle through my mind: the Scorpion Throne. Now that the thought of taking the throne has entered my mind, it's all I can think about. I would only have to keep power for a day—long enough to get to the Island.

After that I'd gladly give my command back, or at least gladly give Riser the *chance* to take it back. A giddy smile finds my face, and I nod along to Lash's diatribe about breakfast being the same old slop.

Maybe when I have the throne I'll change that too.

Despite the pleasant breeze outside, my room is stuffy and hot, and it doesn't take long for a headache to foul my mood, although luckily no voices. I put on another dark, elaborate dress with red embroidery along the bodice. The curve of the neckline is meant to accentuate my assets, and I squirm, tucking and lifting my itchy prison of crinoline and lace to no avail. Sweat immediately dribbles down my back.

Along with my newfound desire to take the throne comes the burning need to find Brogue. He's the only one who can train me to beat Riser, and currently the only person I can trust.

But only a handful of people might know where he is, and I've already questioned all of them . . . except Rhydian Pope.

Plus, I need to get Bramble back from him before a Rebel decides to use him as spare parts.

It takes the better half of an hour to find Rhydian. He's training outside in what was once probably a beautiful court-yard, but now there's only a patch of gravel pocked with weeds and mossy, broken sculptures, their features all but eaten away by the harsh ocean air.

As soon as Rhydian sees me, he hands his sword off to another Rebel and runs over, ignoring the disapproving glances of his friends. Lash, propped against the castle wall and squinting against the afternoon sun, waits in the background.

Once we might have been genuinely glad to see the other. But that was before I refused to execute Prince Caspian and Rhydian took me prisoner.

Now we perform an awkward, tense handshake that hints at our shared loss of Merida and nothing more.

Neither of us has gotten better at pleasantries, so I get straight to the point. "Where's Brogue?"

Rhydian's eyebrows lower. "Graystone, I don't think—"

"Yes, I do. I want to see him. I'm not a child; I can handle whatever mess he's in."

"Let it go."

Sucking in my lip, I glare at him. "No. And I'll visit you every day, sometimes three or four times, until you tell me where he is." I glance over at his buddies still frowning at us. "But I'm sure your new Fienian friends will overlook your associations with a *traitor*."

He lets out a sigh. "Look, last time I saw him, he was near the old servants' quarters."

The servants' quarters? My mind races to remember what Lash said about that part of the castle while on our tour. I'd only half-listened, but I recall something about the Rebels incapable of working being stashed there.

I pivot on my heels, ready to head that way. Bramble will have to wait.

"I tried to help him, Graystone," Rhydian calls after me. "But he's too far gone."

I ignore his words as I rush through the halls. Brogue is strong. He might have problems, but none so bad that he's beyond help. I'm nearly running, buoyed by a sense of hope swelling my chest and lightening my steps.

Brogue will help me get a weapon. Help me prove my innocence and win the Blood Court.

I slow my feet as the hallways narrow and darken. The pungent tang of overflowing chamber pots and unwashed bodies chokes the air.

Nausea creeps up the back of my throat.

I throw a hand over my nose and mouth, my eyes watering. It's dark here, completely windowless, a few meager torches skittering shadows across the walls.

"Gods above, this place reeks," Lash mutters, slipping up behind me and nearly giving me a heart attack. "Next time you try to sneak away, pick the mess hall or something."

But I barely hear him. For a moment, I'm back inside the Trials. The tight walls closing in, the groans of finalists filling the air. My mouth goes bone-dry, my stomach tight.

The Trials are over. Over. But no matter how much I say those words, it feels as if I'm there, about to be smashed between those heavy walls, and my heart rams my sternum with bone-shaking force.

My fear shifts to anger as I see bodies packed onto the beds. A few people lift their heads to gaze at me, their eyes glazed and unfocused, before turning back to stare at nothing. Around the corner, a boy sits against the wall, a smile plastered on his face below unseeing eyes.

Why is no one helping these people?

"Brogue?" I call, voice cracking as I pick through the rooms.

No way Brogue is here. He's a Twitcher, sure, but not like these addicts. Not—

My chest tightens. A man is spread out across the floor, head lolled to the side, scraggly beard crusted with old, dried vomit. His eyes are black slits.

It's not him . . . It's not. It can't be.

He would never—never let himself fall this far. My heart skips a beat. There's a tattoo peeking from his torn shirt . . . a . . . a noose.

A hangman's noose.

"Oh, gods no," I whisper, dropping to my knees. As soon as I get close, I gag on the odor. "Merc, what have you done?"

Brogue blinks, slowly, his Twitcher-black eyes rolling around his sockets. "Mfth, uh . . ."

"How could you do this?" I plead, every word a tearless sob. "How could you let yourself go? You abandoned me! Coward."

Lash drags me back and to my feet. "Easy, love."

Fienian hell, I was hitting him. The realization makes me sick. I drag my forearm across my wet cheeks, collecting my tears.

"Are you crying?"

"No," I sniffle.

"Aw, don't do that."

"What? Do my tears offend you, Fienian?"

Instead of answering, he leans down, his face wrinkling at the smell. "Are you going to help me carry him or what?"

Despite Lash's hurt leg, he's strong, and we manage to move Brogue up two floors to an empty room with a yellow-stained mattress. Other than a few unintelligible shouts, Brogue is quiet.

Too quiet. As soon as his body sinks into the mattress, he starts convulsing. Rolling him onto his side, I lay over his chest to keep him from falling to the floor and hurting himself. I whisper soothing words.

When I run out of things to say, I recite some of my mother's poems.

All at once, he relaxes with a sigh. His flesh is hot, mottled. I remember somewhere hearing that when Twitchers start getting feverish, it means the nanites have already invaded the part of the brain that regulates temperature.

It means it's too late.

Lash presses a hand against Brogue's forehead. "He's hot. We need to undress him and lower his temperature."

Lash scrounges up a basin with water and strips of cloth, and we get to work. I give myself simple commands. Take off his shirt. His pants. Rinse his left arm. Now his right.

Anything I can do to keep from thinking about the proud, strong man this shell of a person once was. In the short time since I last saw him, he's become impossibly gaunt. Deep shadows collect in his collarbones, his ribs sharp against his bone-white skin.

The fever breaks, and Lash helps me find some dusty, moth-eaten blankets to cover Brogue with.

It takes a while for Lash to convince me there's nothing else to do but wait. I don't want to leave Brogue. I feel like I'm abandoning him.

I kiss his forehead. It's clammy, cold.

"Get better, Merc," I whisper. "That's an order."

EIGHTEEN

Lash tries to cheer me up with idle chit-chat as we walk the corridor to meet Teagan and start my job. Although I can't shake the image of Brogue lying half-dead on the floor, I'm looking forward to working, if only to forget about everything else.

"Listening, love?" Lash says as we round a corner.

"How can I not?" I tease, thankful for the distraction. "You won't stop talking."

Grinning, he dives back into the conversation. According to him, everyone helps out. Even the fighters have tasks when they're not training, or leaving the compound on missions.

"There are no servants here," he explains. "No Colors. We all pull our weight."

Yet it doesn't feel that way when I come across my first waste bucket. I curse at the putrid stench that hits me from across the room, eyeing the mound of tunics and leathers balled on the floor. But the worst part is that I don't even get a key. *Lash* does.

He chuckles from the doorway. "That bucket isn't going to empty itself, love."

I gesture obscenely at him as I pick through the clothes. "Care to help?"

"Not a Fienian chance in hell." He throws a lazy wink my way. "Even if you are pretty."

Standing as far away from the waste as possible, I grab the handle. The bucket sloshes in my hand. I swallow down vomit, making a face. "Oh, gross."

I haven't decided yet if I'm going to steal the key from Lash or just ask him for it. If I steal it and he finds out, he'll never trust me. But if I ask him for it and he says no, there's a chance he'll inform on me.

Both scenarios are not optimal, but I need that key. Assuming it unlocks all the doors, it would give me direct access to the war room where I last spied the hologram map. I have to figure out what they're planning and how dangerous it is.

I have to protect Max. I know he's old enough to take care of himself, but I can't help the feeling that he's going to be taken away from me again.

More rooms, more buckets. Sometimes I can talk Lash into helping, but mostly he just watches and makes snarky comments, the key snug in his vest pocket.

The last room down the hall is tidy, at least, and there's no waste to empty. Lash waits out in the hall this time. He doesn't say why, but I notice the longer he stands, the more pronounced his limp becomes.

After smearing the thick legion of grime around with a duster and sweeping the worn stone floor, I sink into the bed, relishing the rare moment alone.

But it's not enough. I need sunlight. Judging by the greenish tinge to the light seeping through the veiled window, dinner should be soon.

Maybe I have time to sneak outside, just for a minute. I need to feel the breeze on my face again. Smell the ocean.

My breath catches, the hairs on my neck lifting one by one.

I turn to see Riser sitting in the chair in the corner, steeped in shadow. My boots hit the ground and I raise the duster, sending motes snowing through the air.

"Going to throw that at me too?" Riser drawls.

I slide my gaze up and down him, pushing back the emotions that come roaring. "What would you do if I did, Prince?"

A dangerous grin carves his jaw.

I lift an eyebrow, tempted. His smile taunts me, daring me to. But the duster's too light; it wouldn't have much impact.

Tossing the feathers onto the bed, I grab the closest item on his nightstand and—

Somehow, without seeming to move, Riser has crossed the floor and has my wrist in his hand. His face is unreadable as he plucks the picture frame from my fingers and sets it back onto his nightstand.

It's then I notice the woman inside it—the same woman depicted in the library painting.

His mom.

His eyes are bright as they pierce me, his fingers strong and warm around my wrist. "I wouldn't do that if I were you."

I sneer at him. "Let go of my wrist, Pit Boy."

His grip loosens, but he doesn't let go. "What did you call me?"

"I'm sure you've been called worse." I can smell him, his soapy, leather smell infused with sweat, and I grind my teeth at its familiar pleasure.

"How do you know about the pit?"

I shrug, blinking back the whisper of tears as I remember our shared history. "Common knowledge."

His focus skims my lips, flicking away before resting there

once again. "No. The prison, maybe, but only my friends know about the pit."

I used to be one of those, before you erased me. My heart thuds so hard it shakes my chest. "Riser, do you remember me at all?"

His jaw tightens, the artery just below it pounding. "Should I?"

This close, I can see the smooth muscled flesh beneath his vest, already golden from the sun. But his scar is still there, the one he told me he was proud of, cresting his collarbone and riding down below sight.

Without thinking, I reach for it with my unbound hand. A small gasp escapes him, and he turns his head to the side and watches as I lightly graze his collarbone with my finger, his flesh shivering beneath my touch.

"But wasn't there a girl on the Island? Someone you cared about?"

His chest heaves beneath my fingers. "Her name was Everly."

"Where is Everly now?"

Something inside him seems to close off, the light inside his eyes dimming. "Dead."

His words are like an arrow through the heart. I pause my finger over the smooth, firm mound of his pectoral muscle/

I could try to tell him who I am, what happened, what he let them do to him. But it wouldn't matter. All he knows about me now is that I'm a suspected traitor with a habit of throwing things at him.

It wouldn't be like before—whatever we had, that connection, that *bond*, it's gone.

And it was his choice to take it away. His *choice*. I have to remember that.

This is how he wants it.

Propelled by fury and sadness, I push off my tiptoes and

find his mouth, capturing his lip between my teeth, my tongue flicking over his.

There's a soft hiss as he inhales, and then I bite down, hard, twisting my wrist from his grip as the tang of blood fills my mouth.

I wrench away from him and stalk into the hallway, leaving all my stuff. Lash nearly collides with me in the doorway, his gaze going from me to the prince.

I glance over my shoulder. "Don't get too used to the throne, Pit Boy."

To my utter delight, his eyes are wide, and he drags the back of his hand across his bloody lip.

Then his injured lip curves into a roguish grin. "If you plan to win by those means, Graystone, I'm very much looking forward to tomorrow."

I frown, the door clicking shut before I can shout any insults back at him.

Lash's gaze slides from the blood on my lip to the closed door. "Should I go sort him out?"

I sigh. "No sorting anyone out today, Lash. Besides, it's the prince's blood, not mine."

Lash's focus falls back to my mouth, now splayed in a silly grin. "Are you upset or happy? I can't tell."

I shrug. "Both."

The opportunity to steal the key comes a few rooms later, when Lash lifts it from his neck, fiddles with the chain, and then dumps the key in his pocket, making it much easier to steal undetected. I blink, looking away before he notices my attention.

Time is short. I need to do this now. Yet, I hesitate. Lash has grown on me. His silly belief in the gods, his willingness to be nice to me despite his near certainty I'm a traitor.

I don't want to hurt him.

You have to figure out what they're planning. This is the only way. Do it for Max.

My tongue feels like limp cardboard as I set my things down and approach Lash. His eyebrows lift in surprise, and I hesitate.

My impromptu plan—to flirt as a distraction—suddenly feels cruel, so I switch tactics and trip into him, slipping my hand into his pocket and snagging the key.

"Whoa, love." He steadies me with his hands. "If you want to feel my manly chest, just say so."

Despite the joke, there's something in his face I can't quite put my finger on, his lips tugged down into a weird frown, as if he knows I took the key.

Stop being paranoid.

I force a hollow laugh. "Sorry. Got a bit woozy. I think I'm still not right after the Blood Court."

"Go," he whispers in a conspiratorial voice. "Lie down for a bit. I won't tell anyone."

His kindness kills me, but not enough to make me give back the key. Can I get it back to him without him noticing?

Somehow that feels just as dishonest as stealing it in the first place.

My nerves have me racing through the hallways—and ignoring the way Lash's gaze followed me down the corridor. No way he knows. My grab was smooth as glass.

A little ironic, actually, considering I used to be horrible at pick pocketing.

The sound of my heavy breathing fills the air. *Slow down.* It's hard enough staying inconspicuous with the stupid dress tangling around my ankles. But even after I force myself to walk, I feel like every Rebel I pass knows I'm about to break into the council room.

I lower my head, studying the faded scarlet roses on the thin, black carpet runner.

It takes longer than expected to find the war room, mostly because the chambers and hallways aren't connected in any rational sort of way, but rather cobbled together, as if several different architectural plans were spliced into a complex, nonsensical maze. But the wall panels and dark drapes look familiar, and finally the heavy oak door appears.

As soon as I retrieve the key, palms sweaty and hand shaking, a sound makes me turn.

Teagan stands in the corner, arms crossed. She wears a disappointed expression. "Lash just lost ten denaris."

"I don't know—"

"Stop. You're caught. Don't make it awkward."

"This was a . . . a trap?"

"More of a *test*."

And I just flunked.

Releasing a deep breath, I pull out the key, feeling like a child caught stealing candy. "Here."

Teagan crosses the floor, plucks the key from my palm, and shoves the last of my plan into her pocket. "Thank you."

"So, what now?"

Teagan blinks at me. "What? Will I turn you in?"

I nod.

"No."

"Thank y—"

"But next time, I *will*."

I stare at the floor. "Okay."

"Look, darling, I know you're not a traitor, but the others don't. They're looking for any reason to condemn you, and you keep trying your hardest to give it to them."

Shifting on my feet, I glance at the door. "Do you know what they're planning?"

"Why are you so interested in Rebel plans?"

"I—I'm not." I shake my head for emphasis.

"Hm. O-kay." She flicks a dubious gaze at the war room I just tried to break into and then back to me. "Don't you have some cleaning to finish?"

End of discussion. *Fine.*

Pivoting on my heels, I march down the hall, winding the maze back to the last room I cleaned. Lash waits for me with a hurt look and a too-full bucket.

Without a word, he thrusts the disgusting thing at me and then storms outside to wait, arms crossed, by the door.

I throw my frustration into finishing the last set of rooms. When they're clean-*ish*, Lash allows me to visit the washroom to remove the day's filth. He even smiles at me—a martyr's smile, but I'll take it.

It's a reminder, though. I have to be more careful. With so much at stake, I can't afford to mess up like this again.

And I can't alienate the few people who don't hate me.

TWENTY

Teagan looks spectacular in an emerald-green tunic and black leather pants cinched down the legs with green ribbon. Like most of the others, black leather wristlets adorn both her arms, decorated with the same green ribbon. She reclines on the bed, unfolding her long frame. We've been discussing the upcoming ceremony and pretending I didn't just try to break into the war room.

"But I'm tired of brands and oaths and people messing with my head, Aster." I realize I've just called Teagan by her last name, like the other Fienians do to those who haven't taken a Fienian name.

I wonder if eventually I'll be expected to do that, too.

Her long fingers flutter over the new Fienian mark at her neck, tracing along the ruby-red scorpion entwined with her old Bronze phoenix.

"We're all tired of something, darling. I, for one, am tired of the kitchen's stale excuse for food and pissing in a bucket." She flicks her amber gaze to me. "But I still eat, and I still have to pee."

"So you're saying I don't have a choice?"

Red lips form a fierce grin over snow-white teeth. "The question isn't whether you can choose. It's what happens when you do?"

I shiver. There's very little doubt what will happen if I refuse the Fienian oath. If I don't publicly become a Rebel, they won't trust me. Without trust, I'm useless.

And without a use, they will dispose of me rather than set me free to talk.

But I've already sacrificed nearly everything for them, and I'm not ready to give the little I have left. "So how did you, Teagan Aster III, become a Fienian Rebel?"

Something dark flashes across her face. "I won't bore you with that story. C'mon, I'm *starving*. Let's go choke down some Fienian slop."

Lash finds us by the stairs, his hair combed for once, pulled back into a knot. A golden scorpion cuff winds down his right ear.

His white tunic gapes open at the top, revealing a strong, muscled chest. Tall black boots gleam with daggers.

Teagan whistles. "Well aren't you a dandy, Lash. Forget your purse?"

Grinning, he pulls at the red ribbon cinching his vest. "Yeah, love. I left it with your girlfriend on my bed."

I tense, expecting Teagan to bite back, but she laughs. "She'll be disappointed when she finds out you have the wrong parts."

Lash runs a finger over his lips. "Still prettier than you, Aster."

I snort. "Since when do Fienians care about fashion?"

Lash crosses his arms over his chest, refusing my gaze. He still hasn't forgiven me.

"Darling," Teagan says as she drapes her lanky arm over my shoulders, "you have a lot to learn."

She's right. Along the way to the Great Hall, we pass Rebels dressed in all manner of leathers, their bodies glittering from head to toe with weapons of every kind. Ornate iron cuffs adorn their wrists, dazzling arm chains jingle and glitter from their bare arms, and festive, metallic-red tattoos zigzag over their exposed flesh.

After living most of my life around dull fabrics, and then being immersed in a strictly Colored world of petticoats and corsets, the display is like a bright, angry, chaotic explosion of metals and every hue of red imaginable.

Then there's me, with my heavy sweeping skirt and itchy, corseted top. I couldn't stand out more if I tried.

To have any chance of winning the Scorpion Throne and gaining the trust of others, I'll need clothes I can move in that don't make me look like a Royalist.

A fireplace swelters and rages inside the Great Hall, blasting an invisible wall of heat as we enter. I feel Riser's gaze from his place at the head table near the back, but I pretend not to notice him as I scan the room. The two tables from lunch have become twenty tables in four rows of five. The sound of laughter and plates clanging and chairs scraping form a loud din that makes it hard to relax.

The few Rebels I make eye contact with either scowl or immediately look away. As the whisper of traitor follows me, I wonder how many times I'm going to have to prove myself before the others accept me.

Entering the Blood Court obviously wasn't enough—hopefully winning it and taking the throne will be.

Riser's burning gaze draws my focus to him, and I ignore the spark between us as our eyes meet.

Instead of looking away, he continues to stare, watching me with deep, unabashed interest, like an animal he's yet to categorize as predator or prey.

I throw a lazy wink at him.

A slow smile flickers across his face.

Just wait until tomorrow, Prince, I think, taking a place at the back table.

As soon as we settle in, I search for Max. The tables nearest the fireplace brim with fighters. They crowd around the food, chanting and slapping each other on the back.

Pale golden hair catches my eye, and I look to see Max perched atop a table on one leg, a glass mug balanced on his head, sloshing amber liquid onto his friends around him. Just like when we were little, Max is the center of attention.

The red-haired girl from the arena calls out bets, while some of the boys around her pelt Max with biscuits, yelling as more beer spills onto the table. The older-sister part of me wants to march over there, yank Max down, and scold him for his bad table manners.

But the cowardly part of me wants to watch him. Soak him all in. Alive. Vibrant. Flushed with youth. He's holding out his arms now. Singing a song I can't hear.

My heart swells. He looks so much like my father, the way his chin dimples as he laughs and his eyes crinkle in the corners.

Watching him, a bittersweet hole of regret splits open inside me. I might have been his sister once, but now these people have replaced me, and I have no idea where I fit into the equation.

The glass mug topples from Max's head and shatters on the floor, drenching everyone around him in alcohol and eliciting a collective cheer from his buddies.

I tear my gaze away, focusing on my fingernails, the grain of the wood table, anything but the stranger who was once my little brother.

The clamor around me grows louder, and I frown at the crass yells and laughter from the Rebels, wishing for peace and quiet. The others must be used to the din, because they talk and joke between steamy bites, while behind them, curses fly at a dice game being played.

Manners and decorum don't belong in this hall of Rebels. Just like I don't belong. Not here . . . maybe not anywhere.

To cheer myself up, I watch Lash and Teagan argue over a corn-silk-haired girl near the middle who keeps glancing at us.

"She's not looking at you, Aster," Lash says, chucking a wicked grin that could melt an iceberg at the poor girl.

"Gods tell you that?" Teagan purrs.

"Oh, I don't need the gods to know when a girl fancies me."

"Apparently you do."

"Settle this, Graystone," Teagan says, turning to me as she winks. "Who's she looking at?"

I'm seconds from cracking a joke when . . . oh. She's giving me a chance to make up with Lash. Sucking my lip, I glance over at the girl. "Hmm. She's pretty."

"That she is, darling," Teagan purrs.

Lash glowers at his bowl of slop.

"I would have to say . . ."

Lash peeks up at me.

I lean over and kiss his cheek, begging him with a glance for forgiveness. "She has to be looking at Lash. I mean"—I run my fingers through his hair—"look at this beautiful mane the color of, erm, rust."

Teagan cackles. "Flirt much, darling?"

"Nope." Lash shakes his head. "Can't win me back with a few compliments, Graystone, even if they are true."

"No?"

"No."

But he's grinning now, and I know I've chinked the icy thaw around his heart, at least.

I'm about to rise and leave when a crackling noise gives

me pause. A rift screen flares to life in the high ceiling above us. The image flickers and hisses, slowly solidifying into a face I know all too well.

The emperor.

TWENTY-ONE

The emperor sits on an ornate gold throne, his thin lips twisted into a cruel sneer, his near-pigmentless eyes piercing the screen and boring straight into my soul. I try to still my racing heart as I take in the wall of deep blue-black behind him, rife with stars cut from glass.

Hyperion. He's on Hyperion.

"Several days ago, the Fienian horde attacked the palace." His voice booms over the mess hall, forcing every single Rebel to watch. "Terrorists hell-bent on destruction, even in a time like this."

The screen cuts away to a golden casket, its smooth metal surface shimmering as if afire. Pale-white roses adorn the top, brushing the shoulders of the pallbearers carrying it. My throat tightens at the sight of Caspian at the front, looking elegant in all black clothing piped with golden accents, his face somber and tight. Wind whips his hair and clothing.

Princess Ophelia rests inside the casket. I'm surprised the emperor doesn't have the lid open so the world can be reminded of her innocence, her ethereal beauty.

Then again, maybe he's afraid by now the bruising from his hands on her neck will show, shadowy whispers of the emperor's murderous secret.

Something makes me glance at Teagan. Her face is frozen into a hard mask, but her chin quivers, her hand pressing against her stomach.

Perhaps she and O were better friends than I imagined?

The entire hall is riveted to the Rift screen. Do they know Princess O was one of them? Do they mourn her too?

Someone wails on the screen, and the noise cuts the air like a knife.

Steel-gray rock backdrops the mourners as they follow the casket to the mouth of a cave. Snow reflects the sun's rays at their feet. In the distance, the palace appears, the size of a cherry. They must be somewhere high up on the Ivory Mountain ranges that shadowed the valley where the first Shadow Trial was held.

"I gave every citizen a chance at life," the emperor continues. "I allowed you into my home, gave your children peace, and this is how you repay me. With the savage and brutal murder of my daughter."

A shiver goes through me as another figure enters the screen. My mother. I blink away tears that rise unbidden and blur her sleight figure. Her features have become sharp, her brown hair drab and brittle, the hollows around her eyes deep and pooled with shadows.

"With much regret, I must inform you that the Shadow Trials have been canceled," my mother says in a strong voice that contradicts her fatigued appearance. "The court will begin preparing for exodus to Hyperion. All Sleepers uploaded to Finalists have been transferred to the Chosen." She hesitates for a moment, her gaze collapsing to her lap. A muscle jumps below the tight skin of her jaw before she addresses the screen once again. "Because of a few cowardly Fienian scum, all of the Finalists for the Trials will be hanged by the neck until dead, along with their attendants and any other Bronzes on the Island not originally slated for Hyperion. Consider this a mercy." She places a hand over her heart, fingers together, and then snaps her hand out. "All hail the emperor."

The hall erupts into a roar of anger. Chairs scrape as everyone jumps to their feet, some hopping onto the tables and throwing whatever's handy at the screen. Metal goblets and plates sail through the air, spilling liquid and slop as they pierce the screen, momentarily disrupting the images and the inevitable.

The din quiets after a minute. Some of the Rebels sob as the Finalists march to the wooden scaffolding by the cherry trees. Only ten can hang at a time.

I fight back tears. The ones in line will be forced to watch as their friends die, forced to witness the horror they're about to experience.

The Rebels drain from the mess hall, shoulders slumped and cheeks slick with tears. Teagan taps my shoulder in a silent plea for me to leave, too, but I shake my head.

I once thought I could look away from the horrors of the empire. That somehow, if I didn't see the atrocities they committed, if I didn't experience the horror and nausea from watching, somehow I had won a small battle against them.

But that's not true. I know that now.

Flame rounds the table, followed by Riser. Both wear hollow expressions mirroring my own.

She glances up at the screen before flicking her angry gaze at me. "They broadcast this every few hours. They were executing traitors, but I guess after you left, they ran out of those."

Her footsteps echo across the stone. I watch her make it to the door before a familiar voice trickles from the screen and wraps cold fingers around my heart.

Flame twitches as she halts, just for a moment, long enough to tell me she recognized the voice too.

But she slips out the arched doorway, and I drag my attention back to the screen, cringing at what I know I'll see.

Flame's best friend, Cage, is pale and thin, blood crusting his tunic. A black, swollen mound makes up his left eye, purplish-blue bruises spreading across both cheeks. His lips are bloodied to a pulp.

"Please," he whispers. "No more."

I gasp as the Archduchess draws up behind him on the scaffolding. Even without seeing her, he must know she's there because he begins to shake, his broken, swollen fingers twitching at his sides. He stares at his feet, and even when the Archduchess prods him with her hatpin and he's forced to walk up to the lever that will drop the trapdoors at the Finalists' feet, he refuses to look up.

That was supposed to be me.

"Do it, worm!" the Archduchess orders.

Still, Cage hesitates. His whole body seizes with fear, *but* he hesitates.

"Don't fight her," I whisper.

A wild moan escapes his lips as the Archduchess presses the tip of the hatpin into his flesh, her eyes feverish and bright.

"Do it!" she says.

His hand trembles on the lever. The Finalists look straight ahead. They've already accepted their fate.

She whispers something into his ear. I know she's threatening to hurt him.

Cage blinks, looks up, and presses the lever. The trap

doors snap open with a loud, horrifying *clack,* and the Finalists drop.

I watch them wiggle and flop before the horror of it all makes me turn away.

Something inside me breaks open. How many times has Cage had to do that? How many times has he been forced to pull the lever and execute innocent people?

That could have been me.

"I stay and watch too," Riser says in a hard, emotionless voice.

But beneath the coldness, there's a thread of sadness. A thread that if I choose to pull might unravel his façade completely.

"Why?"

"To remind myself our actions have consequences. And because it's practice for when the nightmares come." He turns on his heels to leave, throwing a look back at me. "I don't look away from those anymore either."

Something pulls my attention back to the screen.

The Archduchess fills up most of it, so close I can almost see the pores marring her white flesh. Her cheeks are red with excitement, her eyes wide and her breathing fast.

A mangled smile stretches across her face. "I'm going to find you, maggots. There's nowhere you can hide, no hovel you can disappear to. I'm going to find you."

I stop breathing as she suddenly cocks her head, her pupils enlarging, her intense focus directed at me. "Maia of the stars—"

Even though I know she can't see me, even though I know it's a ploy to instill fear, I flee, my heart pounding so hard that my entire body pulses with each beat.

She can't see me. She can't find me. And yet, I know deep down that she will eventually, and when I finally calm down enough to take a deep breath, I'm curled on top of my bed.

I slip into a nightmarish sleep full of voices begging me to save them. Yet even in my nightmare, I know how absurd the idea that I can save *myself* is, let alone millions of people, and I plead with them to find someone else, someone stronger to help them until I wake up tangled in my covers and soaked in sweat.

TWENTY-TWO

I've barely stumbled out of bed before Lash knocks on my door.

I wrench open the door and gaze blearily at him. "What do you want?"

He turns on his heels. "Follow me."

"Where are we going?" I call as I slip from my room, running my fingers through my sweat-soaked hair.

"Nicolai demands a word." Lash's voice quivers with a mixture of fear and respect.

A pounding headache splits my skull, and I realize I'm grinding my teeth so hard my jaw muscles have begun to spasm. Nicolai has that effect on me.

Still, I need to talk to him about retrieving the Mercurian. If there's even a small chance that it's real, how can he not want to find it?

Although I suppose the real question is will I trust Nicolai with my father's device if we find it.

No, absolutely not. But at this point I don't have a choice.

Lash makes conversation as he leads me to the west side of the castle. According to my chatty guide, Bloodwyn Castle has seven separate sections cordoned off by thick, arching wooden doors enforced with rusting iron bars and armed Rebels.

This part of the castle is spacious compared to the other two wings, with high, shadowy ceilings and enormous chambers separated by rich tapestries. Just like the others, the windows to the outside have been covered with scorpion-carved panels. But somehow, even with a wall-full of burning candles it seems darker here, the shadows colder and longer, and I stick close to Lash's side.

The bustle of Rebels is nonexistent. In fact, as I follow Lash up a sweeping staircase inlaid in gold and veiled in cobwebs, I realize we haven't seen a single person since we entered this part of Bloodwyn.

We're deep in the heart of the castle by the time we find Nicolai. Draped in his usual robes, his face partially hidden behind a metallic red mask, he stands with one hand behind his back in the middle of an enormous chamber. His other hand is gloved in deep-scarlet silk and rests on top of a scorpion-handled cane.

Despite a fire burning in the fireplace, the room is cold. An iron chandelier hangs above him, but the candles have long since melted, the floor covered in dull red splatters of wax. Flickering candles clump in the corners, casting wild, lurching shadows across the cracked parquet floor.

As I approach Nicolai, my boot steps shattering the eerie silence, the door clicks shut behind me. I turn and look for Lash, but he's gone. Two guards stand against the wall.

I shift nervously on my feet, unused to seeing Nicolai in person. As a hologram, sure. As a disembodied voice inside my head, yes.

But the burned flesh and blood man staring at me now as if I am nothing more than a pawn, a body to use and discard, this Nicolai terrifies me.

The Puppet Master's cape slithers behind him as he takes my arm inside his silky, gloved half-fingers and guides me to the back wall, his cane tapping loudly against the floor. He walks slowly, with care, as if each step pains him.

Except for an aged wooden piano in the corner and a few armchairs draped in dingy white covers, the huge chamber is bare.

"Hello, Maia." Nicolai's electronic voice rattles my nerves and echoes through the hollow, chilled space. He performs a mock curtsy. "Or is it Everly now?"

"Maia," I say. "I don't want to have anything to do with your other creation. What, did you think you could take pieces of me and create your own little monster?"

"Now, Everly, don't be dramatic." With a muffled groan, he bends and picks up a candle, sweeping its rich amber light over the wall. "Out of curiosity, what drivel did your tutor teach you about our world before the Everlasting War?"

I scan the wall, shrouded in a layer of cobwebs and dust, and shrug. "It was governed equally by the barons of the wealthiest houses."

"An interesting notion. And the war?"

"The lower-class factory workers revolted, using the current technology to fight the barons and destroy their warehouses."

"What if I told you everything they said about the war was a lie?"

I rock back on my heels. "But how could they just erase history like that?"

Yet, even as the words leave my mouth, I know how easy it would have been for the Royalists to take our collective past and manipulate it. They burned all the books. Destroyed thousands of recordings and videos in the Great Purge.

The emperor could tell us anything; we have nothing to refute it.

"Yes, how could they have destroyed the technologies it took hundreds of years to create, all the wondrous inventions that defined us as a people? How could they have enslaved an entire class of citizens? How could they have murdered and plundered and suppressed a nation? I'll tell you how. They taught us to fear."

Nicolai sinks a gloved hand into his pocket and pulls out a small, triangular device nestled in his palm. He presses the top of the device with his finger; it emits a quiet hiss, and then it begins to glow.

"This is a Lumin," he says. "Every household used to have one."

At first the light is soft, like a match head erupting. But then it whirs, lifting from his palm, and the glow brightens until it's as if a piece of the sun burns inside the triangle.

I gasp as the light from the device illuminates the room and brings murals to life on the walls. Brilliant, larger-than-life scenes full of color and beauty scream for an audience beneath their silvery web.

I brush as much as I can from the one directly above. Its ancient map with seven landmasses in varying shapes speckled over a vast blue ocean. Each continent bears a symbol.

I recognize the sigils of the four most prominent Houses immediately: The House Laevus' sphinx, two doves for my mother's House Lockhart, the Bloodwood House's terrifying black Cerberus, and the Croft House red scorpion.

The three smaller continents include House Aster's lightning bolt, House Pope's smiling gray fox, and the House Riverjoy harpy.

One large mass of all the continents exists on the next panel, the shapes of the old landmasses still visible and delineated with dark-red lines from where they joined. In the center of this new continent sits the boot-shaped territory for the Crofts, marked by the bright-red scorpion.

I walk the wall, marveling at the illustrations. Great scenes of war and change, depicted by the House sigils. The sphinx chasing after two doves. Cerberus clawing and biting at the fox, the lightning bolt poised above. The scorpion's sharp tail sunk deep into the poor House Pope fox.

Some murals are more graphic and detailed, showing men battling, their armor coated in blood.

Once I make it to the other side of the room, the warring disappears, replaced by great cities of steel and glass rising to the ceiling.

Nicolai shadows me. When we get to the cities, he pauses. "The Technological Age, when the Houses stopped fighting over territory and began a race to build the most advanced technologies imaginable. Oh, to have been alive then."

Now machines of every conceivable type fill the walls. The kind I could only imagine in a dream. They fly, race, and travel. They crest the mountains and swim among the stars. Older versions of cloudcrafts appear above the cities, hundreds of them in what look like invisible roads in the air.

I squeeze past a covered sofa, brushing sticky cobwebs off my leg, and take in the next painting. The factories that made up every Diamond City shine from their spot on the wall, a horde of people spewing from their doors. A sphinx as large as the factory buildings waits for them, its mouth open and sharp teeth glittering. The sigils of each House encircle the factories and the people.

"When the workers beneath the Houses revolted, the Baron of House Laevus suggested they share their technology to create weapons that could quell the rebellion."

The next painting sends a shudder down my spine. Great whorls of fire and smoke fill the wall, broken up by dark silhouettes of people caught in the flames. "The factory workers never stood a chance. When the other Houses realized what Laevus had planned, it was too late. The destruction was total."

The last mural is the largest. The sigils form a circle around the Royalist phoenix. A crown sits atop the phoenix's head, its eyes dark in the low light. "In one fell swoop, Marcus Laevus not only stopped a rebellion, he gained control of the weapons that would catapult House Laevus into the House of Emperors."

I step back. "But . . . but they said the workers used the bombs. That's why we were labeled Bronzes and forced to work. Why the tech was banned."

Firelight dances inside Nicolai's mask, his burned lips pulled into what could be a grin. "Yes. A lie that allowed them to withhold the very technology that kept them in power and the other Houses obedient. All the books were burned, and anyone who questioned the lie or talked about it was killed."

I struggle to breathe. Everything I've known has been rocked to the core. I've always believed deep down that the Great Purge that destroyed our technology was a necessary evil. That we could not be trusted with it.

To some extent, I even believed that the Bronzes deserved their low Color for the bombings and horrors we were responsible for.

But it was all a lie.

The Lumin drops slowly into Nicolai's open palm. He glances down at the thing. "This is only a fraction of the wonders our world once contained. But it was stolen, manipulated into weapons, and used against us."

Steeling my resolve with a deep breath, I plant my hands on my hips. "Speaking of devices made into weapons, can we talk about the Mercurian?"

He closes his fingers over the Lumin, throwing the room back into near-darkness. "Of course."

"Give me ten Rebels, and I can get inside Laevus Castle and find the Mercurian. I can stop the asteroid. I mean, isn't that what we should be focusing on? Not some . . . some impossible war?"

"Oh, Everly. How naïve you are. I have plans for you and the Mercurian, but those plans don't involve the asteroid. Not yet, anyway."

"I don't know what in the Fienian hell that even means, but I will never let a bastard like you get your hands on the Mercurian."

But Nicolai waves me away, and when I make a move toward him, the two Rebels come out of the shadows and force me back.

"Fine," I snarl, swallowing down my anger. "Go down in history as a warmongering idiot if you want."

Nicolai's shoulders stiffen, and slowly, slowly he turns to me. "Maia, history will remember me as the man who made the emperor finally pay for the sins of House Laevus. Everything else will either be forgotten. Or erased."

TWENTY-THREE

After the frustrating meeting with Nicolai, I check on Brogue in his makeshift chamber. He's still sleeping, his form sunk into the mattress, chest rattling with heavy snores. I wipe his face, cover him up, and follow Lash to my room. I don't question Lash's order for me to go inside until he pulls out a key.

"Please," I beg, wedging my boot in the door frame. "I won't go anywhere. Just—just don't lock me in."

The others are going to the nightly dance, while I'm being ordered to my room. Lash and I heard the music thumping from the stairs on the way up. Sounds and instruments I've never heard before bounced off the high ceilings and worsened my now ever-constant headache.

He runs a hand through his hair, eyes pleading with me not to make trouble. "Like earlier?"

"I'll go straight to bed. Rebel's honor."

"Don't be a pain in my ass, love. Not tonight."

"Tonight special?"

He grins wickedly, a promise some girl will have her heart broken tonight, and I wonder how he got this way.

"Please, you don't understand." I slip my fingers over his wrist, trapping the hand holding the key. "I've been locked away, a prisoner in one way or another, for nearly as long as I can remember. I can't do another night."

I despise my pleading. How powerless it makes me feel. But I don't want to be alone right now. Especially in this room, locked in with my thoughts and fears and memories.

"Please, Lash."

Pity wells inside his eyes as he shakes his head. "I hate this too."

"Then don't do it."

His fingers flutter over his Fienian brand.

"Please—"

I cry out as the door closes and the key grates inside the lock.

"I'm sorry." His muffled voice sounds a thousand miles away.

I try the handle, but it won't budge beneath my fingers. Even so, I continue jiggling it, my palms slick with sweat.

No, no, no.

I stagger back. My erratic heartbeat reverberates through my skull as I stumble through the dark room. The shadows are cold.

Candles. Where are the matches? I scrape all the contents off the desk near the bed. No matches. Slivers of moonlight trickle from the veiled window, teasing me.

And inside the shadows . . . inside the shadows I see Merida, crushed and broken. I see the creatures from the pit. I see Caspian's sword plunging into Riser's back.

More light. I give up on the matches and pry on the wood latticework entrapping me, the glass cool beneath my fingertips. The cobalt night sky peeks from the small holes, the moon full and beautiful and taunting.

I need air.

I need *out*.

I no longer have any thoughts but out. This is like the pit, like the labyrinth, like the Tower. I barely escaped each time. Barely scraped and dug out from the darkness and confines. Barely survived—

I claw the wood over the windows but can't get a grip. I need something sharp. I rip open drawers and fling all the clothes out, dresses and petticoats sailing over my head as I search for a hidden weapon. With all the blades around, there has to be one stashed away.

Has to be.

I lunge to the bed, tearing off the heavy duvet, the sheets, using all my strength to upend the mattress. *Give me something.* I ransack the pillows, spilling their soft gray feather-guts into the air. I yank the heavy wooden night-stand on its side, spilling old letters and a dried-up vial of ink.

Hopeless. A wave of darkness and fear washes over me. I fall into the mess I've created, chest heaving with breaths that seem to have no effect. As if the walls, the air, are closing in on me, constricting my chest, smothering me.

My body shudders and my throat tightens as I drag another pitiful trickle of air into my chest.

Just breathe, breathe . . .

My panting only grows faster, reminding me of how powerless I am. I can't even control my own breathing.

What happened to the girl who was going to fight? The girl who promised her father she would do whatever it took? Even in the pit I held out a tiny kernel of hope. And trapped in the Tower, with my chains and my injuries and the knowl-edge that the emperor would make me suffer in gruesome ways, I still had a spark of fight inside me.

But that was when I still had friends to fight for, still had a brother to protect. Before people I cared about called me a traitor and I witnessed Cage bearing the torture meant for me.

Before Riser scraped me from his heart like a cancer.

I would have told him so many things. How I was sorry for not trusting him earlier. I had been an idiot, a fool. Probably a jerk. How inside the Tower, I prayed every day to whatever gods still exist that he survived. That he wasn't suffering. That he didn't hate me.

And maybe I would tell him of the guilt I felt for begging him not to kill Caspian. Even if I was glad Riser hadn't. Even if I'm not sure I could have forgiven him if he had.

Perhaps . . . perhaps Riser did us both a favor when he erased me . . . and us. This way things will be easier.

Simpler.

Not that he's forgiven. I'm still pissed he took the easy way out. But I remember how it felt to be comforted in his arms, how scary it was when he asked me to trust him, how vulnerable he made me feel.

Three times I thought Pit Boy died. And three times that pain gutted me.

Caring for someone comes with a price. And in my world, caught beneath Pandora's shadow and the Archduchess's murderous reach, with no foreseeable future and an emperor intent on letting over half the world perish, that's a price I can't afford.

Not right now—maybe not ever.

In fact, maybe Riser set us both free.

I draw in my anger and use it to get to my feet. The smothering feeling has leaked away, leaving cold emptiness. I will find a way out of here, make my way back to the tunnel leading to Laevus Castle, and search for the Mercurian on my own.

Somehow I hadn't noticed the small oil painting leaned against the wall in the corner. The frame is weathered, the paint yellowed and cracking. The lonely woman inside looks out to the sea, her dark hair wrangled together and draped over her shoulder like a mass of sleek serpents. A red scorpion crests the nape of her exposed neck.

Amandine.

A slash gapes from the back of the matted frame, and I slip my fingers into the hole, retrieving a small journal.

On the next try, I discover a dagger. The blade is five inches of jagged, cruel serrations that curve into a fine point, an oval of rich amber set inside its handle. I twist the knife, a ray of moonlight catching on the bright-red scorpion encased inside the amber, its body seeming to glow from within.

The knife is sharp and bites easily into the grate locking me in. The blade's teeth make quiet, glorious sounds as pulverized bits of wood rain over me.

When I'm done, sweat coats my chest, and I'm covered in a fine layer of dust. I wrap the dagger in shreds of my ivory sheet and slip the bundle inside my corset.

As I pull the slab away from the window and behold the dark sea below, the great expanse of wide nothingness that unfurls to the horizon, my heart releases something dark and bitter I hadn't realized was there.

I'm not sure I have ever seen a sight so beautiful. The moon is huge, its radiant light trapped along its charcoal nest of clouds.

Pandora is lost to the night, veiled in clouds and shadow. It's like she isn't here. Like maybe she was just a horrible, horrible nightmare I had.

I feel along the edge of the exposed window, flip the lock, and pry it up. The old frame groans, and cool air washes over me as I push into the night, the sweet, briny scent of the ocean bringing tears to my eyes.

I peer below, my gaze traveling down, down, *down*. A

hollow feeling swirls around my belly. From this height, I can hardly hear the waves bashing against the cliffs.

From this height, if I fall, I'll have a very long time to scream before I die.

With one last glance at my cell, I hoist myself through the window.

TWENTY-FOUR

I clamp my fingers over the smooth windowsill, searching for a better grip as chill air swirls through the layers of my skirt and around my thighs. Large, uneven stones give me something to hold onto, but they're damp and worn slick. Strips of my hair slice across my vision.

Curiosity draws my gaze to the cliffs below, and the little I've eaten today threatens to come back up. A gust of wind slams me into the wall. I cry out, automatically reaching for the window ledge.

But I've already committed. The ground—and freedom—lies eighty feet down to the left. *Don't look down.*

My hands scrabble against the rock, fingers cramping, my toes digging, searching for crevasses. Slowly, slowly, I descend, cutting toward the east side of the castle, adrenaline urging me on. Any pause will increase the likelihood of freezing up.

My chest burns, an ache cording through the muscles of my arms and legs and winding around my spine. I can hear the ocean below. The comforting death song of the waves smashing against the cliffs, the seagulls calling from their rocky nests. I cry out as the rough stone scrapes tender flesh from my fingertips.

Keep going, keep going, keep going—

Just as my hands go numb and I know I'm about to fall, I lunge to the left, grunting as I land ten feet below on a sliver of land. Tall grass tickles my legs and reminds me how much I hate my dress.

Massaging life back into my stiff hands, I glance up at my red curtains fluttering in the breeze like tongues of fire.

A chill ripples down my spine. *Foolish. You could have died.* But I would do it again to be free.

I glare at my window. "No one will ever lock me away again. Hear that, Flame? You'll have to kill me first."

Gliding along the cliff's edge, I take in the view. The hole inside me fills a little more with each defiant wave that breaks below.

Now that I have a clear view of Bloodwyn Estate, I see how good its defenses are. The manor rests atop a hill, with 360-degree views. A dark, thick wall of pines forms a shadowy buffer to the north and east, while the ocean and cliffs defend the estate from the other sides.

From my vantage point, I can make out the faint smudge of a wall in the distance.

The perfect, fortified castle for an army.

How have the Fienians hidden here for so long? They couldn't have prevented every captured Rebel from talking. Not with monsters like the Archduchess roaming these hills.

The sound of faraway voices makes me pause, and I drop to my knees in the tall grass as the girl with the copper braid rounds the side of the castle, trailed by others. Max. Rhydian. A few Rebels I don't know.

When Riser appears side-by-side with Lucy, I duck a little lower. The others may not notice me, but he certainly will.

I'm breathless as they pass twenty feet from me, Max

cracking some idiotic joke before they slink along the cliff's edge and then seemingly disappear.

What could they be up to?

Whatever they're doing, I'd bet a Fienian tooth it's dangerous. Postponing my plan to sneak into Laevus Castle, I follow their trail down steep stairs chiseled into the side of the cliff, determined to ensure Max doesn't die doing something stupid before I leave. My boots grind softly against the sandy stone. A strip of pale, wet sand waits below, the waves lapping at my poor dress.

There's no one here. I scan the sliver of beach—soon to be gone with the tide—looking for footprints, but they must have traipsed the shoreline, the sand wiped smooth with every crashing wave.

Perhaps they're swimming?

Silly. These are the kind of waves someone would *drown* in, not swim in. And the water would be freezing—

Footsteps crunch the sand behind me. I try to whip around to face the noise, but it's too late. Strong, warm arms encircle me, one across my chest, the other slinking over my stomach. There's a strange second where my body reacts, somehow recognizing the scent, the feel of my captor, and instead of fighting, I lean back into him.

And then my survival instincts break through and I strain, trying to break free of my warm prison.

A soft laugh tickles my ear.

Pit Boy.

TWENTY-FIVE

Riser's arms lock around me, constricting a little more every time I struggle until we are tangled into a lump of flesh.

"Out for a walk?" His soft, breathy voice hints at a smile . . . and makes me want to throttle him.

"Perfect night for it. Stars. Waves. Belligerent boys."

"Boy?"

I squirm as another soft chuckle caresses my ear, the hard muscles pressing into my body calling me a liar. *Boy, my ass.*

"Let go, Pit *Boy*."

And maybe it's the way I say it, but his body goes absolutely still, and he pauses, his rapid heartbeat pounding against my shoulder blade. "Why do you continue calling me that?"

Yes, why, Maia? To get under his skin? Make him remember? But despite knowing he did me a favor when he forgot me, despite everything, part of me still demands he acknowledge I was real.

"Did *she* call you that?"

Any warmth I might have imagined disappears as his

arms constrict, once again becoming chains. "Why were you following us?"

"I was bored."

"Being a traitor getting old, Graystone?"

Jerk! I try to breathe, but his embrace is too tight. *"Let . . . go."*

Desperation makes me drop. My weight should loosen his grip, but it doesn't.

I'm *trapped*. Panic kicks in, and I fight a trickle of air into my lungs.

Once Riser would have cut off his own arm rather than hurt me. But this is what would have happened once his Reconstruction wore off anyway. Flame just sped up the inevitable.

A spark of rage lights inside my heart, catching fire, incinerating the panic until only fury is left. "Let. Me. Go."

"No."

"You have two seconds, Pit Boy."

One.

Another arrogant chuckle. "Or you'll—"

Two.

I clamp one hand over the arm constricting my neck, slide six inches to my right, drop to my knee, and throw Pit Boy over my shoulder and into the waves.

One smooth motion has him on his feet, arms hanging loose and ready, legs planted wide. His teeth flash. "Neat trick."

"Not as cool as this." I kick sand into his face and then throw a jab hook combination. The sand stuns him long enough for both blows to land, but they're sloppy and glance off his wet jaw. Next jab meets his fists, held defensively in front of his face. "Or this." He grunts as I land a body shot just below the ribs. "Or—"

A leg sweep nearly catches me, and I stumble back.

"Are we fighting or chatting?" He cracks his neck, a roguish grin splitting his handsome face. "Or is this how you flirt? After yesterday, I'm not sure."

I throw a jab, hook, jab combo to distract from the leg I swing at his head. The side of my boot catches his shoulder. He uses the half-second it takes me to recover my stance to deliver a volley of soft, lazy strikes at my head.

He's assessing my defenses.

Fine, Prince. Let's see yours.

I step up my game, countering blow for blow. We trade a few more rounds, testing each other, our breaths merging into a soft cadence—

Riser drops to one knee and lunges, wrapping his arms around the back of my legs and leveraging his shoulder into my hip.

No. I'm helpless to do anything but let him fold me gently to the sand.

A freezing wave pounds my face. I snatch a breath, close my eyes, and roll back on my left shoulder, fighting the sodden weight of my dress and the feeling of suffocating. My legs are wet and slick and slip from his grasp.

I snap to my feet, stumbling as a wave smashes into the back of my knees, shreds of my now-tattered skirt billowing in the water between Riser and me like slippery eels.

Saltwater stings my eyes, and my lungs burn. Riser watches me with a lazy half-grin, his black hair plastered to his skull.

He's not even worried.

He clicks his tongue, as if he can't decide to be angry or amused. Four feet separates us, but it feels like a chasm as deep and wide as the sky.

I'm wet, freezing, and pissed.

This will only end with violence. Perhaps that's the only way we can both find closure for a relationship founded on the bond of a shared past, entangled with lies and half-truths and Reconstructed feelings embedded so deeply that only bloodshed can remove them.

Riser glides a step closer. He can feel it too. This need to finish the inexplicable thing between us, the bond Flame with all her machines couldn't fully sever. His chest is heaving, his eyes riveted to mine.

Eyes I once looked into and believed when he promised he would never hurt me.

Lying bastard.

I snarl, lunging for him—

I take two steps before my boots entangle with my water-logged dress and send me sailing to the ground. I try to roll, but he's too fast and pins me to the wet sand.

In a last-ditch effort, I wrap my legs around his waist, but his abs are hard and unflinching beneath the bare flesh of my thighs, and I can't move him.

His eyes dance with amusement as he leans down until there are only inches between our lips. Hands that once stroked my back pin my arms to the ground. Frigid waves lap at my head and shoulders, sand and water dripping from his dark hair onto my cheeks.

His blue eye darkens to the color of the sea. "If this is how you plan to win tomorrow, I have to say, I'm disappointed."

I arch my back, bucking against his weight and hard, unforgiving muscles. "Give me proper clothes, and you'll enjoy it more. I promise."

"I"—his eyes drift low—"highly"—lower—"*doubt it.*"

"Pig." Ugh, how did I ever like him? "Get off me."

He lifts a night-black, daggerish eyebrow. "Magic word?"

Bastard! I squirm, his hands the only thing keeping me from slapping the belligerent grin off his face. "*Please.*"

He stands, and more sand cascades over me as he holds out his hand. I ignore his offer for help as I clamber to my feet. My dress sits sideways, and I shift it around, frowning at the dirty, sodden skirt weighing me down.

Stupid, idiotic dress. I should burn you to cinders.

Clapping fills the air. I turn to see the others watching us. They're *laughing*.

My jaw locks. Is that what I am now? Amusement for Rebels? A traitor to be imprisoned, laughed at, ridiculed?

Any anger burned off by the fight comes roaring back, building inside my chest, as real as the waves, the sand, forcing its way up, up . . .

I launch an assault on the beach, kicking up clouds of sand until I'm too winded to continue.

Teagan saunters toward me and perches a long hand on her sharp hip. "Feel better now, darling?"

I glare at Riser, my throat raw. "Immensely."

"Good. Now what in the Fienian hell are you doing here?"

"You knew they locked me in?"

Teagan taps her foot. "I was going to talk to Flame about that tomo—"

"You *knew*."

She winces. "Graystone, simply admitting to not killing Caspian when you were ordered to warrants banishment, at the least. Then there's the video of the hangings."

"I thought you didn't believe the rumors and propaganda."

"I *don't*."

I roll my shoulders. "Well, they'll have to kill me next time they want to lock me up."

They all stare at me. I catch Max's gaze, and he looks at his feet. Lucy and Hugo Redgrave stand next to him where I should be, their identical black eyes full of malice above the same poisonous smirk. Even Rhydian stands there just gaping at me.

My jaw locks, and I swallow down my urge to punch the sneers from the Redgrave twins' faces.

"We're wasting time, Aster," Lucy purrs, Hugo nodding along with her words.

Teagan releases a breath. "I'll have Lash escort you to—"

"No!" Lash and I shout at the same time.

"Take me with you," I plead. "Wherever you're going."

Teagan crosses her arms, blinking at me. Then she throws a questioning glance at Riser, who gives a lazy shrug. "Can you keep up?"

"Yes."

She sighs. "You're in."

"Where are we going?"

"The caves first, then—"

Lucy stalks to us, the seven blood-red braids on her scalp matching the scorpion on her neck. "But she hasn't accepted the Microplant."

"If she's caught," Teagan says, hardly acknowledging Lucy, "I will take care of it."

What the Fienian hell does that mean?

"Does Flame know about this?" Lucy persists.

As Teagan gives Lucy a quiet, terrifying stare, I almost feel sorry for her.

Teagan glances pointedly over the landscape. "I don't see her. Where is she?" She nods to the waves. "There?" The cliffs. "There? Unless *you* want to challenge my decision? You can, you know. This isn't like the emperor's Island where titles and Color rule. Blood is the only law at Bloodwyn."

Behind Lucy, Hugo chuckles nervously, his hand snaking into his waistband where his push dagger undoubtedly lurks. Riser's attention shifts to Hugo's hand.

Of course Pit Boy noticed. *Some things haven't changed.*

Lucy's eyes go wide, her nostrils flaring, rage and something else, something *ugly*, stirring just below the bone-white surface of her face. Slowly, she shakes her head.

"It's settled then."

Teagan's words drip with lethal finality. Frowning, Lucy kicks the sand and stalks away.

With a devilish grin, Teagan turns to me and winks. Then she leans into my ear. "You almost had him, darling."

TWENTY-SIX

There are several groupings of caves along the shoreline. According to Lash, who's been assigned to catch me up, they're hidden by the tides during the day and only accessible for four or five hours at night. Already, dark fingers of the sea lap at its shadowy entrance.

"There's also a secret maze of tunnels that lead to the dungeons of Bloodwyn Estate," Lash says. "But you have to be special to access it."

The similarity to the Laevus Castle tunnels is striking, and my mind spins as I try to marry the new information with what I know about the Island tunnels. Perhaps they all connect somehow?

A starburst of pale-purple light erupts around the group as they don glowing orbs around their necks. Lash hands one to me. The spark begins to spit, sending purple tendrils to probe its glass prison. I quickly hang it on a leather strap that goes over my head.

The name of the forbidden technology eludes me, but somehow I know it isn't just for illumination; these are Hot Weapons supposedly eradicated from the earth.

As we enter the darkness, the cave walls amplify the sound of the sea and disorient me, the walls growing closer, forcing us into a single file line. Finally our lavender light diffuses inside a huge chamber, glistening off the water running down the high walls.

Atop a natural dais of rock are countless Swifters, their metallic bodies smooth and sleek. Their engineering screams speed. Max is the first to the machines, whooping as he straddles a champagne-gold monster with a sharp nose.

The copper-haired girl he follows like a shadow shoves him off, sliding her leg over. "This baby's mine, Graystone."

Max shakes his head and takes the silver one next to her. "That Swifter's too powerful for you, Rivet."

Her lips twist to the side. "Bet?"

My little brother smiles like an idiot and lifts the orbs around his neck. "Two enders says she dumps you on your leathers."

"Four." Her teeth gleam above the long row of what must be enders around her neck. I'm willing to bet my one ender some of those are my brother's.

I find a small Swifter the color of black opal next to Max. He regards me from the corner of his eye, frowning. His friend, Rivet, rolls her eyes as she laughs. "Need a body-guard, Maxi?"

Max glares down at his hands, his cheeks growing a dark shade of red. "Do you have to sit by me?"

"Yes, Max," I say, forcing down any guilt for embarrassing him. "That's what siblings do. They protect each other."

"Huh. So where were you when I was scavenging waste bins for food? When I was fighting other kids in the street for scraps of moldy bread?"

"You know where I was." I cringe at how defensive I sound.

"No. I just thought you finally abandoned me. That you . .
. never mind. It doesn't matter."

"It does," I insist, wishing he would look at me. "And I'm
trying to make it up to you now, but you won't let me."

He sighs, finally making eye contact. "It's too late. Why
can't you see that?"

This time, I'm the one to look away. Max is my little
brother . . . and even if he's not so little anymore, I'm still
going to protect him like I should have then. He can just deal
with it.

Lash straddles a silver Swifter just behind mine. "You
know, Graystone, you actually have to get on it to make it
work."

I run my hands over the cool, shimmery shell before me.
"But how do I—?"

Lash thrusts silver goggles into my lap, and a rectangular
wand into my face. A handheld uploader.

"Hold still," he orders.

There's a blue flash, a prick of electricity behind my eyes.

"There," Lash says. "Now try."

I drape my leg over my Swifter, the seat firm but
comfortable, and wrap my fingers around the handlebars. A
familiar feeling comes over me—as if I've done this a million
times.

I press the glowing white button in the center, and my
Swifter purrs beneath me. Though I hardly felt it move, I'm
hovering a foot in the air. A faint-blue light illuminates the
ground.

The goggles are tight as I slip them over my head.
Through their smoky green lens, my world becomes bright
and clear. Energy from the Swifter growls into my muscles,
my bones. Adrenaline burns my veins, my chest lightening.

I feel like I could fly.

"Careful with your dress," Teagan says from the lithe

bronze Swifter beside me, nodding at the silent thrusters below.

My dress. I've never hated a garment more. Especially now, its heavy, cloistering folds weighted with seawater and gritted with sand, strands of dried seaweed clinging to the lacy hem. Another way for them to lock me up, weaken me.

I retrieve the scorpion dagger from my bodice and slash at my skirt, watching heavy panels of dark fabric slip beneath the Swifter and incinerate in a flash of blue. When I'm done, gooseflesh pimples my snowy thighs, the air cool and lovely as it swirls around my bare skin.

"There." I grin at Teagan, ignoring the heat of Riser's stare from his metallic-red beast at the front. "Problem solved."

Lash's gaze glides over my legs. "Never, ever hide those again, Graystone. That's an order."

I snort. "Are there any girls you wouldn't bag?"

"Depends. Do you consider Aster a girl?"

Teagan snarls at him. "In your wet dreams, prick."

We both share a laugh at Lash's expense.

As if on command, all the voices go silent. Riser has turned around and is straddling his Swifter, his hands in his pockets, a casual expression on his face.

For half a heartbeat, my breath catches in my throat. Chiseled cheeks trap shadows below bright eyes that seem to glow from within as they claim command over the fighters—over *me*—as easily as I hold a knife.

"We're all itching to get out there and wreak some havoc, so I'll be quick." A scattering of Rebels whoop in agreement. "Drones are heavy tonight, so we take the tunnels to the edge of the city, forming two groups once we hit the streets. Our target is rumored to be a Purge collector specializing in Hot Weapons. We get in, get out. Hot Weapons for dandies and drones, no touching the Sleepers. If separated, meet back at Bloodwyn." His fingers find the row of Nano-shredders gleaming from his baldric. "May the gods favor chaos over tyranny, Rebels over Royalists, and a quick death for the brave."

"Blood for freedom!" The Rebels chant.

"Death for honor!" Riser answers, his deep voice echoing against the walls.

After witnessing how rowdy the Rebels can be, I'm shocked as they silently await his command. Two days was all it took for Riser to gain their allegiance and trust. Two days to win over the entire Rebel army.

If Caspian was born to rule the well-disciplined Royalist armies, then surely Riser was meant to lead this savage, unruly group of Fienians.

I'm also surprised to find Riser's words have stirred something inside me too. I'm doing this to ensure Max's safety, and because I need to earn the Rebels' trust.

But some part of me needs *this*. To make the Royalists pay.

I grip the handlebars of my Swifter, my naked thighs clenched around its sleek body purring with energy. Excitement electrifies the air.

Our machines are silent as they streak through the tunnel, their bodies flashing like a school of minnows. Max surges ahead, so fast I can barely keep up. Although I've never used a Swifter, my mind knows what to do. I deftly manipulate the throttle, leaning forward with soft, smooth movements that steer exactly where I want to go.

I spot Max's blond mop ahead and gently tease the throttle—

A sharp bump sends me flying into the cave wall. On instinct, I hit both thrusters, clinging to the Swifter as it shoots straight up and skims the wall. As I glide over the ceiling, upside down, I see Lucy laughing.

By the time I've completed my circle and guided the Swifter back to the ground, she's gone.

They're all gone.

I stare into the yawning hole. I don't know these tunnels.

I could get lost.

I could never find my way *out*.

But I have to make sure my brother doesn't do anything stupid. That means I follow, even if it leads me to hell, I'll follow him.

I'll keep him safe.

TWENTY-SEVEN

Fear-sweat slicks my palms. Even with my night goggles, the tunnels all look the same, a blur of watery-black walls streaked green with moss and lichen. Panic makes me go fast, too fast, missing forks . . . Does it matter?

I have no idea which way they took. I stick to the main tunnel, trying to keep my cardinal directions straight. Dominus is southwest from Bloodwyn Estate, which means I just need to keep going straight—but a million curves and turns make that impossible.

Fast, faster. I shove back my fear, swallowing it down as I glide along the walls, attuning my senses to the tunnels until my reactions become lightning fast. Left, curve, straight up, direct right.

I hardly blink, hardly breathe.

A flash ahead. I whoop in triumph as Lash whips a glance back at me. "Keep up, Graystone."

I cut in front of him, aligning with Teagan as I scan the others for Max. I relax a bit at the sight of him folded over his Swifter, smiling ear-to-ear. He had that same look when he was eight and we visited the Hall of Shadows where they keep the pre-Reformation Act artifacts not destroyed in the Purge.

Compared to a life slaving in the bowels of the mines, this is better. Max wouldn't have lasted a day in that rigid, structured life of hard labor. But here, he shines.

Still, he's too young to be a Rebel. Too innocent to fight and kill people.

And too good to survive for long.

Without warning, the tunnel lifts, and we funnel into the night. The fat moon shines down on a valley just outside Dominus, hundreds of tall, domed buildings silvery-blue in the background. Dozens of black spires pierce the low-strung clouds.

The Rebels split into two groups. I glue myself to Max's side, ignoring his sullen glower and the taunting smile Rivet gives him.

After this is over, Rivet, you and I are going to have a talk.

Riser leads us up a hill, and I glare at his back as we glide over the swaying blue-green grass and into the city.

Is he really so different from before, or did I only see what I wanted to see because he was Reconstructed to care for me? Because he would have done anything to protect me?

It had felt good, so good to be cared for again, to have someone think I was worth protecting.

But it had also blinded me to his real character. Relationships blind us. And I'm done not seeing things for how they really are.

Dominus is a maze of alleyways. Bleached houses stack ten deep, dove-white buildings crammed together for miles. The cobblestone streets are quiet, and an eerie feeling scuttles down my spine as we pass the empty shops with goods still laid out for the taking.

The fact that nothing *has* been taken says all I need to know about the drone presence here. We slip into a single-file row, buzzing along the walls of the shops and taking advantage of the awnings.

Teagan puts a finger to her lips and nods up, and I glance two silver drones flying low at the roofline, their red lasers pulsing over the streets.

Fear fills my chest. The Archduchess is searching for me. All it would take is for one of those lasers to dip low and to the right, over my face. A small, simple action that will put me back in the Tower, in her clutches . . . and yet the fear ebbs as soon as it hits.

The cool air on my face, the smell of the sea in my hair, the wicked machine purring between my thighs—all of it has stirred something inside me.

After years of being ruled by my fear, by others, after being forced to fight and grovel, this feels like freedom.

I have a choice. I will fight to protect Max and find the Mercurian, by myself if I have to. And I'll probably die for it. But that's my *decision*.

We lose sight of the drones near the temples. *Mausoleums of dead, forgotten gods*, my father called them.

Tall moonstone pillars reach to the sky, a deity for each one engraved into the worn rock. Though not as large as some of the buildings, the two temples stand on their own, surrounded by parks and overgrown gardens. The famous Dominus aqueducts intersect the dark sky behind them, leading deep into the city.

My heart clenches and flutters as we streak between the statues and unruly hedges toward the temples, silent and swift, the only noise a *whoosh* like a strong wind. The smells of jasmine and honeysuckle fill the air.

Graffiti mars the pocked, crumbling walls of the first temple. The dead idols look down at us with disapproving frowns as Riser slips one of the enders from his neck, the electric light shifting from a deep purple to bright red.

From the careful way he holds the weapon, I know it must be armed. He tosses it against the stone. As soon as the glass shatters, there's a huge pulse of red, and the wall crumples into itself as a man-sized hole appears.

Other than a light cloud of dust, there's no trace of the stone.

Lash grins at me as the others file inside the church. "Cool, right?"

Not the word I'd use. Effective, maybe—but scary as hell.

Long rows of stone pews stretch across the sanctuary, facing what once must have been an enormous statue of Hera, Zeus's wife. Most of her upper torso and head are gone, a headless idol reaching up.

As soon as my focus flickers over the high, curved ceiling, I suck in a sharp breath.

A deep, rich blanket of unnaturally bright cerulean stretches over the temple, so perfect it could almost be the midnight sky. Stars twinkle from its depths, laid out in a perfect rendering of the western constellations.

Glancing at the stars, I realize my mother must have come here as a child. Most of the old Houses still visited the temples in the largest cities. By then, it was more for tradition than actual worship.

It's hard to believe in invisible, absent gods when men were accomplishing miraculous feats on their own.

My mother once told me this had been her favorite place as a child, a refuge she could escape to. An ache spreads inside my heart as I think of her looking up with the same wonder I have now.

From my periphery, I catch Riser watching me.

I quickly look away from the constellations. "What?"

"They're beautiful, aren't they?" Leaned against his Swifter, head angled to the fake stars, his voice is soft. "Not like the real thing. But, still. My mother looked up at this same sky. Did she feel the awe I feel? Did she smile?"

The fact that we shared the same thought makes me uneasy. But his mother loved him. Died protecting him, even.

Mine left me to die. Not the same thing at all.

"Is there something we should be doing other than stargazing?"

Tearing his gaze from the ceiling, he sifts through a black bag and tosses me a heavy silver baton. Then he faces the other Rebels waiting for instruction.

"That"—he nods to the baton in my hand—"will detect Hot Weapons. Check everywhere. The walls, floors, pews. Pair up. Five minutes and we meet back here."

I move to follow Max, but Riser calls out, "You're with me, Graystone."

Max casts a look back at me before disappearing with Rivet down one of the corridors near the back.

"I'm going with my brother," I insist, crossing my arms.

"No, you're not."

"But—"

Riser shakes his head. "Max will be fine."

"Fine, how?" I ease the anger from my voice, trying to sound pleading instead. "He's barely fifteen."

A sigh escapes his lips. "Do you know why so many have joined the Rebels against the emperor? Freedom. Freedom to fight . . . or not fight. Freedom to marry who they want, wear what they want, love who they want. Max is *free* to choose to fight, and to die, because he believes freedom is worth dying for."

But all I hear is the word die. My throat clenches at the thought of Max against the Centurions, or worse, in the Archduchess's clutches. I won't let that happen. I owe it to Max to protect him.

I step forward, prepared to argue, when Lucy inserts

herself between us, a concerned line etched into her forehead. "Are you sure that's wise, Prince?"

I stiffen as her fingers play over his collar. Hugo has come up on Riser's left.

"Yes," Hugo adds, his voice slippery soft, "she's a traitor."

Lucy leans into him, her dark eyes flicking over me. "Dangerous."

"Untrustworthy."

The two of them circle Riser, taking turns whispering and donning oily smiles. They move as if one entity, finishing the other's sentence, taking turns plying Riser with smiles and nods.

"Oh, she'll behave." Riser sidesteps the twins, a wry grin on his face as he locks eyes with me. "And if she doesn't, I think I can manage."

The twins slink away, the air lightening noticeably with their absence. Riser leads me through the temple, past a set of heavy, hammered gold doors, and into a catacomb of chambers.

"Manage?" I wave my baton at Riser. "If you haven't noticed, my dress is no longer a hindrance."

Riser pushes the baton away. "Easy. That goes on the wall, not me." He leans over a shelf of scrolls, passing his wand over the yellowed texts. "And I noticed," he murmurs. "So did every male with a pulse."

I force the blush from my cheeks and concentrate on the rack of scrolls on the other side of the room. "How do we know the weapons are here?"

"We don't. But one of the acolytes from this temple was a notorious Purge collector. We searched her house already, so this is our next guess."

"Why don't you just *ask* her where they are?"

"Can't. They hung her after the last uprising."

Of course they did. I bend over and run my wand over the

gilded floor tiles. "So . . . you're just going to hand Nicolai a bunch of banned weapons? That implies trust."

I feel Riser's gaze flick over me. "I don't trust anyone." A pause. "Nicolai is a means to an end."

End? More scrolls line the next room. "You're a Fienian, then?"

He ignores me, and I decide to let it rest. But a few minutes into our search, he straightens, his baton loose at his side.

"The Royalists killed my mother. But first they made her suffer in horrible, unimaginable ways." Although soft, his voice has a hard, cruel edge that sends shivers down my spine. "So I'm whatever I need to be to make them suffer the way she did."

He looks through me to whatever memory he's reliving. I remember how Riser once told me I was the only thing that made him want to be better. Is this what he's like without someone to anchor his morality to?

Perhaps that's why Flame agreed to erase me; now he's a blade they can wield against the Royalists.

A weapon without a conscience.

When we switch to the next chamber, it's so tiny I can barely move without brushing against Riser. He smells of leather and smoke and spice. I offer to do the next one, but he just chuckles under his breath and keeps waving his stupid baton over the stone. At least there's a window.

I press against the glass, doing everything possible to not touch him, but the heat emanating from his flesh calls to me, and I have to fight the urge to press into him, the air thickening between us until it becomes hard to pull in air.

He shifts, his breath caressing my cheek.

I concentrate on the green light in front of me. What good is desire anyway? What function does it serve, except to make you weak?

I reach to the far wall, and my arm brushes his side. The fabric of his shirt is thin, and I can feel the hard muscle beneath. He stiffens, air hissing through his teeth.

So he feels it too.

Use it. The voice is a remnant of Everly March. The girl who's as comfortable with her sexuality and the power it holds as any man. I shift, pressing the inside of my thigh into Riser's leg. Warmth spreads over the spot our flesh touches.

His knuckles grow white around his baton. When he looks up, I flick my tongue over my lips.

"What are you doing?" His voice is breathy, his eyes settling on my lips.

I reach out, touch the brow bone just above his green eye. My heart throbs wildly inside my chest. I let my hand fall to his cheek.

Surprise and something else, something wicked, flickers across his face, even as he moves into my hand.

Did I kiss him, or did he kiss me? It doesn't matter. His tongue slips into my mouth, parting my lips, and a hollow feeling tickles my belly. Our teeth scrape together as he pushes my mouth open wider. Warmth fills the emptiness, spreading, burning.

This wasn't part of the plan. *I have to stop.* I pull back to face him, my breathing uneven. "Are you . . . are you going back to the Island?"

As soon as I ask, I know I've shown my hand. Most guys might not notice, but Riser would. So why is he grinning?

I gasp as he presses his knee between my legs, pinning me, his lips inches from mine. His palms encircle my waist, ensuring I can't move. "I was wondering how far you would go, but I have to say, I didn't realize how much I'd *enjoy* it."

"You knew," I hiss, "and you let me . . ."

He chuckles, his eyes dancing with amusement. "Kiss

me?" His stare lingers on my lips. "I was curious to see if you could do it without using your teeth."

"Bastard."

"Don't you mean, irresistible bastard?" Suddenly his eyes flutter, and he pulls away from me, his mouth set in a tight line. "They found the weapons. Let's go."

Let's go? That's it?

I open my mouth to respond, but a red light pulses over his forehead. Before I can scream, he drops, yanking me down on top of him. The explosion reverberates through my chest, my bones. Glass shards rain over us.

In one motion, Riser flips me over and shields me with his body.

Sweat and adrenaline gush from every pore as my ears pick up the buzzing coming through the broken window, one word clanging inside my head.

Drone.

TWENTY-EIGHT

A slick, silver teardrop whirs in the air above. I blink against its sensor as its laser probes my face . . . disseminating my features.

Riser swings his baton at the drone, sending it thudding against the wall. I scramble backward, get to my feet, and yank the ender from around my neck. A chill goes through me as the orb changes to red.

Riser makes it to the doorway before the drone is back in the air. Its laser grows from a thin thread to a thick weaponized beam as it arcs toward him.

Praying for aim, I release a breath and lob the angry red ball at the drone. There's a delicate chinking noise as the glass shatters, followed by a quiet crumpling noise. A dark hole appears where the drone was, the air around it warped and spiraled like twisted folds of fabric before slowly straightening back out to normal.

"Good shot," Riser says, smiling absurdly as we rush to find the others. "I thought you might be aiming for my head."

I cut my eyes at him. "Who said I wasn't?"

The others are already waiting for us beneath the false

starry sky, scurrying to load three large duffels with golden obelisks and triangular prisms. *Nano-weapons.* A ring of Rebels draw their weapons and encircle the duffels. Somehow, they know about the drone.

I open my mouth to ask how, but Riser, of course, has already read the expression on my face.

"Microplant." He taps the side of his head. "Nicolai informed the others."

"So he saw you kiss me?" My cheeks redden at the thought.

Riser slings a leg over his Swifter, his gaze focused on the instrument panel at the top, but the corner of his lip twitches. "As I recall, Graystone, you kissed me."

I swallow my witty comeback and scan the room for Max. He and Rivet are already on their Swifters, a bulging duffel strapped to the back and weighing them down. They'll be slower than the rest of us.

"Give me Max's duffel."

Riser glances at them. "Not enough time."

"They'll be too slow."

He shakes his head. "They knew the risks."

"Maybe more drones won't come." But I know it's a lie as soon as I say it.

Riser swallows. "Maybe." In one graceful leap, he hops on top of his Swifter. "All right, we need to move fast and careful. Those carrying the duffels in the middle; everyone else on the outside. Drones out, weapons out. Let's do this."

A soft hum fills the chamber as we glide to the exit, pale light from the full moon seeping across the dusty stone floor. Battering through the line of Rebels, I take a spot to the right of Max, ignoring the jut of his jaw as he glowers at me.

The exit will only take one at a time, but I plan to be as close as possible so I can flank his side once we're through.

"Sorry, kid," I whisper. "You're stuck with me."

Riser is the first to the hole, Lucy and Hugo flanking him. Head scanning the sky, he guides his Swifter forward—and then stops. Without thinking, I glide closer, until the outside comes into view.

A quiet gasp escapes my lips.

Two large cloudcrafts settle on the ground. Their doors pop open, spewing Centurions. Too many to count.

Which means too many to fight.

Even with our newfound cache of weapons and our technology, we'll be trapped inside the temple. We may hold them off for minutes, even hours, but eventually they'll find a way in.

I glance behind me at Max. His eyes are wide, glimmering with excitement. He's either too young to understand the gravity of our situation, or too eager to prove himself to care.

As I turn back around, my breath hitches at the sight of the Archduchess stepping down the metal stairs of the craft, her gray cloak trailing in the wind like smoke. Five enormous golden Swifters shadow her. Caspian sits tall in the middle, Delphine and Roman flanking him.

"Here's our chance to kill the False Prince," someone whispers. A few Rebels beat their chests with their fists in bravado.

I release a long sigh. *We're doomed.* They have no idea how outmatched we are. Or they don't care. But I know. And I *care.* And I'm not going to let them kill my brother.

I refuse.

My body shivers with every racing beat of my heart, filling me with spikes of adrenaline. The drone scanned *me.*

The Archduchess is here for *me.*

They don't know about the others . . . yet.

I slam into the side of Lucy's Swifter, forcing a spot between her and Riser, and ignoring her muttered threats.

Riser's curious gaze slides over my face, his eyebrows

lifting as he reads me like no one else can. "Planning some-thing I should know about?"

"I need a weapon," I say, skirting his question, afraid he'll try to talk me out of it.

Frowning, he reaches for one of the Nano-shredders strapped to his baldric, but I shake my head and gesture to the lethal string of enders throwing purplish light over his face. A pause. Just when I think he's going to refuse me, he lifts the strand of death over his head and onto mine.

"Your sword too."

"Demanding, aren't you?"

"Now."

He obeys with a suspicious glare. The blade shivers beneath my trembling fingers. I glance back at Max one more time, greedily soaking him in. The flaxen hair I used to twirl between my fingers, the stubborn half-smile I used to hate.

An ache fills my chest as I realize that once again I'm abandoning him.

And, once again, it's to keep him alive.

"In one minute have someone make another entrance near the back." My fingers tighten on the throttle. "And tell Max . . . tell him I still love him, and to stop doing stupid stuff."

A grin finds Riser's face.

"What?"

"Nothing. I just thought, you know, I was in charge."

Rolling my eyes, I nudge my Swifter through the hole before he can stop me. *Here we go.* The outside air feels cool against my sweaty flesh. Somehow I make it almost to the hedges before any of the Royalists notice.

The drones come first. The eerie buzz they make as they converge on me settles deep in my bones. I swallow back nausea, feeling both light and heavy as I continue on.

The Archduchess locks eyes with me, a crooked smile warping her pale face.

"Get her!" she orders in a breathless shriek. "Now! Now! *Now!*"

The drones whir, their lasers gliding over the grass toward me. Behind them, the Gold Swifters form a V, Caspian in the lead.

I keep going. Ten feet away. Nine.

The Archduchess isn't smiling anymore. Her wide eyes are fixed on what's around my neck. I round the hedges and come face-to-face with Caspian, my breathing shallow and uneven as I halt.

A part of me is already scolding myself for being so impulsive. Everything rides on assumptions. That the Archduchess's need for me fully intact means the drones can't touch me. That there's no one posted near the back.

That surprise and distraction will make up for lack of a real plan.

Caspian has his right hand up, palm forward, halting the other Chosen riders. Just like the Archduchess, his focus is on the weapons around my neck.

He tears his gaze from the enders to my face, his golden eyebrows lifted above a you-wouldn't-dare expression.

Oh, Prince, but I would. I slip the four orbs from my neck, fitting two in each hand. Their bright-red glow warms my cheeks. The energy inside pulses against my palms. Begging me to release it.

"Stop her, you idiots!" the Archduchess screams, scrambling backward. "Stop—"

I loose the first two Hot Weapons. Time slows to a crawl as they arc over the Chosen on their Swifters, the Centurions, their heads angled to watch the orbs. When they hit the craft, a frantic heartbeat passes before I hear the horrible crumpling noise. The craft groans as it folds in on itself, the Centurions yelling and diving away from it.

The second throw hits the other craft.

More yells. More running. The drones close in, whirring louder, their lasers flickering around me. Perhaps there's an override if I'm deemed too dangerous to capture.

I don't want to find out, so I turn back the throttle and flee, Caspian and the other Chosen on my heels.

TWENTY-NINE

My palms are sweaty as I grip the handles and zigzag through the maze of hedges, trying to escape my pursuers. Other than the noise of my heavy breathing, the wind, and the soft purr of my craft, my world is quiet. Too quiet.

They've probably split up, which means my odds of losing them are low. I need to find a long, hidden stretch where I can discover how fast this thing goes. Maybe if—

A golden blur. On instinct, I pull up and to the right just before a Swifter rams my side. Branches rake against my cheek as I clip the hedges. I whip around, sword in hand, barely repelling Delphine's blade meant for my neck.

She attacks again, her short curtain of blonde hair plastered to one side of her head with sweat, grunting with each stroke meant to cleave some part of me from my body.

"Roman!" she screams.

A feverish excitement flashes inside her cruel blue eyes as she whacks her sword against mine over and over, nearly knocking me out of my seat.

I gaze back just as Roman glides behind me with a spiked flail. Shit. Apparently they didn't get the don't-kill-me talk.

"Hello, worm," he says, ramming his Swifter into the back of mine. His fat lips quiver as he looks past me at Delphine. "Ever wondered what a worm's insides look like, Del?"

Delphine's eyes light up. "Five gold denaris I get her first."

I look from one to the other. *Who's the biggest threat?* My heart races as I scan the hedges, looking for a way out, a weak spot, but there are none. I'm going to have to go through one of them. *Which one?*

A thought comes over me, and before I can think it through, I bring my blade down onto the leafy green wall. I hack wildly, grunting with each blow, leaves flying everywhere.

In my periphery, I see Delphine lift her sword.

A large chunk of sky and garden appear. Big enough to fit through—maybe. *Hopefully.*

As I turn my Swifter to try, Delphine's craft slams into its side, and the shock rattles my spine. I duck as her blade whispers over my hair.

Roman charges, swinging his flail, and I rip back the throttle—

The force of acceleration yanks my head back, and I cry out, squeezing the handles with a death grip to keep from flying off. My neck aches, but I force my body low until I can feel the machine's purr deep within my chest.

Everything around me becomes blips. The fountain. The abandoned shop fronts. The buildings I slip between.

Despite my dangerous speed, I tease the throttle back farther, sweeping and gliding over cobbled hills, maneuvering sharp hairpin turns with ease. Euphoria mixed with terror surges through me as I goad the machine faster and gobble up the road.

This feels good. So, so good.

But how long until my uploader wears off and I lose my ability to operate my Swifter? I need to shake off my pursuers. And where are Caspian and the others?

I lean to the left, forcing the Swifter around another sharp turn. As I round the building, I focus on a concrete bridge peeking from the bottom of the hill. Below that is a river that travels straight through Dominus.

Straight. No turns, which means fast. And I would be hidden below.

I head for the river, checking my tail before dipping over the side. My nose burns from the pungent smell of carrion and waste flowing through the high water clogged with trash. I pick up speed, my belly flip-flopping as I repeat the words:

Max is safe, Max is safe, Max is safe.

I glide for miles, my breath evening out, my heart finding its natural rhythm. My brother's safe. I may not be any closer to the Island or the Mercurian, but I did this one thing right.

The moonlit city rises on both sides of the river. I skim between the thick, graffiti-strewn legs of bridges, antsy to find my way back to the estate.

Something catches my attention, and I glance to my right as two Gold Swifters drop quietly to the river and head for me. Two more break off to my left.

Fienian hell. How'd they find me?

They move with impossible speed. Even as I rev the throttle all the way back, even as I meld myself to my craft's body in a desperate bid for more speed, they grow closer like hunters quarrying their prey.

Pleas rattle around inside my head. To the dead gods. The ghost of my father. My mother. *Help me get out of this, and I'll find the Mercurian. I'll do it. Whatever it takes.*

Something makes me glance back. Caspian is bent low over his machine mere feet away, his golden hair whipped straight back in the wind. Our eyes lock. Other than a slight flare of the nostrils, his face is emotionless as he gains ground.

They're forming a noose around me. I want to sink into the refuse below and disappear into the river. Drowning in filth would be better than my fate if they catch me.

Way out. Way out. Roman looms to my right. He's grinning, flail in the air, ready to knock me off my machine, probably kill me. I can feel his stare linger on my bare legs from behind his thick goggles.

"After the Archduchess is done with you, worm," he calls, "maybe I'll pay you a visit."

"I'd rather die!" I growl.

Something rams my Swifter, hard. At some point while I was looking at Roman, Delphine snuck up on my left side . . . Roman was a diversion! The two other Chosen take their places in the front.

That leaves Caspian behind me. I search for a way out, my gaze flitting desperately over the steep embankments. But even if I somehow slipped away, I would get trapped in the meshwork of city to the right. To the left, a sharp decline that leads to more houses. No way to outrun them. No other direction to go but down . . . into the water. But maybe if . . . maybe if I didn't really drown . . .

The aqueducts rise to the left and snake along the river. Could I lose my pursuers long enough? I try to gather the thoughts ricocheting through my mind. Water. Drown.

Hide.

A glance over my shoulder confirms Caspian's Gold Swifter has blocked me in. I need him to move.

Look at me, Prince.

He focuses on me, his eyes flat. Uncaring. I killed Ophelia; of course he's not going to help me. Delphine slams into my Swifter, but I hold his gaze. *Look at me. See me.*

Something flashes inside his eyes, a spark of emotion.

Suddenly a space opens between us. Small enough that it could be an accident, but enough to slip through.

I brake my Swifter and make a steep cut to the left. At our speed, a second is hundreds of feet. The others grow small as they whiz past.

I gun it up the embankment and hurtle into the air, steering over the scum-slick side and onto the brown, five-foot wide canal of the aqueduct.

My pulse thunders inside my skull. I can hardly think. Hardly breathe.

The city unfolds a hundred feet below, the houses like a little miniature town I once saw in a Royalist shop when I was five, only missing the people.

Time to die, Maia.

All my senses fire at once as I hop on top of my speeding Swifter, arms windmilling for balance, lungs rapidly pulling in air to overload my blood with oxygen, and eye the curve ahead. Five. Four. Three. Two.

One.

I jump right as the craft flips over the side and sink under the cold water, eyes closed in some juvenile belief that if I can't see my pursuers, they can't see me. The water is murky, but it's also shallow, and I force the last of my breath out to keep from floating to the top, hoping they don't notice the bubbles.

Although I can't see anything, I can hear the Swifters pass over me, feel their heat.

I busy my brain with every thought under the sun but air. Bright, perfect stars. Max's rich, madcap laugh. Riser. Our kiss. My lungs burn and burn. I grasp onto my father's memory. The way he looked at me like the only thing in the world that mattered. I clench my teeth, grinding against the need, the primal urge to find air.

Not yet.

The darkness whirls behind my eyelids.

Not yet.

My brain screams.

Not yet—

My gasp is low and hungry as I part the water and find air. I rest my head on the side of the canal, panting to catch my breath. A shiver trills through me.

It worked. Thank the gods, it worked.

I drag myself to the edge of the aqueduct and peer down, drops of water bleeding from my hair and spiraling to the street below. A fire smolders over the black wreckage of my craft. I count the Chosen Swifters surrounding it.

Four—

By the time I turn, Caspian's sword is at my throat. The heat from his machine warms the water where it touches, sizzling and hissing steam as it rises around him. A too-long second passes.

Even now, I stare up at his face, unable to ignore the feeling of belonging, of home in his honey-gold eyes. His comforting beauty, a masterpiece of genetics and bioengineering. His DNA, mannerisms, quirks, and basically everything that makes Caspian *him*, a perfect match to *me*.

My heart flutters against my rib cage. It's over. But I refuse to go back. Releasing a breath, I lean forward until the point of his sword presses into the sensitive flesh of my neck, the pain steadying me.

"I won't let the Archduchess have me," I say in a soft voice, my intention clear.

Kill me or release me.

The prince's fingers twitch over his sword's pommel, just below the emperor's phoenix, the sigil that has marked his family as the most powerful in the nation for three violent, bloody generations.

A muscle trembles in his jaw. "We're even now." His eyes

are hard as they tear away from my face, focusing on something beyond. "Next time I see you, I'll treat you like the terrorist you are."

I gasp as he removes the sword from against my neck and buries the blade in the leather scabbard at his waist. He departs without looking back, but my gaze lingers long after his Swifter takes him round the curving aqueduct and out of sight.

Gone is the golden prince from my childhood. In his place stands a lonely, confused, angry boy. A boy I created when I killed his twin sister and betrayed him not once, but twice.

When I promised salvation but delivered bloodshed and death.

Every ounce of fight drains from my body. I sink back into the murky water, submerging everything but my nose, mouth, and eyes. I weakly grip the sides of the canal as the current tries to drag me down.

I don't know how long I stare up, focusing in and out on the stars peeking from the dissipating clouds. I'm shattered and broken as surely as the mangled pile of wreckage smoldering below.

I almost died tonight. And if I hadn't run across Max on the beach, I would be at Laevus Castle by now . . . either imprisoned or dead from a failed attempt to find the Mercurian.

What madness made me think I could infiltrate the emperor's castle alone?

My eyes fall upon the North Star. Once, I curled up in my father's lap and stared at the same brilliant star. He told me it was actually multiple stars so close together they appear as one.

"By itself," he said, "each star is average, easy to overlook, but together they command the night."

I want to stay in my safe little world, where the only

person I trust is myself. But I can't do this alone. I just can't. Not anymore, not with so much at stake. To have any shot at infiltrating the Island and finding the Mercurian, I need friends I can trust.

But how can I do that when almost everyone thinks I'm a traitor?

THIRTY

The silence of the long-abandoned Gold city weighs on me as I navigate the thin, maze-like streets. Wet, pale, and shivering, I feel like a wraith, a memory of the people who once populated the shops, with their fur-lined capes and over-the-top fascinators worn during hallow-Friday at the temples and every other occasion under the sun.

As the largest and wealthiest Gold city, most occupants are now either with the court on Hyperion, on the Island, or under the mountains in their caskets.

Deeper into the old city, bleached residences speckle the cliffs that shadow Dominus until early afternoon. The oldest city in the empire, Dominus is the last remnant of a dead era where gods ruled and technology had yet to be discovered. Ancient families like House Lockhart and House Laevus once ruled here as barons over all the surrounding lands.

Dominus was the only city protected from change when technology transformed all the others into cold, looming structures of steel and glass, as if it knew someday those cities would perish in the Everlasting War, the few that remained called Diamond Cities.

New cities and towns were built, but none were ever as beautiful or as regal as Dominus.

Dawn whispers its arrival on orange fingers of light. By the time I make it to the cave entrance, a pale blush has chased away any hints of night, and the birds sing from the nearby woods.

At some point during my walk, the voices began, and now they form a quiet hum in the back of my mind. I'm starting to get used to them, and I can't decide if that's a good thing or a bad thing.

Donning my night goggles, I lift the pine needles and brush used to camouflage the entrance to the cave and slide down the rough stone, cursing. I make it ten feet into the cave before I notice the figure waiting for me.

Despite her tall, gangly body, Teagan has a dancer's grace, and she leans sublimely against the wall, watching me. "So you survived, darling."

"Appears so."

"Well, I'm glad. When they told me the stupid thing you did, I searched for you."

I roll my shoulders and stifle a yawn, the beginning of a headache nipping at my brain. "Why? I mean, why do any of this? Help me?"

She pushes off the wall. "That's a conversation for another time."

"Please. I—I need to know why because . . . because I need to trust someone, and I think that person could be you."

"That's fair." Every part of Teagan is a study in composure, except her long fingers, which fidget over the gold buttons of her blouse, twisting and plucking. "Do you remember when that brute Roman stormed our table during the Culling and hurt O?"

"Yeah. He was an ass."

"Right." Her eyes are tight over an angry smile. "He was

an ass, but he was also a Chosen, a very powerful one at that. And you stood up to defend her despite it."

The image of the angry red marks Roman's brutish fingers left on O's mouth blisters against my brain, and my hands ball into fists. "I wish I'd killed him."

"So do I." Her voice wavers, and somehow, *somehow* I understand.

"You and Princess Ophelia were friends?"

"Friends . . . and more." Part of her mouth twists, her gaze hesitant as she watches me for my reaction. "Does that bother you?"

It takes a second to understand. More than friends. Lovers. Two girls . . . in a relationship just like men and women have.

Subversive. The word whispers in my head, the word I first heard whispered about Teagan on the day we entered the Island.

A nasty, hateful word.

In my world, being a Subversive is worse than a Bronze. Worse than a worm. Subversive is the lowest of the low.

Most Subversives with money were stripped of Color and title and sent to camps, but the vast majority of ones without means, the ones who couldn't afford the expensive Reconstruction therapy enforced at the camps, well, those citizens were drained like refuse into the pits below the prisons and forgotten about.

I realize Teagan's gaze hasn't left my face as she awaits my verdict. A childish vulnerability hides beneath her cool mask, one I recognize, and it makes me angry she would be made to feel less than human. I don't care who she loves, or who she kisses.

For me, she's still the exact same person.

"Teagan," I say, cringing at the way she winces, "there are

a million things that bother me right now, but who you choose to love is *not* one of them."

"Good." But her voice remains clipped. "Not everyone is so . . . *open-minded*." She turns. "C'mon, let's leave this damp hole behind."

I wonder suddenly if she has nightmares about the labyrinth too. If cramped, dark spaces fill her palms with sweat and make her feel like she's dying one strangled breath at a time.

"Do you still think about the first Trial?" I ask quietly.

She pauses. "When I was seven, my parents sent me to a special clinic for Subversives." She turns around to face me. "After five years there, undergoing procedures I can't even bring myself to talk about, I thought I would never know that kind of fear again. But the maze proved me wrong."

We walk in silence to her Swifter. Even after what she's told me, I don't hesitate to crawl on behind her and sling my tired arms around her slim waist, thankful for her warmth.

I don't care what they call her, or who she loves. I don't. In fact, the idea feels so pointless and silly that I almost laugh . . . except now that I know how Teagan felt about O, I can't help but feel empathy for her.

"I'm sorry, Teagan," I say. "About Ophelia."

Teagan stiffens. "Me too, darling."

"You're okay?"

"Peachy."

She's lying, but I won't push her. No one is immune to tragedy and pain in the emperor's world. We've all lost someone. And none of us want to talk about it.

"What I said earlier about you and O," I say. "I mean it. And I'm glad she had someone who cared about her. Someone who gave her hope."

A long, heavy pause.

"What? Did I say something wrong?"

Her body shudders, and I realize she's laughing. "I knew, darling. From the moment I saw you at Royalist Headquarters in that horrible ivory dress, I knew we'd be friends. And I don't have many of those."

"Me either."

Teagan stiffens, shifting in her seat. "Look. There's a reason you didn't see me on the mission . . . and why I searched for you earlier."

I lean back a little.

"On Oath Day, you're forced to take Nicolai's Microplant. One reason for this is so Nicolai and some of the higher commanders can communicate with the Rebels quickly. The other is for some of the more complex Sims used in training."

"And the third reason?"

"During every mission, there's a Watcher, someone who hides in the shadows and watches. I was the Watcher last night. If the Royalists had caught any of us, I would have terminated their Microplant before they could have divulged any information about Bloodwyn Estate or Nicolai."

I shiver. That's how they've kept it a secret for this long. "But I haven't taken the Microplant."

"And if you'd been caught, I would have been forced to take you out another way."

I don't ask how she would have done it. I trust that someone like her, someone with access to the kind of weapons I'm starting to learn exist, could have made it happen.

"What about Cage?" I ask. "Why isn't he, you know, terminated?"

"Flame refuses to do it. They were orphans together by the time they were five. He's the only person she trusts not to break, although we both know eventually the emperor can break anyone."

A sick feeling washes over me. "And if I refuse to take the Blood Oath and the Microplant?"

"Just don't, darling. Okay?"

"Okay," I murmur. But I know it's a lie; so does she, I imagine.

Without waiting for my response, the Swifter purrs to life and glides through the darkness, taking us back to the Fienian stronghold. A Subversive and a liar pretending everything's okay.

By the time Teagan and I make it back to the castle, the sun has risen and warms my cheeks, and the voices have faded to a biting headache. I tilt my head up to soak in the sunlight, and my gaze snags on Pandora. Once this simple act would have set my heart racing, but I'm used to the sight of Her now.

Deep down, I know some part of me has come to terms with Her. She's not going to miss us. She will not deviate from Her path of destruction. She's coming, she's going to kill millions of people, and there's almost nothing I can do about it.

To even hope otherwise is foolish.

And yet . . . I have to try. What other choice do I have?

Rebels come and go from the estate. A small group hunches over the rows of tomatoes and sweet potatoes behind a crumbling stable. Others are trudging back from the orchard in the distance with buckets full of apples. I stare, unable to reconcile the image of Fienians working outside in a garden with the stories I've always heard.

Fienians are scavengers. Fienians are lazy. Fienians cause

destruction and death. They don't pick tomatoes from a garden. They don't host balls and wear fancy leathers and follow rank.

And they certainly don't form regimented armies and wage war against the empire.

Few people notice as we enter Bloodwyn Estate and trace the long meandering passageways to our rooms. Teagan leaves me at the stairs with a bleary nod. When I get to my door, I yank it open, prepared to flop onto my bed and sleep off my fatigue.

Instead, I come face-to-face with Lash.

"How could you be so stupid?" he demands. His arms are crossed over his chest and his hair disheveled, as if he's been running around all morning.

"What? No glad you're alive, Graystone?" I say, brushing past him. "Thanks for saving my life?"

He follows me to my bed. Sand patters to the floor as I rip off my boots and sink into my weary mattress, rustling up a cloud of dust that sparkles inside the light from my broken window.

Lash frowns down at me. "There are rules to friendship."

I raise an eyebrow. "Like not locking people inside near-windowless rooms?"

"Like . . . Like, I don't know! Not getting yourself killed."

"One, I'm alive. So you can stop saying that. Two, you locked me in a room."

"After you stole my key!" Lash waves his hands. "And why the hell didn't you ask me to help you? I would have, you know."

He's not going away, so I sit up. "Lash, there just wasn't any time."

He lets out a long sigh, plopping next to me on the bed. "I know everyone thinks my bum leg means I can't do things.

But that's a mistake. This"—he holds up his injured leg —"means I have to do things better, smarter."

My heart clenches at the sight. "What happened?"

His jaw tightens, his gaze flicking to the headboard. "I loved above my station."

"And the Royalists hurt you?"

"Twenty lashes." He swivels to look me in the eye. "The penalty for a Silver that falls in love with a Gold. Except the father of the girl I loved paid the overseer extra to make it fifty. He forced his daughter to watch. Even after I fell, half-conscious, the overseer continued lashing wherever he could, ripping chunks of flesh and muscle as I seized—at least, that's what they tell me." Tears shine in his eyes. "When I woke up, I was a piss-stained Bronze cripple. I'd lost my Color, the job that waited for me with my father, the girl, everything. The shame on my family was so bad that my father . . . well, he chased the black until one day we found him dead."

His dad used Tar? Maybe that's why Lash was so helpful with Brogue.

I bite my cheek against all the things I want to say. How I'm sorry he was hurt for loving someone. How I'm sorry about his dad. But the last thing Lash needs is my pity.

"There are other ways to fight them," I say. "You can heal people, that's—"

"No." He shakes his head, a distant glaze to his eyes. "It's not enough."

The door clicks shut, and we both turn in time to see Riser casually lean against the wall, his hands in his pant pockets.

As Lash gets up to leave, he gives Riser the once-over. "The Prince has been hanging around your door for hours, love," he whispers. "Want me to send him away?"

I cast a glance at Riser. His hair, pulled back in a failed half-knot, is messier than I'm used to, his tunic rumpled and open at the neck. It looks as if he hasn't slept much either.

I put a hand on Lash's shoulder, drawing Riser's gaze. "Give us a minute?"

As soon as Lash leaves, Riser rakes a hand through his hair, freeing the rest of it in a wild tangle around his chin. "I heard your door open."

I rock back on my heels. "Your chamber is close?"

"No . . . not really." A tired half-smile. He takes a step closer, eyeing the broken window. "What you did probably saved our lives. So, as your king, thank you."

Without thinking, I perform a mock curtsy. "Anything for you, King."

He crosses his arms, and I almost feel bad as he frowns. If I had to guess what was running through his head right now, I would say he's wondering why I threw a book at him the other day. Why I taunt him every chance I get but ended up kissing him *twice*.

He chuckles drily. "Anything?"

"Oh, get out!" I say, tossing the only thing I can find—a pillow—at his face. And missing.

He laughs again, this time a real laugh that comes from his chest, his gaze drifting to the edge of my bed. Throwing up his hands as if to ward off more pillows, he crosses the floor and plucks what looks to be dark leather pants and a peach-red tunic from the covers, holding them in the air.

He cuts his gaze at me, a perfectly neat black eyebrow arched sharply over his green eye. "I guess you've been forgiven, Graystone."

The sight of the clothes makes me almost forget about Riser standing only feet away, or my bare legs, pale against the bright-red duvet. I hold out an expectant hand.

Riser's gaze slides over my legs. "Uh-uh."

I jump onto the bed and swipe at the clothes, barely missing as he moves a step back. "Give them to me."

"Nope. I'm going to burn them."

I rest a hand on my hip and frown sternly at him. "Now."

"No."

I'm about to jump and tackle him when the door swings open and Lucy saunters in. The white streak in her hair has been dyed red, all of her thick, wavy black hair pulled up into a braid that forms a crown around her head.

When she sees me, her eyes widen. She doesn't even bother to hide her disappointment that I'm alive, her lips curling, until she notices Riser.

Then her face brightens, a forced smile baring a flash of teeth. "Oh, good." She flicks her focus to me. "I was just checking to see if she made it back."

Liar. More like seeing what stuff she could steal. "Well," I say, hopping down from the bed and straightening my poor, mangled dress, "here I am. Safe and sound."

Lucy ignores me and turns her attention to Riser. I want to rake my nails down her face as she flashes him an oily smile, her gaze lingering on his face for a second too long before falling to the clothes still dangling from his hand.

"Ready, Riser?" She gestures to the door. "We'll miss breakfast if we don't hurry."

The girlish sound of her voice, the fluttering of her eyelashes, all of it worms under my skin. At first I thought it was jealousy, but now . . . now I'm beginning to suspect there's another reason entirely.

I stare at Lucy until she's forced to glance my way. *Hurt him and I'll kill you, bitch.*

Her eyes go flat above a smirk, and she slips her hand over Riser's elbow, urging him to the door. Riser tosses the clothes onto an old cherry wood chest on the way out.

Just before he disappears, he glances back, and our eyes meet. There's a tug inside my stomach, and I want to scream at him to stay. I want to tell him to stay away from Lucy. To be careful.

But my mouth can't seem to form any words, and he slips out.

As soon as the heavy door shuts, I throw a pillow at it, wishing it were Lucy's head.

Toeing into the pants, I sigh as the soft, smooth leather slides up my thighs and settles comfortably around my rear. *Burn them, indeed.*

Well, from this moment forward, my legs are off limits to you, Pit Boy.

THIRTY-TWO

I can't stop toying with the heavy blade of the scorpion dagger hidden inside the waistband of my pants as I stroll to Brogue's chamber. A weapon. Regular clothes. I've accomplished two of the things I set out to, but I'm not any closer to finding the Mercurian than before, nor am I any closer to tempering the sense of urgency that has my heart beating wildly at even the calmest moments, or figuring out what to do about the voices and my headaches.

I run my fingers along the walls as I walk. How many days left until D-Day, the day Pandora hits? Ten? Twelve?

Not enough. There are simply not enough days to stop Her.

I've requested a meeting with both Flame and Nicolai twice this morning, in between emptying waste buckets and tidying rooms and carrying laundry downstairs to the vats. Twice I've been rejected.

Not that I think they would listen to my proposal for a team to enter the Island. At this point, they're hyper-focused on war. A war we have no hope of winning. Maybe that's what they want anyway. Who the Fienian hell knows?

The door to Brogue's chamber is slightly ajar, the sound of humming drifting from the room. *Perhaps Lash is inside*, I think as I enter . . . and find Brogue leaning over a green tub full of water, scraping a straight razor over his jaw. Clean clothes hang over his thin body, and his gaze is sharp and clear.

I wrap him in a hug. "You're okay," I murmur. "I knew you would come back."

"Lady March—"

"Maia," I correct, pulling away slightly so I can really look him over. "Call me Maia . . . or girl. Just not Everly."

"Fine. *Maia*. I like the sound of that." He steps back and sighs through his teeth. "They said you took the prince hostage and escaped?" A rough chuckle scrapes from his chest. "I taught you well."

We sink onto the limp mattress, and I catch him up on what he's missed. When I get to the part about Riser having me erased, three lines crease his forehead, and he pulls on the end of his thick, gray-shot braid.

"So," he says after I've finished, "you went and entered the Blood Court, did ya?"

"I did. And now I need you to help me train to win it . . . that is, if you feel up to it."

He smiles, flashing his gold tooth. "For you, I think I could manage."

"And I need you to find a way for me to beat Riser."

"Now that might be a little harder." He rubs his hand over his newly shaved chin and stands, groaning with the effort. "Follow me outside, Maia. I need to show you something."

We slip through the quiet halls, the smell of breakfast tightening my stomach. Brogue pauses once we're outside, his face tilted to the sun as if soaking it all in. Voices and the clang of steel trickle from just beyond the garden, and we follow the shouts to a large group of Rebels gathered beneath the shade of an ancient oak tree and watch fighters dance across the unkempt lawn.

Despite having just returned from a Twitcher's death, Brogue pushes and shoves a path to the front of the crowd, drawing suspicious glances from everyone in the yard.

I make sure to sneer at the faces we pass. If I thought after last night I'd be treated differently, I was wrong. Even though I'm dressed like the others, even though I one-handedly saved the mission, the Rebels still skirt around me, their doubt evident as they trail me with their heavy gazes and sharp whispers.

My good mood from Brogue's recovery dissolves. Max still doesn't trust me. Lash still won't give me the key. And, even if all those things change, I still have no idea how to activate Max's map to the Mercurian. My only hope is to take Riser's throne today during Shadow Fall. Then, by their own law, they'll have to listen to me.

Not such an easy task, I realize, as I watch Riser glide across the grass without seeming to move his feet, whipping his sword against the blades of three other fighters. Even with three against him, Riser maintains his lithe, predatory grace, calmly deflecting the blows and evading his attackers. He's not even out of breath.

Did they enhance his skills when they Reconstructed him last? Or perhaps without me in his life, the one person that reminded him to be human, he's even more deadly.

"I watched from a window when I could," Brogue says, squinting against the sun. "He comes here four times a day to train when the weather allows. When he's not fighting or training, he's going on missions. It's like there's something inside him that won't let him rest."

I jut out my chin. "So, what? You're saying I can't beat him?"

"I'm saying he's changed. It's like he doesn't even know

me anymore, like they took out the memory of me along with yours, and . . . and changed him somehow. So don't count on him taking it easy on you."

"Oh, I've met this new Riser, and I'm definitely not counting on it. But I am counting on *you* finding his weakness. There has to be something I can use to beat him."

Brogue coughs a sarcastic chuckle that doesn't provide much hope. "Look at him, Maia. That boy's a machine."

The Rebels around me hoot and yell, banging their boots on the ground for the fighters. When Riser strikes a blow, a collective cheer reverberates through the crowd.

I look around. Most of the Fienians look to be my age, and they drip with daggers and Hot Weapons. They flaunt bright pops of color in their accessories and hair and gleam with metal adornments that pierce their flesh. Many are scarred in one way or another, tokens from the empire, I assume. Some drink from mottled bronze cups, the rich amber liquid dribbling down their chins.

"Amberblood," Brogue explains, wrinkling his nose at the lavender-haired girl next to him with a half-empty cup. "Rebels drink it in the weeks before battle."

A baby-faced boy around Max's age hands me a cup. The warm, thick liquid seems to glow from within. As I watch, it begins to move, churning and swirling as if alive.

I shove it back into the young boy's hands.

He laughs and takes a huge gulp, his eyes unnaturally bright. "It only tickles the first few sips."

My stomach roils as if I've actually swallowed some. "Nanites?"

Brogue nods. "Numbs their fear."

Has Max taken some? My chest tightens, and I immediately want to find him and scream myself hoarse. Idiot! Why would he want to take something that can permanently damage his mind? Stupid! And he's just a kid . . .

A boy, not a kid—and one that's about to go to battle, a voice inside me whispers. *A boy who's experienced more pain in his lifetime than any ever should.*

A cheer rises from the crowd, jarring me from my thoughts. Riser has his last opponent on his knees, a blade at his throat.

The cheers meld into a chant that grows louder, filling the air, a hundred voices poured into two words: *Azkar Rex.*

I frown, trying to remember where I've heard those words before, but nothing comes to me. *I'll have to ask Lash later.*

The balmy sunlight highlights the inky-blue undertones of Riser's dark hair and slips down the length of his sword. Squaring his shoulders, Riser lifts his sword to the sky, perhaps to Pandora, and the chant becomes a pulsing roar. Somewhere in the distance, thunder rumbles.

A storm is coming.

The jet-black clouds pool across the horizon, spreading like blood in water. No one else seems to notice or care. The group of Rebels surge around Riser as fresh fighters circle him. The air is thick with whispers of the storm and something else, something dark and violent.

I suck in a deep breath. In a few hours, I have to fight Riser. Not Riser, my friend. Not Riser, the boy who kissed me and promised to protect me. This *Pit Boy* . . . this lethal, seemingly inhuman killing machine.

"I . . . I have to go," I mutter to Brogue. When he moves to follow, I shake my head. "Stay. See if you can find his Achilles heel."

I slip away from the fighters, running across the lawn toward the castle, my boots sinking into the soft ground.

On the crumbling steps leading up to the massive iron doors, I glance back. Five fighters dart around Riser, their blades a flash of silver. He slips through them like black smoke, the crowd vibrating my chest with their screams.

I tear my gaze away. In my wildest dreams, I never imagined I would have to fight Riser. Now that it's a reality, it feels more like a nightmare.

THIRTY-THREE

The darkness of the castle engulfs me. I never thought I would be happy to be back inside this mausoleum of dust and ghosts, but the sight of Riser fighting those Rebels bothered me. All those blades that could easily pierce his flesh.

I shut my eyes against the memory of him falling to the ground on the Island, Caspian's sword covered in blood. In a few hours, I have to fight Riser in the Blood Court and win.

But as much as my brain tells me I have to hurt him, I have to *beat* him, my breath still catches at the thought of him getting injured.

Why can't I let Pit Boy go?

Maybe it's the stress of my upcoming battle, but the voices suddenly flood my mind. I hear a little girl crying. "I want to wake up," she begs. "Please help me."

"I can't," I say, rubbing at my head as I rush to the stairs. "I don't know what you want."

Lash's familiar dragging steps scuff behind me. "Talking to ghosts, Graystone?"

Turning to face him, I flash a weary smile. "Do you ever feel like you're drowning in bad memories?"

"All the time, love. You okay?"

"Yeah, just . . . can't shake this stupid headache, or the voices." I frown at my feet rather than see his worried expression. "What were they saying out there?"

"Blood King. It's the old language of the Croft dynasty, Mythian, spoken before the first emperor united the Houses under his banner. They say the Crofts were originally from the lands across the sea, before the ocean swallowed it."

I blink, trying to remember what my tutor taught me. The world used to be divided by oceans, with different cultures and races swarming huge landmasses. But eventually the oceans rose and the landmasses shifted to merge one huge continent and one race.

They say all the great Houses can trace their descent from one of those long-forgotten masses of land. Even Lockhart, my mother's House, claimed to hail from the northernmost continent, a land of snow and ice and darkness.

Before I can answer, a Rebel with bored eyes approaches. "The Commander requests your presence, Graystone."

Despite wanting to see Flame, my throat tightens as I follow him. Lash tries to shadow me, but my guide waves him away, and he still stands in the exact same spot when I glance back from the top of the wide foyer stairs.

Then we're winding through the catacomb of dim hallways and cramped chambers. I swallow the dread I get from this place, the weak light and feeling of being entombed, the ancient, dead smell—as if rats and other things have died in the walls. Even the rich, polished wood panels bring to mind dark memories of the pit.

I hate this place. Maybe not as much as the Tower, and certainly not as much as the pit. But I can't shake the overwhelming feeling that Bloodwyn should be burned to its foundation.

If Pandora has her way, it will happen soon enough.

The stairs winding and curving up each level have no concern for logistics or common sense. Each one is different. Some carpeted, some ornate with wrought-iron railings and sleek marble stairs. But the higher we climb, the more bare-bones they become.

By the time we scale the last stairway to reach the rooftop veranda where Flame awaits, the steps are cracked wooden boards held together by a few rods of iron.

The storm rages behind Flame, fingers of wind rippling her milky-white cape and tugging her wild tufts of dark hair, spiked blood red to match the scorpion crest on her back and neck.

She bares her teeth in a grin that hints at madness. At war and death and the end of everything safe and good. Four Rebels surround her like the four points of a weapon, their eyes flicking from the storm to her, as if not sure where the biggest threat lies.

I don't have that trouble as I square my shoulders to face Flame.

"Princess." She has to shout over the raging wind. "You did good this morning."

A four-foot stone barrier stands between the roof and the cliffs hundreds of feet below. I follow her to it, more than a little suspicious she plans to throw me to my death. Instead, she looks out and sucks in a heavy, rabid breath, her wild gaze slowly devouring the angry black clouds spitting blue, the white caps smashing against the rocks, and beyond, to the thick smudge of forest.

"I need to talk to you!" I shout.

"War is coming! The empire is weak, half the court hides in the stars, and alliances are shifting."

"Did you know kids are doing nanites?"

"It's our time to make the Royalists bleed."

"Flame—"

Thunder booms, rattling my bones. The Rebels glance around, shifting on their feet, obviously questioning the safety of standing on a roof in a lightning storm. But Flame seems to grow taller, pale-blue eyes glowing as if feeding off the energy.

"Wicked, right?" Flame calls, flicking her gaze to the steel thunderheads above us. "The storms are a gift from Pandora. They keep the drones from the sky and the Rebels from searching."

"Flame, look. I need to know if you did something to my head when I was given my Microplant."

Her lips twist to the side. "Princess, you were given the standard Microplant that allows for Sim interaction."

"With that one, would I hear . . . voices?"

"Voices? Not until you receive your Rebel Microplant, which you get when you take the oath. You're taking it, right?" Her small hand vices around my wrist. "The emperor's court is weak. It's going to fall when the world does. In a few days, we go to battle, and anyone not with us is against us. Prove you're not a traitor, Princess, and stand with us."

Rain pelts our faces. The sky churns, a roiling mass of darkness. Blue flashes of lightning pierce the landscape, followed by a staccato of booms that shake the earth.

"Get me back to the Island," I say. "Give me a few Rebels. Help me find the Mercurian to stop Pandora before it's too late."

Flame blinks. The rain has plastered her wild mass of hair around her forehead and half her face. Her pupils focus on me as if just now seeing me. "Why would I want to stop it?"

"You can't really want half the population to die."

I can't tell by Flame's slack face if she heard me or not.

A blue flash blinds me for a split second, followed by a roar. Brushing the rain from my eyes, I focus back on her. "Give me the men, Flame, and I'll bring Cage home."

"Cage is gone. *Lost.*"

"How can you, of all people, say that?"

"That's the price of this world. Haven't you figured that out by now? If you care about someone, they'll be taken from you. It's only a matter of time."

"So you've totally given up hope?"

Her pupils narrow as she finally looks at me, really looks at me. "You're either with us or against us. Choose one. And don't mention the Island or Cage again."

THIRTY-FOUR

The storm bathes the inside of the castle in green-tinged darkness. Thunderclaps sound like faraway bombs rocking the earth. If I believed in the gods, I would think Zeus angry and venting his rage. Maybe he is. Perhaps he's tired of us.

Perhaps he's warning of the end. That's where Flame is dragging us. There's no way we can win a war, even with our tech. Besides, wars last days, months, years even.

We have less than two weeks.

The thought is like a freezing shadow over me. It doesn't matter where I go or what I do, I can't escape its dark warning of doom.

I'm so wrapped up in my thoughts that I barely see Riser until I nearly crash into him at the bottom of the stairs. I fling out my arm just in time, pushing off his chest to keep from bowling him over.

The ghost of a smile teeters on his lips as he looks sideways at me.

"Sorry," I say, glancing around. "I'm looking for—"

"Max?"

I bristle at how easily he reads me, hiding my annoyance with a tight smile. "Know where he is?"

"Maybe." He arches an eyebrow. "What are you willing to do for it?"

Fienian bastard.

I plan to shove past him, but there's something about the boyish amusement in his eyes that begs me to play along. And perhaps being around him will remind me that he chose to forget me, so I can finally *choose* to forget him.

"What do you have in mind?"

He shifts slightly on his feet, still watching me, a surprised yet pleased expression on his dark, chiseled face. Without a word, he turns, and I follow.

It feels stupid at first, letting him lead me down a near-hidden passageway behind the stairs, then several flights of stairs, each one damper and darker than the last. I focus on his shoulders, wide inside a black leather jacket, his smooth, feline movements as he glides down the stairs.

I'm wet, cold, but a trickle of warmth burns inside me as I take in the pale flesh of his neck peeking above his high red collar, his raven-black hair, pulled back and gleaming. The scent of leather and cotton and rain that drift in his wake.

With each step into the darkness, I shed a layer of worry. With each breath, I forget we're dying. With each exhale, I purge some of the darkness that's been dragging me down into despair.

I follow, he leads. Nothing else matters.

The air is chilly, the sweet, briny scent of the ocean filling my head. My boots scuff against smooth, slick rock. The caves. I'm awash in darkness.

I slip, reaching out my hand—

Warm, strong fingers twine through mine, steadying me, the pad of his thumb tracing the tender line that runs down my palm. Sending ribbons of warmth unfurling up my wrist and arm and into my chest. And it feels good. Right.

He doesn't let go; I don't try to pull away.

Is he playing a game? Is this his residual, pre-reconstructed feelings?

I bury my doubts. I need this moment. I need to trust someone. I need to not feel alone for once since the pit. I need to feel something good and *normal*.

The muffled sound of thunder echoes through the caves. The Swifters come into view first, a bright array of metals, like playthings made by the gods, bold reds and vibrant blues and gold so rich and buttery it feels decadent just to look at it, much less slide my leg over its glass-smooth surface.

Riser takes the flame-red one.

Waves lap near our feet, the water the color of dark steel.

There are no words. Riser flicks his Swifter on and I follow. My uploaded memory is long gone, but I remember anyway, and my body yearns and aches for the power of my machine.

The sound of my heart pounding, the ocean shattering against rock, and the gentle purr of my Swifter merge into a lulling cadence.

Riser hands me sleek silver goggles and a tiny metallic plug. After I slip the goggles over my head, I watch him insert the plug inside his ear.

He turns and watches me as I do the same.

An instant, electric shock of pleasure hits me as my head is filled with sounds. It's music, I realize. Not just one instrument, but several, as if each string, each key, represents an emotion. The notes rise, growing angry, chaotic, a crescendo of rage.

Forbidden music. Rebel songs.

My throat aches as a voice dances through the chaos,

reaching straight to my heart, filling me with a blinding array of feelings I've managed thus far to keep locked away.

Although Riser can't see my eyes, something on my face must tell him what I'm thinking, because he gives me a small, understanding nod.

We enter the storm full speed. A wall of wind and rain slams into us, but we slip through as if the water and gusts slip right off our bodies. Angry whitecaps shiver beneath us. The world is dark, enraged, electric daggers of lightning impaling the water and splitting the murky air.

I meld my body with my Swifter, streaking beside Riser, paralleling the dark, looming cliffs. Inside me, a white flame sparks and grows, feeding off the tragic, furious melody, warming every cell, every molecule of my flesh, shivering and burning and screaming and forcing me *faster, faster, faster*.

We streak toward the storm, arrows from the gods. White flashes dance around us, electricity raking my skin, tickling my marrow, reminding me of who I am, *what* I am. Waves rise and fall, tall as buildings. The wind howls in our faces.

The curtain of rain parts, encircling us in a sheet of dark silver. We're stopped in the middle of the ocean, the cliffs and castle a tiny blip through the gale.

The eye of the storm.

Pit Boy grins at me beneath his smoky goggles, his dark tunic pasted over the ropy muscles of his chest and abdomen, hair sculpted in every direction. Water clings to his skin.

Lightning skims the horizon, illuminating the red of the scorpion on his neck wrapped around the dying phoenix.

I've never seen him so radiant, or so alive.

Rain and seawater drench every part of me, rivering down my breasts and back. My hair is every which way, my breath uneven, my heartbeat so rapid it feels like one long pulse. But I feel weightless, as if all the molecules that make up my body have expanded.

For the first time since I broke out of the pit, I haven't looked up at the sky for Her. Every single piece of me is focused on the present.

Not D-Day. Not Oath day for the Rebels. Not the day we go to war. Even my constant headache has faded to a whisper.

I'm in the now. Savoring the ache spreading through me as Riser lets his gaze slowly roam my body, every inch of me revealed through my wet tunic and leathers. The way my stomach hollows out with every wave—and every hungry look from Pit Boy.

It's different from before, when I occupied some part of his mind that equaled redemption. When I was an intangible ideal he had to protect to liberate his tormented soul.

Now I'm just a girl, and he's just a boy. And the world is ending.

I spin toward him. He reaches out, but my slick fingers slip from his grasp. I know that if it weren't for the heaving ocean and the violent gusts of wind, I would align my Swifter with Riser's, press my body into his, and kiss him. And not because of what we were before, or the chance of a relationship.

But because I want to live.

I want to fight and experience and feel. I want to shut off my mind, all the what ifs, and listen to my body. I want to burn and burn for something that has nothing to do with survival and everything to do with me.

Suddenly an obsidian wave smooth as glass flings us apart. As I ride the wave, it's as if a freezing hand closes over my heart, killing any happiness I might have felt or imagined.

Reality hits me hard. I have to forget him the way he did me. Whatever *this* is, it will leak away like the seawater drains from our clothes, and when we reenter the castle and prepare for the Blood Court, I'll maybe remember scraps from this moment, until they fade into a faint shadow of a memory that evanesces in the breeze of Her destruction.

I'm not allowed happiness, not while Pandora is still up there. I have to fight him. And I have to win.

I start back for Bloodwyn without him. I can feel his questioning stare as he trails behind, his gaze boring into my back.

As painful as it is, I need to let Pit Boy and the bond we share go. In a few hours, I'm going to fight him for command and make decisions he won't agree with.

In a few hours, the only thought when I look at Riser needs to be violence.

THIRTY-FIVE

Going out in the storm was stupid. It will take hours in this humidity for my clothes to dry, which means I'll have to either wait in my room until my pants and tunic dry, or wear another dress. I rip off my clothes and hang them on a chair by the open window and then flop onto the sagging excuse for a bed.

It doesn't take long to slip into a restless sleep.

Darkness. Walls everywhere. I can't find my way out. Merida is calling for me, but then her voice changes, becomes hundreds of voices, begging me to help them. Screaming and clawing through my mind. "Help us," they shout. "Set us free!"

They're real, so real . . .

I tear from my nightmare into reality. Sweat pools over my chest and soaks my sheets, my breathing ragged. I blink at the sunlight pouring in from the broken window and remind myself where I am.

It was just a dream.

Stretching to a stand, I wonder if I'll ever be able to sleep without the nightmares and the voices. Maybe Teagan is right. I have to do something traumatic to bring them to the surface and set them free.

My clothes are still damp, especially my pants, but anything is better than another Royalist gown. When I'm fully covered in clingy pants and my limp tunic, I set out and find Brogue.

For the next hour, we train in the garden outside, sharpening the reconstructed skills I learned what seems like years ago. It feels good to fight, and I don't hold back, even though Brogue's health isn't top notch.

Not that he needs me to hold back. Despite having been near death barely a day ago, he doesn't even break a sweat against my attacks. We cover swordplay, striking, groundwork, and when we're done, my bruised, tired body feels good, like I've actually accomplished something.

"Why you smiling, girl?" Brogue demands, toying with the hilt of a long sword at his side.

I stretch my neck. "I don't know . . . It just, felt good."

"Good? I was going easy on you, but if you fight like that in the Blood Court, Riser will destroy you."

"Then show me his weakness!" I kick at the gravel. "Surely he has one."

"Not that I've seen."

His words send my heart into a tailspin. While I appreciate Brogue's honesty, I was hoping he would be more optimistic.

I place a hand on Brogue's dense shoulder. "Well, you'll just have to find one, won't you?"

Before Brogue can get off a cynical reply, I mention breaking for lunch, and we head to the mess hall. My tunic sticks to my back with sweat, but I don't have time to bathe. I didn't realize how hungry I am until I step into the warm, loud hall and the rich smell of meat hits me. Teagan and Lash sit at their usual table near the back. My stomach rumbles as Brogue and I slip in between them.

As usual, Riser sits at the head table next to Flame, his back to the wall where he can see everything. He hasn't bothered to fix his hair since our outing, but it somehow adds to his raw, untamed look. A lank red banner hangs from the rafters above them.

I nearly lose my appetite as I spy Lucy sitting on his right, her chair pulled closer than a normal acquaintance should sit. The humidity has loosened her kinky black hair into long spirals that snake down her back.

Her creepy brother, Hugo, watches them, his arms crossed over his chest. His dark gaze slides to me, and he leans forward, whispering something to Lucy. Her eyebrows draw together as she glances my way.

Not wanting to stare at them while I eat, I switch seats so that my back is to Riser. *Problem solved.* Lunch is nearly over and the room isn't as crowded as last time, which makes it easier to talk without shouting.

Teagan raises an eyebrow at me. "Heck of a storm, right?"

I pause from scraping the ladle against the bottom of the clay cauldron in the middle of the table. If there was any meat, it's all been picked out, leaving a mush of potatoes and soggy brown vegetables. "Um-hmm."

"Dangerous, too." Lash grins like an idiot. "I heard a few Rebels decided to ride the storm."

Teagan shoots me a teasing look. "Let's hope that's all they rode."

"Gods, Teagan!" I drop my spoon into my soup. "It was just a way to unwind."

Lash digs an elbow into my ribs. "I'm good for unwinding, Graystone. Dandier than the prince, too."

"By the gods, boy," Brogue says, cutting his eyes at Lash. "There ain't much room here with that ego."

Teagan howls with laughter, and I bite back a chuckle. "You have no idea, Merc."

Rebels from the other tables turn to stare, and Lash flashes an aggrieved scowl. "Why don't you alert the entire Rebel army? Lash is not unwind-worthy."

"That's not why they're staring," Teagan says in an amused drawl. "They're watching Graystone."

I glance around. "Why?"

"They heard about what you did this morning."

"Yeah," Lash says, drumming his fingers on the wood table. "Heard you went balls out and made the others look like real dandy assholes."

"That and your plan to *dethrone* the prince has made the rounds." Teagan's red lips curl, and I glare down the raunchy joke she's about to make.

"Already done that, hasn't she?" Lash quips.

I glare him down too.

And so does Brogue. "Enough with the inappropriate jokes about Maia, boy."

A flush creeps up Lash's neck, and he looks away from the Merc as I grin.

"They underestimated you, darling," Teagan explains. "Now they're trying to size you up."

I take a minute to really look at the other Rebels, to size them up the same way they're doing me. On first glance, the Rebels hadn't looked like anything special.

But now, I notice that the Rebels grouped in the center at the fighters' tables are surprisingly athletic and muscular. Not just that, but by the way they monitor the door every few minutes—similar to Mercs—and drip weapons, they are more than capable of violence.

"Those," Lash says, following my gaze to a raucous group of boys, "are your competitors for the Scorpion Throne, Graystone. Ex-miners, dock laborers, and Hawks."

I cringe. "What are Hawks?"

"A bunch of genetically engineered freaks is what they are," Brogue says, frowning at the men.

"My father used Hawks," Teagan says. "It was a barbaric and cruel form of slavery. Young Bronze men, conscripted and trained to be Centurions and then sold instead to the highest bidder, usually Gold factory owners who needed guards to keep their warehouses safe from the starving masses."

"Do they all fight in the Blood Court?"

"Most haven't . . . yet. But it's rumored the fighters plan to join the last Blood Court on Oath day. I guess they all want the honor of commanding during the battle."

My shoulders slump. I hadn't factored in so many contenders to the throne. Two days till Oath Day and the last Blood Court. Two days to win and gather a crew.

I have to win today, in a few hours. There's also the Blood Court tomorrow, but I still need time to use my one day of influence to gather other Rebels, form a viable plan, and find a way into the castle.

"Don't look so glum, darling," Teagan says. "My money's on you, although I cannot figure out why you want the throne."

Lash snorts. "Keep at it, Aster. The girl's head will be as big as a blue-bomb."

"Boy," Brogue says in a biting tone, "this *girl* made it out of a hell that a lot of men and women smarter and more cunning than those muscled-up dandies didn't ever leave."

"The Trials." Lash's gaze falls to the table. His mouth parts as if to say something else, but then his brown eyes flick up to someone behind me.

On instinct, I whip around, not knowing who it is or what threat they might hold. Max pauses a few feet away, his hands stuffed deep inside his pockets, his blond eyebrows gathered together.

For a moment, as he works to control his emotions, I want to jump to my feet and wrap him inside my arms. But I don't dare.

"I don't know who you are," he says, rocking back on his feet. "But . . . erm, you were pretty wicked at the temple."

Stop fidgeting, I want to scold him. *Look me in the eye.* It takes all I have to force those old instincts away. "Thanks."

"Is it true about the Scorpion Throne?"

"Yep."

He frowns. "Why?"

"Yes, darling," Teagan drawls, lifting her eyebrows at me. "We'd all like to know the answer to that question."

A million words come to mind as I stare at Max. Because I need to get inside Emerald Island and infiltrate the castle, somehow find the Mercurian, and finish the impossible mission our father put us on. Because if I don't, you're going to die horribly in a war.

Because I love you.

But if I tell him all that now, he'll become defensive, so I force a smile and shrug. "I always liked bossing you around. Why not an entire army?"

A muscle jumps in his jaw. "You're nothing at all like the sister I remember."

"Is that good or bad?"

"I don't know yet."

I watch him cross between the tables with Rivet in tow, unsure if I know the answer to my question either.

AFTER LUNCH, Teagan and I train outside for the last hour

before the Blood Court as Lash and Brogue watch, helping with weapon changes and pointing out things I can't see with my stance and movements. We're supposed to go light, but I train hard. In spite of Brogue's dire outlook, I feel good, and even Teagan, who's nearly as good at swordplay as my mother, gives me an impressed once-over a few times during our session.

When we're nearly done and sweat moistens my temples and trickles down my back, Teagan sheathes her sword. "Why are you doing this, Graystone?"

I shrug. "Why not?"

But my excuse falls flat, and she twists the sides of her lips up as she studies me. "It's just, you're not the type to want power, and you certainly don't relish bloodshed. So why enter the Blood Court again?"

I examine the worn pommel of my sword, wishing I could tell her everything. But where would I start? I have to win the throne so I can gather Rebels to invade Laevus castle and find a device I've never seen and don't know where it is.

More importantly, if I told her that, what would she do? Because something like that could be considered traitorous by Nicolai or Flame, and the last thing I need is more suspicion on me.

Before I can say anything, though, Flame appears, leaning against the large oak shading us, her hooded eyes following my every move.

"Want a turn?" I call out, glad for the distraction.

"No thanks, Princess. Wouldn't want to embarrass you."

My mouth parts, ready to sling an insult right back at her, but then I think better of it. Why bother? When I've beaten Riser and won the Blood Court, she'll have to eat her words anyway.

Teagan swipes her forearm over her sweaty forehead. "I think that's enough for now, darling. You good until the Blood Court?"

"Yeah." I hand my sword to Lash and wipe my sweaty palms on my pants. "I'm good."

Teagan drapes her arm around Flame, and they immediately begin to whisper and laugh as they walk toward the castle.

I gesture at the two girls. "So . . . how long has that been going on?"

Lash shakes his head. "It's a new development."

"Huh."

"So," Lash says, his playful smile fading, "what happens if you win the throne, Graystone?"

I go to shrug the question off, but his intense gaze tells me that won't work. "Can't a girl have some secrets?" I brush the hair from my forehead. "And you mean 'what happens *when* I win the throne.' Not if."

Brogue winks at me from beside Lash. "Atta girl."

I leave training and spend the rest of my time walking the castle grounds, trying to clear my head. The weight of my responsibility grows heavier with each step. So much rides on me winning the Blood Court and taking the Scorpion Throne.

Stealing a calming breath, I follow the steady trickle of fighters to the arena, pumping my hands into fists in time with my thumping heart.

I can do this. I know I can. All my Reconstruction and training was for moments just like this. I have to win.

Failure is not an option.

THIRTY-SIX

The line for the Blood Court is long, too long. Rebels swell the cramped passageway that funnels directly out to the arena, their excited taunts filling the air. The smell of cramped, sweaty bodies tightens my gut.

I feel Riser before I see him, and his gloating smile tells me he's been behind me for a while. "Graystone," he says, "your situational awareness needs some work."

I grin, pretending his taunt doesn't bother me. "How are you so sure I didn't know you were there?"

"Because," he reaches over and brushes my hair off my shoulder, "when I'm around, you act . . . different."

"Different how?"

His eyes find my lips. "Your breathing speeds up." His voice is uneven, ragged. "You watch me from the corner of your eyes." He leans in, so close I can smell his familiar scent. "Your body draws into me when I'm close . . . like right *now.*"

A horn sounds, the doors grate open, and the line begins to move.

Riser's green eye sparkles with amusement. "Are you sure you can swing a sword at me when the time comes?"

He's messing with me! "Rebel bastard," I hiss, stepping back.

"Oh, but you *like* this bastard."

He turns on his heels and lopes into the arena. I rush to catch up, cursing and trying very hard not to disqualify myself by pulling out my real dagger and lodging it in his back. He was trying to throw me off balance and mess with my concentration. And it almost worked.

Except his stormy-blue eye didn't dance with amusement. It pierced me. It begged me to . . .

Shut up, Maia, and focus on taking the bastard's throne.

But I'm not feeling it. Besides Pit Boy's coy distraction, all I can see is him fighting outside the castle. Slipping through the Rebels, a lethal figure I hardly recognize.

Focus. It has to be now.

I crack my neck and enter the arena, the sand still wet from the storm as the Rebels fan out, backs to the wall, eyes scanning the others. I find Max with Rivet and align myself with them. Who knows if they'll ally with me or try to kill me, but I need numbers to win.

Someone presses their shoulder into mine—Rhydian. He gives a quick jerk of his head, and I nod back, hiding my relief at having a skilled fighter on my other side.

Shadow Fall is coming. I can feel the sunlight ebbing like the tide, sucking all the warmth from the arena and stilling the Rebels' voices until silence reigns. I take deep breaths, my senses heightened, picking up the sweaty tang of the Rebels, the rapid breathing of Max and Rivet, the way some dig their boots into the sand in preparation.

Darkness falls, the torches whoosh to life, and my brain tingles as my fingers fill up with . . . with . . . I stare at the tiny silver button inside my palm, the device's two sides flat, like a denari.

What in Fienian hell am I supposed to do with this?

Max and Rivet face off on either side. Max holds what at first looks like a long gun, a small silver canister at the bottom. At least Rivet's weapon, a Nano-shredder, is familiar.

"What is this?" I shout to Rhydian.

But he's too busy ducking the sword of the Rebel next to him to hear me. I shrink back, heart thudding in my ears, trying not to panic as my brain whirs to understand. Some Rebels have normal, Royalist-approved weapons. Others have Hot Weapons.

Mine has to be Hot. I roll the small, unconvincing weapon inside my palm. But what do I do with it? Throw it? And how do I arm it?

Adrenaline shrinks my vision as I stare at the button, sucking in ragged breaths. A blur to my right. Before the Rebel girl running at me can run me through with her sword, Rhydian knocks me back, and she staggers past me. He smashes a fist into her face and she stumbles, giving him time to level the large metal mitt over his right hand at her torso. Something shoots from the mitt, whirring through the air.

The girl screams as the projectile hits her and boomerangs back to Rhydian's mitt. When the object stops turning, I make out a circle of blades.

A sudden wave of heat scorches my back, and I whip around to see greenish fire roaring from Max's gun. A Rebel falls to the ground, writhing in the sand and swatting at the simulated flames.

As Rebels fall left and right, my allies spread out. Growling in frustration, I do the same, my boots sinking in the sand. The others are too busy fighting to explain my weapon, so I scan the other fighters, using my momentary protection to look for a weapon I *understand* to steal.

I don't have to look far. A lanky boy with a white mohawk and ice-blue eyes behind me holds a sleek crossbow down low at his die, three red arrows lined up in a pretty row, his left arm trapped in the teeth of a long black whip.

Without a usable weapon, the ten steps I take to him seem like a hundred. He jerks his head as I latch onto the crossbow, his eyes huge. The metal is cold inside my palm, calling to me.

His face crumples in anger . . . but then, his eyes flick up and behind me, and a hand of dread squeezes my heart.

I pivot around, but too late.

The gold pyramid inside Hugo's palm splits open, spewing hundreds of red metal scorpions. They scuttle and click, making ominous plopping sounds as they drop to the sand in an angry swarm.

A hyena-like laugh spews from Hugo's lips, his black eyes wide with excitement. "This is going to hurt a bit."

In the dark recesses of my brain, something primal screams with fear as the scorpions converge on me, scrabbling over my legs, a bloody wall of pain. Their tails stab over and over, piercing my clothes, embedding splinters of fire that burrow down to my bones, injecting my marrow with lava.

Tears of pain and frustration blur my vision. *I'm dead already, just stop,* I want to plead, but the scorpions keep coming. Keep stabbing. I shrink from the pain, shrink into myself, a defeated shell, unable to move or escape.

A form appears over me as I groan. Lucy, her dark, braided hair glimmering red and orange from the torchlight, leans close.

I swipe at Lucy, but my arms are too weak from the stings. Why won't the Sim end? I try to scream as the fire inside me rages, but nothing comes out.

And then Lucy clamps her fingers over my jaw, my skin burning wherever she touches as she wrenches my head to the right.

A scream dies in my throat as I'm forced to watch Hugo dump Max to the ground beside me and smash a boot into his throat. Max's mouth gapes open, his eyes panicky-wide as he claws at Hugo's leg.

His focus rolls over me, his eyes blinking, begging me to help him. *Pleading.* Like when we were on the run in Cypher. Like when I left him, and deep, deep down he knew I wasn't coming back.

"You're killing him." I buck and flail and kick trying to get to Max, to protect the only family I have left.

Lucy kicks me in the stomach, doubling me over, but I hardly feel it as I dig and claw my way closer, screaming his name. Hugo's high-pitched laugh burrows into my ears. He swings his crossbow down, the glittery-sharp metal arrow point a hair's breadth from one of Max's wildly blinking eyes.

No. No. No! It's a headshot—

Lucy's voice washes over me. "What kind of worm can't even protect her own brother?"

My stomach heaves. The voices inside my head are screaming, ricocheting inside my skull. Forming a maddening din of chaos. Max's terrified breathing fills the air.

The arrow's not real. It will only hurt for a moment, and he'll be okay.

He'll be okay. He'll be okay. He'll be okay . . .

Hugo shoots the arrow into my brother, and every nightmare I've ever had about Max dying comes true.

THIRTY-SEVEN

I can't stop writhing and flailing against the hands gripping my body, carrying me. I arch my back and peer up, my gaze rolling off wood-beamed ceilings and scorpion walls.

Scorpions. Gods, I've never hated anything more.

The voices inside my head have quieted to a throbbing whisper. I fight whoever carries me, trying to squirm to my feet, even though a part of me knows I'm in no shape to stand.

Every time I think I'm getting better, I see Hugo release an arrow into my brother's head, and I hear his scream as if I'm right there beside him still.

Through my hazy vision I see Teagan and Brogue at my feet, each carrying a leg. I twist around to stare up at the person by my head . . . Lash. Sweat glistens from the coppery stubble on his jaw.

"Stop fighting, love," he orders. His voice is firm, cutting through the ones in my head, his eyes gentle. Russet eyebrows lift in a silent plea for compliance. "You're safe now, and so is Max. But we need to get you to your room."

But I can't stop seeing Max get shot. Can't stop the panic clenching my heart.

Get it together, Graystone.

My friends begin to talk as if I'm not hanging from their arms, their agitated voices breaking through my panic. Hugo and Lucy went too far. Surely Flame will punish them this time. Surely they'll be banned from the Blood Courts—

My friends dump me onto my bed.

Shivering, I roll to my side, a horrible ache spreading through me. "Max?" They said he was fine, but they could be wrong. Or I could have misheard. "Brogue, check on him. Please?"

Brogue hesitates before nodding and striding out the door.

"He's fine, darling." Teagan crawls onto the bed, folding her long limbs up beside me.

"But it was . . . It was a headshot."

Lash fills up the other side of the bed, his shoulder warm against my back. "He's tough, love. Like you."

"He means everything to me. I can't . . . I can't lose him." I bite the inside of my cheek to keep my voice from breaking. "No one said there would be Hot Weapons in the court."

"That was new."

"They're trying to make me fail."

Teagan lays her cheek on the duvet, inches from my face. "That's why you have to be strong." Her eyes glimmer, but her voice is hard. "They're trying to break you; don't let them. If they knock you down five times, rise up six. Mourn the fall after you've risen and stomped them to ash."

"You don't understand. I *needed* to win today."

Tears threaten to fall, and I gouge my knuckles into my eyes.

I can't do this. How could my father have even considered

I was strong enough to find a weapon the emperor would kill to destroy?

Once again, I'm failing. I can't do it. It's too much.

Teagan reaches over and squeezes my arm. "Darling, nothing is worth your tears, least of all the Scorpion Throne. So why do you cry for it?"

I release a ragged breath, studying Teagan the way I once did Riser. He had begged me to trust him, and I didn't. Look how that turned out.

I have to trust someone.

I exhale. "When I was younger, before I was sent to prison, my father implanted me with . . . well, a key of sorts. It's supposed to unlock the Mercurian, a weapon *supposedly* hidden on Emerald Island . . . a weapon that can also stop the asteroid."

Silence. Lash sits up behind me, but Teagan just stares at me as if I claimed the earth was square.

I push up onto my elbows. "Max holds the map to the Mercurian, but so far Nicolai can't figure out how to make it work, and he refuses to even consider sending Rebels back to the Island to find it." I wipe my nose on my forearm, dropping my voice to a whisper. "But that's because he doesn't know there's a way inside Laevus Castle."

A knowing look comes over Teagan. "And if you win the throne, you can gather Rebels to help you sneak inside and find the device."

I nod.

"Why not join the soldiers and fight in the battle? If they make it to the castle, you can look for it."

I sigh. "They won't make it that far. And I don't trust Nicolai. He can never get control of the Mercurian. Never."

Lash blinks at me. "Wait, I'm still stuck on the part where the emperor knew about the device the whole time."

I must be feeling a tiny bit better because I snort. "Yeah,

and he's done everything in his power to destroy it. But it's hidden . . . for now."

His gaze rolls to the heavy paneled ceiling.

"Checking with the gods?"

"Love, they agree. The emperor is an asshole."

Thumps boom in the hallway as Rebels celebrate the Blood Court winner, hooting and roughhousing, reminding me of how badly I failed. I slide to the floor and pad to the broken window, where the remnants of Shadow Fall bathe the world in greenish-silver mist. A cool, salty breeze blows back my hair.

"Could you maybe talk to Flame," I say over my shoulder, "persuade her to lend me some men?"

Teagan's boots lightly strike the floor as she joins me. She smells of expensive flowers—roses and gardenias. "I'll approach her tonight at the dance. I'll make her listen."

Lash chuckles. "I bet you will, Aster."

"If she happens to say no even to *you*," I say, giving Teagan a dubious look, "then I'll need someone to help me train for the next Blood Court."

As they both agree, an ember of hope sparks inside my chest, chasing away some of the darkness that's weighed me down. We stare out across the sea, Pandora's shadow relinquishing its grasp over the world, sunlight streaking across the sky and cresting the jagged waves.

I lean through the opening, the fresh breeze and briny ocean scent calling to me.

Now that I have a sort-of plan and a sort-of team, I need to get out, do something. I need to forget the dank clamminess of the castle. I need to forget the sound of my jagged screams in the arena.

But first I need to see my brother.

THIRTY-EIGHT

After reassuring Lash and Teagan that the simulated scorpion stings had no lasting effects, I search the castle for Max. The mess hall is closed, and he's not in his room. Eventually someone tells me there's a chamber near the indoor arena where fighters unwind after the Blood Court.

It's actually an old saloon lacking windows, with a tall wooden counter and sleek metal barstools. A haze of turquoise smoke wafts through the shadows, a potpourri of herbs and chemicals and spices. Wild music drifts from speakers in the corners, purple and yellow lights pulsing over the crowd.

Although I'm looking for Max, part of me begs to see Lucy or Hugo. Either would slake the rage I feel from the Blood Court. Both would be better, albeit trickier and with more risks. But a quick search tells me they're not here.

Hopefully that means Flame has them on their knees for what they did.

Max is easy to find; his golden hair is like a beacon amidst a hundred darker heads. Gone is the terrified boy who pleaded with me to save him. He's in the middle of a cadre of Rebels, entertaining them with his usual juvenile jokes.

Rivet sits on the stool beside him, her glorious mahogany mane wrangled into a thick, ropy braid that falls to her lower back.

One black, dusty, knee-high boot is propped on the counter. Gods, if only I had been that cool at her age.

Brogue appears from the crowd, scowling. "I've already given your brother my peace. I'll let you deal with it."

He storms away before I can ask what he's talking about, and my gaze flits to the mottled bronze cup in front of Max. As soon as he spots me, he tries to hide the drink, nudging it toward another Rebel, but I've already seen the churning amber liquid inside.

I shove past thick, muscled shoulders and plant my feet in front of him. "Tell me that's not yours, Max."

The others go quiet. Rivet lifts a pierced red eyebrow.

Max tries to shake me off with a laugh. "What, you don't like—?"

"No. No jokes. I'm not our parents. You can't just say something funny and get away with doing whatever you want."

"That's right." His smile is gone. "You're not our parents —because father's dead, and mother's a Royalist dandy-whoring bitch who left us to die for the emperor. And that Twitcher you sent to check on me, whoever he is, he's not our parents either."

"His name is Brogue," I say, frowning at Max's crass Rebel talk.

I have to remind myself that he's been a Rebel for years. This is all he knows. *Don't embarrass him. Not in front of his friends.*

But then Rivet mutters something beneath her breath, her

sharp green eyes flitting over me in a quiet challenge, and Max reaches for the cup full of Amberblood—

I knock the goblet from his hand. The cup clangs against the barstool and then spins across the floor. I know I shouldn't have. I'm embarrassing him.

But I can't shake the horror from earlier when I thought he might die, and I'll be damned if I let him die from that slow poison.

The slick, oily amber liquid drips down his chin and spreads over his red doublet, the nanites scurrying in every direction with a barely-audible hiss. He looks down at it for a moment, his jaw tight. How can he not see that it's dangerous?

With a steely scowl, Rivet turns to the girl behind the counter with pupils in the shape of scorpions. "Another, please."

The girl looks to me. I flash her a smile-that-isn't-a-smile. *Do it and die.* Apparently deciding I'm the bigger threat, she ignores Rivet and goes back to wiping down the dingy counter.

I pin Rivet with my glare. Beneath her iron façade, something hesitates, a whisper of blush coloring the smattering of freckles over her pale cheeks. Satisfied she understands my silent message, I do a full circle, making eye contact with every Rebel even close. "This is Max, my brother. He gets water. Anything else, I'll find you and I'll gut you, *slowly*."

Max's face has turned a dark shade of red, even his ears, and angry tears wet his eyelashes. "You're an asshole."

I lean in and kiss his hot cheek. "I love you too."

On the way out, Rivet grabs my arm. I whip around, prepared for an argument.

She throws up her hands. "Whoa, Graystone. I'm not here to fight. I just . . . I want you to know I don't want Max drinking that poison either."

"Then why not defend my decision?"

"Because it's not yours to make. It's his."

I frown. "But he's too young to know—"

"Look, he's a lot of things—an idiot most of the time, actually—but when it matters, when it counts, he makes the right decision. You can't live years of your life on the streets of Cypher dodging Centurions and not develop a survival instinct."

Her words are like a kick to the stomach, reminding me what happened after I left. "Okay. I'll try. Good enough for you?"

"Yeah. And one more thing. Max is fifteen, not the little kid from your past. Stop treating him like a child. And give him some space. He wants to have a relationship with you, just on his own terms."

She slips through the crowd without a goodbye, nudging a few interested Rebels back with a sharp elbow. *Well, she's a strong-willed one.* Despite our history thus far, I feel a newfound respect for Rivet. If anyone can keep Max out of trouble, it's her.

I'm almost to the underground stairway when the hairs on the back of my neck stand up. Someone is following me.

The breath freezes in my lungs as I grab my dagger and turn, ready for confrontation.

THIRTY-NINE

Riser steps from the shadows of the dark hallway. "Easy, there. The Blood Court's over."

"Sure about that?" Without a word, I turn and begin to walk.

"Where are you going?"

"Out."

"Does Nicolai know?"

I chuckle. "No. Are you going to tell on me?"

"No, I'm going to *chaperone* you."

I bristle at the amusement in his voice. "No, thanks."

"Wait, is that . . . manners I hear coming from your lips?" The sharp planes of his face soften as he smiles.

I ignore the flirty tone of his voice, the invisible butterflies that swell my belly with every second he beams at me, determined not to fall for it *again*. "I don't need protection."

"Protection? No, no. I'm simply going to make sure you don't get caught and give up the entire Fienian army."

"Noble of you."

"I try, Graystone."

We slide into a comfortable routine of sarcasm, poking

lightly at each other with words as we wind through the mess of hallways, tracing our steps from the other day, brushing past Rebels with buckets and mops, some carrying weapons, some loaded down with firewood for the kitchens. The noises fade as we enter the last stairwell that will take us to the caves.

By the time I sling my leg over my Swifter, our banter has faded into silence.

It's hard to pretend the Blood Court didn't just happen. That I wasn't about to battle him for his crown.

We don't do the music this time, but I don't mind. The sea purrs a beautiful melody, serenaded by screeching gulls and breaking waves. Sea spray wets my cheeks and creates fleeting rainbows. My hair slaps back and forth in the wind.

Except for the influx of storms, Pandora hasn't affected the north as bad as the south, and I marvel at the pristine beauty of the steel-gray cliffs and bone-white sands bordered with thick clumps of sea rush. We stay in the cliff's shadow, skimming the white, frothy line of surf.

Once we're free of the rocky cliffs and on the grassy hills south of Bloodwyn, I lean forward and open my Swifter up, chest tingling with pleasure as the sleek machine warms and growls beneath me. The sandy hills are spotted with the lavender blooms of tree mallow, yellow-and-white sand pansies peeking from the thin wisps of grass.

We pass by abandoned towns, one after the other. Some are still inhabitable, like the meandering city that stretches across the hills, the faded orange roofs bright against the grassy slopes, green from all the rain. But most have been damaged beyond repair, roofs torn off presumably by storms, a few even burned to ash.

As we slow down to skirt the rim of a giant crater, Riser explains a small meteor the size of a Swifter hit this area a few weeks ago, leveling the town and surrounding houses. More broken up rocks hit the ocean, sending a tidal wave that decimated some of the lower elevation cities farther east.

But I don't want to think about Her right now, so I avert my gaze from the destruction and glance at Pit Boy. His eyes are hidden behind dark leather goggles, the sharp red tailcoat he wears whipping behind him.

A dark grin spreads across his face as he flicks his gaze to me. "That all you got?"

I dart in front of him, gliding down a rocky hill and skimming an algae-filmed pond. On the left side of the hill, a town of quaint, tile-roofed houses spreads out, fenced in by a crumbling brick barricade.

This was a fishing village, and the old markets remain. There's a town square with a dried-out fountain of a whale, part of its tail broken off. Whitewashed buildings with open windows make up the bulk of the residences.

Other than a few mangy, skeletal dogs, the town is empty.

Riser catches up to me near the market, and we quietly glide through the old stalls. Besides the glass displays where hundreds of types of iced fish used to be presented, we pass flower shops with dead flowers still on display, and even a Reformation-approved toy shop with wooden dolls carved in the image of Centurions and Gold ladies of the court.

Riser slows beside me, his eyes flicking over everything. "I can't believe places like this existed once. There were so many . . . things."

His words remind me what his new, regal image almost made me forget: the only civilization Riser has ever known is the pit. Nearly every experience in this world is new to him. I remember the way he stared at the stars the day we escaped.

He's come so far from the confused, ignorant boy from the pit, and yet part of that savageness remains. He still refuses to sit with his back to the door. Still startles at small noises and watches everything.

Just like he's watching me right now. I blush under his gaze. His goggles are off, his Swifter inches from mine. A breeze ruffles his hair. In the waning afternoon light, both eyes are unnaturally bright, emerald and topaz gemstones set deep in moonstone flesh.

"You kept your throne, I take it?" I ask, careful to keep the disappointment from my voice.

His knee brushes mine as he glides closer. "Indeed." A muscle cords in his neck. "I thought I would have to fight you for it, but then I heard you screaming and saw Aster and Lash carrying you off the court."

"I thought . . ." My hands tighten over the cool silver handlebars. "The Redgraves put an arrow to Max's eye and loosed it." A bitter laugh slips from my lips. "You must have been relieved."

"I was. I thought I was going to have to hurt you, and for whatever reason, that bothered me." A long pause stretches out. "Graystone, why are you so intent on taking my throne?" He searches my face, a frown trembling his lips. "Do you truly think I'm not deserving of it?"

My throat tightens at the hint of hurt in his voice. "Riser, I . . ." I swallow down the truth. As much as I want to trust him, I have no idea what Nicolai did to Riser when he was reconstructed the second time. "It's complicated."

"Please don't enter again."

I stop my Swifter. We're at the end of the market, the last two booths a café and an herbal shop that still retains a sharp, sage aroma. Dried laurel and lemon grass hang just above my head. Rain clouds have brought dusk early, spitting sideways rain onto the streets and making a soft drumming patter on the metal pavilion roof.

"Are you afraid, Prince?"

Ahead of me, he turns around, guiding his machine forward until we're face-to-face, our knees touching. "When I heard your screams, everything else fell away. There was no sound but you. And every scream ran me through, the pain as raw and real as if I'd been pierced with a sword through the gut."

My focus shrinks to the sound of the rain, the feel of my Swifter rumbling beneath my legs, and his sharp gaze poring over me, demanding answers. I open my mouth, but my throat closes over any words I might have spoken.

"Don't enter," he says again, this time a command. Somehow he inches closer without seeming to move, his knee sliding between the Swifter and my thigh, pressing into the tender area there. "Trust that I can lead us. That I am worthy of the throne. That I can win against the emperor."

The rain has become a downpour, his knee a lightning bolt of white-hot energy. For half a heartbeat, I imagine pushing into him, feeling his hard body flush against me, his mouth hot against my lips, my hands twining in his hair.

For a crazy moment, I imagine the world isn't ending.

His eyebrows gather together above beautiful unblinking eyes as he pierces me with his intense gaze. "I will kill the emperor, Graystone. I will defeat his army, kill the False Prince, and bring his corrupt court to its knees. And then I'll claim the birthright my mother could never give me." He reaches out his hand. "Stand with me, not against me."

"Believe me, if I had a choice, I wouldn't want the throne."

"Is this about the device you keep talking about?"

I suck in my bottom lip. "What if it does exist? Don't we have an obligation to find it?"

"The only obligation we have is to wipe the Royalists from the earth. After that, we'll find our way to the caves beneath the mountains where the Silvers hide. The Redgraves know where they are, and they have supplies to last for hundreds of years. And when the smoke clears, the emperor and his court will be gone and we can rebuild into what our world should be."

I chew my lip to keep from screaming at him for listening to Lucy. She saves his life and now she's trustworthy?

"What if I found that device, but it was also a weapon? Would you use it to destroy the asteroid, or the emperor?"

"If it was one or the other?" He shoves a hand through his hair. "We can survive the asteroid. But we won't survive the emperor. If I had to choose, I would destroy the empire."

"And let millions of people perish?"

"You don't understand, do you? I have to kill my father. I have to avenge my mother. I see her in my nightmares, see them . . . see them tearing her to pieces. Her screams fill my head. I . . . never mind."

"Riser, killing the emperor and taking his throne won't make the nightmares go away."

His jaw tightens. "We'll see, won't we?"

My gut clenches. Was Riser always this filled with rage and somehow I missed it? Or maybe being inside his mother's childhood home, surrounded by her things, dredged up the past.

Either way, Riser won't help me. But, more importantly, I can't trust him.

My mouth goes dry as I realize perhaps he's more like his father than he knows. As soon as the thought enters my mind, I force it out.

Riser is nothing like the emperor. Not yet, at least. But if Flame and Nicolai and the Redgraves continue to influence him . . .

Horses whinny in the distance. Both of our heads whip in the direction of the noise as the sound of a carriage clattering down the pocked street fills the air.

We have just enough time to get on our Swifters and pull into the toy shop, wood shavings bursting into flame beneath our machines, before a shiny black carriage pulls in front of a large domed building down the alley.

"Dandies," Riser spits, his voice dripping rancor as he reaches for whatever horrible weapon is stashed inside his waistcoat.

As I glance over the carriage again, a shiver of recognition passes over me, and I freeze. The carriage doesn't belong to *just-dandies*, but to one of the most important Royalists in this war.

Prince Caspian Laevus.

"Let's get back," I say, hoping Riser doesn't notice how quick the words come out.

But Riser barely seems to hear me, his gaze locked onto the carriage. "I need to blow off some steam first."

My heart slams into my throat. I grab his arm, ignoring the way his muscles twitch beneath my fingertips. "I don't want to fight anymore today, Riser," I say. "*Please.*"

Sighing, he turns to go. There's no time to question Caspian's presence before we're slinking out the back, draped low over our machines. I can tell from Riser's stiff body, the way he continues to glance back, that he'd rather be fighting than fleeing. I shudder, knowing if he saw who was inside that carriage, his actions would have been much different.

We slip away unnoticed. Luckily the air is free from drones, and we're able to make it back to the cliffs quickly.

But one question burns at me. What is the prince doing in this tiny, abandoned seaside town? I turn the mystery over and over in my mind, searching for a way to use it to my advantage.

If the Fienians have taught me anything, it's that information can be the most effective weapon of all.

FORTY

More Rebel garments await me in my room, along with Lash and Teagan reclining on my bed. I tell them about the Royal carriage as I dress, ignoring the interested look from Lash as his gaze roves my body.

"*The* Prince Caspian Laevus?" Lash rests his head in Teagan's lap and wags a dubious eyebrow at me. "What, was he tired of veal and mutton and decided to go for a bit of pickled herring?"

Rolling my eyes, I slip on a black, knee-high leather boot with a gleaming gold buckle. "I'm only telling you what I saw."

"No, no," Teagan says, her long, magenta fingernails stroking the gold-red stubble along his jaw. "Some of those towns used to cater to Golds from prominent houses."

She jumps from the bed and disappears out the door. A few minutes later, she reappears with a yellowed map in hand. "Show me where you were when you saw the carriage."

We plop down on the bed beside Lash, and Teagan spreads the map out, the papers crinkling. I find Bloodwyn on the map and trace my finger along the cliffs, turning inland and marking a trail over several towns.

"There was, um," I muse aloud, frowning as I press my finger over hills, "a town around here hit by debris a few months ago."

Teagan clicks her tongue as she studies the map. Then she moves my finger a few inches south. "That's where the meteor hit."

Sucking in my lip, I push my finger a half-inch to the right to rest on the icon of a fish. "There."

"Are you sure?" Teagan asks.

"Yes. That's the town."

"Hm. I heard rumors about Rowell. There were . . ." She waves her hand as she tries to remember, "black market Sim boutiques that operated there. They ran specialized Sims for wealthy Golds and courtiers."

"Right," Lash says. "A black market Sim in a tiny fishing village."

Teagan grins at Lash. "And that's exactly why they did. It was the perfect place to hide an outlawed Sim."

"Even if that were true, surely the prince would have access to a Sim on the Island, where he could—"

"No," I interrupt, my heart racing. "The Sim on the Island doesn't work."

"Huh." Lash sits ups, his eyebrows meeting above suddenly interested eyes. "If the Crown Prince really is venturing outside the protection of the Island, that means he's vulnerable and we can grab him."

"No."

"No?" Lash says.

"No." I shake my head. "No one touches the prince."

Lash cuts a curious glance back at Teagan. "Why not?"

"We take him hostage, then what? The emperor would let Caspian die before he negotiated with Fienians. So, we torture him? Hang him? What does Flame think that will accomplish, except turn any potential allies against us?"

Lash grins at me.

"What?"

"So you're pretty *and* smart."

"Shut up, Lash!" Teagan and I groan.

"Wait." Lash rubs a finger over his jaw. "You addressed the prince by his first name."

Teagan smacks the side of his head. "Aw, pretty and smart."

"Ow." He rubs his head with dramatic flair. "So . . . That's why you ignored the order to kill him on the Island?"

"We were, um . . . ." I search for the words to explain *us*. "We were matched, at least based on our DNA mapping. He was nice, kind, even."

"Uh, huh," Lash says, his mouth parted.

"But then the emperor labeled my father a traitor and executed him, and here we are."

"Yes, here we are." Lash wears a crooked grin. "Tell me, Graystone. How does one manage to juggle two princes? I imagine it's—"

"Lash!" Teagan and I both yell, pelting him with the plethora of fancy red pillows strewn over my bed.

He ducks beneath the avalanche of red, covering his head with his hands. "Okay, okay! Enough, girls. You'll get me all excited."

I cross my arms over my chest. "Lash, I'm being serious. I have a plan." I wait until I have both Teagan's and Lash's attention to continue. "We hack into the Sim, I talk Caspian into sneaking us into Laevus Castle, and we find the Mercurian."

They're staring at me as if I've lost my mind. Maybe I have. But with Caspian to get us inside the castle, we won't need a crew, which means I don't have to fight Riser in the Blood Court.

Lash's shoulders slump as he turns to Teagan. "She's serious, isn't she?"

"Told you not to underestimate her." Teagan jumps up from the bed. "We'll need to find a way to access those Sims and see how often Caspian uses them so we can be ready the next time he visits. We need a house close by to set up the Sim, a Sim operator capable of patching you in, and—"

"Aster, do you actually think this could work?" Lash demands. "I've made loads of idiotic decisions in my lifetime, too many to count, really, but this . . . this will not be one of them. I'm rash, not suicidal."

"Lash, another word and I'll take your panties and gag you with them."

"Look," I say, "I wouldn't ask you to do this if I thought it wouldn't work. Prince Caspian wants to stop Pandora as much as I do. He just needs a little convincing that we're not trying to use it as a weapon against his people . . . and that I'm not tricking him . . . *again*."

"Again?"

"Well, twice now, actually. I mean, the first time was unintentional, there was a bombing . . . and the second time I had to escape"—Lash's skeptical look makes me change direction—"But the important thing to remember is that we were matched. Every time we're together, there's this . . . I don't know. This feeling, like nothing else exists but us. I think it's in his DNA to *want* to trust me, no matter how many times I've hurt him."

"Huh." Lash slides off the bed. "Good luck with that."

Teagan and I roll our eyes. "Lash!"

He makes it all the way to the door before he stops, shaking his head. "Fine! I'll help you two insert your pretty heads into a Royalist noose. But don't say I didn't warn you."

I cross the floor and give his stubbly cheek a kiss. "Thank you."

Teagan joins me on the other side, although she has to bend down a bit. She leans in for a kiss—and proceeds to lick the side of his cheek. "That's my brave *little Lash.*"

Lash wipes his cheek with the edge of his cuff. "By the gods, you two will be the death of me."

The grin on Teagan's face dies. "Don't say that, Lash. Why would you even tempt the gods?"

"It was a joke, Aster. Loosen your corset. The gods assured me I might come out of this alive—but you two are screwed."

After that, I finish getting ready in silence. I'm confident this new plan makes the most sense, especially after the Blood Court today. But I also know that if one element of the plan goes wrong, the stakes aren't losing face in front of a bunch of Rebels.

If everything doesn't work perfectly, all three of us are dead.

FORTY-ONE

We discuss the details of my plan on the way to dinner. Even though Lash swears he can get me into Caspian's Sim, Teagan insists we ask someone more experienced to help. I argue, because the last thing I want to do is put my trust in another Rebel—and if it got out we were sitting on this kind of information, we would all be labeled traitors—but Teagan insists. She knows the perfect person, too. But I don't find out who until we enter the great hall for dinner, and Teagan points a finger toward the middle of the room.

Max stands on top of a table beside Rivet, half-drunk already by the looks of it, his gold locks teased into a wild mess around his head, stomping to whatever Fienian ballad the others sing. Each time the word rebellatis comes up in the song, Max and Rivet swill down a thimbleful of golden brown liquid.

"That's Rivet," Teagan elaborates. "Besides Flame, she's the best Sim manipulator there is."

I cross my arms over my chest. "No way. She's impulsive and unpredictable, and she'll get us killed."

"You say that like we have a choice."

"Don't we?"

"If you count using Lash, then sure. But, darling, do you really want Lash mucking around inside your head?"

I sigh, rubbing a hand over my temple. "Well, when you put it *that* way."

We stare at Max and Rivet, frowning as they wrestle on the tabletop, knocking plates and goblets to the ground.

"I'll talk to Rivet tonight at the dance," Teagan says. "You know we have to include Ma—"

"No. Out of the question."

The Rebels at Max's table cheer as he traps Rivet in a bear hug. With a wild grin, she drops low and flips, sending Max spilling from the table in an avalanche of plates. He jumps to his feet, covered in slop, and bows to more applause.

"I mean, just look at him," I say. "He's never taken anything seriously his entire life."

"Graystone," Teagan says, dabbing a napkin over her red lips that somehow never smear, "I've been a Rebel for a long time. Don't take this the wrong way, but I've watched Max since he got here. He puts on a good show, but behind his humorous exterior is a smart, brave kid."

Even though she didn't mean it as a slight, her words sting. I don't know my brother, they imply. I was the one who taught him how to say his letters, button his shirt, and tie his shoes. I was the one who held him every night after my mother left. I was the one who carried him from our bed when the Centurions came and murdered our father.

Not the Rebels. Not Nicolai. Not Rivet. Me.

"I didn't mean to—"

"It's okay," I lie.

"Of course it's not okay, darling. Your feelings are written all over your face." Teagan pushes her plate of mush away and leans in. "I can't imagine how hard this is for you, seeing

Max after all these years. But know this. Even after all the other young recruits did the name change, he refused. Do you know why?"

I chew my lip, shaking my head.

"When he was twelve I asked him, and he told me that he was afraid if he ever saw you again, you wouldn't recognize him. But if he kept his real name, you might."

I look away so she won't see the pain in my eyes. "Thanks."

"Of course. Now, ready for the party tonight?"

When I look back to answer, I catch Teagan's attention on the high table where Riser, Nicolai, and Flame dine. Flame is mid-conversation with Lucy, but that doesn't stop her from letting her gaze wander to Teagan, a shy, un-Flame-like smile twitching her lips.

I bite back my grin. "You still going to mention the Mercurian to Flame tonight? You don't have to now that—"

"Yes," Teagan murmurs from the corner of her mouth, her eyes still on Flame. "Might as well plant the idea, just in case."

Lash and I share a knowing look.

"Right," I say.

Lash grins. "Just in *case*."

We leave the mess hall and make our way to the party. Music pounds through the castle, rattling the teardrop crystals on the chandelier swaying above our heads as we climb the last set of stairs to the ballroom. Fienians mill about the wrought-iron stairs, dripping bright jewelry and stylish daggers and holding cups swirling with glowing liquid. Two girls with matching red mohawks are locked in an embrace.

I must watch them longer than polite as we pass because one of the girls breaks off their kiss to smile at me, her eyes illuminated like the liquid in her cup.

"Stop staring!" Teagan yells into my ear over the music.

"I'm staring at their drinks," I protest, even though part of me is curious about other things.

I've never seen two women kiss, but I've also never really seen that level of passion. My father never touched my mother like that. At least, not in front of us.

Riser comes to mind, despite every effort to block him. Both times we kissed, it was brief, raw, as if our bodies were trying to get used to the other.

But those two girls did it . . . differently, somehow. Softer, more tenderly. Like their bodies were in tune. Like they had *time*.

Time to explore the other person, discover. Time I don't have. An ache opens inside me, a deep, nagging desire to have that intimacy with another person.

As soon as the heavy iron doors to the ballroom open and we step inside, my mouth falls open. Lumins similar to the glowing device Nicolai used to show me our history flit around like butterflies, spewing jewels of light in sparkling magentas and blues and pinks that dance over the crowd and gleam across the bone-white marble floor. The domed ceiling shimmers with images of sunsets from around the world, making the room feel huge.

An enormous stone balcony overlooks the sea, gossamer red drapes separating the balcony from the ballroom blowing idly in the sea breeze, but it's the stage I can't rip my gaze from. Five Rebels dance together, clutching strange instruments I've never seen before, their faces red and shiny with sweat. When the sounds blend together, they create an other-worldly melody similar to the music Riser introduced me to on the Swifter. The beat swirls through my chest and sinks low into my pelvis, and without a thought, I sway my hips.

Beyond the dance floor, plush chairs are grouped around tables. A tall girl with long pink hair serves the luminous drinks, her eyes so bright I can see them all the way over here. She places a goblet brimming with sparkly gold liquid onto a silver platter with three other full goblets.

My eyes go wide as the platter suddenly lifts into the air, makes a soft whirring noise, and then glides a slow path through the room. The platter doesn't get very far before Rebels take all the drinks, and it returns to the bright-eyed girl for more.

Lash grabs a goblet from the tray, and then we find seats by the balcony. I sink into my chair, the breeze soft and cool on my skin. Lash offers his cup to me.

"Moonblood," he says with a devilish grin that tells me all I need to know about his offering.

Teagan clicks her tongue. "Remember, Lash, we have a mission tomorrow."

But she's hardly looking at us, her gaze drifting to Flame with a clump of Rebels near the balcony.

"Go talk to her!"

Teagan runs a finger over the sharp line of her collarbone, toying with her pearls. "It's not the right time."

Lash opens his mouth as if he's about to tease her but pauses. I meet her gaze, and I suddenly understand her hesitation.

I touch her fine-boned shoulder. "Are you thinking about O?"

A frown trembles across her lips. "How can I even think about someone else when she's hardly been gone a week?"

"These aren't normal times, Teagan. We live knowing most of us won't survive the week, so for us, a day *is* practically a lifetime. Besides, being happy is a slap in the face of the emperor. So, go."

She swallows, craning her long neck back at Flame before pinning Lash with a stern look. "Be good, Lash-y boy, and keep an eye on her."

As soon as Teagan's gone, Lash offers me the drink again.

Shaking my head, I stand, the music calling to me. Teagan has already disappeared somewhere in the crowd. I do the same, drawing near the Rebels dancing, the ceiling images changing to angry, steel-gray thunderclouds above my head. Bright pulses of lightning flash across the tangled, sweat-glistened bodies.

I'm halfway through the crowd when I spot Riser. He's near the stage, seemingly transfixed on the music, the only one standing still in a sea of people vibrating with the beat. I smile, remembering the day he stood in the garden with the peonies after we fled my house, the stupid, boyish smile like the one he wears now.

Riser laughs at something, and I follow his gaze to a girl dancing beside him, the storm clouds above painting her dark hair and skin a light, enchanting blue. Lucy.

Riser and Lucy notice me at the same time. A small frown twitches his lips, our eyes lock together, and for a heartbeat, something sparks between us.

But then Lucy leans into his ear to whisper something, and I turn on my heels, slipping through the dancing Rebels.

I clench my jaw, fighting back the urge to turn around and smack the grin off Lucy's smug face. If Riser wants to get chummy with her, fine. Let her grind her pasty body all over him. I storm through the crowd and run into Lash and some blonde, doe-eyed girl. His irises radiate with Moonblood, and he flashes me a sloppy grin.

I grab one of the goblets, iridescent drops spilling over my fingers, and gulp the contents before I can change my mind. My throat tingles, cold and hot, but I finish the entire cup.

"I don't feel anything," I say, holding out my goblet. "This stuff is . . ."

My words fade away as a loose, falling feeling spills down my middle and floods all the way to my toes. The world slows. I see Lash, his lips moving slowly, so slowly.

"Too much." The words tumble from his lips.

"Too much?" I say, my voice echoing in my ears. "I want more."

I already know I'm in trouble, that I'm no longer in control, but I don't care. I touch Lash's shoulder. It's warm, hard. Doe-eyed girl disappears. Lash is grinning at me. His lips . . . I want to kiss them.

When did he get so beautiful? His skin is moonbeams. His eyes are stars.

My body sways with love.

A laugh ripples from my throat.

Lash smiles at me, and the music wraps around us, and I lean my head on his chest, and he presses his hands into my back, the warmth pooling in my belly and spilling down my legs. The leather of his vest caresses my cheek. We both wobble as I nuzzle my face into his chest, chuckling as our bodies meld and sway together.

I've never felt this wonderful in my life. Everything is going to be okay. I can let go. I'm floating. My body empty yet full. The music speeds up, and my heartbeat aligns with the tempo. I run my fingers through Lash's thick hair, and he presses his head into my hands, like a cat. Makes a purring noise.

We've somehow made our way to the corner of the room, and I can see the ocean unfurling beyond the balcony.

Lash follows my gaze. "Do you want to go swimming?"

"In my clothes?"

"No, silly. Not in your clothes." Lash tweaks my nose, a playful smile dancing across his lips, but his eyes hold a burning question. "We could forget our pain for a night. Enjoy life. Be free."

Free. Through the writhing bodies, I see Teagan and Flame near the doors, deep in conversation. Good. Everyone deserves love.

Love. I love everything. The ocean. The instruments making this amazing music. The supple leather clinging to my legs. Lash. Teagan. Max. Where is Max? I spin around, calling his name.

"Whoa!" Lash grabs my elbow, pulling me upright. How did I fall? The room spins, a hurricane of black and electric blue.

"Max!"

Lash turns me to face him. "Easy, Graystone. You took too much, and now you're having a bad trip."

I rip from his grasp. Where is Max? I'm supposed to protect him from something, and I've been having fun instead. How could I forget?

There. In the crowd. Surrounded by people. Was that a weapon? "Max!"

I'm still calling his name as I dart into the crowd. My legs wobble and my head spins, my stomach churning. I reach out, but there's nothing to grab and I crumple to the floor.

A blazing light shines down. The music stops. I look up at the thing the others are staring at. The Rift screen flashes. A woman materializes as I watch. Silver wig. Black top hat. Cruel red lips.

Not real. Not real. Not real.

The Archduchess sneers as she slowly peels first her arms, then her legs, and finally her head from the screen and stalks toward me. "I told you I would find you, maggot."

FORTY-TWO

Someone grabs me, wrenching me from my hallucinations. The Archduchess is gone. I try to find a face through my blurry vision, but I can't focus. I go weightless as the person scoops me from the floor and carries me. I fight, squirming and kicking.

"Stop," the male voice orders.

"Let me go," I say.

Leaning my face into the neck of my captor, I recognize his leather and soap scent. His muscles tense as I reach into the open collar of his tunic and feel the skin of his chest. My fingertips trail along the faint, raised scars the Reconstructor couldn't erase.

"Riser?" My panic fades away. Everything fades away.

"Shh." Riser's voice is soft, gentle. "I'm taking you outside where you can breathe."

"Max."

"Safe."

Up and down. Boot steps on stairs.

"Where . . . are we?"

"Roof."

Cool air caresses my face, drying the sweat clinging to my flesh. I anchor myself to the cloudless sky above. To the stars that wink down at me. Stars like eyes. Like souls. "That was a . . . a hallucination, wasn't it?"

"Yes and no." Amusement warms his voice. "You saw the Archduchess, just on a Rift screen. The giant goblet of Moonblood you swilled made you think she was here."

Embarrassment stings my cheeks. "Down, please."

He cocks an eyebrow.

"Please."

My feet land quietly on the graveled roof. I look up at Riser, studying his features in an effort to take my mind off the Archduchess. His mismatched eyes—one bright like the sun, the other dark like night. The sharp edge of his peaked hairline, the midnight-black a striking contrast against his ivory flesh.

"Just breathe," Riser commands, and I realize my breath is coming out hard and fast.

The world spins. I throw out a hand, Riser's fingers sliding around my waist as he steadies me. I shiver beneath his fingertips, warmth spreading to my middle.

"Why the roof?"

"It's quiet up here. Safe."

The stars. Did he remember? His hand is still on my waist. Part of my sheer tunic has pulled free of my pants, and his thumb slips beneath, making a slow circle over my bare flesh. My mouth parts at the sensation.

"Safe?"

"Yes. Safe." His thumb presses. "And private. So now I get to ask you some questions."

"Questions?"

"You know. A sentence worded to elicit information."

"Right. Ask me anything."

"Anything?" He leans in, so close I can feel his breath on

my cheeks. "Why did the sight of you with Lash infuriate me? Why did seeing you in a puddle on the floor fill me with terror, when nothing scares me?" His eyes hold mine. "Why do I have this overwhelming feeling that we know each other? That—that I care about you?"

So many words, and yet no way to make him understand. At least, not right now, not when my brain is jumbled into sensations and colors and stars and everything *but* words. I don't want to talk. I want more of him touching me. More of him and this feeling. I want, for once, to stop thinking rationally and just do what feels good.

The realization is like the answer to a puzzle.

I want him.

The pad of his thumb flicks below the waist of my pants, and I release a breath, leaning into him.

"No talking," I order, my lips brushing his.

His hands stiffen around my waist, but he pulls back slightly. "You're twisted on Moonblood."

"No." I flick my tongue over his parted lips. "Talking."

He groans and tries to retreat, hands holding my hips in place, but I capture his bottom lip between my teeth. I want to feel what the two girls on the stairs felt. I want to be lost in something.

In Pit Boy.

A deep growl rises in his throat, his fingertips pressing into my waist, pleading. Slowly, I free his lip and slip my tongue into his mouth. He tastes salty and sweet.

Like the ocean.

With a heavy sigh, he pulls away. "Not until the Moonblood is out of your system."

I grunt and try to kiss him again, but he holds me in place, his pupils so large he barely has any iris left.

"It doesn't matter," I say, squirming beneath his hands.

"It does to me. When I kiss you, I want you to remember

it." He bares his teeth in a roguish smile. "Tomorrow you can do anything you want to me."

I growl. "Anything? Because now I just feel like hitting you in your smug mouth."

"That could be fun too." One of his eyebrows quirks. "If you enter the Blood Court tomorrow, you'll get your chance."

It's his way of asking if I'm still going to fight him. But if everything goes well tomorrow, then there's no need. And if it doesn't go well, then I won't be here to fight anyway.

"I won't be entering the arena tomorrow." As soon as I say it, a heavy weight leaves my shoulders.

"Good. Because the idea of having to hurt you, even simulated hurt, makes me sick to my stomach."

His protectiveness reminds me of our relationship before —and why I cared about him. This Riser is loyal and kind. This Riser would have done anything to keep me safe. Placing my hands on either side of his jaw, I bring my mouth up and brush my lips over his. If I can just kiss him again . . . maybe he'll remember.

But he pulls away. With a deep sigh, he removes his hands from my waist, his fingers clenched into fists. "Tomorrow, then, Maia Graystone."

He holds out his arm, and I begrudgingly take it, allowing him to lead me back to my room. I concentrate on the walls rather than let him see my disappointment. When we stop outside my door, I think he'll change his mind and come in, but he watches me enter and then leaves.

Lash and Teagan wait for me on my bed. Moonblood still emanates from Lash's eyes and illuminates the room. Teagan, sober and more annoyed than usual with Lash, explains between eye-rolls that Rivet agreed to help us hack into Caspian's Sim.

When I raise my eyebrows, she adds that Rivet promised to try to keep it a secret from Max.

The thought of Max in danger literally makes me sick to my stomach, but at this point, there's not much I can do. If I tell Max he has to stay, he'll go to spite me. I'll just have to hope Rivet can sneak away without being noticed.

After a few minutes of teasing me about Riser, they leave with Lash propped up on Teagan's shoulders. I lie in bed, my world spinning softly, and remember the sensation of Riser's thumbs over my hips and stomach. A deep ache spreads open inside me.

I grin, smashing a silky pillow into my face.

I've never felt this way. How I can even feel *anything* under the circumstances is a mystery. But I have this sense that everything will work out in the morning. Caspian will agree. I'll make him, whatever it takes. I won't have to fight Riser in the Blood Court.

And then Riser and I can continue what we started.

FORTY-THREE

Flames claw and jump inside the Shadow Murk. The Blood Court sand tugs at my boots. My eardrums ache from the clash of swords and metal, the air swollen with the metallic tang of blood. Riser's face appears from the shadows. He wields a long sword black with blood. I hold up my hands, but they're empty.

No weapon.

Riser advances on me. His eyes contain no recognition, only the shrewd look of someone who relishes killing.

"It's me, Riser! Stop."

But he keeps coming with that predatory stealth, flickering in and out of the shadows, stalking me. He's going to kill me. I scream as he pins me against the wall, lifting his sword—

I wake up yelling Riser's name. A nasty headache wraps around my brain, and a strange tingle lingers in my nose and cheeks. *Moonblood.*

I'm never, ever drinking that crap again.

Checking my reflection in the small dressing mirror, I notice my green eyes are still rimmed in a sparkling glow. I dress, brush my hair, pull it into a loose braid, and meet the others for breakfast, shoving the nightmare down deep with all the others.

The mess hall is quiet this early in the morning. I scan the room, taking a particular interest in Riser's table near the smoldering fireplace, but the table sits empty. Lash leans over our usual table, his head resting on his arms.

He affords me a sleepy half-grin as I take my place next to him. "Morning, gorgeous."

I elbow his ribs. "Why did you give me that horrible drink last night?"

"I seem to recall you stealing it from the girl I was dancing with."

"Doe-eyes?"

"Yes, her. The one you chased away. We had a beautiful night planned."

Teagan and I roll our eyes.

"Are there any girls you haven't slept with, Lash?" I demand.

"Well, you, Graystone. Although last night you wanted to go skinny dipping—"

"No! That was your plan, not mine. And, by the way, the water would have been freezing."

He flashes an impish grin that makes me want to murder him. "Oh, we would have warmed the water—"

I chuck a spoon at his head.

He ducks just in time.

"Shut up, Lash."

He lowers his lip into a pout and then pushes his head into my lap, purring.

I burst into laughter, running my fingers through his wild mop and shaking my head. "You're such a child!"

Teagan hands each of us a steaming bowl of porridge. Even though it smells delicious, with the faint hint of nutmeg and honey, my stomach protests, and I push the food away. Lash doesn't have that problem and wolfs his down with his usual grace, only to double over on the table once he's through.

"Big day today," Teagan says, tapping her nail on the table. "Think you two can manage?"

"Yes," I say.

Lash salutes with his head still down. "Always."

As Teagan outlines the plan, the buzzing in my head recedes, and I start to feel like myself again. Rivet has already found a cottage in the village near the Sim boutique with a Casket for us to use. Teagan explains that Rivet's been there since last night—which explains where Max was—rifling through the system to see how frequently Caspian visits. This morning she reported that he comes nearly every day, usually before Shadow Fall hits.

Which means we need to leave right now. As we make our way through the castle, we run into tons of people preparing for the Blood Oath that comes before the Blood Court, and I duck my head, relieved I won't have to decide now.

If all goes well, by the time the Blood Oath starts, we'll be in the castle with Caspian.

We leave the crowded halls behind and cross through the courtyard on the way to the caves. My heartbeat drums inside my skull. Deep down I know there's a chance—maybe a *good* chance—we're not coming back. And if the Royalists do catch us, Teagan will terminate everyone, including herself.

Everything is riding on this one interaction with a prince who probably hates me.

But if it works . . . If it works, everything will change for the better.

The sight of the Swifters turns my mouth to cotton. *This is happening, so get your shit together, Graystone.*

It's raining fat drops outside, the ocean dark blue and

frothy. Silver rainclouds drape the sky, blanketing Pandora and seeping the landscape in shadow. I shiver beneath my clothes as adrenaline washes away the lingering Moonblood from my system, making me sharp and alert.

By the time we reach the abandoned city, my wet clothes and hair are pasted to my body, cool water dribbling down my back. With each rumble of thunder in the distance comes the nagging whisper that this will not end well.

The house Rivet has chosen is a two-story cottage with a rotting roof, near the marketplace, off the main street, and relatively hidden behind a large, abandoned tin warehouse. We hide our Swifters inside the warehouse next door and then cut through the alley to the backside of the house where Rivet waits by a yellow, peeling door.

The house is little more than a kitchen and stairs that lead up to a loft. My boots sink into the old, rotting floorboards. Garlic and something long dead permeate the moist air. The wooden stairs quake as Rivet runs down to meet us, frowning, her hair wild, as if she hasn't slept.

I don't dare ask about Max, or even utter his name. As if just by saying it, I'll conjure him.

Rivet brushes a sweaty, tangled lock out of her face. "Took you long enough."

"Late night," Teagan offers, cutting a quick glance my way.

Rivet glowers at me, and I wonder if my eyes still shine. But then she turns on her heel and heads back upstairs. We follow single file, the warped, sagging boards groaning under our weight. As soon as my head tops the second story and I see the dull glint of the oblong Casket that takes up nearly the entire space, my heart lodges in my throat.

I scan the room, my gaze trailing the mass of wires and silver box in the corner. The rest of the cramped room is empty, and I sag with relief. Max isn't he—

A blond head pops up from behind the Casket. My brother peers at me, the glimmer of a smile on his lips below knit brows. "Hey. Don't be mad . . . okay?"

Blood drains from my face as a horrible feeling comes over me.

I can't decide who to be angrier with: Rivet, for leading Max here, or Max for coming. I glare at Rivet and raise a pointed eyebrow. She shrugs.

Twisting the hem of my tunic, I struggle to manage my anger. *Don't be mad?* Doesn't Max know his being here compromises everything? That if he were captured, they would have a map to the Mercurian?

Besides the fact that I wouldn't survive the Archduchess having him. I just wouldn't.

I open my mouth to order him to leave, but as soon as I do, his smile vanishes and his body goes rigid, prepared for a fight. *Fienian hell.*

Closing my mouth, I swallow down my protests and force my attention back to Rivet. "Will the prince be here today?"

"There's a seventy-two percent chance." She narrows her eyes. "You're really going to do this?"

"Yep." I stroll around the Casket.

"Wicked."

I raise my eyebrows.

"I mean," she says, opening the Casket. "It takes nerve to ask the Royalist Crowned Prince to betray his side."

"I'm not asking him to join us—"

"Then what?" She chews a worn fingernail as she roots around the Casket, hopefully ensuring everything works properly. "He's just going to waltz us into Laevus Castle and show us where the thing your father built is because you ask?"

Max takes a seat on the rotten windowsill behind her, pieces of the wood crumbling to the floor. "They were Matched, Riv. The prince even did a sketch of her."

I cut my eyes at him. "How do you know about that?"

Max's face dimples as he grins. "Found it in your drawer."

"Imp!" I smack his head. "I knew you looked in my stuff, even if Mom and Dad never believed me."

Max stiffens. "So, when you were on the Island for the Trials . . . did you see her?"

"Mom?" I tense at the memory. "Yeah, a few times. But she didn't know who I was."

"How'd she look?"

His voice is emotionless, but no matter how hard he tries, he can never hide the pain from his expressive eyes. I grit my teeth, biting down hard to stem the fury I feel at how little my father's death and our absence seemed to affect her.

"Tired."

There's the sound of steps and Teagan tops the stairs, her tall frame hunched slightly to fit. "All right, young bloods, the generator's working."

Rivet performs a respectful nod I'm apparently not worthy of and begins fidgeting with a compact square device. The air shivers and hums and a three-foot-by-three-foot screen solidifies. Max pulls the musty blue drapes closed, and we gather around the image as Rivet's fingers whir over tiny silver buttons, the video rewinding.

She pushes play. I lean in closer.

An impossibly blue-green ocean. Three riders on beautiful white horses gallop along the surf, leaving a trail of hoof-prints in the vanilla sand. They wear emerald green cloaks, their cowls knocked back in the wind. The two flaxen-haired riders I recognize immediately: Caspian and Ophelia.

"That . . . that's Maia," Lash blurts behind me. "With frizzy hair and . . . different features."

I blink at the image of the old me. "Is this . . .?"

"His personalized Sim." Rivet pushes a button, and the screen skips to another video. "It's whatever he wants. I've gone over the last three. They were all different—but that version of you is in all of them."

The next video is worse. Ophelia and I lie on a golden blanket somewhere in the grasslands, laughing amidst a scattered horde of food. Caspian sits beside us, telling some story that makes us laugh.

I look away, unable to watch the rest. Caspian could choose any Sim experience, and yet, out of all the possibilities in the world, he chose for Ophelia to be alive and me to be there.

Me. Not yet a murderer. Not yet a terrorist.

The old, weak, scared, *innocent* Maia.

"That's good then, right?" Lash nudges me with his knee. "This means the prince will listen to Graystone."

"Or," I say, "it means he knows we can never be together except in a fantasy world."

Lash frowns. "Use your feminine wiles, Graystone." He leans down to whisper in my ear. "Like last night."

Max snorts. "My sister, flirting? Yeah. Right."

I glower at Max before shifting my gaze to Rivet. "Can

you retrieve the programmed Sim for today before it happens?"

Rivet shakes her head, freeing a knot of hair she'd managed to pull out of her face. "No. Only after it happens. But I can see they've pulled you and Ophelia's Sim identities again, and I've already prepped the exchange. Once you're in the system, you'll immediately replace your Sim identity with the real you, and no one will be the wiser."

"And when will that be?" Teagan asks.

Rivet sucks in a breath, her eyebrows tugged low as she blinks at a red light flashing on the bottom of the screen. "Now."

Everyone looks at me as I go queasy all over.

FORTY-FIVE

The Casket feels cold, impersonal, a metal cage. I fight the rush of dread that washes over me as Rivet hands me the Headbox. The others stand around with nervous expressions. Max is the only one smiling, but even his annoyingly sunny disposition can't prevent the anxious lines puckering his mouth.

Rivet explains the Sim. Because she didn't have enough time to set up a buddy link, I'll be going in blind and alone. But even though we can't directly communicate, they'll be watching me on the screen.

If something goes wrong, I'm to say the word Cleo—Max suggested the name of his old cat—and they can manually pull me.

Same rules apply as before. If I die in the Sim before they pull me, there's risk of injury, coma, or even death. I'm less worried about that than I am Caspian discovering I'm real before I can convince him to help us.

The next logical conclusion would be that we're close. The drones could find us from there.

No reason to worry about that now.

I should be contemplating the things I'm going to say to Caspian to convince him. *Don't think about Riser or how much you want to get back to him. Concentrate on Prince Caspian, the boy who drew you.*

Make him listen.

Right before we start, Max leans down and hesitates for a moment before touching my shoulder, carefully.

"I won't break, Max," I say.

"Promise?" His blond eyebrows draw together. "If the False Prince hurts you, I'll kill him."

"Everything will be fine," I say with more confidence than I feel. *It has to be.* Sliding my fingers over his hand, I nod, biting my cheek to keep the emotions at bay. "But if something happens, Max, don't leave this room."

He nods and pulls his hand away. "Fine."

I glance up at Lash and Teagan hovering around the Casket, and an ache spreads inside my chest at the thought of the emperor hurting them. And Max.

If anything happens to him . . .

I close my eyes as the headgear clamps over my skull. A whisper of panic trills through me. I hate this part. My teeth clench. I open my mouth to speak—

One second I'm in the room with my friends. The next, I'm under a starry sky with a cold wind blowing against my cheeks and ripping my hair across my eyes. I shiver, my breath spilling into the air in a white cloud.

Where am I?

All around me is empty space. Dark, cold. Snow crunches below my boots, a pristine sheet of it rolling down a ridge and into a midnight abyss. Below, white-peaked steel-gray bluffs peer from the darkness.

We must be on the tallest peak in the Ivory Mountains.

"Cold?" a male voice asks.

I know it's Caspian without turning around. My heart

leaps into my throat. I inhale a lungful of crisp air, reminding myself to act like a simulated version of myself as I turn to face him.

"A bit," I say, hoping my voice doesn't tremble.

"Here." He shrugs off his coat, a fleece-lined leather thing with gold buttons, and offers it to me. He wears mahogany leather gloves and a heartbreaking smile.

Shouldering into his offering, I marvel at the Sim's ability to replicate details. The leather smell of the coat, infused with Caspian's scent of horse and sweat and the cinnamon/clove smell of Laevus Palace. The pearlescent gleam of moonlight dancing across the snow.

Even the constellations are aligned perfectly, the tapestry of sky between them a deep, rich indigo.

My heart thrums in my chest. Not yet ready to face Caspian, I look out into the landscape. Laevus Palace sparkles to the right, dark smoke drifting from its white chimneys. From here it looks beautiful, serene. Not the palace of horrors I remember.

Intending to survey behind me, I turn, my right boot stepping out, crunching through the hard crust of snow—

Suddenly my foot slips, my stomach lurching as I fall toward the abyss. My head snaps back as Caspian grabs my hand, his fingers slipping through mine. He pulls me into his chest. I tilt my head back, inhaling his frost cloud of breath and breathing it back out.

"I'm sorry," he says. "Not much room to move here. But what it lacks in room, it makes up for with beauty."

I blink up at the stars, my heart skipping a little with every winking diamond I see. "They're like tiny holes to another world of pure light."

"That's just like something I'd imagine the real you would say."

"And if I was the real me? What would you tell me?"

A shadow passes over his face. "That will never happen."

"Never?"

Swallowing, he glances past the mountain peaks at the palace beyond. "Ophelia had these silly dollhouses. Dozens of them. In the springtime, she would set them up outside in the main garden with hundreds of her wooden dolls. Every castle and every doll had a name." He runs a hand through his golden hair, a few snowflakes falling to the inside of his black collar and melting into tears against his tan skin. "She begged me to play with her, but I told her it was stupid."

My breath catches. How should I respond? Is Ophelia still alive in this Sim?

"Sometimes, that's how I feel. As if everything in this world is fake. We're wooden puppets on a string, forced to love certain people and despise others, told where to go, what to feel, who deserves to live or die. After a while, it feels like nothing is real anymore." His eyes, a dark, rich gold beneath the stars, rest on my face. "Do you know what I mean?"

"Yes."

"After I learned we were Matched, Maia, I used to stare at your picture for hours. I hadn't expected to feel much for you, but when I read your poem, it was as if, for the first time in my life, someone spoke the truth. Unlike the courtiers and Chosen, with their too-perfect faces and too-perfect smiles, always saying the right thing, you were real, Maia. Your freckles, your half-smile, your wild mess of vibrant hair. But then they took you away and made you like the others."

I fight back tears. I hate that I hurt him. "Caspian—"

"Shh." He runs a gloved thumb over my cheek. "I have to say goodbye now. Everything is about to change, and I have to get you out of my head."

"But—"

He leans down, and before I know what's happening, his lips brush against mine. I don't know how long we kiss. It could be seconds, or hours. As if inside the Sim time doesn't exist.

The frigid breeze, the stars, the mountains, they all disappear. And it's just Caspian and Maia, the girl he used to love; the girl I used to be.

He pulls away. "Goodbye, Maia of the stars."

He presses his fingertips into my shoulders and pushes. Arms windmilling the air, my vision swells with stars as I fall.

Then I'm plummeting backward down the mountainside, Caspian's face leaning down to watch me.

FORTY-SIX

I come to screaming inside the dark, stuffy room, my clammy hands clenched on the Casket's rim, Teagan and Lash gazing down at me with frowns. Sweat beads down my back.

Did Caspian really just push me off a cliff?

Someone has already lifted my Headbox, so nothing restrains me from trying to get out, only to fall with an unceremonious thump to the dirty wooden floor.

Both Teagan and Lash are on me in a flash.

Lash grins at me. "That must have been some kiss, Graystone."

"It wasn't the kiss, idiot," I say, ignoring his offer of help as I get to my feet. "He was trying to find closure."

"By throwing you off the top of a mountain?" Teagan demands, hands on her hips and elbows jutted out like daggers.

Her neat eyebrows gather in a scowl that hints at murder.

I rub my hip and try to plaster on a smile to hide how upset I am. *How was I so wrong about him?* "Some girls leave a lasting impression, I guess."

Rivet finishes messing around with the Casket screen as she calls over her shoulder, "Well, your lasting impression nearly got you killed. I barely pulled you in time."

"Good thing you're as competent as Teagan said. Now, where's the imp?"

"Max? He's right here . . ." Rivet's words trail away as she scans the tiny room.

I do the same. "Max?"

He's nowhere to be found.

"When did you last see him?" I ask.

They glance at each other, their confusion slowly transforming to panic.

Heart in my throat, I hurdle the stairs. "Max!"

The others follow, the sound of their boots pounding the steps, mimicking my racing pulse as they call him. I yell for him again, but as soon as Max's name leaves my lips, his promise whispers through my mind: If he hurts you, I'll kill him.

Max has gone to find Caspian.

Rivet gets the door open first, but I slip past her. I'm sprinting. Puddles of water splashing beneath my boots onto my pants. A light misting of rain wets my cheeks. Rounding the corner of the house, I glance over the building where the Swifters hide.

No time.

I spy the marketplace through a gap between two rows of houses and head that way. As I run, I slip out the scorpion knife, clenching it inside my palm. I don't dare call Max's name, conserving my breath as I will every molecule of my being faster. My footsteps echo over the adobe walls, my breathing fast and choppy.

Deep, deep down, I'm shattering. Fragmenting with terror. Piece by piece, everything I have ever feared comes crashing down, the silent prayer that reverberates inside me growing louder with each terrified beat of my heart.

Don't let him die, don't let him die, don't let him die.

It doesn't matter what happens from here. It doesn't matter if I save the world. If Max dies, I'm dead too.

And I'll kill anyone and everyone to protect him.

The others catch up by the market, the purr of their Swifters slowly breaking me from my trance. The old half-empty shops are to my left. The back of Caspian's black carriage is barely visible from the road, parked directly in front of the building where the Sim boutique operates.

The others slow their Swifters, gliding single file along the edges of the marketplace, dodging to avoid the faded-yellow awning drapes whipping in the wind. I manage to keep up. When we reach the end of the market, Teagan holds up a hand, and everyone freezes.

The rain has picked up, drumming the metal awning and making a soothing noise as it hits the cobbled street. Too impatient to wait, I duck low and round the corner, ignoring Teagan's hissing order to wait. I scan the front of the building, blinking away drops of rain.

The knife is cold and wet inside my hand.

A movement. To the left, in the alley between the Sim building and the two-story whitewashed house on the corner. More movements to my right.

Where is Max?

The door to the building opens, and two Centurions rush to the steps. An attendant in all black snaps a gold umbrella over the person leaving before I can see who it is.

But there's only one person it could be.

I retreat a step, prepared to join the others behind the corner, when someone appears by the Carriage. As soon as I spy the head plastered with wet blond hair, my stomach drops. Max.

I begin to run—

All around me, the street churns with movement as shadows flicker from the alleys and bushes. Red shadows glinting with weapons. Rebels!

I halt a few feet from the carriage as the Centurions turn in surprise and draw their swords. The umbrella tumbles from the attendant's hand to the street, a narrow stream of water whisking it down the sidewalk like a golden leaf.

Caspian's hand is already on his sword, half the blade gleaming from the sheath. Our eyes meet. The two Centurions have left his side and are surrounded by Rebels. Time slows down, making the torrent of water pouring from the gutter by his head seem like a sluggish trickle. His gaze flicks to the dagger in my hand.

Something dark and broken flashes across his face, just as a lithe figure slinks behind Caspian on the steps. My throat tightens as I recognize Riser's graceful, deadly movements. Next to Prince Caspian's light, golden appearance, Riser is a dark shadow.

My mouth opens to scream a warning, but it's too late. Riser lifts his pistol above Caspian's head and then brings it down on his temple.

FORTY-SEVEN

Caspian cries out and drops to his knees. He brings a hand to his head before collapsing on his side, the other hand still on his sword handle, his black coat fanning out over the stairs.

I try to run to Caspian, but arms lock around my waist. "Not the best time to interfere," Lash whispers into my ear.

"Let go of me!" I twist, but Lash holds me in a vise grip.

"Easy there, Graystone. Let's not get ourselves hung just yet."

"Let them try!"

"I'd rather not." Lash's solemn voice makes me listen. "Now, time to act like we're part of the plan—not against it."

Hugo appears by the fallen prince, red cloak slinking over Caspian's body as he rips Caspian's sword from his lifeless hand and holds it in the air to the sound of cheers. The two Centurions lie motionless on the cobblestones.

By the gods, this was a trap. A trap I helped lay out.

"Max!" I yell, desperately trying to pick him out from the others.

Max looks up from where he leans over Caspian,

searching for more weapons. Blood trickles from Caspian's head, darkening his hair and seeping into the water around him. Max glances around as he hops the railing and covers the distance between us.

As soon as Max gets close and I see the guilt in his eyes, I know he's the one responsible, yet my heart refuses to believe it.

"What did you do, Max?"

Max rubs a finger over his neck. "I gave the bastard a chance. If he'd agreed to help us, I wouldn't have turned him in."

"He didn't have the chance to agre—"

"Because he threw you down a mountain and almost killed you!" Max crosses his arms over his chest, his voice cracking. "Just like always, you blame me. Why can't you see he wasn't going to help us? Why do you always have to think your way is the right way? He would have turned us in and watched us hang."

He wouldn't have . . . would he? I sag into Lash's arms. "But they'll kill him."

"Better him than us."

Three Rebels surround Caspian, lift him up, and lug him away, his head lolling to the side and boots dragging the ground. His belt falls from his coat, and one of the Rebels, shielded from the rain by a dark, hooded cloak, plucks it from the cobblestones and holds it up like a trophy. I resist the urge to run and fight them off.

How could Caspian have been so stupid to only have two Centurions? Where are the Gold Cloaks? Delphine?

But the answer stares me in the face. As heir to the Crown, he couldn't openly use a Sim, especially a highly illegal boutique Sim. He had to do it in secret, which meant he couldn't use the Gold Cloaks.

My heart breaks a little as I realize he was so desperate to get rid of my ghost that he gambled everything.

And he lost.

The Rebel that nabbed the belt turns around, and I see the face inside. Lucy Redgrave. A nest of black and red braids coil over her head. She flashes a sharp grin, holding out the belt, her thumb stroking the jewels.

"Why do you look so sad?" she asks in a slippery-sweet voice. "Oh. I forgot. You two had a *thing*." She leans in, cupping her hand over her mouth as if to tell a secret. "Well, you won't have to worry about that anymore, once the Rebels lop off his pretty little head. I hear—"

I run at her, forgetting nearly everything Brogue and the Sim taught me. Before I can even lunge two feet forward, Lash has his arms around me, holding me back.

"Whoa, Graystone," he soothes.

One second it was just Lucy, the next, Hugo shadows his twin, their heads bobbing in tandem like cobras about to strike.

"I wouldn't do that," Lucy says.

"Not if I were you," Hugo finishes.

"Unless you want . . ."

"An accident to happen." Hugo parts his cloak to reveal a small golden pyramid. The device rattles as he strokes it. "Remember this?"

My stomach twists into a knot. He shakes the golden cage and the scorpions inside hiss, striking the metal walls with their stingers.

Lash steps in front of me. "You wouldn't dare."

Lucy grins. "Maybe we wouldn't . . ."

"And maybe we would," Hugo purrs.

They turn on their heels and slither away like the snakes they are, and I realize my fists are clenched so tight that my knuckles are ivory stars. Forcing my fingers to relax, I wipe my hands on my pants, working to calm my breathing.

Just as quickly as the Rebels appeared, they melt back into the city. The rain has become a freezing downpour that matches the chill in my core.

This wasn't supposed to happen. I was prepared to fight alongside the Rebels against the empire, if necessary. I was prepared to either storm the castle or burrow my way into it. To bleed and die.

But the one thing I wasn't prepared for was taking the Crown Prince hostage, knowing the Rebels will make him scream before ending his life.

They'll torture him gruesomely, keeping him just alive enough to do it again and again—

Doubling over, I hold my stomach and try not to get sick.

Lash runs over to his Swifter, and I wait for him, shivering, strands of my hair clinging to my face and neck. I try to move, but my feet are rooted to the ground.

Lash has just started his Swifter when Riser pulls his up beside me. Rain rivers down his flesh, his high black collar covering his jaw and lips, so only his bright eyes are visible. Steam hisses from beneath his blood-red beast, filling the chasm between us.

He holds out his hand to me. "I need to talk to you, Graystone."

An hour earlier, this was all I wanted. To be with Riser. To kiss his lips, feel his body press into mine. And more. So much more.

An hour earlier I would have accepted his hand.

But now . . . now all I see when I look at him is his pistol coming down on Caspian's temple. Now my head buzzes with a million thoughts on how to save Caspian and still make it to the Island.

And Riser no longer fits into that plan.

Lash pulls up on my right, facing the other direction. Riser's gaze never leaves my face as he awaits my decision, although his chest rises unevenly, a muscle flickering in his temple.

Turning my back on him, I slide my leg over the back of Lash's Swifter, shivering against the warmth that immediately enters my legs.

I wrap my arms around Lash's waist, leaning my head against his back and glance to where I left Riser. Only, there's nothing but the slanted rain and clouds of steam from his Swifter in his place.

FORTY-EIGHT

Bloodwyn Castle thrums with the cheers of the Rebels. Someone must have informed the crowd gathered for the Blood Oath celebrations about Caspian's capture, because they clog the main hall, pushing and shoving to try and get a peek at the False Prince, making it nearly impossible to get to my room.

Each clap on my shoulder reverberates through me. Each chant to *kill him* burns like poison in my veins.

Only a fool would think this was a victory; I'm surrounded by an army of fools who will be dead in a day.

I finally push my way through the thick mass of celebrators just as the chants calling for his murder grow louder, the sea of faces brightened with the chalices full of Moonblood being passed around. The air crackles with violent energy.

Teagan waits for me in my room, Lash right behind me as I slam the door. "Why?" I scream. "Why would Max do it?"

My friends regard me from opposite sides of the room. Rain puddles on the floor below my broken window. Every piece of fabric on my body is drenched and clammy, too tight.

I want to strip, but I'm too furious to move. Cheers erupt from the hall outside.

Teagan joins me on the bed. Despite the rain, somehow she still looks put together, her hair coiffed and red lipstick immaculate. "It may not seem like it now, but he did it for you, darling."

"You're right. It doesn't seem like that at all."

"Maybe he thought the Fienians were going to find out, and he had to act to protect you," Lash offers.

"That makes my brother a coward."

"You should have heard him when Caspian pushed you," Teagan says, her voice soothing. "The way he screamed."

Hearing that is a punch to the gut, but still I frown. Why can't Max ever listen to me? I told him to stay, and he did the opposite. I grit my teeth. I want to scream my head off at him. But I also want to hug him and tell him I'm never leaving him again.

Someone knocks at the door. As soon as I see Max's dopey face, I'm back to wanting to throttle him. Teagan and Lash slip out the door before I can protest.

Suddenly the air in the room grows thin, the space between us becoming an ocean of raw emotion.

"Maia." Max rocks back on his heels, the same nervous habit he had at seven. "Please don't be mad, okay?"

"Don't be mad? Do you realize what you've done?"

His gaze drops to his feet.

"I needed Caspian to help us sneak into the castle, but now Nicolai and Flame will kill him!"

"He wasn't going to help—"

"You don't know that!"

He kicks at something by my bed. "He hurt you! Just like they did Dad."

"It was only a Sim, Max."

He shakes his head, his shoulders slumping. "I'm just . . .

I'm tired, Maia. Tired of them taking away everyone I care about. And I didn't want them to take you too."

"I . . ." All the angry words I'd planned to say melt away. "Oh . . . oh, Max."

Heart in my throat, I jump to my feet and round the bed. Max looks up at me, shiny tears streaming down his face. We stare at each other for a second.

Then I throw my arms around him. Press him into my chest. He's warm and snotty, his body shuddering in my embrace.

"I'm sorry I left you," I whisper. "And I promise, I'll never leave you again. I'm doing all of this for you. You and Dad."

He pulls away, wiping his nose on his sleeve. "Typical Maia, had to get all mushy."

"Turd breath!" I smack his head.

Rubbing his temple, he frowns. "Will they really kill him?"

"I don't know," I lie. "Flame has to know the emperor won't negotiate with them, even for the Crown Prince. Maybe I can talk to her."

"When I saw the prince push you, I wanted to hurt him back. But . . . I don't want them to torture him. I mean, he lost his sister too, right?"

A heavy sigh leaves my chest. "I'll fix it, okay?"

But my words ring hollow. Fix it how? How the hell can I make this right?

We both look toward the door as it creaks open and Rivet peeks her head in, her eyes scanning Max before landing on me. "So, you didn't kill him?"

"I'm too charming for anyone to snuff," Max says. "You know that, Riv."

Rivet rolls her eyes. "Obviously, or I would have snuffed you years ago. Now, c'mon. The Blood Oath is in a few hours, and we need to practice for the Blood Court."

And just like that, an answer to our predicament comes to me. It takes a while, but I manage to gather everyone in my room. Teagan and Lash are on the bed, Max on the floor by the window, braiding Rivet's damp hair. Rhydian is the last to join, and he's brought two Hawks with him, both with bulging muscles, thick necks, and scowls.

It's a motley crew. Counting me, and assuming Lash can fight in the Blood Court, there are eight of us. Hardly enough to ensure my plan will work.

Rhydian taps his boot on the floor. "So, let me get this straight, Graystone. You want us to . . . to protect you, keeping you alive so that you can win the Scorpion Throne?"

"Yes, but—"

"I'm not listening to this," the Hawk on Rhydian's right says, turning to leave.

"Wait." I hold up a hand. "You haven't heard the rest."

"Don't need to, little girl. I'm not fighting for you."

"Do you have a family?"

The Hawk pauses. "Course."

"What if I told you I could stop Pandora, but first I need to win the Scorpion Throne to do it?"

Interest flickers inside his deep-set eyes.

That got your attention, didn't it? "Get me the throne, and I'll stop Her."

He glances at Rhydian. "You trust this girl?"

Rhydian locks eyes with me. "I do."

"Well, then." The Hawk performs a quick bow. "I'm all yours."

I swallow, masking my relief with a grin. "Max, Rivet?"

Max nods, but a frown twitches Rivet's lips. "If you win, what will you do with the prince?"

"The prince has to come with us to the Island—"

"No." Rivet hops to her feet, her half-braided hair spilling over her shoulder. "Someone has to pay for what the Royalists have done."

"And they will. But not him."

Her lower lip trembles. Max gets up behind her, and he places a hand on her shoulder, whispering something I can't hear.

Finally, she says, "I'll get you your throne. But promise me a few Royalists heads."

Before I understood the atrocities of the emperor, I would have thought Rivet too young to think this way. Now, though, I simply nod before turning to Teagan and Lash.

Teagan arches a neat eyebrow. "You really have to ask, darling?"

Lash's eyes hold a devilish gleam. "Can't let Aster show me up, can I?"

A wave of tension rolls off me as I glance around the room at the people willing to fight for me. A few days ago, most were strangers.

Now I have to trust them with my life, and they have to trust me with theirs.

Now that everyone agrees to protect me, we discuss strategy. Lucy and Hugo will be paired off, as usual, so Rhydian and his men will shadow them and hopefully take them out early. The Hawks are problematic, but if we stick to the outside and let them take out as much of each other as possible, we might stand a chance.

With Rhydian's crew taking care of the Redgraves, the others will form a circle of protection around me. Lash and Teagan will make the first layer, Max and Rivet pronging the outside.

Teagan brings up the catastrophe from last time, and we agree that the last hour before Shadow Fall should be spent familiarizing me with the Hot Weapons that could be used in the arena.

After a final word with Rhydian and his crew, they leave, and I follow the others to the armory. As soon as we enter the small, rectangular space gleaming with weapons of every sort imaginable, the voices start whispering to me, and a headache floods my skull.

I must make a face, because Teagan purses her lips. "You okay?"

"Yeah." I touch the side of my head. "The voices are back. Maybe it's the stress. I don't know."

"Lash can get you something from the apothecary for the pain."

I shake my head. "Nope. I'm fine. Maybe teaching me about the weapons will help with the stress."

She watches me for a second longer and then crosses to a wall filled with strange devices. Ironically, the first Hot Weapon I learn about is the one that made me lose the last Blood Court: a silver, button-sized disc. It's an electrode, I discover. A mean little weapon that, when pressed and thrown, produces an electric cloud with high enough voltage to kill a man and stun a horse. I might get three, maybe four uses out of it before it needs to be recharged.

The problem is retrieving it after the first throw, although if everyone in the vicinity has been killed, I guess it's not that hard.

The Fienians like electricity, I learn, running a finger over the rubber handle of an Electro-Whip near the top wall. Max's flame-throwing gun from the last Blood Court is here, too, near a rack of flammable weapons carefully stored inside a glass cage. Incendier. I memorize the name and its particulars —twenty-five seconds of flame—along with the rest of the flaming weapons available.

The orbs we wore on our necks during the first mission are here. There are Sinkers, Faders, Bleeders, and every other hideous weapon imaginable. I try to remember everything as Teagan paces the room, referring to this weapon or that.

She talks quickly; we're almost out of time.

Near the last rack of Hot Weapons, I spy the pyramid device Hugo used to house the scorpions that nearly killed me.

"Scorpio-Fire," Flame breathes in a hushed voice.

I nod, inhaling a deep breath to chase away the horrible memory of their stingers piercing my flesh, the cruel, torturous poison that turned my bones to fire.

"This time will be different," Teagan promises.

We continue until my brain is overloaded with every killing device seemingly ever made, and I long for the simplicity of a sharp blade or arrow point. There are those, too. They glitter from their perch on the walls near the front, along with the closely guarded vials of poison.

"Tip your blade in that," Teagan says, nodding toward a tiny blue vial with a red scorpion, "and a scratch will be your enemy's doom."

"Hmm." I touch the vial, carefully. "Teagan, how did you become a Fienian Rebel?"

She strolls along the wall, running her fingers over the weapons before answering. "I'll give you the short, sweet version. I'd just come back from the camp. I was messed up, darling. Couldn't sleep, couldn't stomach food. The Royalist pigs had burrowed their way into me and scraped out bits of my soul—private things that they took without asking. The only thing that got me to my twelfth birthday was meeting O. The emperor was hosting an elaborate birthday party for her and Caspian on the Island. I found her cross-legged beneath a huge sycamore by the pond.

"Soon after, my family was called to court to stay while my father worked in the Treasury. O and I were inseparable. She liked to tell these horrible jokes—gods, they were terrible —and she didn't care that I preferred men's clothes, or wasn't like the Chosen. We passed our time reading secret pamphlets in support of the Rebels and making grand plans to change the world. And then one day we were invited to meet Nicolai."

"What was he like then?"

Teagan laughs. "The same. Serious, cryptic, dogged in his beliefs. But he spoke truths no one dared talk about. And he had such passion. He was willing to die for what he believed."

I twirl a light gold dagger between my fingers. "How long were the Rebels planning to infiltrate the Trials?"

"Years. Nicolai has been gathering and training an army inside Bloodwyn Castle since I met him. The plan was to use the Trials to kill the emperor, and then, once the emperor was dead, he would send in the Rebel army."

"How did I fit into the plans?"

"When he announced he was going to spring Amandine's son from Rhine Prison, Max begged him to look for you too. He promised you would cooperate. He must have told Nicolai about the thing your father built, because I can't imagine Nicolai would have bothered otherwise."

I want to ask a thousand more questions, but there's only one that still eats at me. "Who is Nicolai? Why does he hate the emperor so much?"

Teagan shakes her head. "Only the gods know. I've heard he's everything from a disgruntled courtier to a Bronze servant of House Croft."

Footsteps near the door draw our attention to Lash. "Done gossiping, girls? The Blood Oath starts soon."

Teagan chucks a shield at his head, and he ducks just in time, the golden circle ricocheting off the wall of long-swords and skidding across the stone floor.

As we brush past him out the door, Teagan pats his shoulder. "Sharp reflexes, Lash-y boy."

I leave Teagan and Lash to search for Brogue. When I find him holed up in the bar on the first floor, his somber look sets my heart aflutter.

We move to a quieter room by the kitchens, and Brogue drops his head. "I can't give you what you're here for."

I suck my lip. "I've never known you to give up before."

"Maia, this ain't me giving up; it's me being honest. That boy don't have any weaknesses, and if you fight him . . . Well, I refuse to watch."

"Then you're giving up on me?"

"No." He shakes his head, the corners of his lips twitching downward. "No, of course—"

"Why don't you just hide in a corner and shoot up again? Isn't that what you do when life gets too hard?" As soon as I say the words, I regret them, but they hang heavy in the air anyway.

"That you talking, or Lady March?" A vein throbs in his forehead as he holds my gaze. "Good. You're gonna need her to stand any chance against Riser."

"I'm sorry, Brogue," I plead, horrified at what I said. "There's just so much riding on this, and I need you there, in my corner. There's no one else I trust like you."

"Girl, I'll always be in your corner. Always. But I won't watch you get hurt. I can't." He runs two fingers over his chin. "But I can tell you this: Before they stole the memory of you from Riser, you were his weakness. In fact, you were the only weakness I imagine he's ever had, which is probably why they did it. Find a way to make him remember you. That's the only way."

I walk with Brogue to the arena, a sinking feeling weighing me down. How in the world am I going to win now?

FIFTY

R ebels in their Fienian best leathers and weapons clog the hallways and cram into the indoor arena, the only place big enough to hold the Blood Oath. The crowd is packed shoulder-to-shoulder, the room dim, save the large pillar candles strewn over the dais. A wooden structure has been constructed over the three thrones, a silver-and-red tapestry hanging from its beams.

Draped in a vibrant red cloak, Nicolai reclines in the middle throne, sunk deep into the rich wood. I can almost see the bored expression through his mask.

How many of these has he witnessed? A lost feeling comes over me as I realize how much of this dark, mysterious world is still a secret.

How long has Nicolai been planning this entire thing? I wonder as Pit Boy and Flame rise from their thrones in similar ceremonial robes; Flame's the color of fresh snow, Riser's the color of a moonless night.

As we push our way to the front, I'm not surprised when Riser's sharp gaze picks me out from the crowd. I ignore the question inside his eyes.

Even though my heart hurts to see his confusion, I can't deal with that right now. In an hour, I'm going to have to fight him for the throne.

And I can't do that when I'm worried I might hurt him.

Focus, Graystone. Lash and Teagan catch up with us, and I grit my teeth and force Pit Boy from my mind as we press forward, Brogue's meaty shoulders clearing a path through the crowd.

Max and Rivet stand in the line of Rebels waiting along the wall to take the Oath, and my breath catches. Max's shoulders are back, his head held high. Despite my reservations, his confidence makes me smile as I realize how proud my father would have been.

Look, Daddy. Our Max isn't a kid anymore.

Lash leans into my ear. "Normally, they don't require us to take the Oath until age sixteen, but with the battle tomorrow, they're making an exception."

The battle. I pick through the line, a heavy feeling weighing me down with each young Rebel I see. An army of kids.

Sure, we have technology, and some trained fighters, but it's not enough. Not by half.

Nicolai's cane hits the floor, and all at once, the hall goes from a wild din to dead quiet as he pushes himself to a hunched stand. Slowly, carefully, he plods to the front. No one dares breathe, his cloak swishing against the floor.

I'm close enough I can see the blue in his eyes, the fine silver stitching of his pant hem. His breathing is rattled, and it makes a strange, guttural sound as it comes out of his Electrolarynx. He sweeps the room with his slow, burning gaze.

I swear it lands on me and pauses for a moment.

And then, a small murmur pulses through the room and dies as he removes his mask, revealing his ruined face.

"There," he murmurs, hushing the crowd. "That's better."

The mask falls from his gloved hands and clangs against the floor. He takes off his cloak and then his gloves. His mottled, scarred flesh gleams eerily in the firelight.

"The time has come to reveal the empire's many sins. To take those who dared stay awake through the veil of corruption to expose the rotting, gangrenous corpse beneath. There will be no redemption without anarchy! No hope without first burning away the rot."

Wild screams fill the air. *Blood for freedom! Death for honor!*

Nicolai taps his cane, and silence descends like a wave. "Today, when you say your Oath, you're declaring war on this world that has beaten you, starved you, enslaved you, and turned its back on you."

Riser glides from his throne to stand by Nicolai. At first, when I see the dagger in his hand, my heart skips a beat. But Nicolai simply holds out his hand palm first, and Riser drags the blade across his ruined hand, thumb to pinky.

"The only law is blood," Riser says in a strong, clear voice. "There are those who bleed it and those who take it."

Riser produces a red linen and hands it to Nicolai to staunch the blood before returning to his throne. It's only after the line of Oath takers begins to move toward the dais that I realize the red of the linen is old blood.

Nicolai removes the bandage and smears a bright swath of blood over the forehead of the first Rebel, a short, pudgy boy around Max's age. The boy declares his new Fienian name, "Blade," and crosses the dais to where Riser and Flame sit, kneeling beside each and repeating the words, *blood for freedom, death for honor.* I watch until he reaches the back, where he disappears with two Rebels.

"To take the Microplant," Teagan explains.

My dread grows as Max and Rivet near the steps. Nicolai's blood splatters around his feet, his cloak dragging in it, smearing a bright red half-circle into the gray stone.

Max takes the stage. I flinch as Nicolai claims him with his blood, a thin ribbon of red trickling down his nose.

For a moment, I think Max won't take a Rebel name.

But then he turns to address us, his eyebrows bunched in a look of concentration. "Cleo."

I nearly fall over in shock; my brother just named himself after his cat. Fienian hell, I almost wish my mother were here to die in horror.

Rivet goes next. Although she's already privately taken a new name, she announces it again, her voice ringing out loud and clear. "Rivet."

I wonder what the story behind her name is as I watch her walk toward the back along with Max. For once, they aren't horsing around.

At least they're taking the Oath seriously—sort of.

When the final Rebel takes the blood brand and heads to the back, the room stirs with excitement, hushed voices filling the hall. Many of the people in the crowd will probably fight in the Blood Court for a chance at the throne.

I glance around, all the moisture inside my mouth gone as nerves overtake me.

"Wait," Teagan says into my ear over the din. "Something's different."

Flame has joined Nicolai near the front, all her attention focused on a domed enclosure being rolled to the steps on squeaky wheels. All but the bottom of the cage is covered in a ragged burgundy blanket. Hugo is on one side, Lucy on the other, and along with two other Rebels, they lift the swaying pen over the steps and onto the dais.

I know who they have inside the cage, but my mouth parts anyway as Lucy rips off the blanket. The enclosure isn't quite tall enough for Caspian to stand, so he hunches, his fingers clenched knuckle-white around the rusted bars. His lip curls in derision as he glares at the crowd.

The Rebels roar with delight.

Two boys take out their daggers and prod his pen. One cuts off a piece of his cloak like a trophy. Caspian leans to the side to avoid their blades, his face twisted with contempt. Someone spits on him.

With a tired sigh, he wipes his dark shirtsleeve over his cheek.

Flame appears, and the Rebels scatter from the stage. She wears a demented smile that chills my blood. Hugo and Lucy flank her.

"This is the False Prince," Flame says. "He and his father have tortured us, executed our families, and enslaved us. Now it's his turn."

No. Oh gods no. The hall vibrates with cheers, but I'm seemingly frozen as Hugo plucks the pyramid-shaped weapon from his baldric, presses the top, and tosses it at Caspian's cage.

"Scorpio-Fire."

The word has barely left my lips before I see them. The golden scorpions swarm from the cracked device toward Caspian, large metal stingers held high and ready.

They're going to kill him.

FIFTY-ONE

The memory of the scorpions stinging my flesh floods my brain. The agony. The terror. I can't let that happen to anyone else. Lash and Teagan watch me, both waiting to see what I'll do.

"The stage," I say as I push through the crowd beside Brogue.

We kick and punch our way to the front, spilling cups of Moonblood onto the floor. Lash and Teagan help us clear a path. As soon as I'm close to the dais, I hurdle it, my friends right behind me.

The scorpions have nearly made it to his pen. A few scuttle over the bottom. Caspian kicks at them, cursing. One must find him because he screams.

We're running out of time. I stomp and kick the swarm of weapons, but there are too many. Caspian screams again.

How many stings will kill him? I can't remember.

Hugo and Lucy are yelling at us to stop, but they keep their distance. *Cowards.* I press my shoulder into the cage and shove. It barely moves an inch.

"Lash! Brogue! Help me."

When I look between the bars, I meet Caspian's gaze, mere inches from my own.

"What are you doing?" he hisses, his face red and glazed with pain.

"Saving your ass again!"

Lash and Brogue shoulder into the pen, and it begins to move. Teagan gets behind it and pulls. With a loud squeak, it rolls across the stone floor.

When the crate gets to the edge, I glance over at the scorpions. They're still coming, scurrying after their prey with dogged determination.

Lash and I share a questioning look.

"Push," I order.

"I'm confused, Graystone. Are we trying to save him or kill him?"

Teagan joins me. Together, we shout, "Shut up, Lash."

The room has gone dead quiet. The sound of the scorpions' metal bodies scrabbling over the stone lodges deep in my bones.

I glance over at Nicolai. His head is tilted to the side, a curious look twisting his ruined face.

I turn to Caspian. "I'm sorry."

Then, together, we force the cage over the edge. It crashes with a horrible grinding metal sound. The scorpions have stopped their attack and mill in a confused circle, stinging the air with aggressive thrusts. A few start to kill each other.

"Check on the prince," I say Lash as Teagan, Brogue, and I form a barrier between the milling scorpions in case they regroup.

For a heartbeat, there's silence. Heavy, suffocating silence. And then the sound of clapping stirs the air as Nicolai approaches. He walks slowly, his eyes still curious, his mouth twitched up in a bizarre smile.

Everything inside me screams to run.

Skirting around the confused mass of scorpions, he gestures to Hugo—standing near Lucy and Flame by the thrones. Hugo strides to the cruel golden bastards, pushes the top of his device, and they swarm over him and back into their cage. His eyebrows are lowered above a sneer as he glances at me and runs a finger across his throat.

Nicolai comes to a stop in front of me. "What is this, then?"

"I won't let you kill him." My voice comes out strong, even though fear grips my throat.

"Won't let me? How do you plan to *stop* me?"

From the corner of my eyes, I see Max and Rivet joining us. Brogue, too, has come up beside me, and I don't need to look to know his face is murderous.

Nicolai ignores them.

"I have a proposition." I slide my gaze over the Rebels. "If I win the Blood Court and take the Scorpion Throne, then Caspian lives and you release any Rebel that wants to follow me."

Flame and Riser have joined Nicolai. Skipping over Pit Boy, I glance at Flame. Her eyes dance with anger, so I focus on Nicolai.

Nicolai's body shakes. *He's laughing,* I realize.

"And why don't I just put you and all your friends inside that cage with the False Prince right now and release the scorpions? Hmm?"

"The only law is blood. There are those who bleed it, and those who take it." I swallow. "If you don't allow me to compete in the Blood Court, then your laws mean nothing . . . and you're just like the emperor."

Nicolai's blue eyes bore into me as a murmur ripples through the hall, his lips pressed together in a tight line.

"She's right." Riser steps forward. "Let her try. She's tried twice before and failed. I can't imagine this time will be any different."

"Oh, I'm not worried she'll win the throne," Nicolai says. "You forget I've been inside her mind. She's weak, broken. Someone like her could never challenge the throne. No. The question is, what happens if she loses?"

I hadn't even thought about that, but now, I know only one thing will make Nicolai accept. "If I lose, then you can string me up with Caspian. Two executions. The traitor and the False Prince. That should make your twisted heart happy."

Riser frowns at me; I scowl right back.

Curious whispers slither through the Rebels as I aim my glare at Nicolai.

His face contorts into a grin. "As you wish, with a caveat. Anyone who supports you in the Blood Court will suffer your fate. You win, they live. You lose, they die with you."

My stomach clenches. That wasn't part of the plan. I glance at my friends, trying to read their faces. Will they support me now that their alliance could be their death?

I'll just have to trust them. Releasing a sharp breath, I nod.

Just like that, our death warrant is signed in blood.

I jump from the stage, landing near Caspian's cage. The metal gate had broken open, and Lash has Caspian sprawled out on the floor. Blood drips from a lump on his forehead, his eyes glazed with the lingering madness and pain of the scorpions.

I drop to my knees. "Prince."

He blinks at me. "Ma—Maia."

"I explained the Blood Court to the prince," Lash says.

"Yeah?" I quickly check Caspian for more injuries as I talk, ignoring his affronted expression. "And what are the gods saying about our chances?"

Lash runs his hand through his beautiful, coppery mess of hair. "Nothing you want to hear."

"Well, screw them, then."

Caspian reaches out and grabs my wrist. "Why are you doing this?"

"Saving you?" I shake my head. "I'm not *just* doing it for you. I'm doing it for our world. Everything I told you was true. The Mercurian exists. If I win the throne, will you help us find it?"

"Yes." Although his voice is raspy with pain, his eyes are clear, his lips pressed into a thin, solemn line. "I swear, on my honor, Maia. If you survive, I'll do everything I can to help you."

Hugo and Lucy stride toward us, their boots scraping the stone. I immediately find my dagger, but Lash shakes his head as they grab Caspian by his shirt collar and haul him up.

"Look at the little prince now," Lucy whispers into his ear.

Hugo taps the weapon that houses the Scorpio-Fire. "They miss you already, Prince. But don't worry." His gaze flicks to me. "You'll be reunited soon."

After they drag Caspian off, Brogue approaches. Most of the crowd already left for the Blood Court, and the indoor arena is quiet.

Brogue frowns, as if deciding what he'll say to me. "Are you afraid?"

I think about lying, but only for a moment. "Yes. Almost as scared as when I entered the maze during the Trials."

"Because you're afraid of dying?"

"No. I'm afraid of letting my friends die."

"Good," he says.

"Good?"

"Those young Rebels you've surrounded yourself with, they're your family now, much as Max is, and you finally see that. You'll do what it takes to keep 'em alive, girl. And if

Riser tries to get in the way of your family's safety, you end him. Family always comes before love."

I nod, horrified at the prospect. But he's right.

Brogue's palms are rough on my cheeks as he takes my face between his hands. "I'm proud of you, Maia. Always have been. Now remember what I taught you and go claim your throne."

I head for the Blood Court, trying to calm my tangled nerves. Each step closer to that arena of sand and violence feels like a step closer to death.

How can less than an hour of my life define the future of everything? I struggle to breathe as the weight of my situation crushes me. I'm not ready. It's all happening too fast.

I'm. Not. *Ready*.

But then I look around at my friends. Lash, Teagan, Rivet. Other than Max, they're the closest things I have to family. They *are* my family. And if I don't take the throne then they die beside me.

I have to win for *them*.

A sudden calm comes over me. When I stood outside the labyrinth and screamed that I was ready, it was a lie.

No more lies. No more half-truths. I might not be ready, but I'm not alone this time.

With friends, sometimes the impossible becomes possible.

<h1 style="text-align:center">FIFTY-TWO</h1>

The tunnel leading to the arena is packed with tense bodies. The pungent tang of fear permeates the air and roils my stomach. I press closer to Max, fighting the urge to pull him into my arms.

Do that later . . . Make sure there is a later.

Rivet fidgets with her red leather wristlets. Nearly a foot shorter than me, her youth and inexperience becomes hard to overlook. But then she turns to me, her expression forged in steel.

"We won't let you down," she promises over the muffled chatter filling the chamber, her eyes earnest and clear.

I nod, slowly. Some of her mahogany hair has escaped its tight braid, and I realize she could be my sister. How do I not know a single thing about her, this girl who helped my brother and pledged to fight for me?

"What's the meaning behind your Fienian name?" I ask.

She examines her fingernails. "I was five when my father died in the eastern salt mines, and my mother moved us to the Diamond City of Burnside, thinking the textile factories there would be safer for us."

"They weren't?"

"The conditions, sure." A dark shadow falls over her face. "Not so much the overseer. He started visiting my mom every night. She'd stash us in the tiny bedroom we all shared and tell us to hide under our moth-eaten blanket until she came back. Every night, my little sister and I covered our ears while I stared at this one shiny rivet at the top of our metal bunk and pretended it was okay."

Rage threatens to blind me. This is life under the emperor. This is what we're fighting to destroy. Rivet turns her attention on her boots, but I refuse to let her feel an ounce of shame for what happened to her family, and I call out her name.

Her eyes lift to mine. They gleam with tears and unimaginable heartache.

"Thank you for taking care of Max . . . Cleo, when I couldn't."

She shrugs, but the ghost of a smile breaks through her frown. "We took care of each other."

Teagan and Lash fight their way through the bodies to stand next to me. Lash wears a grin that could blind the sun, but Teagan can't hide her worried glances at him. Just the fight through the crowd has drained him, his shoulders tight with pain, left side dragging a bit.

"You good?" I call.

His brow creases. "What, Graystone? You think just because I'm half a man, I can't protect you?"

I stand on my tiptoes and plant a kiss on his cheek, the bristle from his beard scratching my bottom lip. "You're more man than the whole lot of them, Lash."

"Whoa!" Max calls. "I'm, you know, *right here*, guys."

Lash grins. "Anyone ever tell you your sister's pretty?"

"Lash!" I swat his arm.

All at once, a grating noise splits the air, and I whip around, the din melting into silence. It's time.

The crowd of fighters swells forward, and I nearly fall in the ensuing chaos. Fighting my way to the door, I find a small gap of flesh to slip through.

A dim, cloudy sky greets me as my feet hit the sand. Somewhere behind the dirty gray veil, Pandora moves steadily toward the sun.

Shadow Fall whispers in the air, a silent specter of death. Like always, my life is tethered and chained to that falling darkness. I can almost feel Her up there, chanting for my death. As if she knows my intentions to stop Her.

I tilt my face up. "I'm not afraid of you. Not anymore."

Teagan and Lash flank my sides. Max and Rivet push out four feet, using their elbows and knees to carve out a small circle of space. Glancing up, I see the ominous form of Nicolai, Flame on the throne to his left. Caspian has been propped in the middle throne, forced to watch his future unfold.

I die, he dies.

Where are Rhydian and his men? I search the arena, but it's a forest of Rebels.

I have to believe he won't let me down. He *won't*.

Sucking in a deep breath, I force out all negative thoughts and focus on my surroundings. My heart pounds against my sternum. My breath comes out hard and fast. The air is dimming . . .

Right before the shadow falls, before the air grows quiet and the torches flicker to life, an opening between the fighters appears and there Riser stands. For a heartbeat, the sand, the stone around the arena, the crowd all disappear. It's just him and me.

See you soon, I mouth.

His lips curl into a smile.

The shadowy curtain falls, separating us.

Time to fight.

One second, my hands are empty. The next, the smooth handle of a heavy leather electro-whip rests inside my right hand.

Grasping the whip, I immediately bring it up and down, snapping it over the huge Hawk with a shiny sword in front of me. The black cord coils around his fat neck.

He drops to his knees, fingers around the coil as electricity hums through his body.

Lash finishes the Hawk with his crossbow. I grab the fallen fighter's blade from the sand, wielding the weapon in my left hand.

Surprisingly, the Reconstructed me is almost as good with a blade on her left, and I manage to clear out a few more Rebels.

The air rings with the sharp kiss of metal on metal, the sound of fire and screams and the grunt of hand-to-hand combat. As promised, Max and Rivet form a barrier around us, and we slowly carve a small section of the arena for ourselves. At some point, Max throws his ender, taking out two female Rebels, and I toss him my sword.

A cheer rises from the crowd. Hugo and Lucy cut down the middle. Lucy swings a flail just as Hugo lobs an electrode in a blast of blue, three fighters dropping. Rhydian is nowhere to be seen.

Big arena. Big crowd. Still, doubt nibbles at the back of my mind.

Our group spreads out as more fighters drop. Lash runs out of arrows for his crossbow but gains an incendiary a few minutes later. He trades places with Rivet, who's armed with a long sword nearly as tall as she is.

Pressing our backs together, Teagan, Rivet, and I face outward, dispensing with the few Rebels who make it through Max's blade and Lash's fire.

We move through the darkness, the warm pools of fire-light coloring the sand, striking and slashing and burning, tightening and expanding, an entity of one mind, one goal: Survival.

Hope sparks inside my chest, lighting a flame I haven't felt in a long time. The arena is thinning, the sand a mess where people have fallen, the noises dulling as more and more leave.

Every minute or so, a space opens between Riser and me, and we appraise each other. As if all of this is just an act, a game that slowly brings us closer to the finale.

And then, suddenly, I can't locate him. Something tickles the back of my neck.

It doesn't matter. We're winning. Lash is being smart, conserving his little canister of fuel, and—

A sudden charge forces Lash back. Three towering Hawks converge on him with blades. Max counters the closest, giving Lash time to spew a long streak of flames at them.

They fall backward, and Lash finishes them with the last of his fire.

"I'm out!" he calls as another wave descends.

Something thuds in the sand by my feet, and I stumble sideways, the air crumpling to my left, just missing me. Ender.

Our group is breaking apart.

A tall girl with dark skin slips through Max and Lash. She lifts her arm, and I spot the electrode she's about to lob at my face. The butt of my whip bounces off her temple and she collapses.

The electrode feels small and cold inside my palm as I toss the weapon at the wall of fighters grappling a few feet to my right, trying to clear a path.

A blue flash blinds me.

When my vision returns, they sprawl on the sand, groaning.

Panic hits as I realize our group has been forced apart. Spinning around, I retrieve the metal disc, ready to use it again.

Ten feet ahead, Lucy and Hugo appear, their cruel gazes pinning me to the sand. I need them closer before I throw my electrode. I exhale a ragged breath as Rhydian slips behind them.

He lifts an axe . . .

And then a shadow with a sword flickers behind Rhydian. Riser. Before I can warn Rhydian, Riser plunges the simulated sword into Rhydian's back. As Rhydian plummets to the sand, his two friends surround Riser, but he slips through their blades, picking them off easily.

My heart lurches, adrenaline firing through my veins. The Redgraves have disappeared. My friends are falling. And I'm starting to weaken.

My carefully laid plan is unraveling.

FIFTY-THREE

I swivel my head, scouring the arena as I work my way back to the others. Three Hawks have Max and Teagan backed against the wall. One toss of my electrode takes care of them. Two charges left.

Don't waste your charge. Use your whip.

Once again, I can't find Riser.

Where is he? Where is he—?

A grunt sounds behind me. I turn, dropping just in time to miss an axe to my head. The broad steel blade skids off the wall with an ominous scrape, spitting sparks. I swing my hand palm-first into the offender's nose, and he drops to the sand, blood spurting from his face.

But it's not Riser.

I grab the axe and turn just in time to see the arrow spiraling through the shadows toward me. The golden arrow-head bounces off the head of the axe with a *clang*. The girl that fired the crossbow notches another.

She's about to release her bolt when Max tackles her, the shaft whizzing above my head. Rivet finishes her with her sword.

Where is Riser? The Redgraves?

A sudden surge of fighters swarms our little crew. In the span of a breath, a heartbeat, everything descends into chaos.

My brain struggles to process what's happening. Sand bursting the air and pelting my cheeks. Screams and grunts. Metal kissing metal. I lose my electrode somewhere in the madness. My friends have disappeared.

I try to use my whip, but it's useless in close quarters, so I toss it.

I force my way out of the fighting. *Where are my friends?* Very few contenders are left, maybe twenty. For a moment, I'm alone, weaponless and unnoticed, a spectator to the death throes of a violent battle.

Rivet limps off the arena. Max is still fighting, but he disappears into a churning mass of Rebels before I can get to him. I spot Teagan and Lash back to back, fighting off two axe-wielding muscle heads. By the time I run to help them, they've taken care of the fighters, but Teagan is out.

"Just you and me, Graystone," Lash says in a breathless gasp.

"That might be a problem!" I shout, holding up my empty hands.

A flash to our left catches our attention. Lucy wields a longsword, her eyes cruel and cunning as they take in my lack of weapon.

My heart rattles against my rib cage. Where's Hugo?

Lucy's lips curl into a sneer. "A mistake, letting the invalid have the weapon."

Hugo comes at Lash from the right. As Lash turns to counter the blow, Lucy lunges, her blade flashing through the air as it pierces Lash's stomach.

And then, as if time has been frozen, I watch as the tip slowly comes out his flank. Watch the drops of blood splatter the sand.

Blood. *Real blood.*

Lash crumples to the sand and doesn't get up. My mind screams with the memory of Riser falling beneath Caspian's sword on the Island. The dread and anger from that moment well inside me, filling me with rage.

Somehow, Lucy has a real weapon.

I glance up at Nicolai and Flame, watching from their thrones. "She has a real sword!"

Flame jumps from her throne, Teagan right behind her. With a flick of his gloved hand, Nicolai sends Rebels to block the arena entrance and bar them from helping. His eyes are hard, unrelenting, as Teagan grips the side of the arena, her face twisted with fear.

She goes to charge the Rebels guarding the court, but Flame grabs her by the waist and holds her back, whispering something in her ear.

They're not going to do anything. A sick feeling comes over me. I shoot forward, reaching for Lash's Sim sword, but Hugo plucks it from the sand, making a point to step around Lash's blood pooling around him.

A hyena-like laugh spills from Hugo's lips. "Where did all your friends go?"

"Screw you!" I hiss. I try to check on Lash, but Hugo drives me back with his sword. I flick a murderous glance at Lucy. "Everyone will know you used a real weapon. They'll know you're a coward."

Lucy glides closer, firelight flickering over her face. "Real? How could I possibly know that? The darkness hides so much."

I'm trapped. They're closing in. I can't tear my gaze from Lucy's sword, the blood smearing the blade nearly black in the Shadow Murk.

Take out Hugo. Get the bastard's sword. Even in my delusional state, I know that option will fail.

But I have to try.

Something flashes in my periphery. I look, but it's too late. Max charges, sword pointed at Hugo, but Max is rushing, his balance off—

Hugo chops the sword from his hand with a quick arc of his blade. A clang pierces the air.

Dread pools inside my chest as Max stumbles between them, the confidence draining from his face. Lucy grins and raises her sword.

Her *real* sword, darkened with *real* blood.

Everything fades away to my little brother, scared and vulnerable, and the sharp, cruel steel coming at him.

Just as Lucy's sword is biting into Max's neck, he ducks low, her blade clipping the ends of his curls. His face has gone from terrified to confident as he pops to his feet and grabs her sword arm.

While they struggle in the sand, I sprint toward them. I slip past Hugo and lunge for Lucy. Right as my fist connects with her cheek, Max wrenches Lucy's sword from her hands and stumbles back. Our eyes lock, and then his gaze flicks behind me.

Hugo's running at me with his blade pointed at my heart. With a yell, Max jumps in front of me, taking the impact of the weapon.

As he falls, he stretches the sword out at me, a grin on his face despite the pain. "Make them pay for Lash, Maia."

I twirl the real weapon, testing the weight. It feels the same as the others, but it's not. I have to remember that.

The smell of blood haunts the air as the twins circle me, their faces contorted into ugly masks.

"She has the real sword," Hugo hisses.

Firelight twinkles down the blade Lucy plucked from the sand. "So? Look at the way she hesitates. She's weak, afraid of real blood. She won't use it when it matters. She's scared."

Hugo lunges and I jump back, cutting my eyes back and forth between them. Around us, only a few clumps of fighters remain, their weapons clashing in a slow, steady rhythm. My breath pulses from my lungs in short, shallow bursts.

But Lucy is wrong. I'm not scared. I'm furious. Filled with blinding, murderous rage that sends a headache screaming into my brain.

How dare they hurt Lash. How dare they bring a real sword onto the field, almost use it on my brother, and then force me to wield it.

How. Dare. They.

Except now I realize voices other than mine are the ones talking.

How dare the empire imprison us inside these Caskets.

How dare they consign us to die.

How dare they trick us into believing we're safe.

"I don't—I don't know what to do," I whisper to them.

Abruptly a thousand voices pierce my skull. *Now!* They scream. *Free us now!*

For a single heartbeat, nothing. I exist in a vacuum of darkness.

Then the fury inside my head bursts. There's a pulse of energy. A release. I cry out as I feel them draining from me, pouring like a raging river of souls until my head feels hollow and light for the first time in forever, my skull *empty* of strange voices.

But there's something else still inside me, something I can't explain, like a tingling static that I know is somehow linked to the Sim.

Lucy and Hugo's swords shimmer until they are translucent, two-dimensional blue outlines. The other weapons on the field look the same.

All but mine.

A laugh escapes my lips. "They're not . . . they're not real."

Lucy hisses and swings her blade at my head. There's a

tingle and a light *whoosh* as it passes through my skull, but nothing happens. Lucy tries again—and again, nothing happens.

For whatever reason, the Sim weapons can't harm me.

The realization sends my heart into overdrive. A spark of electricity pulses at the base of my brain. I focus on Lucy's weapon, drawn to the way it flickers. The longer I stare, the more it seems to fade.

As if I'm controlling it.

Snarling, Lucy lunges, sword aimed at my chest—

"No more!" My voice echoes through the arena, a lightning bolt of energy barreling down my spine.

A moment later, Lucy's sword evanesces, and she and Hugo fall. They don't just drop; they crumple like dominos, the other fighters melting to the ground until only Riser and I are left. Yells and surprised gasps shift through the crowd.

My jaw hangs open. What the Fienian hell did I just do?

"Neat trick," Riser calls out, gliding toward me. He's the only one in the arena who doesn't seem phased by the bodies spread over the sand.

Why didn't I incapacitate him too? Perhaps some part of me protected him, for all the good it will do me.

I grit my teeth. "Wasn't it?"

My confident voice hides the fact that I have no idea what I did, or, more importantly, how to *reproduce* it. Like now, when I need it the most.

I glance at the fallen Rebels. I didn't just destroy their Sim weapons; I knocked them out cold. They rise slowly and stumble across the sand, rubbing their heads. Hugo helps Lucy up, and she flicks a savage glance at me before they ascend the stairs.

Relief washes over me. At least I didn't kill them— although that sentiment doesn't reach the Redgrave twins. And my stunt certainly didn't improve our relationship. I have the same feeling I would get if I pissed off a very large, very poisonous snake and it was underfoot somewhere, about to strike.

Riser glances up at the stadium. "Sword, please!"

Within seconds, Teagan has thrown her longsword down to the arena floor. It sticks straight up in the sand, wobbling.

As much as I glare at it, I can't will it away like the others.

Riser claims the weapon, tossing it back and forth as he tests the weight. The sight fills me with cold, mindless fear.

He cants his head to the side, a swath of hair falling over his forehead and a feline smile twitching below hard, determined eyes. "Ready to finish the dance we started a long time ago, Graystone?"

Swallowing, I afford myself one glance up at the crowd. Caspian sits on the edge of his seat, his eyebrows lowered. He gives me a tight-lipped smile. My heart swells as I recognize Brogue leaning over the railing.

For the first time since I've known him, he looks truly worried, deep lines etched into his forehead.

That makes two of us.

The others join him. Max, Rhydian, Rivet, and Teagan. They do their best to nod and appear hopeful, but their pale, drawn faces say otherwise.

This is a fight to the death. One that will decide the fate of everyone I care about. If I fail now, I fail them.

But as I glance back at Riser and the tendons in his neck cord, heralding his attack, I know one thing is certain: I've trained for this moment in one way or another my entire life. I was shaped by my father, chiseled by my mother, hardened by the pit, and polished by my Reconstruction, all to make me an unstoppable weapon.

Still, despite it all, I know there's a very good chance the only boy I ever came close to loving is going to kill me.

FIFTY-FOUR

Riser advances a step across the sand, grinning. "Ladies first."

My heart thuds inside my ears. Is it a trap? Should I strike first or make him chase me? But then Lash groans.

He doesn't have much time. I'll have to strike first—

Riser lunges. Grunting and pissed, I manage to knock his blade away with my sword. He lunges again and again. Chopping away at me with a calm, graceful ferocity. My panting fills the air, and I barely manage to deflect his blows, the power from our swords meeting reverberating up my arm and into my shoulder.

I parry and counter, but he's like the shadows around us, flickering and shifting, a dark and deadly specter that defies the rules of space and time.

He moves too fast, too unpredictably.

Out of nowhere, he brings down his sword and clips my shoulder.

I cry out.

"You know, while I enjoy this little dance," he says, hardly out of breath. "I would have preferred your support instead."

I take advantage of his talking to rein down a volley of thrusts and lunges on him.

Laughing, he defends my attack, moving easily to the side.

I square to face him, breathless and incensed. "Did you ever consider supporting *me*?"

"Maybe if you'd asked me nicely."

I lunge, just missing his belly. "This *is* me asking nicely!"

He swings his blade toward my head, but I duck and counter with a stop thrust to his heart.

Deflecting, he feints left and catches me with another good blow to the shoulder. Any pain I'd normally feel is blunted by adrenaline.

Frustration contorts his face. "I don't want to hurt you."

"Funny," I counter, sucking breath and chopping away at his ribs with clumsy, angry strokes. "Because I certainly want to hurt you."

This charade goes on for what could be hours. The cheers and yells from the spectators soon give way to silence. I can feel Lash fading behind me. His blood soaking into the sand.

Yet Riser toys with me.

I stumble, and his blade glances off my left shoulder again. I roar as fire shoots down my arm. My sword hangs in my right hand, but it droops to the sand, my muscles screaming against the weight.

They aren't mortal blows. He's wearing me down. Taking out my arms. He wants me to give up. But I'd rather die by his sword than whatever monstrous weapon Nicolai has in mind for me.

Fury rages in my chest, and I goad my muscles into lifting the sword.

I swing.

I miss.

I swing again.

I miss again.

I growl in frustration, even as a simple truth becomes clear: I can't win this way. I can't beat Riser with my strength. I can't win against him with my skills and speed. Even my Reconstruction isn't enough to best him.

The same feelings I used to have when I was forced to spar against my mother surface. Not fast enough. Not violent enough. Not *good* enough.

Not unless I change the game.

There's a glimmer of silver as Riser swings his sword at my head. I duck to my knees, remembering Brogue's words.

I'm Riser's weakness. Now I just need a part of him to remember who I am so I can break down his defenses and win.

His steel bounces off my blade as I pop to my feet, my sword held low to counter more blows. I wait to strike, conserving my energy for the perfect moment.

"You can't defeat me," I say, circling. "I survived the pit. Don't you remember?"

His lips twist in a frown and he strikes again.

"Afterwards we stared at the stars, and you covered me in a blanket. I thought you would eat me you were so feral."

Riser cracks his neck. "Whatever you're trying to do, you're wasting your breath."

I dodge another blow, just barely, and continue. "I didn't know then that you were the one who saved me." My words come out choppy between labored breaths. "That I was the reason you lost your eye."

Grunting, he attacks twice as hard, his sword coming down in a relentless barrage of strikes, as if his body is lashing out at the painful memories.

I fall back, letting him chase me. Trying to buy myself time. "You begged me to trust you, but I couldn't, remember? I wasn't brave enough."

He's striking over and over now with deadly ferocity, his face an unreadable mask as he grunts and pivots around the sand. It takes everything I have to ward off his fury . . . but I won't last much longer.

"You told me to fight, remember? Fight until my very last breath. That's what I'm doing." I cry out as his sword catches my shoulder again. "I'm fighting you because I have to. I have to, *Pit Boy*."

The onslaught of metal dies. Riser is frozen in place, his eyes wide and searching.

As much as it hurts me, I use this moment to ram my sword into his shoulder. His mouth opens in a silent gasp. There's the sound of the blade tearing through tendons and muscle. Even as I push forward, my gut clenches, my mind replaying images of him falling after Caspian nearly killed him.

I fight through my emotions, shoving them deep down into the hole I've carved out over the years.

As if coming out of a trance, he yanks free from my blade and stumbles backward, but I follow. My sword connects with his, there's an enormous, ear-splitting clang—

His blade jerks from his fingers and tumbles to the sand.

For a breath, I see Riser, *my* Riser, and my heart screams for me to stop.

But my heart stopped mattering the day my father made me responsible for saving the world, so I press the edge of my blade into his chest and say the three words I never thought I would say to him. "Do you yield?"

Riser's chest heaves as he studies me, confusion etched into his face. Blood spurts from his shoulder onto the sand. The silence of the arena magnifies my heartbeat into a booming symphony.

Slowly his confusion gives way to betrayal, his jaw tensing.

Riser's gaze collapses to the sand. "It's yours."

The muscles in my shoulders quiver as I lift my sword high into the air and square to face the crowd.

Nicolai's flapping cloak is the only sound as he makes his way to the side of the arena, frowning down at us. Straightening, I glare up at him, daring him to defy me.

For what feels like an eternity, we stare one another down.

Then he sighs and calls out, "Behold, the Scorpion Queen," and cheers drown the air as hundreds of Rebels stand and applaud.

FIFTY-FIVE

The stadium still thrums with cheers. Teagan runs to take care of Lash. I want to go with her, but first I must face Nicolai. I need to see it in his eyes. That he truly concedes, and I have the Scorpion Throne.

I meet his gaze.

"Release the Crown Prince," I order in a clear, strong voice, even though my body feels seconds away from collapsing.

His gaze flicks to Caspian and then back to me. Even with Nicolai's ruined face and masked expression, I can see the hatred in his eyes. I think for a moment he's going to refuse, but then he nods to the two Rebels guarding Caspian, and they slash his binds.

Satisfied, I stagger to Lash, praying to whatever gods listening. *Don't let him die. Don't let him die.*

Teagan has Lash's head cradled in her lap. His eyes are white and glazed as they find me. His mouth parts in a tight grin. "I know what I want my last wish to be."

I drop to my knees beside him. "Anything."

Lash puckers his lips. "Maybe a . . . a kiss for me?"

I fight the urge to smack him as relief trills through me. If he's joking, that means he's not on the verge of death. Teagan has his bloody shirt lifted, inspecting the bubbling hole in his abdomen. Ripping off her jacket, she presses it over the wound, turning him onto his back.

"Careful, love," Lash groans.

"We need to get him to a healer," Teagan says.

"I *am* a healer."

"No, right now, you're a patient. An annoying one at that."

My breath hisses between my teeth. I try to focus on helping, but I can't tear my gaze from his back, crisscrossed with a mess of thick red scars. It gets worse the lower I look.

Tears of rage brim my eyes. "Oh, Lash."

"Isn't it a little early to be calling out my name?" Lash mutters, his voice tinged with pain. "I think that comes *after* the kiss."

I roll my eyes. "Well, getting run through by a sword didn't do anything for your ego."

We help him up. He's pale but smiling, and the blood has stopped flowing. I can't help but hug him, careful to avoid his injured side. He sags into me. Even though he's joking and moving, he's still in bad shape and probably in more pain than he'll admit.

"So," Lash grunts, pressing a hand into his side. "What's on the agenda now that you're in charge, Graystone?"

"Don't worry about that."

We get him to the stairs, and without a word, Riser takes my place by Lash's side and props him against his shoulder. A shiver runs through me as I make eye contact with Riser.

It's only for a second. A dizzy, terrifying, vulnerable second.

Does he remember now? Does he hate me?

But I can glean nothing from his hard, expressionless

mask—nothing except the fact that when our shoulders brush, he pulls away. It could be because he's injured, because I ran him through with a sword.

Or it could be because he knows somehow that I tricked him.

Biting my lip, I tear myself away, practically sprinting through the mass of Rebels all gaping at me.

Even though he's free, Caspian is slumped in the throne on the left, his face waxy and pale, eyes feverish. Mottled flesh peeks from the top of his ripped tunic. Gripping the chair's thick arms, he tries to stand, but the effort is too much, and he falls back.

"Cong . . . congratulations," he rasps.

"The prince needs a Reconstructor," I order.

For a moment, my command hangs in the air as everyone watches to see if I really have the Scorpion Throne. Frowning, Flame cuts her eyes at Nicolai, impatiently tapping her boot against the base of her throne.

Nicolai gives Caspian a bored once-over and then flippantly waves. "Fine. Attend to his needs."

As Rivet and Max help Caspian up, Caspian nods to me. "Thank you."

But, as I watch my friends assist Lash and Caspian inside Bloodwyn Castle, I can't help but feel it's a little premature to be thanking me just yet. Not until I've gathered anyone who wishes to go with me and we've made it out of this gods' forsaken place, *alive*.

Brogue finds me on the stairs and wraps me in a bear hug. "Couldn't be prouder of you, Maia."

My bruised muscles scream under his strength, and I wiggle from his grasp. "I thought you weren't coming."

"Almost didn't, you know." His lips twist to the side as he runs a hand over his stubbly cheek. "Couldn't stand the idea of you getting hurt and me not being able to protect you.

Now I see you don't need my protection. Not anymore. If only your parents could see you . . . they would be so proud."

He's never mentioned my parents before, but I know he's heard me talk about them, so I brush it off. "If you knew my mother, you wouldn't say that."

With a final kiss against his stubbly cheek, I rush to claim my throne. Already, the Rebels are funneling into the castle in preparation for my crowning. I missed both times Riser was crowned after the Blood Court, so I'm not sure what to expect.

All I know is that I have to make a speech riveting enough to entice Rebels to leave the safety of Bloodwyn and follow me—a task that's sounding more impossible by the second.

I defeated Prince Riser and won the Scorpion Throne, but will it be enough to make them forget I was a suspected traitor?

My mouth is dry as cotton as I slip through the subdued crowd on the way to the indoor arena. Shadow Murk spills from the grated windows, darkening the halls. A few torches flicker in the musty air.

The arena is nearly full by the time I enter, my footsteps echoing in the silence. For a nervous second, I pause, wringing my sweat-slick hands as I survey the Rebels.

Is it normal for the Rebels to be this quiet after the Blood Court?

Just before I ascend the steps, I glance over the crowd, looking for a familiar face. My gaze focuses on the empty throne in the middle. Nicolai and Flame watch me as I hesitate, disdain pouring from them.

Gathering my nerve, I climb the podium, the base of the tall pillared candles along the three thrones pooled with wax. The Scorpion Throne swamps me, the seat hard and uncomfortable against my achy body. I sink back, resting my arms on the huge armrests while keeping my hands away from the carved scorpions beneath my palms, their tail stingers poised in aggression.

I know they're not real, but I still can't manage to touch them.

Silence swells the room, the candle flames from the pillars by my feet sputtering softly. Gripping the sides of the chair, I remind myself to breathe.

Hollow footsteps ring over the dais and break the quiet. Riser glides toward me, his eyes looking just past me, the jagged silver crown in his hands sparkling in the candlelight. He wears an indifferent mask, but the tendon feathering his jaw says otherwise.

When he gets to the throne, he releases an uneven breath and drops to one knee. His eyes are tight as he relinquishes the crown.

Slowly, his gaze slides over my face and locks. "I hope you treat this crown with as much respect as I do."

I bristle at his hard voice but manage to swallow down my hurt with a nod. The crown is heavier than I imagined, and it sits a little too far down my head, pressing behind my ears and instantly spawning a headache.

With a forced smile, I tear my gaze from Riser and stand, ignoring the way my muscles tremble with pain. The way my heart aches as Riser leaves me and stands by Nicolai.

The crowd watches me expectantly. All the moisture in my mouth seems to transfer to my palms, and I clench my fists to keep from wiping my hands on my tunic. My heart thuds dully against my sternum.

"I . . ." I pause, startled by how loud my voice sounds.

Someone clears their throat. I blink, glancing again over the faces, searching for someone I know. Someone who will believe in me.

And then I spot a familiar figure by himself in the corner, and the breath catches in my chest. My father nods to me, a look of pride on his face as he smiles and fades away.

Was it a hallucination? A remnant of the Sim, or maybe a glitch in my Microplant?

It doesn't matter. Unclenching my fists, I once again stare out into the crowd. Except this time, I'm speaking for my father, saying the words he would have spoken if he hadn't been murdered by the empire.

"I know most of you are wondering why I wanted the Scorpion Throne. I'm a traitor, right?" A few people snicker under their breath, but most sit rapt, listening. "I understand why you might think that. But I need you to know, I have every reason to want the empire dead. When I was seven, they took my mother from me. When I was nine, they murdered my father and sent me to a prison I wouldn't wish on my worst enemy. And then, by some miracle, Nicolai rescued me and I entered the Shadow Trials, witnessing more horrors inflicted by the emperor. I was tortured, beaten, abused, and nearly broken.

"So, you see, I have every right to hate the empire. To want to see it burn to the ground, just like you do. But I can't do that yet when I know the one thing that could save our world from Pandora is inside the castle."

Murmurs ripple through the crowd.

"My father created something that can stop the asteroid from hitting us, and I made him a promise," I continue, raising my voice, "a promise to do whatever it takes to gain control of this device. I even know where it is. But I learned something these last few days: I can't do this alone. I need your help." I hold out my hand. "You can stay here if you like and fight a battle you cannot win. Who knows? Perhaps you'll kill a few Royalists, but you will most certainly die. Or you can join me for a cause greater than revenge . . . and maybe, just maybe, save our dying world."

Silence. Nicolai's raspy breathing behind me rattles my bones, and I can feel his stare burning into my back. No one moves. I swallow my disappointment, shifting on my heels as I scour the crowd for one volunteer. One person who believes in my cause, believes in *me*.

Anyone.

But not a single person comes forward.

FIFTY-SIX

Clearing my throat, I knead my thighs and try not to show my frustration. "Well, if—"

"Do I get to kill Royalists in your plan too, Princess?" a female voice interrupts from behind.

Not wanting to look desperate, I force myself to turn around slowly. Flame leans against her throne, one hand stroking her crossbow.

"As many as you like," I answer. "Except the prince, of course."

"Pity." She lifts her pierced eyebrows and strides to stand beside me. "Still, count me in." She leans close. "For Cage."

My jaw hangs open. Then I turn to the crowd, hiding my surprise behind an indifferent mask. A moment later, the doors burst open and relief purls through me as my friends jaunt toward the stage. Teagan helps a limping and bandaged Lash up the stairs, followed by Max, Rivet, and Caspian.

The Reconstructor must have worked because Caspian's face has regained some of its color, and his eyes are clearer, the corners of his lips no longer tight with pain.

Caspian's neck cords as he glances just past me at Riser.

For a too-long second, Caspian glares at Riser with a stare that could melt icebergs. Riser grins at his half-brother, a brutal smile that promises death. Tension crackles the air. I'm preparing to intervene before the two kill each other when Caspian turns away, taking the place to my right.

"How does someone as feral as him wear the crown?" Caspian demands under his breath.

I swallow down a laugh. "It's different here than at your Royalist court."

"Oh, there are savages at the palace too, they just hide it behind a veil of manners and civility." His gaze flits over my face. "So, how does it feel to wear the . . . What do they call it? Scorpion crown?"

"Uncomfortable." I shift the heavy thing back up my forehead, cursing as it tangles in my hair. "Terrifying."

"It looks good on you, if that's any consolation."

"Thanks." I bite my lip, ignoring the searing scowl I feel from Riser behind me. His hate for his half-brother is almost palpable. "Does that mean you're with me too? You'll help us inside Laevus Castle?"

Caspian scratches the back of his neck. "Is it true?"

"What . . . about the device—?"

"No. About my father killing my sister."

I blow out a long breath. "Yes. I'm sorry."

A dark shadow passes over his face, and he nods, his gaze on an invisible spot behind me. "I'll help you take the castle." His distant tone can't mask his pain, and when he finally focuses on me, I want to look away from the torment inside his eyes. "About what happened in the Sim—"

"It's okay. You don't have to say it."

"No. I do. Especially now that—look, I'm not like my father. I didn't want to hurt you, and if I'd known it was the *real* you . . ." He rakes his hand through his hair. "I thought if

I could just forget you, somehow the ache from losing O would get better."

"And did throwing me off a mountain help?"

"No." His lips twitch into a sad half-smile. "I don't think anything ever will."

Loud boot steps draw my attention to the front of the room. Brogue struts down the aisle like a damned peacock. As he lopes up the stairs with the spry movements of someone half his age, I marvel at how far he's come since a few days ago.

It feels good knowing I have him in my corner again. Even if I'll have to worry about him using Tar every second of every day from now on.

The Rebel crowd parts as Rhydian and one of the men from earlier follow behind Brogue. By now, Nicolai's breathing has quickened into rattling, angry puffs, his gloved hands clenched over the arms of his throne.

Beneath his red mask, his gaze darts over me, his nostrils flared and lips twisted to the side.

Suddenly I wish I had kept the sword from the arena. I slip my sweaty hand under my waistband, grasping the scorpion dagger.

Nicolai wouldn't dare challenge me now . . . would he?

No. Of course not. Yet I can't shake the feeling of unease clinging to me. I know I'm just tired, the stress from the last couple days hitting all at once.

As soon as we're out of this gods' forsaken castle, I'll feel better.

My chest loosens, and I breathe a little easier as more people trickle up the stairs. Rebels I've never met. Excitement and adrenaline burn my veins.

Soon we might have enough people to infiltrate the castle.

I glance over to Riser standing just to the left of Nicolai's throne. Although Pit Boy doesn't acknowledge me, I know he feels my questioning stare and refuses to acknowledge me. I suck in my bottom lip and tear my gaze back to the stage, now half full of Rebels.

My Rebels.

The words make me dizzy.

Lash leans in and whispers into my ear, "Happy now, love?"

A wild grin finds my face. "One step closer."

Something in my periphery calls my attention. A blur of dark hair streaked red. But my brain is buzzing with a million emotions and thoughts, and the image gets lost in the shuffle.

Max grabs my elbow, his lips curling into a smile. "You did it."

"No, we did it." But my voice sounds shaky, unsure.

Something is off.

A whisper of warning trills down my spine, too quiet to understand but too persistent to ignore. Silver flashes in the crowd. My gut clenches as my gaze darts through the Rebels, searching out what my body already knows, the reason all the hairs on my neck have risen.

Wrong. Wrong. Wrong.

Teagan approaches, a line creasing her forehead. "Darling . . ."

But I'm whirling around, panic clawing at my chest. My mind has finally pieced together what I saw.

Lucy.

Sword.

Lucy has a sword—

I pivot just in time to see Lucy barreling toward me, lips twisted in a sneer and blade poised over my heart. "The Archduchess sends her regards!"

FIFTY-SEVEN

The world slows. My hand goes to my dagger. But it's too late. I flinch, prepared for the pain of her sword—

From the corner of my eye comes movement. Then I'm staggering to my left as someone pushes me. I barely fall to one knee before popping to my feet, dagger in hand . . .

But it's too late.

Lucy sprawls over the stage, her eyes wide and glazed. A wood-handled dagger sticks from her chest, blood oozing from the wound. Brogue is on his knees, leaned over her.

Before I can say a word, something draws my attention to Riser's throne. Hugo stands behind Riser.

A crossbow rests in Hugo's hand, a shiny arrow pointed at Riser's back.

There's no time to warn him. Taking the blade of my dagger between two fingers, I release a breath and flick the scorpion blade at Hugo's chest. The dagger hits its mark with a dull thud, sinking to the hilt. Riser whips around as Hugo falls, clutching the knife, lips opening and closing like a fish out of water.

I run to Brogue. He's on his knees now.

"Are you hurt?" I demand, sinking beside him.

A laugh bursts from his throat and becomes a hacking cough. "Naw, Maia. Not hurt. Just . . . just tired."

My gaze flits to the red bloodstain blooming over the belly of his white tunic and the giant puddle of blood already pooled around his knees, and my heart shrivels in on itself. "Oh, gods. You're hurt."

"Think I might . . . might lie down for a bit."

Brogue rolls onto his side and then flops onto his back, one hand pressed into his gut. "Gotta be ready for . . . everything. My motto."

I fall over his torso. The sword he took for me must have lacerated an artery because the blood spurts from his wound in time with his heartbeat.

"Someone help me get him to a Reconstructor!" I scream.

"Too late . . ." Coughs rattle his chest. "But I protected you, Maia. I kept my . . . promise. It wasn't enough. We shouldn't have . . . shouldn't have killed him."

I freeze. The world around us shrinks to Brogue and me. "Kill who?"

His glassy eyes roll loosely until they focus in my direction. He licks his dry lips. "Don't make me say your father's name. I want to die proud. Your father and Lillian said it was the only . . . only way to keep the Royalists from getting the device. He knew so much. Too much."

"My father?" My mouth parts, the words heavy and jagged on my tongue. "Brogue, how do you know my parents?"

His words from earlier, that they would be proud, come back to me with new meaning.

His sharp Adam's apple bobs as he struggles to swallow. "I was . . . supposed to protect you all, especially you. But I failed in that duty."

"You . . ." A hollow moan rises in my chest. "Gabriel?"

"Yes." A flicker of recognition sparks inside his dying eyes at the name of my old bodyguard. The man who murdered my father and betrayed my family. "And now you know the reason I had to protect you from Nicolai. I had to . . . to make it right after everything that happened to you from that one horrible decision."

I'm too stunned to do anything but stare at his face, trying and failing to reconcile my bodyguard with my friend.

"It's me, Maia. You're not the only one they . . . they made to look different."

He was reconstructed. "But why?" I grab the lapels of his shirt, torn between grief and fury. "Why did you have to kill him?"

"It was his . . . his final sacrifice." His shoulders tremble with coughs, his breath hissing out in shallow, wheezing spurts. "We . . . We . . . I'm sorry." The fist on his stomach relaxes; his gaze slowly fixes on the ceiling. "Did it . . . all to stop . . . Her."

All at once, the ragged rise and fall of his chest ends. His name dies in my throat. Brogue. No, Gabriel. The name synonymous with betrayal and death and crying myself to sleep.

Yet, still I loved him, this man who trained me, who cared about me when so few did, and whoever he was in the past will die with him.

Throat aching and eyes burning with tears I don't dare shed, I run my fingers down his stubbly face, closing his eyes for the last time.

"Goodbye, friend," I whisper, and it takes everything I have not to fall apart here in front of everyone.

As if I've existed in a vacuum until now, the rest of my world shrieks back to life. The Rebels are in an uproar. People are arguing, screaming. Weapons are out. The Rebels who have pledged to me are accusing Nicolai of trying to assassinate me.

The room is seconds away from chaos.

I run the back of my hand over my cheeks, even though they're dry, slip Brogue's pistol from the leather holster at his waist, and stand, shoving my way through the crowd. One leap and I'm standing on the middle throne.

I lift the pistol to the ceiling and shoot. The sound splits the air and rattles my eardrums. Smoke drifts from the muzzle.

Silence.

"Now that I have your attention, I would like to speak." I lower my pistol and scan the Rebels. "Nicolai didn't try to kill me. The emperor did. And he will keep trying until either he succeeds or I do."

Murmurs stir the stage.

"Now, if you don't mind, I have a friend who needs to be properly sent to the gods, and then I plan to pay a visit to the emperor. Feel free to join me, or stay and die."

As if just now realizing a Rebel has died, the crowd parts around Brogue. Flame is the first to reach him, followed by Teagan and Max. More join them, and they lift him up, carrying him through the room.

I cross the dais to Hugo's body, nudging him onto his back with the toe of my boot. The scorpion dagger sits perfectly between the fifth and the sixth intercostal bones.

"You taught me well, Brogue," I say as I retrieve it.

I notice Riser watching me quietly and offer him the dagger. "This was your mother's, I think. You should have it."

His lips twist to the side as he takes the weapon, wiping the blade clean on Hugo's shirt. "Thank you . . . for saving my life."

"Sure." I lift the heavy crown from my head, wincing as it brushes against my bruised skull. "This is yours, too."

The crown fits him perfectly—the way it was supposed to fit me. The true Blood King. For an agonizing moment, I drink him in, not caring if he wonders why I'm staring, all the words I should be saying lodged in my throat.

Come back to me, Pit Boy. Remember me. I don't want to leave you.

His Adam's apple bobs. "What happened out there between you and me?"

I want to finally tell him everything. Our shared past . . . his broken promises. But how can I, when it's obvious being King of the Rebels and avenging his mother means everything to him?

Whatever I was to him, whatever he felt for me, this is who he is now.

"A trick." I chew my cheek to keep the hurt from my voice.

I count ten beats of my heart before he finally speaks. "You know, once you walk out that door, you are no longer considered Fienian, meaning we're no longer allies."

"I'm aware." I release a ragged breath, still fighting the urge to fall to my knees and beg him to come with me. "You'll make a good Blood King."

"And I have no doubt you'll give the Royalists a Rebel's welcome when you enter the castle."

"I'm not hiding anymore, am I?" I remark, referencing words I said to Riser what seems like years ago, in a tiny, dirty bathtub as he washed my hair. "I'll never hide again."

Something flickers over his face—an emotion, a memory —but I flee before he can see how much leaving him hurts me.

There was a time in our lives when I could have lost myself in Riser and forgotten about our dying world and my promise to my father. But that moment passed, and I have no idea how to get it back again.

Leaving Riser is a worthy sacrifice if it means sparing countless lives, I tell myself. But those words do nothing to numb my pain as I cross the room and out the door, the feel of his gaze heavy on my back.

I thought, no matter what, Pit Boy would come back to me. But I was wrong. He won't stop until he burns the world to the ground.

And I won't stop until I save it.

FIFTY-EIGHT

The faraway promise of a storm flickers along the ocean's dark horizon, rain falling in fat droplets over my cheeks. I hold Max tight in my arms. Even though I can't see his face, I know he's crying by the way his body shakes.

I should be thinking about how to find shelter for my Rebels, but all I can focus on is the tiny ship that holds Brogue's body, now a fiery-red star cresting the dark ocean waves.

"I can't believe he's gone," Max whispers.

I squint against the driving rain. "We gave him a good send off, the way he would have wanted."

It's true. Brogue would have fancied watching his body burning to ashes over the sea, if only to make some deep, sentient speech about it and watch me roll my eyes.

You did good, girl, I hear his voice say. *Now forget me and move on.*

Gods, I want to. From the cliffs, I can barely make out his little wooden boat anymore. I promised myself as soon as it was out of sight I would stop hurting. My eyes ache to cry, to wash his memory away, but I push my emotions down into the hole I've buried all the other tragedies in.

I'll mourn later, when it's safe to feel again. When I can shatter into a thousand pieces and not worry about being seen as weak. When I can be a teenager.

I know there's a huge chance that will never happen, and I'm prepared for that, too.

The distant rumble of thunder rocks the air, and I send Max off to pack. In less than an hour, I'll lead my group of Rebels away from the safety of these walls.

Where, I have no clue. I'm also struggling with how to feed and protect nearly thirty people.

Wind lashes my wet hair as I glance over my shoulder at the other mourners. Most are ones who've chosen to leave the safety of the Rebel stronghold and follow me.

There's only one person missing: Riser. A cold fist wraps around my heart. He might not remember me, but surely he remembered Brogue, so why isn't Riser here?

Forcing Pit Boy down to join Brogue's memory, I whisper one last goodbye to my friend. "I'll miss you, Merc. I really will."

Rhydian finds me as I'm making my way past the other mourners. The rain has slicked his hair, and for a moment, I see Merida's face instead of Rhydian. Then he thrusts something cold into my hands.

Bramble. Despite my heartache, I'm filled with joy at the sight of my old friend.

"I'm sorry," Rhydian says. "I had to turn him off. After the prince escaped and Meadow knocked you out, he wouldn't let us near your body."

A grin finds my face as I run two fingers over his smooth shell, slick with water. "Thank you."

His lips twist to the side, and he nods. "The least I could

do . . . after everything. And you'll need every friend you can get, now."

I watch him jog away toward the castle. Time to leave. I'm gathering the others when I spot Flame cutting through the rain, gusts of wind blowing back her cloak. A quiet warning sounds inside my head as I race to meet her.

Flame never runs.

She pulls me behind an abandoned storage building, raising her cloak over us both to block the rain. "There's been a development, Princess."

My mouth goes dry. "What kind?"

"We caught movement on the surveillance around the front gates. At first it only looked like a few people but . . ."

"But what?" The storm has reached us, and I have to yell over the howling wind. "Flame! Just tell me. Is it an army?"

"In a sense, yes." She blinks, her lips curling at the corners. "Somehow the Sleepers woke up, and now they're asking for you."

Me? For a breathless moment, I'm stunned. "How . . . how many?"

"Thousands. Silvers from the mountains. Bronzes from the cities. They just keep coming."

I slump back against the crumbling wall, barely noticing as the cloak slides from my head and cold rain soaks my face and hair. "They want to talk to *me*?"

Flame nods, her dark hair pasted over her skull. Her spiked eyebrows knit together. "There's more."

I lift my eyebrows. What else could there be?

"A woman leads them. She's . . ."

Something about her hesitation, the strange look in her eyes, and I know who it is.

"It's your mom."

FIFTY-NINE

I have my Swifter topped out way past the one hundred and fifty miles per hour line on its sleek dashboard, riding the curved grassy-pocked road to the gate. Rain shivers in the two long white beams of my headlights, cedars rising on either side.

Thoughts rattle my brain as I take the last curve and the towering iron gates rise ahead. My mother is here. My mother betrayed me. My mother is a Royalist.

This could be a trap.

Lash, Teagan, and Rhydian struggle to follow behind me. Only Caspian manages to keep up, but just barely. My skin is cold and clammy, but a fire rages inside me, burning away the cold.

I see my mother the day she left me. I see her on the Island during the Trials, her face cold and unaffected by the horrors we endured.

My emotions are jumbled and raw, but I know one thing for sure.

If she tries anything, *anything* at all, I'll kill her myself.

The gates begin to part with a massive rumble before we

stop. As the space between the doors creaks wider, my heart gives a wild kick. Teagan pulls her Swifter next to mine, steam rising from the black beast she straddles. She gives me a steadying nod just as Lash and Rhydian glide up on my left. We all have our hands on our weapons.

My mother sits on a snow-white horse, an amethyst cloak falling to her knee-high black boots. Behind her, the sweeping grasslands stir with people. Thousands and thousands milling over the land. My mouth hangs open.

"Fienian hell, darling," Teagan murmurs.

Lash grins and cracks his neck. "They heard I was here."

Suddenly a little girl with a sky-blue dress and corn silk braids breaks from the crowd and runs over. Before I can react, she has her arms round my stomach, hugging me.

"It's really you," she squeals into my stomach.

Holding out my arms, I stiffen and glance at Teagan. She shoots me an amused grin.

A reed-thin woman darts forward and drags the girl off me, apologizing the whole time. "I'm sorry; she wants to be just like you. You . . . you give her hope."

I frown and refocus on my mother as they melt back into the crowd. Swinging a leg over the saddle with grace I've never known, she drops to the road and makes toward me.

For a moment, I'm frozen, my body tensed and trembling. Even the rain seems to stop, as if awed by her presence.

"Stop right there!" Teagan orders.

An ender sparkles inside her palm. Caspian and the others quickly follow, their enders illuminating the night.

My mother halts, cutting her eyes at Teagan with a look that used to terrify me, and raises a sharp eyebrow.

I wait a second longer than necessary, enjoying watching her squirm probably more than I should. Then I nod the okay, and she continues.

My boots sink into the mud as I steal a breath and walk to

meet the woman I've hated for half my life. The soft glow of the lantern she holds paints her high cheekbones orange, and lank bits of wet brown hair fall over her forehead.

Eyes that used to pick me apart with one glance focus on me. Now, though, they simply look tired, weighted down with bags that make her look ten years older.

Her mouth tightens, and she slips off her leather riding gloves. "Maia? It's . . . you?"

Of course she can't be sure. She remembers the pre-Reconstructed me. The timid girl who cowered in her shadow.

I nod, grateful my throat's too dry to work properly. I'm afraid if words do start pouring out, I'll say things I might regret. Things I've wanted to say for years.

Hurtful, hateful, unforgivable things.

"These are your Sleepers." She gestures behind her with a wave. "After being inside your head for so long, they feel a certain loyalty to you. All of them will fight to help you retrieve the Mercurian and overthrow the emperor."

I flick a glance over the sea of people, hardly breathing. I wanted an army, but this . . . this is an entire population of people. "There are so many."

"Instead of uploading them to the Chosen after the bombing, I secretly funneled all the Sleepers from the finalists into you. It was your father's failsafe to wake them up after the mandatory upload. I apologize for any cognitive effects the process might have had. I tried to do it slowly, but I only had so much time, and you were the only one who could wake them."

Right. I think of the headaches I've had recently. The first thing that comes to mind is a sarcastic retort, something about a mother's love and playing a guinea pig, but I bite it back.

"Look, Maia. I know you have questions, and we can get to those soon. But first we need to move before the rain stops and the drones return. So, I need to know . . . Are you ready to lead these people?"

My pulse drumbeats inside my ears. Her voice dredges up all the times she looked at me like she is now, asking if I was good enough, strong enough. All the times she hurt me, pushed me harder, broke me apart and put me back together.

All the times she expected me to be strong, and I let her down.

But this time is different. I meet my mother's steely gaze. "I'm ready. Now excuse me while I gather my people and things."

Ignoring the way her jaw clenches at my defiant tone, I circle my Swifter around and speed to the castle, losing the others. The Rebels are in a state of alert when I enter the main hall, running through the corridors carrying weapons. It's not every day an army shows up outside their doors.

Not *an* army.

My army.

I cross through the indoor arena, now dim and quiet compared to my first day here, and talk a Rebel girl into leading me to Nicolai. I practice what I'll say to him as I lope up the wide set of stairs near the foyer, but as soon as I spot his solemn figure standing at the table inside the war room, the words flee my head.

The bored look Nicolai gives me beneath his mask hints that he was expecting me. He waves the Rebels away, and I flinch as the door shuts with a thud.

"Maia Graystone." Nicolai's Electro-Larynx makes my name sound gravelly and foreign. "Winner of the Blood Court. Champion of the people. And fool."

"Perhaps," I say, running my hand along the table. "But *this* fool beat you at your own game."

Nicolai drums his gloved fingers over the back of his chair. "What makes you think you've won, hmm? My, a few

Rebels join your side and suddenly your head is as big as the hole I found you in. Too bad they don't know what a broken, pathetic creature you are."

I shiver at the rancor dripping from his voice. "You might have dragged me from my hellish prison, reconstructed my flesh, and made me into a lady, but you never controlled me, and that drives you crazy, doesn't it? That I'm not some silly Rebel you can manipulate?" I close the distance between us. "I know what you are now, and I'll do everything in my power to make sure that someday, after I've stopped Pandora and prevented your war, Riser sees it too."

He laughs, a terrifying, half-mad sound. "You cannot stop the inevitable."

"Watch me!" I shout, banging my hand on the table.

"Foolish child. If you play grown-up games, you must expect grown-up consequences. The second you lead those Rebels out my doors, you are no longer Fienians but the enemy. And when the end comes, I will string you up along with the Royalists."

I stalk from the room, calling over my shoulder, "You can *try*."

My breathing doesn't even out until I'm two floors down. I hurry through the hall to my room and slip inside the chamber that was once a prison.

Muffled moonlight spills from the broken window and curves along the carved scorpion walls. I hadn't realized until now how relieved I am to leave this place, with its savage rules and dark secrets.

There isn't much to pack. Any weapons I have are already stashed on my body. I scrounge up a few pairs of pants and an old tortoise-shell brush missing half its bristles. Bramble, of course, gets a safe space nestled in the bottom of my pack.

Last minute, I nab the old journal I discovered from Amandine, Riser's mother.

Still, I pace the room, not ready to leave. I despise this place, so why am I stalling? Perhaps I'm afraid of accepting the responsibility waiting just past the gates below. Maybe my mother is to blame.

Except I know the real reason I can't leave, and he has a boyish smile and murderous tendencies. As soon as I walk out those iron gates, Riser Thornbrook will be lost to me forever.

No, not just lost; he will be my enemy.

"He made his choice," I mutter, grabbing the few items and crossing the floor. The statement becomes a mantra echoing inside my head as I finish gathering my stuff. When everything is packed and ready, I let out a breath.

Goodbye, Pit Boy.

And then the door swings open as I reach for it, bringing me face-to-face with the very thing I'm obsessing over.

Maybe it's the shock, but I retreat four or five steps, my heart punched into my throat.

Riser shuts the door quietly behind him. For a heartbeat, we just stare at each other, our breathing the only sound. I had a million things I wanted to say to him, but now my mind is blank.

He walks toward me slowly, never breaking his gaze, and each step he takes hollows out my stomach a little more, until we're inches apart. We stay like this for countless seconds, his breath warming my cheeks, me staring open-mouthed at him as a thousand emotions seem to flicker inside his mismatched eyes.

His mouth opens twice, as if to say something, then he frowns. "I'm not . . . not good at this."

"At what?"

He falls to his knees, his hood slipping back and dark hair falling over his forehead, and presses his face into my stomach. "Forgive me." Rising, he takes my hands in his.

"Forgive me." His forehead rests against mine. "Forgive me."

My heart pounds in my ears. "Does this mean . . .?"

"I remember you, Digger Girl. It was something you said in the throne room about never hiding again. I just, I couldn't let it go, and suddenly the memory of you came flooding back. *We* came flooding back."

Conflicting emotions rage inside me. Anger. Hurt. Relief. "Why? Why did you let them take me from you?"

He pulls away, his blue eye stormy and dark, lips pressed taut. "I didn't. I assume one of the Redgraves made that up, but the only thing I'll ever know for sure is that I would have died before I let them take your memory from me."

I slip my hands from his, not fully trusting this after being hurt for so long. "What now? I don't want to keep you from—"

"Stop." He finds my hands again and squeezes, hard. "Look at me, Maia. How can you see my face, read the intention in my eyes for you, and still think I would let you leave without me?"

"But you . . . your mom."

A vein throbs in his temple. "Maia, I'll make this simple for you. Wherever you go, I go. Whenever you fight, I fight. And if you die . . . I die too."

It's all happening so fast, and I can't think of what to say.

Seeing my conflicted expression, he growls, pulling me into him. "I will never let anyone take you away from me again. Do you understand?"

Before I can respond, he leans down and captures my bottom lip with his teeth. I practically stop breathing as his tongue slides inside my mouth, slowly, gently.

His breath comes out in ragged puffs as he explores my lips, alternating between deep, passionate kisses and soft, sensual pecks.

"Now do you understand, Digger Girl? I love you, I have since the pit, and my path will always include you, *always*, for as long as you'll have me."

He waits quietly for my response, eyes wide and solemn.

I force back a grin. "Does that mean you'll take orders from me?"

He quirks a daggerish eyebrow. "Perhaps. If you ask nicely."

"And Caspian, your half-brother?"

His lips curl into a frown. "What about him?"

"We need him *alive*. So please, promise you'll get along."

A scowl darkens his face, but he nods. "Fine. If he plays nice, so will I."

"Good." My attention falls over the pack on the bed where the journal hides, and I meet his curious stare. "Don't let me forget, I have something for you."

"Oh?" His voice shivers with amusement as his gaze drops to my lips. "A good surprise, I hope?"

"Could be, but it'll have to be later. Right now, we need to go before Nicolai changes his mind."

"Yeah, about that. We should probably hurry."

A sigh hisses between my teeth. "What did you do?"

"I might have accidentally misplaced a couple caches of Hot Weapons."

I gasp. "A couple?"

He shrugs. "A couple . . . ten. They're in the caves, waiting for us."

"Then maybe you should gather a *couple* of our Rebels and retrieve those?"

Grinning, he salutes. "On it." He pauses for a moment and then leans down to brush his lips over my cheek. "See you soon, Digger Girl."

My toes don't uncurl until he's gone. Gulping a deep breath to steady myself, I float to the window and gaze out.

For the first time since I can remember, things seem to be going right, like the universe is on my side. The tides are against the Royalists; they just don't know it yet.

Gods, I can't wait to see their faces when they do.

I grip the windowsill and search the sky for Her. Nestled in a pool of silver clouds, she's the size of an apple. The promise I made to destroy Her doesn't seem quite as silly now.

Are you worried yet, Pandora? You should be. I have an army. I have friends. I have a plan.

I know there are still a thousand ways I could fail. I still don't trust my mother. Nicolai won't just sit back and let us have the Mercurian. And I'll be lucky if Riser and Caspian don't kill each other before we break inside Laevus Castle—and luckier still if we don't all die the moment we get inside.

Still. I survived the pit. I survived Reconstruction and the Shadow Trials, the sadistic Archduchess and the Blood Court, and Nicolai and countless other things that should have killed me.

I think it's time to find out if the emperor can survive *me*.

The End

Don't forget to grab SHADOW RUIN, the final book in the Shadow Fall series.

Welcome to EVERMORE ACADEMY where the magic is dark, the immortals are beautiful, and being human SUCKS.

After spending my entire life avoiding the creatures that murdered my parents, one stupid mistake binds me to them for four years.

My penance? Become a human shadow at the infamous Evermore Academy, finishing school for the Seelie and Unseelie Fae courts.

Day one, I make an enemy of the most powerful Fae in the academy. The Winter Prince is arrogant, cruel, and apparently also my Fae keeper. Meaning I'm in for months of torture.

But it only gets worse. Something dark and terrible looms over the academy. Humans are dying, ancient vendettas are resurfacing, and the courts are more bloodthirsty than ever.

What can one mortal girl do in a world full of gorgeous monsters?

Fight back with everything I have—and try not to fall in love in the process.

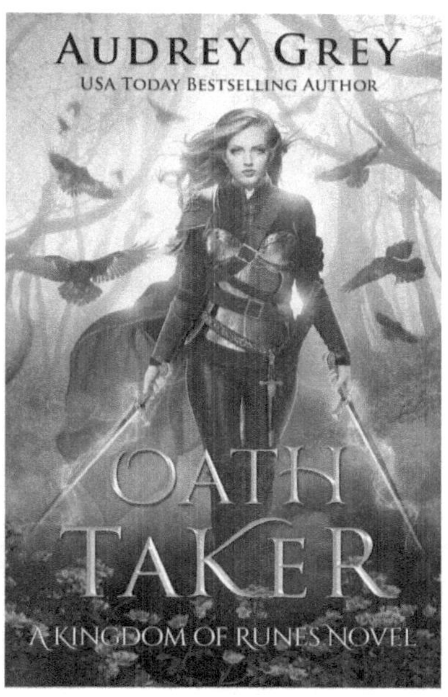

After the Prince of Penryth saved her from captivity, Haven Ashwood spends her days protecting the kind prince and her nights secretly fighting the monsters outside the castle walls.

When one of those monsters kidnaps Prince Bell, Haven must ally with Archeron Halfbane and his band of immortals to rescue her friend.

Her quest takes her deep into the domain of a warped and vicious queen where the rules are simple: break her curse or die.

Lost in a land of twisted magic and fabled creatures, Haven finds herself unprepared, not just for the feelings she develops for Archeron, but for the warring powers raging inside her.

Faced with forbidden love, heartbreaking betrayals, and impossible choices, only one thing remains certain.

Haven must shatter the curse or it will devour everything she loves.

ABOUT THE AUTHOR

Audrey Grey lives in the charming state of Oklahoma surrounded by animals, books, and little people. You can usually find Audrey hiding out in her office, downing copious amounts of caffeine while dreaming of tacos and holding entire conversations with her friends using gifs. Audrey considers her ability to travel to fantastical worlds a superpower and loves nothing more than bringing her readers with her.

Find her online at:

WWW.AUDREYGREY.COM